I0661223

The Ancient Wisdom Collection (Vol. 7)

Meno, Phaedo, Crito, Timaeus, Gorgias & Euthyphro
— Plato on Knowledge, the Soul and Rhetoric

A Modern Translation

Adapted for the Contemporary Reader

Plato

Translated by Tim Zengerink

Table Of Contents

Preface - Message to the Reader

What If You Could Help Rebuild the Greatest Library in Human History?

Thousands of years ago, the Library of Alexandria stood as the crown jewel of human achievement — a sanctuary where the collected wisdom of every known civilization was gathered, preserved, and shared freely.

And then, it was lost.

Through fire, conquest, and the slow erosion of time, humanity lost not just books — but ideas, dreams, discoveries, and stories that could have changed the world forever.

Today, the Library of Alexandria lives again — and you are invited to be a part of its restoration.

Our mission is simple yet profound:

To rebuild the greatest library the world has ever known, and to translate all timeless works into every language and dialect, so that no seeker of knowledge is ever left behind again.

By joining our movement to rebuild the modern Library of Alexandria, you become part of an unprecedented mission:

- **Unlimited Access to the Greatest Audiobooks & eBooks Ever Written:**

   Instantly explore thousands of legendary works—Plato, Shakespeare, Jane Austen, Leo Tolstoy, and countless more. All instantly available to read or listen, placing a complete literary universe at your fingertips.

- **Beautiful Paperback & Deluxe Editions at Printing Cost**

  Own any title as an elegant paperback, deluxe hardcover, or stunning collectible boxset—offered to you at true printing cost, delivered straight to your door. Build your personal Library of Alexandria, crafted for beauty, built for durability, and worthy of proud display.

- **Fresh Translations for Modern Readers—in Every Language & Dialect**

  Enjoy timeless masterpieces reimagined in clear, contemporary language—no more outdated phrases or obscure references. Alongside the original versions, we're tirelessly translating these classics into every language and dialect imaginable, ensuring accessibility and understanding across cultures and generations.

- **Join a Global Renaissance of Literature & Knowledge**

  You directly support expanding our library, publishing deluxe editions at true cost, translating works into all global languages, and bringing humanity's greatest stories to people everywhere. By joining today, you're not just preserving a legacy of masterpieces; you set in motion a powerful wave of literary accessibility.

Become a Torchbearer of Knowledge.

Join us for free now at **LibraryofAlexandria.com**

Together, we will ensure that the light of human wisdom never fades again.

With gratitude and a shared love of knowledge,
The Modern Library of Alexandria Team

Visit:

www.libraryofalexandria.com

Or scan the code below:

Introduction

Plato's Spiritual Geometry:
Knowledge, the Soul, and the Power of Speech

In this seventh volume of The Ancient Wisdom Collection, we delve further into the mind of Plato through six key dialogues: Meno, Phaedo, Crito, Timaeus, Gorgias, and Euthyphro. Each work contributes to a grand mosaic of questions that Plato posed—and in many ways, defined—for all subsequent Western philosophy. What is knowledge? What is the soul? What is justice? What is persuasion? What is the origin and structure of the cosmos?

These are not easy questions. But Plato, more than perhaps any other thinker, understood that the path to wisdom lies not in answering quickly, but in asking rightly. His dialogues are not treatises—they are dynamic encounters, dramatic explorations in which Socrates becomes both a teacher and a mirror for our deepest uncertainties.

The works in this volume cover three fundamental aspects of Plato's philosophy: epistemology (the theory of knowledge), metaphysics (the nature of being and the soul), and rhetoric (the ethical use of speech in civic life). Each dialogue is a self-contained inquiry, yet together they offer a sweeping view of Plato's attempt to align reason, virtue, and reality.

Whether you are drawn to the mysticism of Timaeus, the moral clarity of Crito, the challenge of defining piety in Euthyphro, or the existential reflections in Phaedo, this collection presents a unified philosophical vision—one that is as spiritual as it is logical, as passionate as it is precise. In these texts, Plato calls us not just to think differently, but to live differently.

Knowledge and the Soul's Ascent:
Meno, Phaedo, and Timaeus

Meno begins with a deceptively simple question: Can virtue be taught? But quickly the dialogue turns into a profound exploration of epistemology, featuring Plato's famous theory of recollection. Meno's paradox—that one cannot search for what one does not know—is met by Socrates with the claim that learning is the recollection of truths already known by the soul before birth. This introduces Plato's doctrine of anamnesis: the soul, immortal and pre-existent, has glimpsed eternal Forms, and education is the process of recovering that vision.

This metaphysical idea is developed in full in Phaedo, a dialogue set on the final day of Socrates' life. As he awaits execution, Socrates engages his companions in a discussion about the soul's immortality. He offers several arguments for the soul's continued existence after death, including the theory of opposites (life arises from death), the theory of recollection (knowledge implies prior existence), and the theory of the soul as a simple, indivisible essence.

But Phaedo is more than philosophical argument—it is a meditation on death as liberation. Socrates approaches his end with serenity, convinced that death merely separates the soul from the body and allows it to return to the realm of Forms, the true reality. In this dialogue, Plato fuses logic with myth, reason with spiritual yearning. It is one of the most profound treatments of death in all literature.

Timaeus, perhaps the most complex dialogue in this volume, shifts from the soul to the cosmos. It offers Plato's speculative account of the creation of the universe by a divine craftsman (the Demiurge), who imposes rational order on chaos using the Forms as templates. The world, Plato tells us, is a living being with a soul—a harmonious whole created with intelligence and purpose.

Timaeus also introduces Plato's early physics, including the role of the four elements (earth, air, fire, water), geometric shapes (the Platonic solids), and mathematical proportions. This dialogue reveals the fusion of metaphysics, mathematics, and cosmology that characterized Plato's vision of reality. The universe is not an accident—it is a rational, intelligible structure reflecting the order of the divine mind.

Together, Meno, Phaedo, and Timaeus provide a comprehensive view of Plato's spiritual philosophy: knowledge as recollection, the soul as immortal, and the cosmos as a rational being. They are texts of illumination, designed to lift the soul toward what is eternal.

Justice, Speech, and Civic Life: Crito, Gorgias, and Euthyphro

While the previous dialogues reach toward the heavens, Crito, Gorgias, and Euthyphro bring us back to the ethical and civic challenges of everyday life. They show Socrates engaged in debates about law, persuasion, and piety—not in abstract isolation, but in the context of death, duty, and public opinion.

In Crito, we see Socrates in prison, offered a chance to escape his death sentence. His friend Crito urges him to flee, citing the injustice of the trial and the shame of abandoning his life. But Socrates refuses. He argues that he must obey the laws of Athens, even when they wrong him, because to break them would damage his soul. His reasoning is not based on external outcomes, but on inner consistency. One must never return injustice for injustice. The soul's integrity is more important than survival.

This dialogue exemplifies Socratic ethics: doing what is right regardless of consequence, guided by reason and commitment to principle. It challenges modern notions of justice as mere legality or self-interest, insisting instead on moral self-governance and responsibility to the community.

Gorgias presents a broader critique of rhetoric and the manipulation of public discourse. Socrates debates the famous orator Gorgias, the ambitious politician Polus, and the cynical Callicles, exposing the emptiness of speech divorced from truth. Gorgias claims that rhetoric is the art of persuasion, but Socrates asks: if one persuades without knowledge, is that not flattery rather than teaching?

The dialogue escalates into a confrontation between two worldviews: one that values pleasure, power, and success, and another that values justice, truth, and the health of the soul. Callicles argues that the strong should dominate the weak, that laws are tools of control, and that morality is a fiction. Socrates counters that injustice corrupts the soul and that living rightly is better than mere power. The dialogue ends not with agreement, but with Socrates standing firm in his conviction that philosophy, not rhetoric, is the path to genuine strength.

Euthyphro, a short but provocative dialogue, tackles the question of piety. Socrates meets Euthyphro outside the courthouse and challenges his confident assumptions about religious duty. Is something pious because the gods love it, or do the gods love it because it is pious? This dilemma, known today as the "Euthyphro problem," raises enduring questions about the foundations of morality.

Euthyphro's inability to define piety becomes a lesson in humility. Socrates exposes the fragility of our moral assumptions and the need for philosophical rigor. This dialogue is a masterclass in questioning—unmasking the superficial clarity of everyday beliefs to reveal the depth of inquiry they demand.

These three dialogues confront the real-world implications of philosophy. They ask how we should act, how we should speak, and how we should relate to the laws and beliefs of our society. They reveal Plato's vision of the philosopher not as a recluse but as a moral guide—a gadfly whose sting awakens the conscience of the polis.

The Philosopher's Path:
Integration and Transformation

Reading these six dialogues together is like walking through a philosophical initiation. We begin with the question of whether virtue can be taught (Meno), pass through meditations on death and the soul (Phaedo), witness a cosmic vision of divine order (Timaeus), and then return to earth to examine civic duty (Crito), the ethics of persuasion (Gorgias), and the mystery of piety (Euthyphro).

This arc mirrors the path of the philosopher: from ignorance to knowledge, from opinion to understanding, from complacency to transformation. Plato does not merely argue—he crafts experiences. His dialogues are designed not to inform but to initiate. They turn the reader inward and upward, challenging us to examine our beliefs, refine our desires, and attune our lives to truth.

At the heart of this process is Socratic dialogue: a method of asking, listening, refining, and seeking. It is a practice of humility and courage, of standing in uncertainty without despair. It is the antidote to dogmatism, propaganda, and self-deception.

In today's world—where knowledge is commodified, communication is weaponized, and truth is often contested—Plato's dialogues remain a sanctuary of intellectual and spiritual integrity. They remind us that philosophy is not a luxury but a necessity: the soul's exercise, the mind's training, the heart's realignment.

Welcome to The Ancient Wisdom Collection (Vol. 7). May it challenge and inspire you as it has for millennia. May it draw you closer to the eternal questions—and give you the courage to live your answers.

Meno

Plato

Foreword

Virtue, Knowledge, and the Search for Truth

Plato's Meno, composed around 385 BCE, stands as one of the philosopher's most accessible yet profoundly challenging dialogues. At first glance, it appears deceptively simple—a conversation about virtue between Socrates, the philosophical seeker, and Meno, a confident, ambitious young nobleman. Yet beneath this straightforward premise lies a rich tapestry of philosophical inquiry, examining deep questions about human nature, morality, knowledge, education, and the very possibility of wisdom itself. In contrast to the ambitious political scope of Plato's Republic, the Meno offers a more intimate exploration of philosophical problems that remain central to our understanding of ethics, education, and human potential.

Readers familiar with The Republic will find in Meno a more focused yet no less rigorous investigation into the heart of moral philosophy. New readers, meanwhile, will discover in this dialogue a powerful entry point into Plato's philosophical world. The Meno elegantly demonstrates Plato's mastery of the Socratic method—his characteristic style of probing, questioning, and dialectical reasoning—while also introducing fundamental Platonic themes such as recollection, virtue, and the nature of true knowledge.

This introduction seeks to guide readers, whether seasoned or new to Plato's philosophy, through the central questions and themes of the Meno. By placing the dialogue in historical context, clarifying its philosophical arguments, and exploring its lasting significance, readers will gain a deeper appreciation of Plato's method and message. The dialogue's accessible style and thought-provoking content make it an ideal gateway into the wider landscape of Platonic philosophy.

Plato's dialogues, unlike formal treatises, are living conversations. Through the characters of Socrates and his interlocutors, Plato invites us to become active participants, urging us to question, challenge, and reconsider our assumptions. The Meno exemplifies this spirit of inquiry beautifully. It is not a text that provides definitive answers; instead, it guides readers through the complexities of philosophical thought, encouraging them to reflect deeply on the meaning of virtue, the possibility of knowledge, and the role of education in shaping human character and society.

The Central Question: What is Virtue?

The dialogue begins abruptly, with Meno posing a deceptively simple question: "Can virtue be taught? Or is it acquired by practice, or by nature?" This straightforward inquiry opens the door to one of philosophy's deepest and most persistent questions: What exactly is virtue?

Socrates immediately redirects the conversation, asserting that before one can determine how virtue is acquired, one must first know what virtue truly is. Thus begins an intensive philosophical investigation into the essence of virtue itself. Meno, confident and articulate, offers multiple definitions, each of which Socrates skillfully dismantles through careful questioning and logical critique. For example, Meno initially proposes a traditional definition—virtue as the ability to rule well, to gain power, honor, and prestige. Socrates challenges this notion by demonstrating that it is limited and context-dependent, highlighting contradictions and inadequacies in Meno's understanding.

Throughout the dialogue, this pattern continues: Meno proposes definitions based on conventional wisdom or cultural assumptions, and Socrates systematically reveals their limitations. This relentless questioning exposes the underlying difficulty of defining virtue precisely. Virtue, Socrates suggests, cannot be reduced to mere success, political influence, wealth, or even good actions; rather, it demands a deeper understanding of goodness itself—a universal essence that remains elusive and difficult to articulate clearly.

In presenting virtue as elusive, Plato highlights a critical philosophical issue: the problem of universal definitions. How do we define concepts like virtue, justice, beauty, or goodness? Are these ideas merely subjective, relative to culture or individual preference, or do they represent objective realities accessible through reason and philosophical inquiry? By refusing easy answers, Plato challenges readers to think critically about the nature of morality itself and to question the foundations of their own moral beliefs.

Yet the Meno does not merely critique conventional morality. Instead, it pushes the reader toward deeper philosophical insights about knowledge, truth, and the nature of learning. Socrates' dialectical method reveals not only the difficulty of defining virtue, but also broader questions about human understanding, the possibility of objective truth, and the relationship between virtue and knowledge.

Knowledge, Recollection, and the Paradox of Inquiry

One of the most famous and influential moments in the Meno occurs midway through the dialogue, when Meno expresses frustration at the apparent futility of their inquiry. Known today as "Meno's paradox," he articulates a profound philosophical dilemma: How can we inquire into something we do not already know? If we do not know what virtue is, how can we recognize it if we find it? Conversely, if we already know it, inquiry itself seems unnecessary. This paradox strikes at the heart of epistemology—the theory of knowledge—and poses a profound challenge to the entire philosophical enterprise.

In response to this paradox, Socrates introduces one of Plato's most intriguing and debated theories: the theory of recollection (anamnesis). According to this theory, the human soul is immortal, having encountered eternal truths before birth. Thus, learning is not the acquisition of new information but the recollection of truths already known but forgotten through the trauma of birth. Socrates demonstrates this dramatically through his famous encounter with Meno's slave, who, despite having no formal education in geometry, successfully solves a complex geometric puzzle through careful questioning. The slave boy's ability to arrive at correct answers through guided inquiry serves as powerful evidence for Plato's idea that knowledge is innate and accessible through proper philosophical guidance.

The theory of recollection has profound implications for our understanding of human nature, education, and the pursuit of knowledge. For Plato, true education is not the transmission of information from teacher to student; rather, it is the careful cultivation of the soul's inherent capacity for wisdom. The role of the philosopher-teacher is not to impose external truths but to awaken dormant knowledge within each person. This transformative view of education emphasizes active inquiry, self-reflection, and critical thinking as essential components of intellectual growth.

Yet Plato's theory of recollection is more than an epistemological solution; it carries significant ethical implications as well. If virtue, like geometric truths, is a form of knowledge innate within every human soul, then becoming virtuous is not merely a matter of habit, tradition, or external teaching. It requires deep introspection, critical self-examination, and genuine philosophical inquiry. Virtue becomes not just a set of rules to follow, but an authentic and internalized understanding of goodness that guides moral behavior naturally and spontaneously.

The Conclusion and Its Philosophical Significance

The dialogue concludes somewhat inconclusively. Socrates and Meno fail to establish definitively whether virtue can be taught or precisely what virtue is. Instead, they reach a provisional conclusion: if virtue is knowledge, it can be taught; yet since no clear examples of teachers of virtue exist, perhaps virtue is not teachable after all. Plato leaves the dialogue deliberately open-ended, challenging readers to continue the philosophical inquiry for themselves.

This unresolved conclusion underscores one of Plato's central philosophical commitments: true philosophy is not about definitive answers but about sustained and earnest questioning. The dialogue ends with an invitation rather than closure—a call for readers to engage actively in their own search for wisdom and moral understanding. Philosophy, Plato suggests, is not merely theoretical; it is deeply personal, ethical, and transformative. Virtue is not something passively received; it must be actively pursued, questioned, and internalized.

Reading the Meno Today: An Invitation to Philosophical Inquiry

What does the Meno offer contemporary readers? Far from being an abstract philosophical exercise, the Meno provides timeless insights into questions that remain central to our lives today: How can we live virtuously? Can morality be taught, or must it be discovered individually? How do we distinguish between mere opinion and genuine knowledge?

In an age characterized by moral relativism, skepticism, and educational uncertainty, Plato's Meno continues to resonate profoundly. It reminds us that virtue demands more than mere conformity or passive acceptance; it requires active, ongoing philosophical inquiry. The Meno invites us to reflect critically upon our assumptions, encouraging us to question the foundations of our beliefs and to cultivate wisdom through persistent, thoughtful investigation.

In reading the Meno, we enter into conversation not only with Socrates and Meno, but with generations of thinkers who have grappled with these essential questions. We become part of a timeless philosophical dialogue—a dialogue as vital and relevant today as it was in ancient Athens.

Welcome to Plato's Meno, a profound exploration of virtue, knowledge, and the enduring human quest for truth. Engage fully, question deeply, and you may discover, within yourself, truths that resonate across the ages.

Characters:

Meno, Socrates, Meno's Slave (Boy), Anytus

Meno

MENO: Socrates, can you tell me if virtue is something people learn, or something they develop through practice? Or does it come naturally? Or is there another way people gain it?

SOCRATES: Meno, there was a time when people only thought of the Thessalians as wealthy and great at horseback riding. But now, they're also seen as wise—especially those from Larisa, like your friend Aristippus. That's because of Gorgias. When he visited, all the top leaders, including Aristippus, admired his wisdom. He taught them to answer questions with confidence, just like he does himself. Anyone can ask him anything.

It's not like that in Athens, though. Wisdom seems to have left us. If you asked someone here whether virtue is natural or learned, they'd probably laugh and say, "You think I can answer that? I don't even know what virtue is, let alone where it comes from!" Honestly, Meno, I'm just like them. I admit I don't know what virtue really is. And if I don't know what something is, how could I know what it looks like or how someone gets it? If I didn't know anything about you, how could I say whether you're good-looking or not, or whether you're rich or poor?

MENO: That makes sense. But are you serious, Socrates? Do you really not know what virtue is? Should I tell everyone in Thessaly that?

SOCRATES: Not only that—tell them I've never met anyone who truly does know what virtue is.

MENO: But didn't you meet Gorgias when he was in Athens?

SOCRATES: Yes, I did.

MENO: And didn't you think he knew?

SOCRATES: I don't have the best memory, Meno. I don't remember what I thought at the time. Maybe he did know. And maybe you remember what he said. Why don't you remind me? Or even better—tell me what you think virtue is. I imagine you and Gorgias think the same way.

MENO: That's true.

SOCRATES: Well, since Gorgias isn't here, just go ahead and tell me. Come on, Meno, be generous and tell me what you think virtue is. I'd love to find out I was wrong and that you and Gorgias really do understand it, even though I just said I've never found anyone who does.

MENO: It's easy to answer your question, Socrates. A man's virtue is knowing how to lead a city, helping his friends, hurting his enemies, and protecting himself. A woman's virtue is taking care of the home, managing what's inside the house, and obeying her husband. Each age and role has its own kind of virtue—young or old, male or female, free or slave. There are all kinds of virtues, depending on what a person does and what stage of life they're in. And the same goes for vice.

SOCRATES: Wow, Meno! I asked you to tell me one thing—virtue—and you gave me a whole bunch, like a swarm of bees. Let's say I asked you what a bee is, and you said there are many types. I'd then ask you: are they different because they're bees, or is there something else, like their size or color, that sets them apart?

MENO: I'd say bees don't differ from each other just because they're bees.

SOCRATES: Right. So if I then asked you to describe what makes them all bees—what they have in common—you'd be able to answer that, right?

MENO: Yes, I think so.

SOCRATES: So, with virtue, even if there are many kinds, they must all share something that makes them "virtue." That's what we should focus on if we want to understand what virtue really is. Do you see what I mean?

MENO: I think I'm starting to get it, but I'm still a little unsure.

SOCRATES: You said a man has one kind of virtue, a woman has another, and children have theirs too. But does that only apply to virtue? What about things like health, strength, or size? Isn't health the same in a man and a woman?

MENO: Yes, health is the same in both.

SOCRATES: And the same goes for strength, right? A woman's strength comes from the same kind of strength as a man's?

MENO: Yes, that's true.

SOCRATES: So wouldn't virtue also be the same in a man, a woman, or a child?

MENO: This seems a little different, Socrates.

SOCRATES: But why? Didn't you say a man's virtue is running a city, and a woman's is managing the home?

MENO: Yes, I did.

SOCRATES: But can a house or city be run well without justice and self-control?

MENO: No, it can't.

SOCRATES: So, if someone runs a house or a city with justice and self-control, they're doing it with those virtues, right?

MENO: Yes, exactly.

SOCRATES: That means both men and women need justice and self-control to be good at what they do?

MENO: That's right.

SOCRATES: And young or old people can't be good if they're unjust or lack self-control?

MENO: No, they can't.

SOCRATES: So all people—no matter their age or gender—are good in the same way: by having the same virtues?

MENO: Yes, that's what it seems.

SOCRATES: And they wouldn't be good in the same way unless the virtue itself was the same in all of them?

MENO: That's true.

SOCRATES: Now that we've agreed all virtue is the same, try to remember what you and Gorgias said it was.

MENO: Do you want one definition that fits all types?

SOCRATES: Yes, that's what I'm looking for.

MENO: In that case, I'd say virtue is the ability to rule over people.

SOCRATES: But does that include everyone? Can children or slaves rule over their parents or masters? And if a slave could rule, would they still be a slave?

MENO: No, that wouldn't make sense.

SOCRATES: Exactly. So when you say that virtue is "ruling over others," shouldn't you add "justly, not unfairly"?

MENO: Yes, I agree. Virtue includes justice.

SOCRATES: But do you mean justice is virtue, or just a kind of virtue?

MENO: What do you mean?

SOCRATES: Well, it's like saying a circle is "a shape," not just "shape." Because there are other shapes too.

MENO: That makes sense. And yes, I meant that justice is just one type of virtue—there are others too.

SOCRATES: Then tell me what the others are. Just like if you asked me to name shapes, I'd give you a list.

MENO: Things like bravery, self-control, wisdom, and generosity are all virtues. And there are many more.

SOCRATES: Yes, Meno. And once again, we've found ourselves in the same situation—we're trying to define one single virtue, but we've ended up listing many of them. Still, we haven't figured out what makes all of them part of the same group.

MENO: Honestly, Socrates, I still can't follow what you're saying. I don't understand how all these different virtues could be explained as one thing.

SOCRATES: That's not surprising. But I'll try to get us a little closer, because you know how every kind of thing usually has something in common that defines it. Let's say someone asked you the same kind of question I asked earlier. For example, imagine they asked, "Meno, what is a shape?" And you said, "It's a circle." That person might ask, the way I do, "So are you saying a circle is shape, or a shape?" And you'd probably answer, "It's a shape."

MENO: That's right.

SOCRATES: And the reason you'd say that is because there are other shapes too, correct?

MENO: Yes.

SOCRATES: And if that person asked you what the other shapes are, you'd be able to list them?

MENO: I would.

SOCRATES: Now imagine they asked you what color is, and you said "white." If they asked, "Is white color itself or just one example of color?" you'd probably say, "It's a color," right? Because there are others, like red or blue?

MENO: I'd say that.

SOCRATES: And if they asked what the other colors are, you'd be able to give examples just like with shapes?

MENO: Yes, definitely.

SOCRATES: But let's say they kept pressing for a better answer. They might say, "You keep giving specific examples, but that's not what I'm asking. I want to know what all these things have in common. You say they're all shapes, even though some are round and others are straight. So what exactly is this shared quality that makes them all shapes?" Wouldn't they ask you like that?

MENO: Yes, they would.

SOCRATES: And when they ask, they're not saying that a round shape is more of a shape than a straight one, right?

MENO: Of course not.

SOCRATES: They're just pointing out that both round and straight are equally shapes?

MENO: That's correct.

SOCRATES: So then, what makes something a shape? Try to answer. Imagine someone asks you that same question about shapes or colors, and you say, "I don't know what you're getting at." They might look surprised and say, "Don't you understand I'm asking what these things have in common?" Then they might rephrase it like this: "Meno, what's the one idea that includes all the examples you call 'shapes'— like round ones, straight ones, and every kind?" Could you try answering that question? It'll help you get better at thinking through the question about virtue.

MENO: I'd rather you answer it, Socrates.

SOCRATES: Should I go ahead and explain?

MENO: Please do.

SOCRATES: And after that, you'll tell me about virtue?

MENO: I promise.

SOCRATES: Alright, then I'll give it my best shot. There's a reward on the line, after all.

MENO: Absolutely.

SOCRATES: Okay, here's my try. Let's say this: shape is the only thing that always comes with color. Would that answer work for you? I'd be happy if you could give me a similar definition for virtue.

MENO: But that answer sounds too simple, Socrates.

SOCRATES: What do you mean, simple?

MENO: You just said shape is what always comes with color.

SOCRATES: That's right.

MENO: But what if someone says they don't know what color is either? How would you explain it then?

SOCRATES: I'd just be honest. If the person was someone who liked arguing just for the sake of it, I'd say, "Well, that's my answer, and if you think I'm wrong, then prove me wrong." But if it were a friendly discussion like ours, I'd take a different approach. I'd try to explain things in a way you'd agree with, using ideas we both understand. That's what I'll try to do with you now. So tell me—do you agree that things can have edges or limits?

MENO: Yes, and I think I understand what you mean.

SOCRATES: And you know about surfaces and solids, like in geometry?

MENO: I do.

SOCRATES: Then you're ready to hear my definition of shape. I'd say a shape is what outlines a solid—it's the outer limit of a solid object.

MENO: Alright, now tell me—what is color?

SOCRATES: Meno, you're really putting me through it—asking an old man to answer everything while you won't even try to remember what Gorgias said about virtue!

MENO: I'll tell you what he said—after you answer me.

SOCRATES: Anyone listening to you, even without seeing you, would guess you're attractive and have plenty of admirers.

MENO: Why would they think that?

SOCRATES: Because you give orders like someone used to getting attention. You sound like someone who knows people are charmed by them. And since you know I have a soft spot for beauty, I guess I'll have to go along with you.

MENO: Please do!

SOCRATES: Do you want me to answer in the way Gorgias would?

MENO: That would be perfect.

SOCRATES: Alright. You and Gorgias and Empedocles say that everything gives off little streams or particles, right?

MENO: Yes.

SOCRATES: And there are paths or openings that those particles go through?

MENO: Exactly.

SOCRATES: And some of the particles fit into the openings, while others are too big or too small?

MENO: That's right.

SOCRATES: And we also have the ability to see?

MENO: Of course.

SOCRATES: Then listen carefully, as the poet Pindar would say. Color is a stream of particles, matched to our sight, and something we can physically sense.

MENO: That sounds like a great answer, Socrates.

SOCRATES: Of course you like it—because it's something you've heard before. And I bet you've also realized you could explain sound, smell, and other things in the same way.

MENO: That's true.

SOCRATES: You liked that last answer, Meno, because it sounded serious and traditional. That's why it felt more acceptable than the answer I gave earlier about shapes.

MENO: Yes, that's correct.

SOCRATES: Still, I honestly think the first answer was better. And I believe you'd think so too if you stayed and learned more, instead of needing to leave like you said yesterday.

MENO: I'll stay, Socrates—if you keep giving answers like that.

SOCRATES: I'll do my best—for both our sakes. But I might not be able to give many more answers that are just as good. Now it's your turn. You promised to tell me what virtue really is. Not a bunch of different types of it, but one clear idea. I already showed you how to do it.

MENO: Okay, Socrates. I think virtue is when a person wants good things and is able to get them. A poet once said, "Virtue is wanting good things and having the power to get them," and I agree with that.

SOCRATES: So, do you think wanting good things is the same as wanting what's truly good?

MENO: Yes, I do.

SOCRATES: Do you think some people want bad things while others want good things? Or does everyone want good things?

MENO: I don't think everyone wants good things.

SOCRATES: So, some people want bad things?

MENO: Yes.

SOCRATES: Do they believe those bad things are actually good, or do they know they're bad but still want them?

MENO: I think both happen.

SOCRATES: Do you really believe someone could know something is bad and still want it?

MENO: Yes, I do.

SOCRATES: And when people want something, it means they want to have it, right?

MENO: Yes, they want to have it.

SOCRATES: So if someone wants something bad, do they believe it will help them, or do they know it will hurt them?

MENO: Some believe it will help them, and others know it will hurt.

SOCRATES: But if someone thinks it will help them, do they still see it as bad?

MENO: No, they think it's good.

SOCRATES: Then if they don't realize it's bad, they're not really choosing something bad—they just made a mistake and thought it was good.

MENO: That's right.

SOCRATES: Now, what about the people who do know the thing is bad and believe it will hurt them? They understand it's harmful, correct?

MENO: Yes, they do.

SOCRATES: And they believe that being harmed makes people miserable?

MENO: Of course.

SOCRATES: And miserable people are unlucky or in a bad place in life, right?

MENO: Definitely.

SOCRATES: So, do you think anyone wants to be miserable or unlucky?

MENO: No, I don't think anyone wants that.

SOCRATES: Then if no one wants to be miserable, no one really wants bad things either—because getting bad things leads to misery.

MENO: That makes sense, Socrates. I agree—nobody really wants bad things.

SOCRATES: But didn't you say earlier that virtue is wanting good things and being able to get them?

MENO: Yes, I did.

SOCRATES: But if everyone wants good things, then that part of virtue is the same for everyone. So what makes someone better must be their ability to get those good things.

MENO: That's true.

SOCRATES: So, based on what you said, virtue must be the ability to get good things.

MENO: Yes, I agree.

SOCRATES: Let's look at that more closely and see if it really works. You say virtue is the power to get good things?

MENO: Yes.

SOCRATES: And by "good things," you mean things like health, money, gold, silver, and success in public life?

MENO: Yes, all of those.

SOCRATES: So, from your point of view—since you're close to the king—virtue is being able to get gold and silver. But what if someone gets those things by lying or stealing? Would that still count as virtue?

MENO: No, that wouldn't be virtue, Socrates. That would be wrong.

SOCRATES: Then it sounds like things like honesty, self-control, and fairness have to be included in virtue. Just getting good things isn't enough.

MENO: Right. You need those qualities to truly have virtue.

SOCRATES: So even if someone doesn't get wealth or success because they refuse to lie or cheat, they could still be considered virtuous?

MENO: Yes, definitely.

SOCRATES: So in the end, it's not the act of getting good things that defines virtue—it's how you go about it. If someone acts with honesty and fairness, that's virtue. If not, then it's not.

MENO: I totally agree.

SOCRATES: Didn't we just say that things like justice, self-control, and so on are parts of virtue?

MENO: Yes.

SOCRATES: Then, Meno, I think you're teasing me a little.

MENO: Why do you say that, Socrates?

SOCRATES: Because I asked you to explain what virtue is as a whole—not just a piece of it. I even gave you an example to help you, but now you've told me that virtue is the ability to get good things in a just way. And you already agreed that justice is only a part of virtue.

MENO: That's true.

SOCRATES: So based on your own words, you're saying that doing something using a part of virtue counts as having virtue. You're saying justice is just one part, and yet you define all of virtue using only that one part.

MENO: What's wrong with that?

SOCRATES: Well, didn't I ask for the full meaning of virtue—not a broken-up version? Instead, you're telling me that anything done with a part of virtue counts as full virtue, as if I already knew the whole thing, even though it's been split into little pieces. That's why, Meno, I think we need to start over. I'm going to ask again: What is virtue? Because if we don't know what virtue is, we can't really know what its parts are either, right?

MENO: No, I guess not.

SOCRATES: Do you remember how, when we talked about shapes, we agreed that we shouldn't explain something using words or ideas that haven't already been clearly defined?

MENO: Yes, I remember. And we were right to do that.

SOCRATES: Then we can't define virtue using pieces of virtue that we haven't clearly explained yet. We'd just have to keep asking, "What is virtue?" over and over again. Don't you agree?

MENO: Yes, I do.

SOCRATES: Alright then. Let's start fresh. Tell me, according to you and your teacher Gorgias, what is virtue?

MENO: Oh Socrates, I used to hear people say that you were always full of doubts and made other people doubt things too. And now I really understand what they meant. You've completely confused me—I feel like I've been put under a spell! I used to think I could talk about virtue easily. I've given speeches about it to many people, and I thought I did a great job. But now, standing here with you, I can't even say what virtue is. If I'm being funny, you're like a stinging sea creature that makes people numb just by touching them. That's what you've done to me. My brain and my voice are frozen! And honestly, Socrates, I think it's smart you never leave Athens. If you acted like this in other cities, people would probably throw you in jail for being some kind of wizard.

SOCRATES: You're a clever one, Meno. You almost caught me there.

MENO: What do you mean?

SOCRATES: I know exactly why you made that comparison.

MENO: Why?

SOCRATES: So I'd make one about you in return. I've noticed that good-looking young men like you enjoy being compared to nice things—and I don't blame you! But I won't play along. Now, if the sea creature you mentioned is numb itself and also causes numbness in others, then yes, maybe I am like that. I confuse people not because I have all the answers, but because I'm confused too. I honestly don't know what virtue is, and it seems like you don't know either—even if you thought you did before we started talking. Still, I'm willing to figure it out with you.

MENO: But Socrates, how can you even search for something when you don't know what it is? What are you going to look for? And even if you somehow find it, how would you recognize it if you didn't know what it was to begin with?

SOCRATES: I understand your point, Meno. But think about where that kind of thinking leads. You're saying that a person can't ask questions about something they know—because they already know it—and they can't ask about something they don't know—because they wouldn't recognize it even if they found it.

MENO: Yes, and doesn't that make sense?

SOCRATES: I don't think so.

MENO: Why not?

SOCRATES: I'll explain. I once heard some wise men and women—people who talk about spiritual matters—say something important.

MENO: What did they say?

SOCRATES: They talked about a beautiful idea.

MENO: Who were they, and what did they say?

SOCRATES: Some of them were priests and priestesses who had thought deeply about their beliefs. There were also poets, like Pindar, who spoke from inspiration. What they said was this—see if you think it could be true: they said that the soul never dies. Sometimes it seems to end—that's what we call death—but then it's born again. It keeps living over and over, never truly destroyed. The lesson from this is that we should always live in a good and moral way.

They say that after nine years, the goddess Persephone sends certain souls back to the world of the living—souls that have paid for past wrongs. These souls return as wise people, strong leaders, and even heroes remembered for doing good.

Because our souls are immortal and have been born many times, they've already seen and learned everything, in this life or the next. So the soul already knows all things—including what virtue is. It's just a matter of remembering. That's why learning isn't really about gaining new knowledge, but about recalling what the soul already knows.

So, Meno, we shouldn't believe that argument about how it's impossible to search for something you don't know. That belief makes people lazy. But this idea—that we're remembering what we already know—makes us curious and motivated. That's why I'm happy to search for the truth about virtue with you.

MENO: Alright, Socrates. But what do you mean when you say that learning is just remembering? Can you show me how that works?

SOCRATES: Meno, I just said you were being sneaky, and now you're asking if I can teach you something, even though I just said that real learning is actually remembering. You think you're catching me in a contradiction.

MENO: That's not what I meant, Socrates. I was just asking out of habit. But if you can prove that remembering is how we learn, I'd really like to see it.

SOCRATES: It won't be easy, but I'll do my best to show you. Why don't you call over one of your servants so I can use him to demonstrate?

MENO: Sure. Come here, boy.

SOCRATES: He's Greek and speaks the language, right?

MENO: Yes, he was born in my house.

SOCRATES: Alright, listen closely to the questions I ask him. Watch carefully to see if he's learning from me or just remembering things he already knows.

MENO: I'm watching.

SOCRATES (to the boy): Tell me, do you know that this shape is called a square?

BOY: Yes, I do.

SOCRATES: And do you know that a square has four equal sides?

BOY: Yes, that's true.

SOCRATES: And the lines I drew through the middle are also equal, right?

BOY: Yes.

SOCRATES: A square can be any size, can't it?

BOY: Of course.

SOCRATES: So, if one side is two feet long and the other side is also two feet, what is the area of the square? Let me help—if one direction is two feet and the other is one foot, then the area would be two feet, right?

BOY: Yes.

SOCRATES: But since both sides are two feet, what do we have?

BOY: Two times two feet.

SOCRATES: So how much is that?

BOY: Four square feet.

SOCRATES: Now, could there be another square that's twice as big, but still has equal sides?

BOY: Yes.

SOCRATES: How many square feet would that be?

BOY: Eight.

SOCRATES: So tell me, how long would each side of that bigger square be? This one has two-foot sides—how long should the sides be for the one with eight square feet?

BOY: It must be double—so four feet.

SOCRATES: Do you see, Meno? I haven't taught him anything—I've only asked questions. But now he thinks he knows the answer. He believes a square twice as big needs sides twice as long. Don't you think?

MENO: Yes, I see that.

SOCRATES: But does he really know the answer?

MENO: No, he's just guessing.

SOCRATES: Exactly. He's guessing that doubling the side will double the area.

MENO: That's right.

SOCRATES (to the boy): Okay, let's go over this carefully. Do you still say that doubling the side will make a square that's twice the area? Remember, I'm not talking about a rectangle—just a square, with all sides equal and an area of eight square feet. Do you still think a double-length side gives a double-sized square?

BOY: Yes.

SOCRATES: If we take this two-foot line and add another two-foot line, does that make a four-foot side?

BOY: Yes.

SOCRATES: And four-foot sides on all sides make how many square feet?

BOY: Let's see… four sections of four feet each.

SOCRATES: Right, and how much is four times four?

BOY: Sixteen.

SOCRATES: So instead of eight, we've made a square that's four times bigger.

BOY: That's true.

SOCRATES: So four times four is sixteen, right?

BOY: Yes.

SOCRATES: Now, what kind of line would make a square with eight square feet, like this one made sixteen? Can you figure that out?

BOY: I'll try.

SOCRATES: The small square with four square feet used a two-foot line. Right?

BOY: Yes.

SOCRATES: And we want a square that's twice as big as that one, but smaller than the sixteen-foot square. Correct?

BOY: Right.

SOCRATES: So the line we're looking for must be longer than two feet, but shorter than four feet. Agree?

BOY: Yes, I think so.

SOCRATES: Good. It's great that you're thinking it through. Now, isn't this a two-foot line, and that one four feet?

BOY: Yes.

SOCRATES: So the line that gives us a square of eight feet must be somewhere between two and four feet long?

BOY: It must be.

SOCRATES: Can you guess how long that line might be?

BOY: Maybe three feet?

SOCRATES: Let's test that. If you make a square that's three feet on each side, how many square feet will that be?

BOY: Three times three is nine.

SOCRATES: And how much is two times four?

BOY: Eight.

SOCRATES: So then, a three-foot line doesn't create an eight-square-foot area, does it?

BOY: No, it doesn't.

SOCRATES: Then what length of line does? Can you tell me exactly—or if you're not sure how to count it, can you show me the line?

BOY: Honestly, Socrates, I don't know.

SOCRATES: See that, Meno? He's already made a lot of progress. At first, he didn't know the answer—and he still doesn't—but earlier, he thought he knew and answered with confidence. Now he realizes he doesn't know and admits it.

MENO: That's true.

SOCRATES: Isn't it better for him to recognize what he doesn't know?

MENO: Yes, I think so.

SOCRATES: So by making him question himself, like giving him a little shock, have we done him any harm?

MENO: No, I don't think so.

SOCRATES: It seems like we've helped him get closer to the truth. Before, he would've insisted that doubling the side would double the square. Now, he's unsure and wants to figure it out.

MENO: That's true.

SOCRATES: Do you think he would've ever tried to learn the right answer if he kept thinking he already knew it?

MENO: Probably not, Socrates.

SOCRATES: So getting confused actually helped him?

MENO: I believe it did.

SOCRATES: Now watch what happens next. I'm only going to ask him questions—I won't teach him anything. Let's see if he can figure it out on his own. (To the boy:) This square here is four square feet, right?

BOY: Yes.

SOCRATES: And now I'm adding another square that's exactly the same?

BOY: Yes.

SOCRATES: And now a third one, also equal to the first two?

BOY: Yes.

SOCRATES: Let's finish it off by adding one more square in the corner.

BOY: Okay.

SOCRATES: So now we have four equal squares here?

BOY: Yes.

SOCRATES: And this whole space is how many times bigger than just one of the squares?

BOY: Four times bigger.

SOCRATES: But remember—we were only trying to double the area.

BOY: That's right.

SOCRATES: Now, doesn't this line from corner to corner cut each square in half?

BOY: Yes.

SOCRATES: And aren't there four of these same lines creating the shape?

BOY: Yes.

SOCRATES: Look closely—how big is this new space?

BOY: I don't really get it.

SOCRATES: Each of those lines splits a square in half, right?

BOY: Yes.

SOCRATES: So how many half-squares are there in total?

BOY: Four.

SOCRATES: And how many full squares do those halves make?

BOY: Two.

SOCRATES: And four is how many times more than two?

BOY: Twice.

SOCRATES: So this space is how big?

BOY: Eight square feet.

SOCRATES: And which line created that figure?

BOY: This one.

SOCRATES: The one running diagonally from corner to corner of the original four-foot square?

BOY: Yes.

SOCRATES: That's the line experts call the diagonal. So, Meno's servant, are you saying that a square twice as large is formed from the diagonal?

BOY: Yes, Socrates.

SOCRATES: What do you think, Meno? Weren't all his answers his own?

MENO: Yes, all of them.

SOCRATES: But didn't we agree earlier that he didn't know the answer?

MENO: That's true.

SOCRATES: Still, he had those ideas inside him all along, didn't he?

MENO: Yes.

SOCRATES: So someone who doesn't know something might still have the right ideas deep down?

MENO: That's right.

SOCRATES: And now those ideas have started to come back to him, like a memory in a dream. If we kept asking him more questions like this, eventually he'd fully understand it, just like anyone else.

MENO: That seems likely.

SOCRATES: So just by asking him questions—not by teaching—we helped him remember something he already knew?

MENO: Yes.

SOCRATES: And that kind of remembering is what I mean by recollection?

MENO: Exactly.

SOCRATES: Now, this knowledge he has—he either learned it at some point, or he's always had it, right?

MENO: Yes.

SOCRATES: But if he's always had it, then he's always known it. And if he learned it, he didn't learn it in this life—unless someone taught him geometry. But you said he's grown up in your house, so you'd know if he had.

MENO: And I'm sure no one ever taught him anything like that.

SOCRATES: So even though he was never taught, he still has this knowledge in him?

MENO: That's clearly true, Socrates.

SOCRATES: If he didn't learn it in this life, then he must have learned it at some other time.

MENO: That makes sense.

SOCRATES: So he must've learned it before he was born as a human.

MENO: Yes.

SOCRATES: And if he had true ideas in his mind both when he was a man and before he became one, and only needed to be asked the right questions to remember them, then his soul must have always had this knowledge—because he always existed in one form or another.

MENO: Obviously.

SOCRATES: So if truth has always been inside the soul, then the soul must be immortal. That's why we should stay hopeful and keep trying to remember the things we don't seem to know.

MENO: I think I'm starting to really like what you're saying.

SOCRATES: And I like it too, Meno. I can't say I'm sure about everything I've said, but I'm sure about this: we'll be better people—braver and more capable—if we believe it's worth asking questions and trying to learn, rather than thinking there's no point because we can't really know anything. I'd defend that idea with everything I've got.

MENO: That part especially sounds very wise, Socrates.

SOCRATES: So since we agree that we should explore what we don't know, shall we try to figure out what virtue really is?

MENO: Yes, let's do it. But I'd still like to go back to my first question: Should we treat virtue as something people can learn, or is it something they're born with, or does it come in some other way?

SOCRATES: If I had control over both of us, Meno, I wouldn't ask whether virtue can be taught until we first figured out what virtue actually is. But since you seem to think you can direct me and not yourself—because that's your idea of freedom—I'll follow your lead. So now I'll try to answer a question about something we haven't even defined yet. Still, will you allow me to explore this question by using a guess or starting idea?

Like in geometry, when someone is asked if a triangle can fit inside a circle, they might say, "I don't know yet. But let me make a guess. If the triangle has certain sides or angles, then maybe it can fit. And if that's impossible, then it can't." That's how they start reasoning.

In the same way, since we don't yet know what virtue is, let's try to answer the question—"Can virtue be taught?"—based on a guess. For example: if virtue is a kind of knowledge, then can it be taught or not? Or, if it's something remembered, does that change anything? The wording doesn't really matter—what matters is whether virtue can be taught.

MENO: That makes sense to me.

SOCRATES: Then if virtue is knowledge, it can be taught?

MENO: Yes, definitely.

SOCRATES: So we've answered that question quickly: if virtue is knowledge, it can be taught. If it's not, then it can't.

MENO: Agreed.

SOCRATES: Now the next thing we have to figure out is: Is virtue knowledge, or is it something else?

MENO: Yes, that seems like the next logical step.

SOCRATES: We've already said that virtue is something good, right?

MENO: Yes, for sure.

SOCRATES: So if there are types of good that aren't knowledge, then maybe virtue is one of those. But if all good things are based in knowledge, then virtue must be a kind of knowledge too.

MENO: That sounds right.

SOCRATES: And virtue makes people good?

MENO: Yes.

SOCRATES: And when people are good, they become helpful or useful—because all good things are helpful in some way?

MENO: That's true.

SOCRATES: So virtue is helpful?

MENO: Yes, that follows.

SOCRATES: Now let's look at what kinds of things help us in life—like health, strength, beauty, wealth, and so on. We consider these to be helpful, right?

MENO: Yes.

SOCRATES: But those things can also hurt us sometimes, don't you think?

MENO: Yes, that can happen.

SOCRATES: So what makes the difference? Isn't it how we use them? They're helpful when used wisely, and harmful when used badly?

MENO: Exactly.

SOCRATES: Now think about the qualities of the soul—like self-control, justice, courage, quick thinking, good memory, and confidence.

MENO: Yes, all of those.

SOCRATES: And those qualities—when they don't involve wisdom—can also be harmful, right? Like courage without good judgment can be dangerous. It becomes helpful only when guided by wisdom.

MENO: That's true.

SOCRATES: Same goes for self-control and quick thinking—when they're used wisely, they're good. But without wisdom, they can lead to trouble.

MENO: Very true.

SOCRATES: So in general, anything the soul does—if guided by wisdom—leads to happiness. But if guided by foolishness, it leads to harm.

MENO: Yes, that seems right.

SOCRATES: So if virtue is something that comes from the soul and it helps us, then it must be a kind of wisdom or understanding. Because soul-qualities are only helpful or harmful depending on whether they're guided by wisdom or not. So if virtue really is helpful, then it must be a type of wisdom.

MENO: I totally agree.

SOCRATES: And didn't we say earlier that things like wealth can be either helpful or harmful depending on how the soul uses them? Just like how the soul's own traits—like courage or self-control—can be good or bad depending on whether they're guided by wisdom or foolishness?

MENO: Yes, that's true.

SOCRATES: So a wise soul uses things in the right way, and a foolish one doesn't.

MENO: Exactly.

SOCRATES: Isn't this the case for all of human nature? Everything depends on the soul, and the soul itself needs wisdom to make anything truly good. So we can say wisdom is what makes things beneficial. And since we also said virtue is beneficial...

MENO: Then virtue must involve wisdom, either completely or at least partly. Yes, Socrates, that seems true.

SOCRATES: But if that's right, then people aren't naturally good from birth, are they?

MENO: I don't think they are.

SOCRATES: If they were born good, then we'd be able to tell who the future great people were. And we'd protect them, like treasures—keeping them safe from harm, even more carefully than gold. We'd help them grow up to serve and benefit the country.

MENO: Yes, that's how we should do it.

SOCRATES: But if people aren't born good, then do they become good through teaching?

MENO: That seems to be the only other option. If virtue is knowledge, it must be something we can teach.

SOCRATES: That makes sense. But what if our guess is wrong?

MENO: I honestly thought we were right.

SOCRATES: Maybe we were, Meno. But a solid idea should always make sense—not just sometimes.

MENO: Fair point. So why don't you believe that virtue is knowledge?

SOCRATES: I'll explain. I'm not saying that if virtue were knowledge, it couldn't be taught—it absolutely could. But I'm not sure virtue is knowledge. Think about this: for anything that can be taught, don't there have to be teachers and students?

MENO: Of course.

SOCRATES: And if there are no teachers and no students, then it probably can't be taught?

MENO: That's logical. But do you really think there are no teachers of virtue?

SOCRATES: I've looked hard to find them, and I haven't had any luck. And I've asked others who seemed like they would know. Actually, we're in luck—Anytus is here with us. He's exactly the kind of person we should ask. His father, Anthemion, was wise and earned his wealth through hard work, not luck. He was well-mannered and respectable, not arrogant or rude. Anytus himself was well educated, and the people of Athens clearly respect him—they've chosen him for important roles. So, Anytus, can you help Meno and me figure this out: who teaches virtue?

Let's look at it this way. If we wanted Meno to become a doctor, who would we send him to?

ANYTUS: To doctors, of course.

SOCRATES: And if we wanted him to become a good shoemaker?

ANYTUS: To a shoemaker.

SOCRATES: Same with any other craft?

ANYTUS: Yes.

SOCRATES: One more question. If we say Meno should be sent to doctors to learn medicine, we mean real doctors—people who claim to teach it and are paid to teach anyone who wants to learn. Isn't that what we mean?

ANYTUS: Yes, that's right.

SOCRATES: So wouldn't the same logic apply to flute playing or any other skill? If someone wants to learn, wouldn't it be silly to avoid the teachers who openly teach it and try to get help from random people who've never taught it and don't claim to know it?

ANYTUS: Yes, that would be foolish and ignorant.

SOCRATES: Great. Now you're ready to help Meno. He wants to learn the kind of wisdom and virtue that helps someone run a household or serve the city well—someone who honors their parents and knows when to welcome or send away others. Who should he go to for that kind of learning? Based on what we just said, shouldn't we send him to those who publicly claim to teach it—for a fee—and say they'll teach anyone who's willing to pay?

ANYTUS: Who do you mean, Socrates?

SOCRATES: Surely you know who I'm talking about, Anytus. I mean the people known as Sophists.

ANYTUS: By Heracles, Socrates, stop right there! I hope no friend or relative of mine ever goes near those people. They're nothing but trouble. They ruin anyone who listens to them.

SOCRATES: Are you saying, Anytus, that out of everyone who claims they can improve others, only the Sophists actually make them worse? And even worse—they do this on purpose while charging money for it? That's hard to believe. I know one Sophist, Protagoras, who made more money from his work than the famous sculptor Pheidias, or even ten sculptors combined. Think about it: if a shoe repairman or tailor ruined what he worked on, he'd be out of business in a month. People would notice.

But Protagoras supposedly "ruined" people all over Greece for more than forty years—and no one caught on? He died around seventy years old, and he practiced his craft for most of his life. People still respect his name. And he's not the only one. There were Sophists before him and others still teaching now, and many of them have good reputations.

So, Anytus, do you really think all these men were secretly damaging their students—on purpose? Are we supposed to believe that some of the smartest people in Greece were completely out of their minds?

ANYTUS: Out of their minds? No, Socrates. It's not the Sophists who are crazy—it's the young men who pay them, and even more so the families and guardians who trust them with their education. But worst of all are the cities that let these people in and don't kick them out, whether they're citizens or foreigners.

SOCRATES: Did one of the Sophists wrong you, Anytus? You seem really upset with them.

ANYTUS: Not at all. Neither I nor anyone in my family has ever had anything to do with them, and I wouldn't allow it.

SOCRATES: So you've had no contact with them?

ANYTUS: And I don't want any, either.

SOCRATES: Then how can you say whether they're good or bad if you don't know them at all?

ANYTUS: I don't need to know them to know the kind of people they are.

SOCRATES: Then you must be some kind of mind reader, Anytus, because I don't understand how someone can judge something they've never experienced. But I'm not asking you whether the Sophists are good or bad teachers. Let's say for argument's sake that they're bad. I just want you to help Meno here. Can you tell him who in this city can teach him how to become a good and capable person—the kind we were just talking about? He's a friend of your family, so you'd be helping him out.

ANYTUS: Why don't you tell him?

SOCRATES: I already told him who I thought the teachers might be. But according to you, I'm completely wrong. So now I'd like you to tell us—who in Athens could teach him?

ANYTUS: Why name specific people? Any respectable Athenian—if Meno listens to him—will help him more than any Sophist would.

SOCRATES: So these men became virtuous on their own, without being taught, and yet they're somehow able to teach others something they never learned themselves?

ANYTUS: I suppose they learned from the previous generation of good men. Haven't there always been many good men in this city?

SOCRATES: Yes, Anytus, there have been many. And there are still good leaders and statesmen in Athens. But the real question isn't whether there have been good men—it's whether they could teach others to be good. That's what Meno and I have been trying to figure out. Do you think these great men of the past were able to pass on their virtue to others, or is virtue something that just can't be taught at all? Let's test it. Would you say Themistocles was a good man?

ANYTUS: Of course. One of the best.

SOCRATES: Then surely he would've been a good teacher of virtue too, right?

ANYTUS: Yes—if he wanted to teach it.

SOCRATES: But wouldn't he have wanted to teach it to his own son, at least? He wouldn't have refused to teach his own child out of jealousy. In fact, people say he had his son Cleophantus trained in horseback riding, javelin throwing, and other skills. He was taught well in anything that could be learned from an instructor. Have you heard that?

ANYTUS: Yes, I've heard stories like that.

SOCRATES: So no one ever said his son lacked ability?

ANYTUS: I don't think so.

SOCRATES: But have you ever heard anyone say that Cleophantus was wise or a good man like his father?

ANYTUS: No, I've never heard that.

SOCRATES: So if virtue could be taught, wouldn't Themistocles have made sure his son was trained in that more than anything else?

ANYTUS: You're probably right.

SOCRATES: That's just one example. Let's look at another. What about Aristides, the son of Lysimachus? Would you call him a good man?

ANYTUS: Certainly.

SOCRATES: Didn't he also give his son Lysimachus the best education money could buy? But did that make him better than anyone else? You know him personally. What do you think?

ANYTUS: I know him, yes.

SOCRATES: Then there's Pericles, known for his wisdom. He had two sons—Paralus and Xanthippus. You know about them too, right?

ANYTUS: I do.

SOCRATES: Pericles had them trained in horseback riding, music, physical fitness—all sorts of skills. In those areas, they were as good as anyone. Do you think he didn't want them to be good men, too? Of course he did. But maybe virtue just can't be taught.

And to prove this isn't just true for ordinary people, let's talk about Thucydides. He had two sons, Melesias and Stephanus. He gave them the best wrestling training available—one trained with Xanthias and the other with Eudorus, who were both famous. You've heard of them?

ANYTUS: Yes, I have.

SOCRATES: So don't you think Thucydides would have taught his sons to be good people too—if virtue could be taught? Teaching wrestling costs money. Teaching virtue, if it were possible, wouldn't cost anything. And if he couldn't do it himself, he had the connections to find someone who could. Still, it seems like even the best men weren't able to pass their goodness on to their sons. So again, Anytus, doesn't it seem like virtue might not be something that can be taught?

ANYTUS: Socrates, you talk badly about people too easily. If you want my advice, you'd better be more careful. In every city, it's easier to do harm than to do good. And here in Athens, I think you already know that.

SOCRATES: Meno, it looks like Anytus is angry. And I think I know why. He thinks I've insulted some very respected men—and maybe he even sees himself as one of them. But one day, he'll understand what I meant and, I hope, forgive me. For now, let's come back to you, Meno. I assume your part of the world has respected men too?

MENO: Yes, definitely.

SOCRATES: And are they willing to teach the younger generation? Do they claim to be teachers? Do they say virtue can be taught?

MENO: Not really, Socrates. They can't seem to agree. Sometimes they say virtue can be taught, and other times they say it can't.

SOCRATES: Can we really call someone a teacher if they don't even believe in what they teach?

MENO: No, I don't think so.

SOCRATES: What about the Sophists—the ones who actually claim to teach? Do you think they teach virtue?

MENO: I'm not sure. I've noticed that Gorgias never claimed to teach virtue. When others said they could, he just laughed. He only said he could teach people how to speak well.

SOCRATES: So you're not convinced the Sophists are real teachers?

MENO: I go back and forth. Sometimes I think they are, and sometimes I don't.

SOCRATES: And you're not the only one. Even poets have questioned whether virtue can be taught. Have you heard of Theognis?

MENO: Yes, I have.

SOCRATES: In one of his poems he says:

"Sit with the good, eat with the good, talk with the good—

You'll learn from them. Be around the bad, and you'll lose your wisdom."

That sounds like he believes virtue can be taught, doesn't it?

MENO: Yes, it does.

SOCRATES: But in another part, he says:

"If understanding could be poured into someone,

Those who could do it would be rewarded greatly."

And also:

"No bad child would come from a good parent,

If teaching could really make someone good.

But you can't turn a bad person into a good one by teaching."

So he completely contradicts himself.

MENO: Yes, clearly.

SOCRATES: Is there anything else where people claim to be experts, yet not only fail to teach it to others, but also don't even understand it themselves? Or anything else where even respected people can't agree—sometimes saying it can be taught, other times saying it can't? Can people like that really be called true teachers?

MENO: No, definitely not.

SOCRATES: So if neither the Sophists nor the so-called wise men can teach virtue, then it seems there are no teachers of it at all.

MENO: That seems to be the case.

SOCRATES: And if there are no teachers, then there are no students either, right?

MENO: Right.

SOCRATES: And we agreed earlier that something can't be taught if there are no teachers or students.

MENO: We did.

SOCRATES: And since we can't find any teachers of virtue...

MENO: ...then there are no students either.

SOCRATES: So virtue can't be taught?

MENO: Not if we're right about all this. But, Socrates, I just can't believe there aren't any good people in the world. And if there are, how did they become good?

SOCRATES: I'm starting to think, Meno, that you and I haven't learned much, and that Gorgias was no better a teacher for you than Prodicus was for me. Looks like we'll have to help ourselves and look for someone who can truly make us better people. I say this because during all our talk, none of us noticed that people can do the right thing even without having knowledge. And if we deny that, it's hard to explain how there can be any good people at all.

MENO: What do you mean, Socrates?

SOCRATES: I mean that we agreed good people are helpful and useful. That was true, right?

MENO: Yes.

SOCRATES: And we said that they are useful because they help guide our actions. That was true too?

MENO: Yes.

SOCRATES: But we also said someone can't be a good guide unless they have real knowledge—and that part might've been wrong.

MENO: What do you mean by "wrong"?

SOCRATES: Let me explain. If someone knew the road to a city like Larisa, and led others there, he'd be a good guide, wouldn't he?

MENO: Of course.

SOCRATES: But suppose someone had never been to Larisa, but still had the correct opinion about how to get there. He could still guide people there just as well, right?

MENO: That's true.

SOCRATES: So as long as he believes the right thing, even without knowing, he can be just as useful as someone who actually knows?

MENO: Yes.

SOCRATES: That means a true belief can guide us just as well as knowledge. And we forgot that earlier when we said that only knowledge can lead to right actions. We should have said true beliefs can too.

MENO: You're right.

SOCRATES: So isn't true belief just as useful as knowledge?

MENO: The only difference, Socrates, is that people with knowledge will always get it right. But those with only true beliefs might sometimes be wrong.

SOCRATES: But how can someone with a true belief be wrong while they still hold that belief?

MENO: Okay, I see your point. Now I'm confused why people value knowledge more than true belief—why even make a difference?

SOCRATES: Want me to explain that?

MENO: Please do.

SOCRATES: Have you ever seen statues made by Daedalus?

MENO: No, what do they have to do with this?

SOCRATES: They were said to be so lifelike that, unless they were tied down, they'd move around or disappear. If they weren't secured, they weren't worth much, even though they were beautifully made.

MENO: Interesting. But what's the connection?

SOCRATES: It's like this: true beliefs are useful while you have them, but they don't stay with you unless you "tie them down." If you don't secure them, they can fade away, like the statues running off. But once you understand why they're true—once they're connected to reasoning—then they stay. That's when a belief becomes knowledge. And that's why knowledge is more valuable than just true opinion—it's tied down and won't slip away.

MENO: That makes a lot of sense, Socrates.

SOCRATES: I'm just guessing, really. I don't know much for sure. But I do know this: knowledge and true belief are not the same.

MENO: And you're absolutely right to say that.

SOCRATES: And don't you agree that someone with true belief can be just as effective as someone with knowledge when it comes to action?

MENO: Yes, I do.

SOCRATES: So true belief is just as useful as knowledge in practice. A person with true belief is just as effective as one with knowledge.

MENO: That's true.

SOCRATES: And we've already said that good people are useful, right?

MENO: Yes.

SOCRATES: Then it seems people can be good and helpful to society not just through knowledge, but also through true belief. And since neither knowledge nor true belief is something people are just born with—do you believe either one is naturally given?

MENO: No, I don't.

SOCRATES: Then if they're not born with it, people aren't naturally good either.

MENO: That's right.

SOCRATES: So when we ruled out nature, we asked: can virtue be taught?

MENO: Yes, that was the next question.

SOCRATES: And we said that if virtue was knowledge, then it could be taught.

MENO: Yes.

SOCRATES: And if it could be taught, that would prove it was knowledge.

MENO: Exactly.

SOCRATES: And if there were teachers, then it must be something that can be taught. But if there aren't any teachers, it can't be.

MENO: That's true.

SOCRATES: But we agreed earlier that there are no teachers of virtue, didn't we?

MENO: Yes.

SOCRATES: Then we agreed that virtue isn't something that can be taught, and it's not the same as knowledge?

MENO: That's right.

SOCRATES: But we also said that virtue is a good thing?

MENO: Yes, we did.

SOCRATES: And something that leads us in the right direction is both helpful and good?

MENO: Definitely.

SOCRATES: And the only things that can guide us correctly are either knowledge or true opinion. These are the things that help people make decisions—because random luck isn't something we control. So people are guided by either true belief or real knowledge.

MENO: I agree with that.

SOCRATES: But if virtue can't be taught, then it can't be knowledge.

MENO: That makes sense.

SOCRATES: So out of the two helpful things—knowledge and true opinion—one has been ruled out. Knowledge can't be what guides people in leading public life.

MENO: I guess not.

SOCRATES: That means people like Themistocles and the other leaders Anytus mentioned didn't lead with wisdom or knowledge. And that's probably why they couldn't teach others to be like them—because their virtue didn't come from knowledge.

MENO: That sounds right, Socrates.

SOCRATES: So if it wasn't knowledge, then it must have been true opinion that helped them lead—just like how in religion, people sometimes speak the truth without really knowing what they're saying. That's what fortune-tellers and prophets do: they often say things that come true, but they don't really understand them.

MENO: I believe that's true.

SOCRATES: So, Meno, wouldn't it make sense to call people "divine" when they achieve great things even though they don't fully understand what they're doing?

MENO: Yes, I think that's a fair way to put it.

SOCRATES: Then we could say the same for prophets, poets, and even politicians—especially politicians. They speak and act in amazing ways, but it's like they're inspired by something beyond themselves. They don't always understand what they're doing, but something drives them.

MENO: That sounds right.

SOCRATES: And even ordinary people, Meno—even the women—say a good man is "divine." The Spartans too, when they praise someone, say, "He's a godlike man."

MENO: I think they're right, Socrates. Though Anytus might not like us saying that.

SOCRATES: I'm not worried about Anytus. There will be time to talk to him again. So, to wrap up everything we've talked about: if we're even close to the truth, then virtue doesn't come naturally, and it can't be taught. Instead, it seems to be something people are born with or receive from the gods. And unless there's someone out there who can truly train future leaders, then good statesmen are just acting from some kind of divine instinct—not from reason.

If such a teacher did exist, he'd be like the prophet Tiresias in Homer's story—he was the only one among the dead who had real understanding. All the others were just wandering shadows. This kind of teacher would be a living version of Tiresias—someone truly wise in a world full of guessers.

MENO: That's an amazing thought, Socrates.

SOCRATES: So, Meno, it looks like virtue is something given by the gods to those they choose. But we won't really know the truth about how it's given until we first understand what virtue truly is. I have to go now, but since you're convinced, try to help Anytus see things more clearly too. If you can calm him down and get him to understand, you'll be doing something really good for the people of Athens.

The End

Phaedo

Plato

Foreword

Facing Death, Seeking Truth:
The Last Moments of Socrates

Plato's Phaedo, written around 380 BCE, occupies a unique and profoundly moving position within his philosophical writings. Unlike the grand political vision of The Republic, or the searching inquiry of the Meno, the Phaedo invites readers into a solemn and deeply reflective moment—the final hours of Socrates' life. Yet, despite its emotional gravity, this dialogue is not merely an elegiac farewell to Plato's beloved teacher. Rather, it stands as a rich philosophical exploration of some of the most enduring and profound questions that humanity has ever confronted: the nature of the soul, the reality of immortality, the pursuit of true wisdom, and the significance of philosophy itself in preparing us for death.

For readers already acquainted with Plato's works, especially The Republic, the themes explored in Phaedo offer a deeper, more personal complement to Plato's philosophical worldview. For those encountering Plato's dialogues for the first time, the Phaedo presents itself as an accessible yet profound introduction to Socratic philosophy and its lasting impact on Western thought. Unlike many of Plato's dialogues, which thrive on the lively back-and-forth of philosophical debate, Phaedo is marked by a reflective, almost reverent atmosphere—a calm and measured meditation on life's deepest meanings as Socrates calmly awaits execution in an Athenian prison cell.

The dramatic setting of the dialogue significantly enhances its philosophical impact. Socrates has been condemned to death by drinking hemlock, sentenced by Athens for corrupting the youth and impiety—charges explored in detail in Plato's Apology. On this final day, gathered around him are a select group of his closest friends and students, including Phaedo, the narrator; Crito, his loyal companion;

Simmias and Cebes, thoughtful disciples whose probing questions guide much of the discussion; and others who have come to bid farewell to their teacher. Their conversation turns naturally toward the profound themes most pressing at such a moment—the immortality of the soul, the purpose of philosophy, and how one should face death.

In this introduction, we will explore the historical context and philosophical significance of the Phaedo, clarify its key arguments and themes, and illuminate why this dialogue remains not only one of Plato's most compelling philosophical texts but also a profoundly human reflection on mortality, wisdom, and the meaning of life itself. Through a close examination of Socrates' final hours and the philosophical legacy he leaves behind, we gain insight not only into Plato's ideas but into the timeless questions about death, the afterlife, and what truly matters in a life well lived.

The Immortality of the Soul: Arguments and Reflections

At the heart of the Phaedo lies Socrates' exploration of the soul's immortality—a topic of perennial philosophical fascination. With calm confidence, Socrates presents several rigorous arguments intended to convince his friends (and himself) of the soul's continued existence after bodily death. These arguments are neither simplistic nor dogmatic; rather, they are constructed carefully and methodically, allowing the reader to engage with Socrates' reasoning step-by-step.

The first argument Socrates offers is the cyclical or "opposite" argument, based on the observation that all things arise from their opposites: cold emerges from heat, sleep from waking, and life from death. Socrates suggests that life and death similarly alternate, implying that souls must persist after death to re-enter life. While this argument may appear intuitive, Plato's deeper philosophical intention is to highlight the cyclical nature of existence itself, suggesting that the soul participates in an ongoing cosmic process of renewal and rebirth.

Following this, Socrates introduces the famous argument from recollection, which readers of the Meno will recognize. Here, he asserts that humans possess innate knowledge of abstract truths—such as mathematical concepts or ideals like justice and beauty—that we "recollect" rather than learn for the first time. This innate knowledge, Socrates argues, demonstrates that our souls must have existed before birth. If our souls existed before birth, it logically follows that they can continue to exist after bodily death.

Socrates then presents the argument from affinity, observing that the soul is invisible, immaterial, and immortal, sharing these properties with the unchanging Forms—eternal truths that exist independently of the physical world. By contrast, the body is visible, material, and mortal, destined to decay. The soul, therefore, belongs naturally to the realm of the eternal, suggesting that its survival after bodily death is not merely possible but philosophically necessary.

Finally, in response to concerns and objections raised by his companions—most notably by Simmias and Cebes—Socrates develops a nuanced and powerful argument centered on the soul's essential nature. He argues that the soul, as the very principle of life itself, cannot admit its opposite (death). Just as fire cannot become cold without ceasing to be fire, the soul cannot become lifeless without ceasing to be a soul. This final argument powerfully reinforces Plato's core philosophical conviction that the soul, being inherently alive, must therefore be immortal.

Yet these arguments are not simply theoretical exercises. They carry deep ethical and existential implications, challenging us to consider how our beliefs about the soul and immortality shape our lives. If the soul is immortal, what kind of existence awaits it after death? How should we live now, knowing that our souls transcend the material world? For Plato, and Socrates, these are questions of paramount importance, defining how we should pursue virtue, truth, and wisdom in our earthly lives.

Philosophy as Preparation for Death: Socrates' Final Legacy

Perhaps the most profound and lasting contribution of the Phaedo is its depiction of philosophy itself as preparation for death. Socrates calmly explains that a true philosopher spends their entire life preparing for the moment of death—not through morbid obsession, but by cultivating a clear separation of soul and body. For Socrates, philosophical inquiry is fundamentally a process of freeing the soul from bodily desires, sensory distractions, and earthly attachments, allowing it to pursue pure wisdom and truth unhindered.

This vision of philosophy as preparation for death dramatically redefines the purpose of human life and learning. For Socrates, genuine philosophical practice involves a lifelong commitment to truth, virtue, and self-examination, purifying the soul from ignorance, prejudice, and worldly temptations. In doing so, philosophers prepare their souls to exist independently of the body, readying themselves for a seamless transition to the afterlife. Death, in this perspective, is not an end to be feared; it is a liberation, the soul's release from bodily constraints into the eternal realm of perfect knowledge and ultimate reality.

Socrates' serene acceptance of death profoundly impacts his friends and students, both within the dialogue and across generations of readers. Rather than displaying fear or regret, Socrates embodies a remarkable serenity born from his philosophical convictions. His final moments exemplify the power of philosophy to shape not only our understanding but also our emotions and actions. He approaches death not as tragedy but as fulfillment, demonstrating in practice what he preached in theory—a life dedicated to wisdom, moral integrity, and truth.

The Significance of the Phaedo Today:
A Timeless Reflection

Today, the Phaedo remains as compelling and relevant as ever. In a world often marked by uncertainty, materialism, and the avoidance of uncomfortable truths, Plato's dialogue offers a powerful reminder of the enduring significance of philosophical inquiry. Its exploration of immortality, virtue, and the nature of the soul speaks directly to contemporary anxieties about meaning, mortality, and what it means to live a good and meaningful life.

The dialogue's emotional and philosophical depth invites readers to reflect on their own beliefs and attitudes toward death and dying. Socrates' calm acceptance of his fate challenges us to reconsider our own fears and anxieties about mortality. Are we prepared, as Socrates was, to meet death with courage and wisdom? Do we live our lives in a manner worthy of our deepest convictions? The Phaedo confronts readers with these timeless questions, urging us to engage actively and thoughtfully with life's most profound mysteries.

Reading the Phaedo is thus not simply an intellectual exercise; it is a deeply human experience, inviting readers to join Socrates and his companions in contemplating what truly matters. The dialogue provides not only profound philosophical insights but also a compelling model of how philosophy itself can offer consolation, clarity, and meaning in the face of life's ultimate challenges.

Welcome to Plato's Phaedo, a profound meditation on the soul's immortality, the nature of wisdom, and the meaning of life and death. May your journey through its pages inspire you, challenge you, and perhaps even transform your understanding of what it means to truly live—and to bravely face the inevitable journey we all must take.

Characters in the Story:

Phaedo (who tells the story to Echecrates), Socrates, Apollodorus, Simmias, Cebes, Crito, and a prison guard.

Scene: Socrates' prison cell.

Location of the Storytelling: Phlius.

Phaedo

Echecrates: Phaedo, were you actually there with Socrates the day he drank the poison?

Phaedo: Yes, I was.

Echecrates: I really want to know what happened. What did he say in his final hours? We heard he died by taking poison, but we never heard the full story. No one from Athens has visited us, and no one from here goes there anymore.

Phaedo: Didn't you hear what happened during his trial?

Echecrates: We did hear something about the trial. But we didn't understand why he wasn't executed right away. Why the delay?

Phaedo: That was because of a special event. The Athenians had crowned the stern of a ship they send to Delos, and that happened just before Socrates' trial.

Echecrates: What ship was that?

Phaedo: It's a sacred ship. According to tradition, it's the same one Theseus sailed to Crete in when he rescued fourteen young people and saved himself. It's said that back then, the survivors made a promise to Apollo that if they returned safely, they would send a mission to Delos every year. That tradition still happens. While the ship is gone, the city must remain "pure," meaning no public executions are allowed. If bad weather delays the ship, the waiting period can be long. Since the ship was crowned the day before the trial, Socrates had to stay in prison until it returned.

Echecrates: So how did he die? What happened that day? Were his friends allowed to be with him, or was he alone?

Phaedo: No, he wasn't alone. Many of us were there.

Echecrates: If you have time, I'd love to hear everything that happened.

Phaedo: I'm free, and I'd be happy to tell you. Talking about Socrates always brings me joy—whether I'm sharing memories or listening to others.

Echecrates: I feel the same, and I hope you can tell me everything you remember, as clearly as you can.

Phaedo: It was a strange experience. I couldn't believe I was watching a friend die. But I didn't feel sorry for him—he was calm, brave, and kind. It seemed like he had been called by something divine. He looked peaceful, like someone going to a better place. It didn't feel sad in the usual way. But at the same time, I couldn't enjoy the conversation like I usually would, even though we talked about philosophy. There was a mix of happiness and pain, knowing this was his last day. We all felt that way—sometimes laughing, sometimes crying. Especially Apollodorus—you know how emotional he is?

Echecrates: Yes, I do.

Phaedo: He was completely overwhelmed. The rest of us were also very emotional.

Echecrates: Who was there?

Phaedo: Besides Apollodorus, there were some Athenians: Critobulus and his father Crito, Hermogenes, Epigenes, Aeschines, Antisthenes, and Ctesippus from Paeania, Menexenus, and a few others. Plato was sick, I think, so he wasn't there.

Echecrates: Were there any guests from outside Athens?

Phaedo: Yes. Simmias and Cebes from Thebes, and Phaedondes, along with Euclid and Terpsion from Megara.

Echecrates: What about Aristippus or Cleombrotus?

Phaedo: No, they were said to be in Aegina.

Echecrates: Anyone else?

Phaedo: I believe that's everyone.

Echecrates: What did you talk about?

Phaedo: I'll try to tell you everything, starting from the beginning. For several days before, we had been meeting early at the court near the prison, waiting for the doors to open. Once we were let in, we spent the day with Socrates. On his final day, we arrived even earlier than usual because we heard the sacred ship had returned, meaning he would likely die that day. When we got there, the jailer came out and told us to wait—Socrates was with the officials who were removing his chains and giving orders for the execution. After a short while, we were allowed in.

Inside, we saw Socrates just freed from his chains. His wife Xanthippe was sitting with him, holding their child. When she saw us, she cried out, "Socrates, this is the last time you'll speak to your friends, or they to you!" Socrates turned to Crito and asked him to have someone take her home. So Crito's people gently led her away as she cried and hit herself in sorrow.

After she left, Socrates sat up on his bed, bent his leg, and started rubbing it. He said, "Isn't it strange how pleasure and pain are connected? They never happen at the same time, but when one comes, the other usually follows. It's like they're two bodies with one head. I think if Aesop had written about them, he would have told a story about how the gods tried to separate them but couldn't, so they tied their heads together instead. That's why I feel pleasure now that the pain from my chains is gone."

Cebes said, "I'm glad you mentioned Aesop. Just a few days ago, Evenus the poet asked me why you, someone who never wrote poetry, are now writing Aesop's fables and that hymn to Apollo. He'll probably ask again. What should I tell him?"

Socrates replied, "Tell him the truth. I wasn't trying to compete with him or become a great poet. That's not easy. I was just trying to clear up something that had been bothering me. Throughout my life, I've often had dreams that said, 'Make music.' I always thought they meant I should keep studying philosophy, since I believe philosophy is the truest kind of music. The dreams were encouraging me to do what I was already doing—like telling a runner in a race to keep running. But as my death approached, I started to wonder: what if the dreams meant music in the usual sense—actual songs and poetry? So I decided to play it safe and write something before I die. First, I wrote a hymn to Apollo, since this festival is in his honor. Then, since a real poet needs to tell stories and I'm not good at making things up, I turned some of Aesop's fables into verse. Tell Evenus this, and encourage him to follow after me if he's wise—and not to wait too long. The Athenians say today is the day I must go."

Simmias said, "That's quite a message! I've spent a lot of time with Evenus, and from what I know of him, I don't think he'll follow your advice unless he absolutely has to."

"Tell me," Socrates said, "isn't Evenus a philosopher?"

"I think he is," Simmias answered.

"Then he, or anyone with a truly philosophical mindset, would be willing to die—but he wouldn't take his own life. That's considered wrong."

Socrates shifted his position, placing his feet on the ground, and stayed sitting like that for the rest of their talk.

"But why," Cebes asked, "do you say someone shouldn't take their own life, even though a philosopher should be ready for death?"

Socrates replied, "Haven't you and Simmias, who both studied under Philolaus, ever heard him talk about this?"

"Yes," said Cebes, "but honestly, what he said was hard to understand."

"I don't claim to understand it perfectly either," said Socrates, "but I'll share what I've heard. And since I'm about to die, it makes sense for me to spend my last hours thinking and talking about where I'm going. What better way to spend the time before sunset?"

"Then please explain," said Cebes. "Why is suicide considered wrong? Philolaus said that too when he stayed with us in Thebes. Other people agree with him, but I've never really understood why."

"Don't worry," Socrates said. "Maybe one day it'll make sense. You're probably wondering why, if some bad things can sometimes be good for certain people, death is always treated as something to be avoided. Why can't someone end their life if it would be better for them?"

Cebes smiled and said, "Yes, that's exactly what I've been thinking."

"I get why it seems strange," Socrates replied. "But maybe it's not really a contradiction. There's a quiet belief that people are like prisoners and shouldn't open the door and escape unless they're told to. I'm not sure I understand this completely either, but I do believe the gods are watching over us, and we belong to them. Don't you agree?"

"Yes, I do," said Cebes.

"So, if one of your animals—say an ox or a donkey—decided to end its life without your permission, wouldn't you be upset?"

"Of course," said Cebes.

"Then maybe that's why people shouldn't end their lives unless the gods give a sign. Like now—they're calling me."

"That makes sense," said Cebes. "But if that's true, how do we make sense of what we just said—that philosophers are ready to die? If the gods are such good caretakers, why would wise people want to leave them? It sounds like only foolish people would want to escape. The wise would want to stay with the gods, who care for them better than they could care for themselves. A fool might try to run away, not realizing he should stay. So doesn't it seem backwards? It sounds like the wise should be sad to die, and the fools should be happy."

Socrates smiled and said to the group, "Cebes is always asking good questions. He doesn't accept something just because he hears it once."

Simmias added, "I agree. What he's saying does make sense. Why would a truly wise person want to leave the gods, who are better than us? I think Cebes is talking about you, Socrates—he thinks you're too ready to leave us and the gods."

Socrates replied, "That's a fair point. So you think I should defend myself, like I'm in court?"

"We'd like that," said Simmias.

"Alright then," said Socrates. "I'll try to explain it better than I did at my actual trial. First of all, Simmias and Cebes, I would be upset about dying if I didn't believe I was going to be with other gods—who are wise and good. I'm as sure of that as I can be about anything. And secondly, even though I'm less certain, I believe I'll also be with better people than those I'm leaving behind. That's why I don't feel sad—I actually feel hopeful. I believe that death holds something better for good people than for bad ones."

Simmias asked, "But Socrates, will you share your thoughts with us before you go? It would help us, and we deserve to understand too. And if you can convince us, that'll answer some of the doubts we've raised."

"I'll do my best," said Socrates. "But first let's hear what Crito has been wanting to say."

Crito spoke up, "The guard who's supposed to give you the poison told me to remind you not to talk too much. He said talking gets you worked up, and that might make the poison less effective. Sometimes, when people get too excited, they need more than one dose."

Socrates replied, "Then he should be ready to give me two or even three doses, if that's what it takes."

"I knew you'd say that," said Crito. "But I had to pass on the message."

"Forget about him," said Socrates.

He turned back to the others and said, "Now, friends, I want to explain why a true philosopher has good reason to be calm about death. In fact, he can even look forward to it. And after death, I believe he can hope for the greatest rewards. Let me try to explain why. I believe real philosophers are often misunderstood. People don't realize that they are always preparing for death throughout their lives. So if they've been longing for death all along, why would they fear it when it finally comes?"

Simmias smiled a little. "Even though I'm not really in the mood to laugh, Socrates, you made me laugh. I can already hear people back home saying, 'Look how right we were about philosophers—they really do want to die!' They'll say philosophers deserve the death they get, since that's what they seem to want."

"And they're not completely wrong," said Socrates. "Except they misunderstand what kind of death we mean. They don't know what real death is for a philosopher, or why we desire it. But let's not worry about what other people think—let's talk about it ourselves. Do we believe death is a real thing?"

"Of course," said Simmias.

"And isn't death just the soul separating from the body? When the soul is no longer connected to the body, and the body to the soul—isn't that death?"

"Yes, that's right," Simmias replied.

"There's another question that might help us understand what we're talking about," said Socrates. "Tell me, Simmias—do you think a real philosopher cares about the pleasures of eating and drinking?"

"Not at all," Simmias replied.

"What about romantic pleasures—do you think he values those?"

"Definitely not."

"And what about nice clothes, fancy shoes, and other things that make the body look good? Wouldn't he ignore anything beyond what's truly needed?"

"I think a true philosopher would not care about those things," Simmias said.

"So wouldn't you say that a philosopher focuses only on the soul, and tries to stay away from anything related to the body?"

"That's true," Simmias agreed.

"In fact," Socrates continued, "philosophers seem to go out of their way to separate their soul from the body in every way they can."

"Yes, that's very true," said Simmias.

"But most people in the world think differently. They believe that a life without pleasures like these isn't worth living. They think anyone who doesn't enjoy the body's pleasures is as good as dead."

"That's also true," Simmias said.

"Now let's think about how we actually learn things," Socrates continued. "When we try to understand something, is the body helpful or not? Can we trust what we see or hear? Aren't our eyes and ears often wrong? And if our best senses can be misleading, what about the rest?"

"You're right," Simmias answered. "Even our best senses aren't perfect."

"So when does the soul actually discover the truth? Clearly, not when it's relying on the body."

"That's true."

"Then isn't it through thought alone that the soul comes closest to the truth?"

"Yes."

"And isn't thinking best when the mind is focused only on itself— when it isn't distracted by sights, sounds, pain, or pleasure? When it turns away from the body and its desires, and instead aims for truth?"

"Certainly."

"So a true philosopher actually avoids the body. His soul tries to be as separate from it as possible."

"That's true," Simmias said.

"Let me ask you something else," Socrates continued. "Would you agree that things like perfect justice, perfect beauty, and perfect goodness really exist?"

"Yes, absolutely."

"But have you ever seen them with your eyes?"

"No, I haven't."

"Or felt them with any of your senses? I don't just mean justice or beauty, but also things like perfect strength, perfect health, or the true nature of anything. Have you ever fully understood these through your body? Or wouldn't you say that the best understanding comes from someone who uses only their mind to clearly think about what each thing truly is?"

"Yes, that's how someone gains real understanding," Simmias agreed.

"And the person who understands best is the one who uses only their mind—not their eyes or ears or any other sense—just clear thinking, without distractions from the body. He believes that senses only confuse the soul and get in the way of knowing the truth. So who could possibly understand reality better than someone like that?"

"What you're saying makes a lot of sense, Socrates," said Simmias.

"So when real philosophers think about this, don't you think they end up saying something like this: 'We've found that as long as we live in these bodies, and the soul is mixed with the body's problems, we'll never be fully satisfied in our search for truth. The body needs constant care, like food, and it gets sick and tired, holding us back. It fills us with desires, fears, and silly distractions. As people say, it makes thinking almost impossible. Where do war and fighting come from? The body and its desires. People fight for money, and they need money to take care of the body. All this gets in the way of real thinking. And even when we do get a quiet moment to think, the body still interrupts us. It distracts us, confuses us, and stops us from finding the truth. We've learned from experience that we'll only reach true understanding once we're free from the body—when the soul is alone, seeing things as they truly are. That's when we'll finally gain the wisdom we've been seeking—not during life, but after death. Because if the soul can't gain pure knowledge while in the body, then we have two options: either we never find truth, or we find it only after death. That's when the soul leaves the body completely. So, while we're alive, the best we can do is stay away from the body's distractions as much as possible. We must keep our souls pure until the gods choose to free us from the body. Only then, once we've escaped the foolishness that the body brings, can we meet the pure truth and finally understand it ourselves. For only the pure can understand what is pure.'"

"These are the kinds of things true philosophers say and believe," Socrates concluded. "Don't you agree, Simmias?"

"I absolutely do, Socrates."

"My friend," said Socrates, "if all this is true, then I have a good reason to feel hopeful. Where I'm going, I might finally reach what I've been searching for my whole life. That's why I'm happy as I go—not just me, but anyone who feels they've prepared their mind and purified their soul."

"I agree," said Simmias.

"And what does it mean to purify the soul?" Socrates continued. "It means separating it from the body—learning to focus on the soul itself, pulling away from the body's distractions. In both this life and the next, a purified soul lives in its own space, free from being controlled by the body."

"That's true," said Simmias.

"And isn't that separation what we call death?"

"Exactly."

"And aren't true philosophers always working toward this kind of separation? Isn't that what they focus on most?"

"Yes, that's right."

"Then wouldn't it be strange," Socrates said, "for someone who's been preparing for death their whole life to be afraid of it when it finally comes?"

"Very strange," agreed Simmias.

"Real philosophers practice dying all the time, which is why they, more than anyone else, have no reason to fear it. Think about it: if they've spent their whole lives turning away from the body and focusing only on the soul, why would they be upset when death gives them what they've wanted—freedom from the body? Wouldn't they be glad to go to a place where they hope to find what they've been seeking—wisdom—and to leave behind what they've always seen as an enemy?

"Some people have looked forward to death just for the chance to see a loved one again—a spouse or child—and to speak with them. But wouldn't someone who truly loves wisdom be even more eager to go, believing that only after death can they fully be with her? If so, they would leave this world with joy, not fear. If they are truly wise, they must believe that wisdom exists in its purest form after death. So it would make no sense for such a person to fear dying."

"Agreed," said Simmias.

"So if you see someone afraid of death," Socrates said, "doesn't that show they aren't a lover of wisdom? That they probably care more about their body, or maybe money, power, or both?"

"Yes, that makes sense," Simmias replied.

"And wouldn't you say that courage is something that belongs especially to philosophers?"

"Definitely."

"And temperance too," Socrates added. "Even most people say temperance means controlling your desires and rising above them. Isn't that something you only find in people who look down on bodily pleasures and spend their lives on philosophy?"

"Absolutely."

"But look closer," Socrates continued. "Most people's courage and temperance are full of contradictions."

"What do you mean?" asked Simmias.

"Well, most people see death as a terrible thing, right?"

"Right."

"And don't most people only face death bravely because they're even more afraid of something worse?"

"That's true."

"So they're being brave because they're scared—which is a pretty strange kind of bravery."

"Yes, very strange," said Simmias.

"And it's the same with temperance," Socrates went on. "People seem self-controlled, but really they're just afraid of losing other pleasures. They give up some pleasures because they want to hold onto others. So in a way, they're controlled by pleasure, not free from it. That's not real temperance. It's like they're being self-controlled because they're not self-controlled."

"That's what it looks like," Simmias said.

"But trading one fear or pleasure for another—like swapping one coin for another—that's not real virtue," said Socrates. "There's only one true coin, and that's wisdom. Only wisdom makes courage, temperance, and justice truly valuable. Without wisdom, those things are just imitations. But when someone has real wisdom, all those virtues are purified and true. That's why people in the ancient mystery religions used to say that anyone who dies without being purified will be stuck in darkness, but those who are purified will live with the gods. When they said, 'Many carry the ritual staff, but few are true initiates,' I think what they meant was that only a few people are real philosophers.

"I've spent my whole life trying to be one of them. Whether I've done it right, I'll soon find out—once I cross over to the other side, if the gods allow it. That's why I don't feel sad about leaving you or my teachers. I believe I'll find more good friends and wise teachers after I die. Most people don't believe this. But if I can explain it well enough to convince you—better than I convinced the Athenian judges—then that would be a success."

Cebes said, "I agree with most of what you've said, Socrates. But people still doubt what happens to the soul after death. They worry that as soon as the soul leaves the body, it just disappears—like smoke or air—and vanishes into nothing. If the soul really stayed whole after death, then what you're saying would give us strong hope. But I think it takes a lot of proof and good reasoning to show that the soul still exists and can think after the body is gone."

"You're right, Cebes," Socrates said. "Shall we try to explore whether that's really the case?"

"I'd really like to hear your thoughts," said Cebes.

"Well," said Socrates, "I don't think anyone listening to me now—even my old critics, like the comic playwrights—could accuse me of talking nonsense about things I don't care about. So, if you're ready, let's continue."

"Let's talk about whether souls continue to exist after death," he said. "There's an old belief that souls leave this world and go to another, and from there they return and are reborn. If that's true—if the living really do come from the dead—then souls must still exist after death, or else how could they be reborn? If we can prove this idea, then we'll have strong evidence. But if not, then we'll have to look for another explanation."

"That makes sense," Cebes replied.

"Then let's think about this more broadly," said Socrates. "Not just with people, but with all living things—animals, plants, everything that's born or changes. Don't all things that have opposites come from their opposites? For example, good comes from bad, and bad from good. Just like big comes from small, and small from big. Isn't that how change happens?"

"Yes," said Cebes, "that's true."

"And anything that becomes smaller," Socrates said, "must have once been bigger, right?"

"Yes," said Cebes.

"And what becomes weaker must have been stronger before, just like something faster must have come from something slower."

"That's true."

"And the worse comes from the better, and justice comes from injustice."

"Of course."

"So wouldn't you say that all opposites are created from their opposites?"

"Yes, I'd agree with that," said Cebes.

"And between all opposites, don't there always seem to be two things happening—going from one to the other and back again? For example, between bigger and smaller, there's growing and shrinking. What grows is increasing, and what shrinks is decreasing."

"Yes, that's right," Cebes replied.

"There are many other examples, like combining and separating, heating and cooling. These are all ways of changing from one opposite into another. Even if we don't always describe them in words, they really are opposites moving between each other."

"Very true," Cebes agreed.

"Well then," Socrates said, "isn't life the opposite of death—just like sleeping is the opposite of being awake?"

"Yes," said Cebes.

"So what's the opposite of life?"

"Death," Cebes replied.

"And if they are opposites, then one must come from the other. That means life must come from death, and death must come from life. Do you agree?"

"I do."

"Let's look at one pair of opposites together," Socrates said. "I'll take sleep and waking. Sleep is the opposite of waking. We fall asleep to go from waking to sleeping, and we wake up to go from sleeping to waking. Do you agree?"

"Yes, I do."

"Then do the same for life and death. Is death the opposite of life?"

"Yes."

"And one must come from the other?"

"Yes."

"Then what comes from the living?"

"The dead," said Cebes.

"And what comes from the dead?"

"Well... the living."

"So the living are born from the dead?"

"That's clear."

"Then that means souls must exist in the world of the dead, right? Otherwise, how could the living come from them?"

"That makes sense."

"We see one half of this process—dying—is clear and visible," Socrates said. "But we must accept that the opposite is also happening, right? Life must come from death too."

"Of course," said Cebes.

"So what would that process be called?"

"Coming back to life."

"And if people come back to life, that means the dead are being born again into the world of the living?"

"Yes, exactly."

"Then this gives us another reason to believe that souls continue to exist after death, and they come back from that place to live again."

"Yes, Socrates," said Cebes. "That seems like a clear conclusion from what we've just said."

"And I think," Socrates continued, "that we weren't wrong to believe this. Because if everything just kept changing in one direction with no balance, then all things would eventually end up the same and there would be no more change."

"What do you mean?" asked Cebes.

"Let me explain it with sleep," said Socrates. "Imagine if everyone just kept falling asleep but never woke up. Then the story of Endymion—a man who sleeps forever—wouldn't mean anything, because we'd all be asleep too. Or imagine if things could only combine but never break apart. Everything would turn into one big mess, like the chaos Anaxagoras talked about.

"Now think about life. If everything that lives eventually dies, and nothing ever comes back to life, then eventually everything would be dead. There would be no life left anywhere. If the living only come from other living things, and all living things die, then sooner or later, death would take over everything."

"There's no way around that," said Cebes. "And honestly, your argument seems absolutely right."

"Yes," said Socrates. "I really believe that life comes from death, and the souls of the dead exist in another place. And I also believe that good souls are better off than bad ones."

Cebes added, "Socrates, your idea that learning is just remembering—if that's true—it also means that our souls must have existed before we were born, so we could learn things that we now remember. That would be another proof that the soul lives on."

"Tell me more about that," said Simmias, jumping in. "I'm not sure I remember the reasoning behind that idea."

"One strong example," said Cebes, "is how people answer questions. If you ask someone the right kind of question, they can give the correct answer on their own. How could they do that unless the knowledge was already inside them? You can really see this when they look at a drawing or a shape."

"But if you're still unsure," Socrates said, "maybe I can explain it in another way. I don't think you're truly doubtful, Simmias—I just think you want to hear the idea more clearly so you can understand it better."

"That's right," said Simmias. "Cebes helped remind me, but I'd still like to hear how you explain it."

"Well," said Socrates, "I think we agree that if someone remembers something, then they must have learned it at some point before."

"Of course," said Simmias.

"Now let me ask you this," Socrates said. "When a person sees or hears something, and it makes them think of something else— something different from what they saw or heard—can't we say they're remembering that other thing?"

"What do you mean?"

"Take this example," said Socrates. "Knowing what a lyre is isn't the same as knowing a person. But imagine a person sees a lyre or some clothes that belonged to someone they loved. Don't they immediately think of that person? Isn't that remembering?

"In the same way, someone might see Simmias and think of Cebes. And there are lots of examples like this."

"Endless examples," Simmias said.

"Exactly," Socrates replied. "And memory usually works like that—it brings back something we forgot because of time or distraction."

"Very true," said Simmias.

"And sometimes you might see a picture of a horse or a lyre and it makes you think of a person. Or maybe a picture of Simmias reminds you of Cebes."

"Yes, that happens."

"Or it might just remind you of Simmias himself."

"That too."

"So we can remember things because of things that are similar to them—or even things that are totally different."

"That's right."

"And when we remember something because it looks like something else, isn't it natural to ask whether the thing we're looking at really matches what we remember—or if it falls short?"

"Yes, that's definitely true," said Simmias.

"Let's take this a little further," said Socrates. "Would you agree that there's such a thing as perfect equality—not just comparing two sticks or stones—but a kind of perfect, unchanging equality beyond all physical things?"

"I agree completely," said Simmias. "I'd even swear it's true."

"And we understand what this perfect equality is, right?"

"Of course."

"But where did we get that understanding?" Socrates asked. "Was it from seeing equal things—like sticks or stones—and realizing that perfect equality is something different from those? Because clearly, those things aren't always exactly equal. Sometimes two things might seem equal, but at another time, they might look unequal."

"That's true," Simmias agreed.

"But the idea of perfect equality—does it ever change or become unequal?"

"No way, Socrates."

"Then the physical things we compare can't really be the same as perfect equality."

"Definitely not."

"And yet, even though those things fall short, they still help us understand what perfect equality is."

"Exactly."

"Whether what we're looking at is similar or not doesn't matter—if seeing one thing makes you think of another, that's still remembering, right?"

"Yes, it is."

"So, when we look at two pieces of wood or two stones and say they're equal, we're still noticing that they don't measure up to perfect equality."

"That's very true."

"And if someone looks at a thing and realizes that it's trying to be like something else—but falls short—they must already have some idea of what that 'something else' is, don't you think?"

"Yes, of course."

"And that's exactly what's happening when we compare things and recognize that they're not truly equal—we're measuring them against our idea of perfect equality, which we must've already known."

"That makes sense."

"So that means we knew about perfect equality before we ever saw anything with our eyes or touched anything with our hands—because we're comparing our physical experiences to that idea."

"That must be right," Simmias said.

"And we started seeing and hearing and using our senses right when we were born, didn't we?"

"Yeah, of course."

"Then we must have learned about perfect equality before we were born."

"Yes."

"And if we knew that before birth, then we probably also knew other ideas before we were born—like beauty, goodness, justice, and holiness—all the big ideas we talk about when we ask or answer deep questions."

"I think that's true."

"And if we never forgot what we knew before birth, we'd still remember it all now. We'd always have that knowledge with us. Because knowing something means holding on to it and not forgetting it. Forgetting is just losing knowledge, right?"

"Yes, that's true," said Simmias.

"But if we did forget all that knowledge at birth, and then later started remembering it by using our senses, wouldn't that mean that learning is really just remembering things we already knew?"

"Exactly."

"So when we see or hear something and it makes us think of something else—something we had forgotten—that's what remembering is. That shows us that either we already knew things from birth and never forgot them, or that what we call learning is actually just remembering."

"I see what you mean, Socrates. That sounds right."

"Which one do you think makes more sense, Simmias? Did we know these things at birth, or did we remember them from even earlier?"

"I'm not sure. I need to think more about it."

"Well, let's try it from another angle. Someone who knows something should be able to explain it, right?"

"Yes, of course."

"But do you think everyone can explain these deep ideas we're talking about?"

"I wish they could, Socrates. But honestly, I don't think anyone alive tomorrow will be able to give a full answer."

"Then you don't think everyone really knows these things?"

"No, I don't."

"Then maybe they're still in the process of remembering what they once knew."

"That sounds right."

"So when did our souls learn all this? Not after we were born."

"Definitely not."

"Then it must have been before."

"Yes."

"So, Simmias, that means our souls had to exist before we were born—without our bodies—and they must have had intelligence."

"Well, unless you think we somehow got all this knowledge right at birth. That's the only other option."

"But even if that were true," said Socrates, "when would we have forgotten everything? It's agreed we don't have this knowledge at birth, right? So how could we lose it the very moment we received it?"

"That wouldn't make sense," Simmias admitted. "I guess I was talking nonsense without realizing it."

"Then let's say this, Simmias: If there really is such a thing as perfect beauty, goodness, and truth—and we recognize these ideas by comparing our experiences to them—then those ideas must have existed before we were born. And if the ideas existed before, so did our souls. If not, then neither the ideas nor our souls existed before birth."

"Yes, Socrates," said Simmias. "I really do believe now that both things are connected—our souls must have existed before we were born if those ideas like beauty and goodness truly exist. And I feel like the argument clearly proves that."

"Good," said Socrates, "but what about Cebes? Is he convinced too?"

"I think so," said Simmias. "Even though Cebes is one of the most doubtful people I know, I think he now believes that the soul existed before birth. But whether the soul continues to exist after death—that part still isn't fully clear, even to me. I still feel that same worry Cebes mentioned earlier, that when someone dies, the soul might just scatter and vanish. Even if the soul came from somewhere else before entering the body, why couldn't it be destroyed after leaving the body again?"

"You're right," said Cebes. "Half of the question has been answered—we know the soul existed before birth. But we still need proof that it survives after death too. Once we have that, the whole argument will be complete."

"But that part," said Socrates, "has already been answered—if you put together both arguments. Remember, we agreed that all living things come from the dead. So, if souls existed before birth and living things are born from death, then the soul must still exist after death in order to be reborn. So we already have the proof. But I understand—you and Simmias still want to go deeper, don't you? It's like you're scared, like little kids afraid of ghosts. You're worried that when the soul leaves the body, it might just get blown away in the wind, especially if someone dies in a big storm instead of a peaceful moment."

Cebes smiled. "Yes, Socrates. We want you to talk us out of our fears. Though honestly, it's not us who are afraid—it's that childish part inside all of us that's scared of the dark and death."

Socrates replied, "Then we need to use comforting words, like a song that calms someone who's scared. We should repeat it again and again until the fear goes away."

"But who will do that for us after you're gone, Socrates?" asked Cebes.

"Hellas is a big place," said Socrates, "and there are good people everywhere—even in other lands. Look for them far and wide, don't be afraid to spend money or time on it, because nothing is more important. You should also look within yourselves, because you might be the ones best able to find the truth."

"We'll make the search, no doubt about it," said Cebes. "But for now, can we go back to where we left off in our discussion?"

"Of course," said Socrates. "What else would we do?"

"Alright," he continued. "Let's start by asking what kind of things we think can be scattered and lost—and which things we believe stay together. Our hopes and fears about the soul will depend on how we answer that."

"That makes sense," said Cebes.

"Now, things that are made of parts can usually fall apart too, right? But things that are not made of parts—things that are simple—don't fall apart."

"That seems reasonable," Cebes said.

"And things that are simple and whole are usually unchanging. But things made of parts are always shifting, never staying the same."

"I agree."

"Now, let's go back to those perfect ideas we talked about before—like perfect beauty or perfect fairness. Do those things ever change? Or are they always exactly what they are?"

"They never change," said Cebes.

"But what about things like beautiful people, or clothes, or anything else we call beautiful or equal—don't they always change? Don't they look different from time to time, or to different people?"

"Yes, they're always changing."

"And we can see or touch those changing things with our senses. But the unchanging things—like perfect beauty or perfect fairness—we can only understand with our minds. We don't see them with our eyes."

"That's true."

"Then it seems like there are two types of things: the ones we can see and the ones we can't see."

"I agree."

"The ones we see are always changing. The ones we can't see are unchanging."

"Yes."

"Now, we each have a body and a soul, right?"

"Of course."

"Which of those—body or soul—is more like the things we see and touch?"

"The body, clearly."

"And the soul—can we see it?"

"No, we can't."

"So the soul is more like the invisible and unchanging things?"

"That makes sense."

"Didn't we also say earlier that when the soul uses the body's senses—like sight or hearing—it gets pulled into the world of change and becomes confused, like someone who's dizzy or drunk?"

"Yes, we said that."

"But when the soul turns inward, thinking on its own, it enters a pure world—a world of unchanging truths, things that are eternal. That's its true home. When it's not distracted by the body, the soul becomes calm and clear. That's what we call wisdom, right?"

"Yes, exactly."

"Now, based on all this, which one is more like the unchanging world: the soul or the body?"

"Definitely the soul," said Cebes.

"And the body is more like the changing world?"

"Yes."

"Let's look at this in another way. When the soul and body are together, who's supposed to be in charge? Doesn't the soul naturally lead, and the body follow?"

"Yes, that's true."

"And which sounds more divine—the one who rules or the one who serves?"

"The one who rules."

"So which one is more like something divine—the soul or the body?"

"The soul is like the divine, and the body is like something mortal."

"Then, Cebes, based on everything we've said, isn't this the conclusion? That the soul is like something divine, immortal, wise, and unchanging—and the body is like something human, mortal, unintelligent, and always changing?"

"That's the only conclusion we can reach."

"And if that's true, doesn't it follow that the body will break down quickly, while the soul won't—or at least, not easily?"

"Yes, that's clearly true."

Now think about this: when someone dies, their body—what we can see—stays in the physical world. We call it a corpse. You might expect it to break down and fall apart right away, but that doesn't always happen. If the person was healthy and the weather is good, the body might last for quite a while. In places like Egypt, where they used to embalm people, the body could stay mostly intact for thousands of years. And even when it does decay, parts like bones and tendons don't break down easily. Would you agree?

"Yes," said Simmias.

"So, if that's true of the body, which is visible, isn't it even more likely that the soul—something invisible—wouldn't just fall apart right away after leaving the body? Especially if the soul is going to a place like itself: invisible, pure, and full of goodness, which is what people call the true underworld. If the soul is really made from something pure and noble, how could it suddenly be destroyed after death like some people believe?"

"That doesn't make sense," Socrates continued. "A soul that leaves the body clean—one that hasn't gotten tangled up in physical desires, one that's focused on deeper things and avoided worldly pleasures—that soul is ready. That's the kind of person who has practiced separating their soul from their body during life. And what do we call that practice? Philosophy. Isn't philosophy really just preparing for death?"

"Definitely," said Simmias.

"So a soul like that—clean and invisible—goes to a place that's also invisible and divine. There, it's safe and free. It escapes the confusion, fears, and madness of the human world, and it lives forever in peace, in the company of the gods. Isn't that right, Cebes?"

"Yes, absolutely," Cebes replied.

"But now think about a different kind of soul," said Socrates. "One that is unclean when it leaves the body. This soul spent its life chasing after physical pleasures—things it could touch, see, and taste. It got so attached to the body and its cravings that it started to believe only what it could physically sense was real. It hated the kind of truth that comes only through thinking and reason—the kind that can't be seen or touched. Would a soul like that leave the body clean and pure?"

"No way," said Cebes.

"That kind of soul is stuck," Socrates explained. "It's so used to the body and physical things that it can't let go. It's weighed down— heavy, earthy, and pulled back toward the physical world. It's afraid of the invisible world it's supposed to go to, so it hangs around the places it knows—tombs and graves. That's why people say ghosts appear there. They believe these souls didn't leave clean and pure. They were too tied to what they could see, so they stay behind and become visible themselves."

Like the poet Milton once said:

When a person gives in to lust—through inappropriate looks, rude gestures, or filthy talk—

and especially through repeated sinful actions,

it brings a kind of dirtiness deep into the soul.

The soul becomes weighed down and sick from the inside.

It becomes trapped in the body, acting more like an animal than a divine being,

and loses the purity it once had.

These kinds of souls—dark, heavy, and lost—

are the ones people say appear around graveyards and tombs,

lingering near fresh graves,

unwilling to leave the body they once loved.

They became stuck because of their attachment to physical pleasure,

and ended up in a lower, more broken state of being.

That sounds very likely, Socrates.

Yes, Cebes, it does. These must be the souls of bad people—souls that are punished by being stuck wandering around in certain places as a result of the way they lived before. They continue to wander because they're still attached to physical things, and eventually, they get trapped in another body again. Most likely, they're reborn into a body that matches the kind of life they lived before.

What kind of bodies do you mean, Socrates?

I mean that people who gave in to gluttony, wild behavior, and drinking—without ever trying to avoid these habits—might come back as donkeys or other animals like that. What do you think?

That sounds very possible to me.

And people who lived unjust lives—those who were violent or tyrannical—might return as wolves or hawks or other fierce animals. Where else could they end up?

Yes, I agree. Those kinds of souls would match those kinds of lives.

And it's not hard to imagine every type of soul being reborn into a body that matches its habits and personality, right?

Right.

Some souls, though, are better off than others. The happiest ones are those who practiced fairness and self-control in life—not through deep thinking, but by good habits and attention to doing the right thing.

Why are they the happiest?

Because they'll likely be reborn as gentle, social creatures, like bees, ants, or even as humans again—especially humans who are just and balanced.

That makes sense.

Now, no one can enter the realm of the gods unless they've studied philosophy and lived a pure life. That's why true lovers of wisdom stay away from physical pleasures. They don't avoid them because they fear being poor, like people who chase money. And they don't do it because they fear shame, like people who crave power and honor.

No, Socrates, that wouldn't suit them at all, said Cebes.

Exactly, said Socrates. That's why people who care about their souls—and not just about shaping their bodies—say goodbye to all those distractions. They don't want to live blindly. When philosophy offers them a way to clean their souls and be free from evil, they listen and follow her lead.

What do you mean, Socrates?

I mean this: People who love wisdom realize that the soul is stuck to the body. Before discovering philosophy, the soul can only see truth through the body, like through prison bars. She's stuck in ignorance, dragged around by desire, and helping to trap herself. That was her situation.

But when philosophy finds her in that state, she comforts her and gently leads her toward freedom. Philosophy shows her that the senses—like sight and hearing—can't be trusted. She encourages the soul to stop relying on the body and instead look inward, to trust her own pure understanding of what's real. Things we see and touch are always changing. But what the soul understands deep down is unchanging and invisible.

So the true philosopher doesn't fight this process. Instead, the soul avoids pleasure, desire, pain, and fear as much as possible. Why? Because when someone feels intense joy or pain, they start to believe that what they feel is what's most real—but that's not true. What we see and feel can fool us.

That makes sense, said Cebes.

And don't you think the soul is most chained to the body in these moments?

What do you mean?

Think of it this way: Each intense pleasure or pain is like a nail that pins the soul to the body. Over time, the soul starts to agree with the body about what's true. She likes the same things and goes to the same places. And by the time she dies, she's too attached to the body to be free. So she ends up entering a new body and starting the cycle all over again. That's why she misses out on living in a pure, divine state.

You're right, Socrates, said Cebes.

And this, Cebes, is the real reason why true philosophers are brave and self-controlled. Not because they're afraid of being poor or embarrassed.

Definitely not.

Right. A philosopher doesn't want to be freed by wisdom just to fall back into the same old traps. That would be like weaving a cloth only to unravel it again, like Penelope in the old story. Instead, the soul wants to calm her passions, follow reason, and focus on truth. She finds strength by staying connected to what's truly divine—not just opinions, but real understanding. That's how she lives her life. And after death, she hopes to go where she truly belongs—to a place of peace, free from human suffering.

So don't worry, Simmias and Cebes. A soul that's lived this kind of life won't just scatter like dust or be lost. It won't disappear into nothing.

After Socrates stopped talking, there was silence for a while. He seemed to be thinking, and most of us were too. Only Simmias and Cebes whispered a few words to each other.

Socrates noticed and asked what they were thinking. "Do you have doubts?" he asked. "There's still plenty we could examine more closely, if you want. If you're thinking about something else, I'll stay quiet. But if you're unsure about anything, don't be afraid to speak your mind. If you have better ideas, I'd love to hear them. And if I can help, let me."

Simmias said, "Honestly, Socrates, we do have questions. We were encouraging each other to ask, but we both hesitated because we didn't want to bother you at a time like this."

Socrates smiled and said: "Simmias, what are you saying? How can I convince others that I don't see my death as something bad if I can't even convince you? Don't you think I have the same sense of what's coming as swans do? Swans sing all their lives, and when they know they're about to die, they sing louder and more joyfully than ever—because they're excited to go meet the god they serve. But people, because they fear death, wrongly think the swan's last song is one of sadness. They forget that no bird sings when it's cold, hungry, or in pain—not even the nightingale or swallow or hoopoe. And swans are sacred to Apollo. They've been given the gift of prophecy, so they sing with joy knowing they're about to enter a better place. I feel the same. I believe I serve the same god and that he gave me the power to sense what's coming. So I welcome death like they do. Don't worry about asking your question—go ahead and say what's on your mind, while the city's officials still allow it."

Simmias replied, "All right, Socrates. I'll speak my mind, and Cebes will too. I believe it's really hard—maybe even impossible—to be absolutely certain about things like the soul and the afterlife during this life. But I also think it's cowardly not to explore these questions fully. We should try everything to understand the truth—either find solid proof or stick to the most convincing explanation we can find and live by it. Unless a message from the gods comes and tells us something more certain, we have to hold on to that explanation, even if it's risky. So, since you gave us permission, I'll ask what's been on my mind. If I didn't, I'd regret it later. Honestly, Socrates, even after all you've said, I still don't feel completely convinced."

Socrates replied, "That's fair, Simmias. But can you tell me what part of the argument seems weak to you?"

Simmias answered, "Well, imagine someone says the soul is like the harmony that comes from a lyre. The soul is invisible, divine, and perfect—just like harmony. The lyre and its strings are like the body: made of material things, earthy, and bound to decay. Now, if the lyre breaks or its strings are cut, the harmony disappears. That person might argue the same with the soul: when the body falls apart through illness or injury, the soul—like harmony—must also vanish. Even if the body lasts a little longer after death, the soul, being a kind of harmony, could be the first thing to go. What would we say to that?"

Socrates looked at us, smiled, and said, "That's a good question, Simmias. You make a strong point. Maybe someone else here is better suited to answer. But before we respond, let's hear what Cebes has to say too. Then we'll look at both arguments together and decide what makes the most sense."

Socrates turned to Cebes and asked, "So, what's your concern?"

Cebes said, "Here's my issue. I agree that you've made a good case for the soul existing before birth. But I'm not convinced that the soul keeps existing after death. That's still unproven. I don't think, like Simmias, that the soul is just a harmony. I believe the soul is stronger than the body. But I'm still not sure it survives after death. Think about this example. Imagine someone says, 'Look, this coat is still here, so the man who wore it must still be alive.' That's clearly silly. A person can outlive many coats, and just because the last coat remains after his death doesn't prove the man is still alive. In the same way, the soul might outlast many bodies during a long life, repairing and replacing them as needed. But maybe in the end, the soul uses up its last body and finally dies for good. So even if the soul is strong and lives many lives, what if it eventually wears out too? If we can't prove that the soul is completely immortal and can never die, then anyone who's sure it survives death is just being overly confident."

All of us felt uneasy hearing this. We had been so convinced before, and now we were confused and unsure—not only about what had just been said, but about how we could trust any argument in the future.

Echecrates interrupted: "Phaedo, I feel exactly the same! When I heard that, I started to wonder if I could trust any argument at all. I've always liked the idea that the soul is a harmony—it's something I've believed before. But now I feel like I have to start over and find a new reason to believe that the soul lives on after death. Please tell me what Socrates said next. Did he seem upset or worried? Or did he stay calm and answer their arguments strongly? I want to hear everything."

Phaedo replied, "I've always admired Socrates, Echecrates, but never more than I did that day. It wasn't just that he had answers. It was how calm and kind he was when he listened to the young men's concerns. He understood exactly what was troubling them and responded with care and confidence. He reminded me of a general gathering his troops after a setback, urging them to stay in the fight for truth."

Echecrates asked, "What did he say next?"

Phaedo said, "I was sitting right next to him. He reached out and gently smoothed down my hair—he used to play with it sometimes— and said, 'Phaedo, I suppose your hair will be cut tomorrow.'"

Yes, Socrates, I guess they will be, I replied.

"Not if you take my advice," he said.

"What should I do?" I asked.

"Well," he said, "if this argument dies today and we can't bring it back to life, then both of us should shave our heads today—not tomorrow. If I were in your place and lost to Simmias and Cebes in this debate, I would swear, like the Argives once did, not to grow my hair again until I had returned to the argument and won."

I said, "But even Hercules couldn't fight two opponents at once."

"Then call on me," he said, "and I'll be your Iolaus until the sun sets."

"I'd rather call you like Iolaus would call Hercules," I joked.

"That works too," he replied. "But before we continue, let's be careful not to fall into a trap."

"What kind of trap?" I asked.

"The danger of becoming misologists," he said—"haters of arguments. That's one of the worst things that can happen to someone. Just like some people become haters of humanity (misanthropes), others become haters of reasoning. And both come from the same root—disappointment caused by lack of experience. People trust others too easily and then feel betrayed when those people turn out to be false or dishonest. After being hurt by a few, especially close friends, they begin to hate everyone, thinking no one is good. Have you seen that kind of person?"

"I have," I said.

"Isn't it sad?" he said. "It just shows they didn't really understand human nature. With more experience, they'd realize that only a few people are truly good or truly bad—most are somewhere in between."

"What do you mean?" I asked.

"Think about it," he said. "Extremes like very tall or very short people are rare. The same goes for anything—fast or slow, beautiful or ugly, dark or light. Most things fall in the middle. Don't you agree?"

"Yes, that's true," I said.

"And the same goes for evil. If there were a contest for being the worst, there'd still only be a few who win that title."

"That's likely," I said.

"Exactly," he said. "But arguments aren't quite the same as people. I got carried away there. What I meant was, when someone without much experience in reasoning finds an argument they believe in and it later turns out to be false—whether it really is or not—they lose trust in all arguments. And after being disappointed a few times, they start thinking that everything is shaky and unreliable, like the tide constantly changing direction."

"That's very true," I said.

"And it's sad," Socrates said, "because if there is such a thing as truth and knowledge, it's a tragedy for someone to give up just because they were misled by a few arguments. Instead of blaming their own mistakes, they blame reasoning itself and end up hating it. That way, they lose any chance of ever finding real truth or understanding."

"Yes," I said, "that's a real shame."

"So let's be careful," he said, "not to let that idea into our minds— that there's no truth in arguments. Instead, let's admit that we ourselves haven't reached that understanding yet, and we must keep trying. You and I and everyone else must keep working to clear our minds and become wiser—not just for today, but for the rest of our lives. And in my case, for the little time I have left before I die. Right now, I don't claim to be a perfect philosopher. Honestly, I'm just like any other person trying to prove a point. The only difference is that I'm not trying to convince others—I'm trying to convince myself. Whether others agree with me is secondary. And here's the benefit: if what I believe is true, then I've gained something valuable. But if it turns out I'm wrong and nothing happens after death, well, I'll still have lived these last moments in peace. I won't make my friends suffer by watching me fear or cry, and my ignorance will die with me—so no harm done.

"This is the mindset I bring to this discussion, Simmias and Cebes. So I ask you, don't focus on me, but on the truth itself. If what I say makes sense to you, agree. If not, argue back as strongly as you can. I'd rather be corrected than mislead you and myself. I don't want to sting you like a bee before I go."

"Alright then," Socrates said, "let's continue. First, let me make sure I understand what you both said earlier. Simmias, if I'm remembering correctly, you were worried that the soul—though more beautiful and divine than the body—might still be like harmony, and could be destroyed first. Cebes, on the other hand, agreed that the soul lasts longer than the body, but you said no one can know if the soul eventually wears out after going through many bodies, and that death could be when the soul itself is finally destroyed—not just the body, since the body is always decaying. Are those the points we're focusing on?"

They both agreed.

"Now," Socrates asked, "do you reject the whole argument we made earlier, or just part of it?"

"Just part of it," they said.

"What about the part where we said learning is really remembering—recollection—and that the soul must have existed before being born in a body? Do you still believe that?"

Cebes said that argument still convinced him completely. Simmias agreed and added he could hardly imagine ever thinking otherwise.

Socrates responded, "But Simmias, if you still believe the soul is like harmony, then your two beliefs can't go together. You can't say the soul existed before the body if you also say it's like harmony, which only comes after the body's elements are arranged. You wouldn't say harmony existed before the strings of the lyre, right?"

"Of course not," Simmias replied.

"But that's what you'd be implying if you say the soul existed before the body but is also a harmony. Harmony is created last and is the first to disappear. So that idea can't match the belief that the soul existed before the body."

"You're right," Simmias said.

"And yet," Socrates continued, "shouldn't there be harmony in an argument that talks about harmony?"

"There should be," said Simmias.

"But there isn't any harmony," Socrates said, "between the idea that knowledge is recollection and the idea that the soul is harmony. So which one do you believe more strongly?"

"I believe in recollection much more," Simmias said. "It's been clearly proven to me. The harmony idea sounds nice, but it hasn't been proven. It just sounds likely, which is why many people believe it. But arguments based only on what seems likely can be misleading if we're not careful. The idea that knowledge is recollection makes sense to me—because it shows the soul must have existed before birth. So I think we should stop comparing the soul to harmony."

"Let me put it another way," Socrates said. "Do you think a harmony can be in any condition other than the condition of its parts?"

"Certainly not."

"And can it do or experience anything other than what its parts do?"

"No, it can't."

"Then a harmony doesn't control its parts—it only follows them."

"That's true."

"A harmony can't have qualities like motion or sound unless those qualities are in its parts first, right?"

"Exactly."

"And the way a harmony works depends entirely on how the parts are arranged?"

"What do you mean?"

"I mean that a harmony can be more or less perfect depending on how well its parts are put together. A better arrangement makes a better harmony."

"Yes, I see."

"But does that apply to the soul? Can one soul be more or less of a soul than another?"

"No, not at all."

"But we do say that one soul can be wise and good, while another can be foolish and bad, right?"

"Yes, that's true."

"So if the soul were harmony, and if some souls are better than others, then wouldn't that mean some harmonies are more perfect than others?"

"I guess so."

"But earlier we agreed that harmony, if it exists, doesn't come in degrees—it's either a harmony or it isn't."

"Yes, we said that."

"Then no soul could have more or less harmony than another. And if vice is disharmony, and virtue is harmony, then no soul could be more or less virtuous or wicked than another."

"That follows."

"And if that's true, then a soul couldn't be evil at all, because harmony can't contain disharmony."

"Right."

"So if all souls are equally souls, then all souls would have to be equally good."

"That's what your reasoning suggests."

"But that can't be true, can it?" Socrates said. "These are the kinds of problems that come from thinking the soul is a harmony."

"No, it doesn't make sense."

"One more question," Socrates said. "What controls the parts of a human being? Isn't it the soul? Especially the wise soul?"

"Do you know of anything else that could?"

No, I don't.

Now, tell me this: do you think the soul agrees with the body's feelings, or does it go against them? For example, when the body is hot and thirsty, doesn't the soul sometimes stop us from drinking? And when the body is hungry, doesn't it sometimes stop us from eating? That's just one example of many where the soul seems to fight against the body's desires.

That's true.

But didn't we already agree that if the soul is just a kind of harmony, like a tune, then it can't go against the physical parts it's made of? A harmony has to follow the movements of the strings—it can't control them, right?

Yes, that's what we said.

But now we're seeing something very different, aren't we? The soul doesn't just follow the body—it leads it. It pushes back against the body's wants in many ways during a person's life. Sometimes it does this through tough methods like medicine or exercise. Other times it uses softer ways, like warnings or gentle reminders. It talks to our fears, cravings, and emotions as if they were something separate from itself. Remember how Homer described Odysseus in the Odyssey? He hit his chest and told his heart, "Hold on, my heart—you've survived worse than this!"

Do you think Homer wrote that because he believed the soul was just a harmony controlled by the body? Or did he see it as something much stronger and more powerful—something meant to lead, not follow?

Yes, Socrates, I think that's exactly what he believed.

Then, my friend, we can't be right if we say the soul is only a harmony. If we did, we'd be going against both Homer and ourselves.

That's true.

So much for your goddess Harmonia, Socrates said with a smile—she's kindly stepped aside for us. But what should I say to her husband, Cadmus? How do I make peace with him?

I think you'll figure something out, Cebes replied. Honestly, I didn't expect you to answer the harmony argument so well. When Simmias brought it up, I thought it couldn't be answered. But your reasoning completely overturned it. So maybe Cadmus's argument won't hold up either.

"No, my friend," said Socrates, "let's not brag. We might jinx it, and I don't want anything to get in the way of what I'm about to say. Still, we'll leave that to the gods. I'll come forward now, like a hero in a story, and test the strength of your argument.

Here's the issue—you want proof that the soul never dies, that it lives forever. You think that unless someone can prove this, a philosopher who is calm in the face of death is just being foolish. You say that just because the soul is powerful and existed before we were born, it doesn't mean it will live forever. Even if the soul has lived a long time and learned a lot, that doesn't make it immortal. You're wondering if maybe being born is actually bad for the soul—like a sickness that leads to its breakdown—and that eventually, after life's struggles, the soul might just end.

Also, you say it doesn't really matter whether the soul enters the body once or many times. Unless someone can explain clearly that the soul truly lasts forever, a smart person would still be afraid of death. That's your point, right, Cebes? I'm going over it again just to make sure we don't miss anything. Let me know if I got anything wrong or if you want to add something."

Cebes said, "No, that's exactly what I meant. You said it clearly."

Socrates stayed quiet for a moment, thinking deeply. Then he spoke.

"You've brought up a huge question, Cebes. It's about how things are created and destroyed. If you want, I can tell you what I've learned from my own experience. Maybe it will help you understand things better."

"I'd really like that," said Cebes.

"Okay," said Socrates. "When I was younger, I was obsessed with understanding how nature works. I wanted to know the reasons why things happen—why things are born or die. I thought that studying this was a noble thing to do. I used to ask myself all kinds of questions, like: Do animals grow because the heat and cold in their bodies break things down and build them up? Is it our blood that makes us think? Or is it air or fire? Or maybe none of those—maybe it's the brain that gives us sight, hearing, smell, and thoughts. Maybe memory and understanding come from those, and maybe science comes from memory once it's solid.

Then I started wondering how all those things break down. I thought about the stars and the sky and the earth. But eventually, I realized I was totally confused. I'll explain why. I got so caught up in these questions that I started forgetting the things I once believed were obvious. For example, I used to think that people grow by eating and drinking—because when food is digested, it adds flesh to flesh and bone to bone. When things of the same kind come together, a small body becomes bigger, and a short person becomes tall. That idea made sense, didn't it?"

"Yes," said Cebes. "It did."

"Well, let me tell you something else," Socrates continued. "There was a time when I thought I really understood what 'bigger' and 'smaller' meant. If I saw a tall man next to a short one, I thought the taller one was just taller by a head. Or I'd say one horse was bigger than another. I even thought it was obvious that ten is more than eight by two, or that two feet are more than one because two is double.

"And now?" Cebes asked.

"To be honest," said Socrates, "I don't think I really understand any of it. I can't even explain how one plus one becomes two. I don't get how putting two things together makes them two—why were they one before, but now they're suddenly two just because they're next to each other? Or if I separate one thing into two, how does that make two? It's strange that both adding and separating can lead to the same result. I can't explain why anything comes to be, or stops being, or exists at all. Now I have this new way of thinking, and I've stopped believing in the old one."

"Then I heard someone reading from a book by Anaxagoras," he continued. "It said that Mind controls everything and causes all things. I loved that idea. I thought, 'If Mind is in charge, then everything must happen for the best.' I believed that if you want to know why something exists or is destroyed, you need to understand what's best for it. And if you know what's best, you'll also know what's worst, because both come from the same kind of thinking.

"I was so excited—I thought I'd finally found a teacher who could explain everything. I thought he'd tell me whether the earth is round or flat, and explain why it's that way—not just what it is, but that it's the best way it could be. If he said the earth was in the center of the universe, he'd explain that this was the best place for it. And I would be happy with that answer—I wouldn't need anything more.

"I imagined asking him about the sun, the moon, and the stars. I thought he'd explain why they move the way they do, why they change, and how all of it is arranged for the best. I really believed that since he said Mind was in control, he'd explain that everything was exactly the way it is because that's what's best. I couldn't wait to learn what was best for each thing, and what was good for everything as a whole. I was so hopeful. I grabbed those books and read them as fast as I could, eager to finally understand what makes things better or worse."

I had high hopes—but I was completely let down. As I kept reading, I saw that this philosopher totally abandoned the idea that mind or reason caused anything. Instead, he started talking about air, space, water, and other strange things. It was like someone saying, "Socrates does what he does because of his mind," but then trying to explain all my actions by only talking about my body—my bones, muscles, and how they work together.

He'd say things like, "Socrates is sitting because his bones are hard and jointed, and his muscles are soft and stretchy. The muscles move the bones, and that's why his body is bent and sitting." Then he'd explain that I'm speaking to you because of vibrations in the air and sound and hearing. He would give a thousand explanations like this, all about physical stuff—and forget to mention the real reason: that the people of Athens sentenced me, and I decided it was right to stay here and face my punishment.

Honestly, if my body parts acted on their own, they would have taken me to Megara or Boeotia by now! But they didn't, because I chose to stay. I chose to accept my fate instead of running away. So, you see, it's not the muscles and bones that made the choice. It was my mind deciding what was right.

There's a big difference between a condition and a cause. Yes, I need bones and muscles to carry out my decisions, but they aren't why

I do things. Saying they are is careless and confusing. People often mix up the actual reason for something with the things that happen to go along with it. They feel around in the dark and get it wrong.

Some think the earth stays in place because the sky spins around it. Others say the air holds it up like a bowl. But no one stops to ask what makes everything work for the best. They ignore that a guiding force for good could be behind it all. Instead, they search for some stronger force that holds everything together—like a giant, cosmic Atlas. But they forget the true force behind it all: the power of goodness itself. That's what I've always wanted to understand, if anyone could teach me.

But since I've never figured it out, and I haven't found anyone else who has either, I'll show you the next best way I've learned to search for answers—if you want to hear it."

"I'd love to," Cebes said.

Socrates continued, "When I couldn't understand how things truly exist, I started to worry that I might harm my soul by relying too much on my senses—like people can hurt their eyes by staring at the sun during an eclipse. They protect their eyes by looking at reflections in water. I decided I should protect my soul the same way—by not depending on sight or the other senses to find truth, but instead focusing on the mind.

I know that might not be a perfect comparison. I don't believe that thinking with your mind gives you only a vague picture, like looking through a dirty window. In fact, I think it shows things even more clearly than physical experience. So here's what I did: I chose a belief that seemed strongest, and then I accepted anything that agreed with it as true. If something didn't fit, I considered it false. I'll explain more so you see what I mean."

"I'm not quite following yet," Cebes admitted.

"That's okay," Socrates said. "It's nothing new—just what I've always said. I want to show you the kind of cause I think about. I'll start with simple things that everyone talks about: the idea that there is something called absolute beauty, goodness, and greatness. If you accept that, I can use it to show you how I think about causes—and prove that the soul lives forever."

"Go ahead," said Cebes. "I accept it."

"Alright," Socrates said, "do you also agree with this? If anything is beautiful, it's only beautiful because it shares in that pure, absolute beauty. I'd say the same about everything—things are only what they are because they share in the true form of it. Do you agree?"

"Yes," Cebes said. "I do."

Socrates went on, "I don't understand any of those other explanations people give. If someone tells me that something is beautiful because of its shape or color or something like that, I don't get it. I ignore those things. I believe one thing for sure: something is beautiful because beauty is in it—however that works. I may not know the details, but I firmly believe that it's beauty itself that makes anything beautiful. I think that's the safest answer I can give, whether to myself or anyone else. Do you agree?"

"I do."

"And it's the same with greatness," Socrates said. "Anything great is great because of greatness. And things are greater or smaller by how much of greatness or smallness they share in."

"That's right," Cebes said.

"So if someone says, 'This man is taller than that one by a head,' you wouldn't just agree with that way of speaking, right? You'd say, 'No, the taller man is taller because he shares more in greatness, and the shorter man is shorter because he shares more in smallness.' You wouldn't say he's taller just because of the size of a head. That would be silly, since a head is small."

"Exactly," said Cebes, laughing.

"In the same way," Socrates said, "you wouldn't say that ten is greater than eight because of the number two, but because it has more 'number'—more quantity. Or you wouldn't say two feet is more than one foot because of the extra half—it's more because it has more size. Otherwise, you fall into the same kind of confusion."

"Very true," Cebes agreed.

"You also wouldn't say that adding one to one is what causes two," Socrates said. "You'd say that what makes something two is that it shares in 'twoness.' Same with one—it exists because of oneness. I don't want to get stuck solving puzzles about math and measuring. Smarter people can handle those. I want to stick with what I'm sure of—a solid principle. If someone argues with me, I won't listen until I've tested whether the results match that principle. If they don't, I reject it. And if they ask me to explain the principle, I'll move upward to a higher one, and keep going until I reach the highest and best one. That's how I avoid mixing up causes and results. I don't want to end up like those debaters who just argue for the sake of arguing, not for truth. They don't really care—they're just proud of themselves, even when their ideas are a mess. But if you want to be a real philosopher, you have to stick to this method."

"You're absolutely right," said both Simmias and Cebes at once.

Echecrates said, "Phaedo, I'm not surprised they agreed. Socrates explained everything so clearly."

"Yes, Echecrates," Phaedo replied. "Everyone there felt the same way."

"And we feel the same now," said Echecrates. "But what happened next?"

Phaedo continued, "After they all agreed on those points—that ideas are real, and that things only become what they are by sharing in those ideas—Socrates said something like this:

108

'This is how you talk. But when you say Simmias is taller than Socrates and shorter than Phaedo, aren't you saying that Simmias has both tallness and shortness?'

'Yes, I am,' said Cebes.

'But you also agree that Simmias isn't taller than Socrates just because he's Simmias. It's because of the size he happens to have. Just like he isn't shorter than Phaedo because of who he is, but because his size is less compared to Phaedo's.'

'That's true,' said Cebes."

And if Phaedo is taller than Simmias, it's not because he is Phaedo, but because he has more height compared to Simmias, who is shorter?

"That's right."

So, Simmias is both tall and short—but only because he's between the two. He's taller than Socrates but shorter than Phaedo. That's why he's described both ways. Then Socrates laughed and said, "I know I sound like I'm quoting a textbook, but I think what I'm saying is true."

Simmias agreed.

"I'm explaining it this way because I want you to see that absolute greatness can never also be small. And anything in the real world that has greatness in it can't suddenly accept smallness without losing its greatness. When something greater is faced with something lesser, only two things can happen—either the greater thing gives way and disappears, or it steps back and is replaced. But it doesn't change into something smaller and keep being what it was. Just like I don't stop being a small person just because I'm smaller than Simmias. The smallness in me doesn't turn into greatness.

The same idea works in reverse. Something small doesn't turn into something great without losing what it is. One opposite can't turn into its opposite while staying the same. If that happens, the original quality either fades away or is gone entirely."

"Yes," said Cebes. "That makes sense to me."

Then someone else in the group said, "Wait a second—didn't we say earlier that opposites come from opposites? Like how something small becomes big, and something big becomes small? But now it sounds like you're saying the opposite of that."

Socrates nodded and replied, "Good point. I'm glad you brought that up. But you're missing a key difference. Before, we were talking about everyday things that change—like how cold can turn into heat, or how people grow taller over time. Now we're talking about the core ideas themselves—like the idea of greatness or smallness. These ideas don't mix with their opposites. In the earlier case, we were talking about things that carry these qualities, not the qualities themselves. But now, we're talking about the qualities directly, and they never become their opposites."

He turned to Cebes and asked, "Does this bother you?"

"No, not really," Cebes said. "But I admit that sometimes these kinds of arguments can be confusing."

"Well," said Socrates, "can we agree that something can't ever be the opposite of itself?"

"Yes, I think we can agree on that."

"Then let's look at it another way. You know what heat and cold are, right?"

"Of course."

"But they're not the same as fire and snow?"

"Definitely not."

"Right. Fire is not the same thing as heat, and snow isn't the same thing as cold."

"Correct."

"But still, if you put heat near snow, the snow can't stay snow. It will either melt or disappear, right?"

"Exactly."

"And the same goes for fire. If you bring cold near fire, the fire will either fade or go out. They can't stay together as they are."

"That's true."

"And now think about this: sometimes, not just the idea itself, but things that carry the idea also act like this. Here's what I mean—'oddness' is an idea, and 'three' is a number. Three isn't the idea of oddness itself, but it always has oddness in it. So, we call it an odd number."

"Right."

"But three is still different from the idea of 'odd.' It has its own name. Even so, we call it odd because it always has oddness. The same goes for five or any other odd number. They're not oddness itself, but they're always odd. In the same way, even numbers like two and four always have evenness, even though they're not 'evenness' itself. You agree with this?"

"Definitely."

"Here's what I'm getting at: not only do true opposites reject each other, but things that carry those opposites also push away what's opposite to what they have. For example, the number three will stop being three before it becomes even. It would rather stop existing than be something it's not."

"Very true," said Cebes.

"And yet, three and two aren't direct opposites."

"No, they're not."

"Exactly. So, it's not just opposites that can't mix. Even things that have a certain quality won't accept the opposite quality."

"That's right."

"Okay, let's try to figure out what kinds of things behave this way."

"Let's do it," said Cebes.

"Wouldn't you say that there are things that, once they contain a certain idea, not only show that idea, but also naturally push away its opposite?"

"What do you mean?"

"I mean, like what we were just saying. If something is the number three, it's not just three—it's also odd. And since it's odd, it can't be even. The idea of 'even' can't exist in something that has the nature of 'odd.'"

"Yes, that's right."

"So, the number three, which carries oddness, will never accept evenness?"

"Correct."

"Then we can say that three is definitely an odd number."

"Yes."

"And now, going back to our earlier point: some things aren't opposites, but still won't allow the opposite idea into them. Like three won't become even, and fire won't become cold. These examples show us a bigger rule: not only do opposites avoid each other, but anything that brings one quality with it can't accept the opposite quality.

Let me say that again—it's okay to repeat important points. The number five will never be even, and ten, which is twice five, will never be odd. Being 'double' doesn't mean it's the opposite of odd, but it still won't accept oddness. Or take any fraction like 3:2, or any number with a half or a third in it—it will never be a whole number, even though it's not the exact opposite of 'whole.'

Do you agree with that?"

"Yes," said Cebes. "I completely agree."

"Alright," Socrates said, "let's take it from the top again. And when I ask you a question, don't just repeat the usual answer I talked about earlier. Give me a better answer, one based on what we just figured out. So, if someone asks you what makes a body hot, don't say 'heat'—that's the easy but unhelpful answer. Say 'fire.' That's the clearer, stronger answer.

Or if someone asks why a person is sick, don't just say 'because of illness'—say 'because of a fever.' And if someone asks what makes numbers odd, don't say 'oddness,' but say 'the monad,' or the unit, which is the cause behind odd numbers. The same idea works for other things too, but I think you get it now without me giving more examples."

"Yes," he said, "I understand you."

"Then tell me," said Socrates, "what is it that makes the body alive?"

"The soul," he answered.

"And is that always true?"

"Yes, of course."

"So whenever the soul is present, it brings life with it?"

"Yes, definitely."

"Now, is there something that's the opposite of life?"

"Yes—death."

"Then since the soul brings life, it can never accept its opposite, which is death?"

"That's impossible," said Cebes.

"Let's go over something else," Socrates said. "What do we call the thing that refuses to accept even numbers?"

"The odd," he replied.

"And what do we call what refuses to accept things that are unmusical or unfair?"

"The musical and the just."

"So what do we call the thing that does not accept death?"

"The immortal."

"And does the soul accept death?"

"No."

"Then the soul must be immortal?"

"Yes."

"And would you say we've proven this now?"

"Yes, Socrates, it's been clearly proven."

"Now imagine this," Socrates said. "If oddness could never be destroyed, wouldn't that mean the number three can't be destroyed either?"

"Of course."

"And if coldness could never be destroyed, then snow would never melt, even when heat came near. It would stay whole and untouched, right?"

"Yes, that's true."

"In the same way, if warmth or heat could never be destroyed, then fire wouldn't go out when it got cold—it would just leave instead of being destroyed?"

"Exactly."

"So let's say the soul is immortal and can't be destroyed. Then, even if death comes, the soul can't be killed. It would resist death just like three resists becoming even, or fire resists becoming cold. A person might argue, 'Well, even if the odd can't become even, maybe it could disappear and then the even could take its place.' But that idea only works if we don't accept that oddness can't be destroyed. If we do accept that oddness is indestructible, then there's no way the even could replace it. The same is true for fire and heat, or any other quality like that."

"Very true."

"So, if immortality also means the soul can't be destroyed, then the soul is not only immortal but also indestructible. And if that wasn't true, we'd need some other way to prove it."

"I don't think we need another way," said Cebes. "Because if something immortal could still be destroyed, then nothing would be truly indestructible."

"You're right," said Socrates. "And almost everyone agrees that God, the very idea of life itself, and anything immortal, never dies."

"Yes," said Cebes. "Not just people—even the gods believe that."

"Then if the immortal cannot be destroyed, and the soul is immortal, it must also be indestructible."

"Definitely."

"So, when death comes, the part of a person that's mortal dies, but the soul—the immortal part—survives and remains whole."

"That's true."

"So, Cebes, it's clear now: the soul is both immortal and indestructible, and that means our souls will continue to exist after death."

"I believe it, Socrates," said Cebes. "I don't have any more doubts. But if Simmias or anyone else has anything they want to say, now is the time. I can't imagine a better moment to bring up questions."

"I have nothing to add," said Simmias. "I don't see any reason to doubt it either. Still, I can't help feeling unsure. This is such a big topic, and we humans are so limited."

"You're right," said Socrates. "That's a good point. Even when something seems certain, we should still think it through carefully. Once we've checked the beginning of an argument and found it solid, then we can follow the rest of the logic, even if we do so with a bit of hesitation. But if the reasoning is clear and solid, we won't need to keep searching."

"That's very true."

"Now, my friends," Socrates said, "if the soul really is immortal, then we need to take care of it—not just while we're alive, but for all time. Ignoring the soul would be incredibly dangerous. If death was really the end of everything, then the wicked would be lucky. They'd be free not only from their bodies but also from their own evil. But now, since we know the soul lives on, there's no escape from wrong except by becoming wise and good.

When a soul leaves the body and moves on, it takes nothing with it except its character—how it was shaped by the way it lived and what it learned. That's what helps—or harms—it on the journey to the next world, right from the very start."

They say that after someone dies, the spirit or guide that watched over them in life leads them to a place where the souls of the dead gather. There, they are judged. After the judgment, they are taken by a guide to the next world. When they've received what they deserve and stayed there for the right amount of time, another guide brings them back, but only after many ages have passed.

Now, the path to the next world isn't a single straight road, like the poet Aeschylus once wrote. If it were that simple, no guide would be needed because no one could get lost. But the journey has many turns and crossroads, which is why people offer sacrifices at places where three roads meet. The wise and good soul follows the right path and stays aware of what's going on. But the soul that still longs for the body, the one that clings to the world of physical things, struggles a lot. It suffers and fights before it's finally pulled away by its spirit guide. When it reaches the place where all souls gather, if it's full of wrongdoing—things like murder or other awful acts—then everyone avoids it. No one wants to be near that soul. No one will guide it. It wanders alone in misery until the time comes for it to go where it truly belongs. On the other hand, every soul that lived a pure and just life, under the guidance of the gods, also has its rightful home.

The Earth itself has many amazing places, and it's not at all like the maps and descriptions most people believe. That's what I've come to believe, based on the words of someone I trust.

"What do you mean, Socrates?" asked Simmias. "I've heard lots of ideas about the Earth, but I don't know which one you believe. I'd really like to know."

"If I had the skill of the sea-god Glaucus, I'd describe it better," said Socrates. "But even Glaucus might not be able to prove what I'm about to say. And even if I could prove it, I probably wouldn't have enough time left to explain it all before I die. Still, I can at least tell you what I think the Earth is like."

"That would be more than enough," said Simmias.

"Alright," Socrates said. "I believe that the Earth is round and sits at the center of the sky. It doesn't need air or anything else to hold it up, because it stays in place due to how evenly it's surrounded by the heavens and how balanced it is. If something is perfectly balanced in the center of something else that's equally spread out, it won't lean or move in any direction. That's my first belief."

"That sounds right," said Simmias.

"I also believe the Earth is very large, and we only live in a tiny part of it. We live around the sea, from the river Phasis to the Pillars of Heracles, like ants or frogs living around a pond. There are many other places like ours, with people living in them. Across the Earth, there are big and small valleys where water, mist, and lower air collect. But the true Earth is pure and high above us, in the pure sky where the stars are. That sky is what we call the ether. Our part of the Earth, where we live, is just a lower layer, filled with the leftover parts that settled down.

We think we're on the surface, but we're really living in a hollow. It's like if a sea creature at the bottom of the ocean thought it lived on the surface. It would think the ocean was the sky and that it saw the sun and stars through the water, even though it had never actually reached the surface. That's us. Because of our weakness and slowness, we can't rise to the surface of the air. But if someone could go high enough—if someone had wings and could fly up—he'd see the real world, just like a fish breaking through the water sees the world above. And if humans could handle such a sight, they'd see that the real Earth, sky, and light are up there.

Everything down here—our land, our rocks, our surroundings—is dull and damaged, like how saltwater ruins things in the sea. Nothing grows perfectly down here. There are only caves, sand, and endless mud. Even the shore is nothing compared to what exists up there. And the difference between our world and the one above is even greater.

Let me tell you a beautiful story, Simmias, about that upper world under the real sky. I think you'll enjoy it."

"We're all eager to hear it," said Simmias.

Socrates continued, "From above, the Earth looks like a ball with colorful streaks across it—kind of like a fancy ball stitched from twelve colored pieces of leather. Our painters use bits of these colors, but up there, the whole land is made from them, and they shine much brighter and clearer than anything we know. There's a glowing purple, golden light, and white that's even brighter than chalk or snow. The Earth is full of colors more beautiful than anything we've ever seen.

The valleys I mentioned are filled with air and water that reflect light, making the whole place shine with beautiful colors. Everything is full of color and light, blended in perfect harmony. The trees, flowers, and fruits there are far more beautiful than anything that grows here.

The hills have stones smoother, clearer, and brighter than our emeralds, sapphires, or jaspers. What we call precious stones are just tiny bits of what they have up there. All the stones are like jewels—and even better than ours—because they're pure and untouched by the salty, dirty elements that rot things down here. That same bad air and moisture that spoils our plants and animals also ruins the ground and stones.

In the upper world, everything shines with gold and silver. These materials are common and everywhere, making the land a joy to look at. The people and animals there live in harmony with their surroundings. Some live in the middle region, others live in the air, like we live around the sea. Others live on islands floating in the air near the edges of their continent. To them, the air is like water is to us, and the ether is like our air.

Their seasons are perfectly balanced, so they don't get sick and live much longer than we do. Their senses—sight, hearing, smell, everything—are far sharper than ours, just like air is clearer than water and ether is clearer than air. They also have real temples and holy places where the gods truly dwell. They hear the gods' voices, receive answers, and speak with them directly. They see the sun, moon, and stars as they truly are. Their whole way of life is just as blessed as everything else in their world."

This is what the whole Earth is like, along with everything around and beneath it. All over the planet, there are deep hollows—some deeper and wider than the one we live in, some narrower but even deeper, and others that are shallower but broader. Inside the Earth, there are many holes and tunnels that connect these hollows, both wide and narrow. Water flows into and out of them like giant basins. There are underground rivers, both hot and cold springs, thick and thin streams of mud, fiery currents, and great blazes of fire. Some areas are filled with lava-like flows, like those found in Sicily. These rivers and streams spread into the regions they pass through.

Deep inside the Earth, everything moves in a kind of seesaw motion—up and down, back and forth. This happens because of one huge opening that runs through the entire Earth. It's the largest of all the chasms, and it's what Homer called "the deepest pit under the Earth," also known by poets as Tartarus.

The seesaw motion is caused by all the streams that rush into and out of this great pit. The water, having no solid base, sways up and down. The air and wind follow it, moving with the water in constant motion, like breathing in and out. These strong, swirling forces create powerful blasts of wind.

When the water rushes downward into the lower parts of the Earth, it fills the deep regions like water being pumped up. Then when it flows back, it fills the hollows near the surface. From there, it moves through hidden underground paths, forming the seas, lakes, rivers, and springs we know. Some streams take a long journey through many lands before falling back into Tartarus; others take shorter routes. But all of them eventually return, always falling in at a lower point than where they began.

Some rivers come back up on the same side, others on the opposite side. Some twist around the Earth like coiled snakes, flowing as far as they can before diving back into the great pit. None can go deeper than the Earth's center, because there's a giant cliff blocking them.

These rivers are many and powerful, but there are four main ones. The biggest is called Oceanus, and it flows all the way around the Earth in a circle. Flowing in the opposite direction is the river Acheron, which runs under the Earth through deserted lands and into the Acherusian Lake. Most souls go there after death. They wait for a certain amount of time—longer for some, shorter for others—before they're sent back to be born again as different creatures.

The third river flows between the others and pours into a huge fiery area, forming a boiling lake of mud and water even bigger than the Mediterranean Sea. This muddy river twists around the Earth and eventually reaches the edge of the Acherusian Lake, but it doesn't mix with the lake's waters. After winding through the Earth many times, it dives deep into Tartarus. This river is called Pyriphlegethon and shoots fire from the ground in different places.

The fourth river flows out on the opposite side into a wild and dark blue land that looks like lapis lazuli. This is the Stygian River. It falls into the Lake Styx, which gives its water strange and powerful properties. Then the river flows under the Earth, loops around in the opposite direction from Pyriphlegethon, and comes near the Acherusian Lake again. Like the others, its water doesn't mix. It circles back to Tartarus, near where Pyriphlegethon falls in. This river is called Cocytus.

This is how the world of the dead works. When souls arrive at their destination, led by their guardian spirit, they are judged based on how they lived. Those who lived neither good nor bad lives are taken to the river Acheron. There, they find boats to carry them to the lake, where they stay. They suffer for the harm they caused and are rewarded for their good deeds, each person receiving what they truly deserve.

But souls who committed horrible crimes—like murder or extreme acts of disrespect against the gods—are thrown into Tartarus and never come back. They stay there forever. Others who did very bad things but later felt deep regret—like someone who hurt a parent in a moment of rage—also go to Tartarus, but only for a year. After that, the waves throw them out: those who killed others are tossed out by Cocytus, and those who killed their parents are cast out by Pyriphlegethon.

These souls are then carried to the Acherusian Lake, where they cry out to the people they wronged, asking for forgiveness and begging to be allowed into the lake. If the ones they hurt forgive them, the souls are freed from their suffering. But if not, they are taken back to Tartarus and the rivers, and the cycle continues until they are finally forgiven. That is the punishment set by the judges.

As for those who lived truly holy and good lives, they are set free from the cycle of life and death. They rise above this world and go to a pure and beautiful place on the higher Earth. And those who lived in true wisdom—who practiced philosophy and purified themselves—leave their bodies behind forever and live in even more beautiful homes that are too wonderful to describe.

So, Simmias," Socrates said, "when we hear all of this, shouldn't we do everything we can to become wise and good? Isn't the reward worth the effort? The hope is great—and the prize is beautiful."

A wise person shouldn't say with full confidence that everything I've described about the soul and its journey after death is exactly true. But since we've shown the soul is immortal, it's reasonable—and even uplifting—to believe that something like this might be true. It's a hopeful and noble belief, and it brings comfort. That's why I've taken the time to tell this story.

So, I say this: anyone who has let go of physical pleasures and flashy appearances—things that often do more harm than good—and instead has focused on gaining wisdom and knowledge, should feel good about what lies ahead. If someone has decorated their soul not with material things but with its own proper qualities—like self-control, fairness, courage, dignity, and truth—then that soul will be ready for its journey when death comes. It will be dressed in the right kind of beauty.

You, Simmias and Cebes, and everyone else will leave this world eventually. As for me, the time has come. As the poets say, fate is calling me. Soon, I must drink the poison. I think I'll take a bath first so the women won't have to wash my body after I'm gone.

After he said this, Crito spoke up: "Socrates, do you want to give us any instructions? Is there anything you want us to do for your children, or anything else we can help with?"

Socrates replied, "Not really, Crito. I only ask what I've always asked—take care of yourselves. That's the best way you can help me, my family, and everyone else. Whether you make a promise or not, that's the real way to serve me. But if you ignore your own well-being and don't live the way I've taught, then any promise you make now won't mean much."

"We'll do our best," said Crito. "And how would you like us to bury you?"

Socrates smiled and said, "Any way you like—if you can catch me! Just make sure I don't slip away. He turned to us and said with a smile, "Crito still thinks I'm the same Socrates he's known all along. He thinks he'll soon see me lying there, lifeless—and he asks how to bury me! Even after all the things I've said about going to a better place after death, he still thinks I'm just a body. So, I want you all to reassure him, like he once stood up for me in court. But this time, tell him something different. Back then, he promised I would stay. Now, you promise him that I'll be leaving. That way, he won't be so upset when he sees my body being buried. I don't want him to feel sorrow, or to say things like, 'We're laying Socrates to rest' or 'We're following him to his grave.' Those words aren't just wrong—they harm the soul. So cheer up, my dear Crito, and say instead, 'We're burying Socrates' body,' and do with it whatever you think is right."

After saying this, Socrates went into another room to take a bath. Crito followed, telling the rest of us to stay where we were. So we waited, talking about the things he had said and feeling the heavy sadness of it all. It felt like we were losing a father, and that we would be like orphans for the rest of our lives.

When he had finished bathing, his children were brought to him— two young boys and an older son. The women of his family came too. He spoke to them for a bit, gave them some final instructions with Crito present, then sent them away and came back to sit with us.

By then, the sun was close to setting. After some quiet time, the prison guard, who worked under the Eleven officials, came in and stood beside him.

"Socrates," he said, "you are the best, kindest, and noblest man I've ever met in this place. Others get angry and curse at me when I tell them it's time to drink the poison. But I know you won't. You understand that I'm just following orders. So, farewell—and try to bear what must happen as calmly as you can. You know why I'm here." The man then burst into tears and quickly left the room.

Socrates looked at him and said, "Thank you for your kind words. I'll do what you say." Then he turned to us and added, "What a good man. He's visited me often since I've been here, and he's always been kind. And now, see how much he grieves for me."

Then he said to Crito, "Let's do what he said. Bring the cup if the poison is ready. If not, have someone prepare it."

But Crito said, "Socrates, there's no rush. The sun is still up. I know people who've taken the poison long after being told it was time. They ate, drank, and spent time with their loved ones before doing it. Why not wait a little longer?"

Socrates replied, "Crito, those people were right—for them. They thought they gained something by waiting. But I don't think I'll gain anything by putting it off. I'd only be clinging to a life that's already over. I'd rather not do that. Please, do as I ask."

Crito nodded to the servant, who left and came back after a while with the jailer carrying the cup of poison. Socrates said, "You, my friend, know how this works. Tell me what I need to do."

The man said, "You just need to walk around until your legs feel heavy. Then lie down. The poison will take effect."

He handed Socrates the cup. Socrates calmly took it—no fear in his face, no trembling. Looking directly at the man, as he always did, he asked, "Is it okay to offer a bit of this as a gift to the gods? Or is this all I'm allowed to drink?"

The man replied, "We only prepare exactly the amount needed."

"I understand," said Socrates. "Still, I ask the gods to bless my journey to the next world. May it be a good one." Then, lifting the cup to his lips, he drank it easily and without hesitation.

Until then, most of us had held back our emotions. But when we saw him drink the poison, and saw that it was done, we couldn't hold it in anymore. My own tears fell fast, not just for him, but because I knew I was losing a true friend. I covered my face and cried. Crito had already gotten up, unable to control his emotions. And Apollodorus, who had been crying the whole time, suddenly burst into loud sobs that made all of us lose control.

Only Socrates remained calm. "What is this noise?" he said. "I sent the women away so they wouldn't cry like this. I've heard that a man should die in peace. Please, quiet yourselves and be strong."

Ashamed, we stopped crying. Socrates stood and walked around until his legs felt heavy. Then he lay down on his back as instructed. The man who gave him the poison checked his legs and feet, squeezing them and asking if he could feel anything.

"No," Socrates answered.

He continued checking up the body, showing us how it was growing cold and stiff. Socrates felt it too and said, "When the poison reaches the heart, that will be the end."

As his body began to go numb near his waist, he uncovered his face and spoke one last time.

"Crito," he said, "we owe a rooster to Asclepius. Don't forget to pay that debt."

"It will be paid," said Crito. "Is there anything else?"

But there was no reply. After a moment, we heard a slight sound. The man uncovered Socrates' face—his eyes were still. Crito gently closed his eyes and mouth.

And that, Echecrates, was the end of our dear friend. I can honestly say, of all the men I've ever known, he was the wisest, the most just, and the very best.

The End

Crito

Plato

Foreword

Conscience and Civic Duty:
The Moral Struggle of Socrates in Prison

Plato's Crito, written around 360 BCE, occupies a unique and intimate position among his dialogues. Unlike the ambitious scope of The Republic, with its expansive exploration of justice, the soul, and the ideal state, Crito narrows its philosophical lens, concentrating on a profoundly personal moment: Socrates' moral deliberation about escaping his imminent execution. Set in the early hours within an Athenian prison cell, the dialogue captures an urgent conversation between Socrates and his close friend Crito, who desperately implores Socrates to flee and avoid the unjust sentence handed down by Athens.

For readers familiar with Plato's broader philosophical project, Crito provides a focused and dramatic illustration of principles previously discussed abstractly. Yet for readers new to Plato's works, this dialogue serves as a powerful introduction to some of the core questions of moral philosophy: What obligations do we have to the laws of our community? When is civil disobedience morally justified? And ultimately, how do we balance personal conscience with societal responsibility?

The dialogue is short, emotionally charged, and profoundly moving. It is set immediately after Socrates' sentencing, mere days before his scheduled execution by drinking hemlock, as vividly described later in the Phaedo. Socrates' friends, including Crito, are anguished, unable to accept the impending loss of their teacher and companion. Crito, in particular, struggles deeply with this injustice, driven by loyalty and love to save Socrates at all costs—even if it means breaking Athenian law.

Yet, as readers will discover, the seemingly straightforward choice to flee rather than die opens into a nuanced philosophical exploration of justice, citizenship, and integrity. Socrates, ever calm and rational, leads Crito—and by extension, all of us—through a rigorous examination of the ethical implications of his escape, forcing consideration not only of what is personally advantageous, but what is morally right and just. This introduction aims to guide readers through the central themes and arguments of the Crito, illuminating its significance both as an independent philosophical work and as a powerful complement to Plato's larger philosophical vision.

The Urgent Plea of Friendship: Crito's Appeal

The dialogue opens dramatically, with Crito entering Socrates' prison cell at dawn, visibly distressed and insistent upon Socrates' immediate escape. Crito, deeply troubled, presents several compelling reasons for Socrates to flee. First, he argues from personal and emotional grounds, urging Socrates to consider the pain and shame that his friends and family will suffer should he willingly accept death. Crito is not merely concerned about losing a friend; he also fears public judgment. He worries that others will accuse Socrates' companions of cowardice, believing they failed to save him due to greed, indifference, or fear.

Crito's second argument appeals to Socrates' self-interest. He notes that arrangements for escape are already in place—money is readily available, sympathetic friends abroad eagerly await him, and leaving Athens would grant Socrates additional years to continue his philosophical mission elsewhere. To Crito, this escape is not only feasible; it appears the rational and obvious choice. He sees Socrates' willingness to accept execution as absurdly stubborn, almost prideful, bordering on unjust itself.

These appeals set the stage for Socrates' characteristic method of careful, deliberate inquiry. Rather than responding hastily or emotionally, Socrates gently but firmly challenges Crito's assumptions, urging a deeper reflection on the true meaning of justice and moral obligation. For Plato, Crito's arguments represent the intuitive, emotional responses most of us might share: to act on friendship, fear of disgrace, personal preservation, and loyalty. But as readers soon discover, Socrates demands that decisions of such magnitude be governed not by sentiment or expedience, but by reason and moral principle.

The tension between emotion and reason, between loyalty and justice, becomes a central theme, inviting readers to question their own ethical instincts. What is the right action when personal loyalty conflicts with public responsibility? How should we weigh emotional attachments against moral duties? These pressing questions give the Crito its lasting power and resonance, engaging readers deeply in Socrates' personal dilemma.

Justice, Laws, and the Socratic Argument

Socrates' response to Crito forms the philosophical heart of the dialogue. Instead of immediately addressing the practicality or benefits of escape, Socrates redirects the conversation towards the nature of justice itself. He insists that the rightness of an action must be judged independently from its consequences or personal advantages. In his own words, Socrates argues famously: "One must never do wrong intentionally, even when one has been wronged."

This central assertion radically shifts the moral perspective. Rather than evaluating the escape based on personal outcomes, Socrates proposes considering it solely on ethical grounds: would escaping represent a violation of justice? To determine this, Socrates employs a unique rhetorical strategy, personifying the Laws of Athens, imagining them confronting him directly. In a compelling, imaginative passage, the Laws speak to Socrates, challenging him to consider his lifelong contract with Athens. Socrates has willingly lived under Athenian laws, benefiting from their protections, agreeing implicitly to abide by their judgments—even, tragically, when those judgments appear unjust.

Through this powerful metaphor, Socrates articulates the concept of a social contract—one of Plato's significant contributions to political philosophy. By living within a community and accepting its advantages, Socrates argues, citizens implicitly consent to abide by the laws governing that society. This consent is not conditional on always agreeing with individual judgments. Thus, even if the verdict against Socrates is unjust—and Plato clearly believes it to be—Socrates himself must still uphold his moral responsibility to the state by respecting its laws. To escape would constitute an act of injustice, undermining the authority and stability of the community to which he has dedicated his life.

This argument poses profound ethical questions still debated today: What does it mean to respect the law when it conflicts with personal morality? Is civil disobedience ever justified, and if so, under what conditions? Socrates does not deny the possibility of unjust laws, but he insists that violating one's moral commitment to justice is inherently damaging to the soul. By this reasoning, willingly accepting the consequences—even death—rather than betraying his moral obligations, preserves the integrity of his life's mission.

The Timeless Significance of Crito: A Challenge for Modern Readers

While Crito is grounded firmly in the historical reality of Socrates' trial and imprisonment, its philosophical insights transcend the particularities of ancient Athens. Modern readers find in this short dialogue a powerful framework for reflecting on issues as relevant today as in Plato's time—civil disobedience, personal integrity, justice versus loyalty, and the role of law in a just society.

In an era marked by political turmoil, debates over unjust laws, and questions about civic responsibility, the dialogue's central questions are strikingly contemporary. Should citizens obey laws they believe to be unjust, or do they have a moral duty to resist? Under what conditions is civil disobedience ethically permissible? How can one balance loyalty to family, friends, and self with obligations to society and justice?

The enduring strength of Crito lies in Plato's ability to present these profound questions within a deeply human context, grounded in friendship, loyalty, love, and personal integrity. Socrates emerges not merely as an abstract philosopher but as a deeply relatable individual facing profound personal anguish. He confronts injustice not with resignation but with deliberate, reflective courage, guided by reason and moral conviction rather than emotion or convenience.

As you embark on your journey through this dialogue, consider not only the historical Socrates but your own beliefs, obligations, and decisions. The Crito is not merely a historical document—it is an invitation, as relevant today as ever, to reflect deeply upon the nature of justice, personal responsibility, and the ethical foundations of our lives.

Welcome to Plato's Crito, a dialogue that challenges us all to think carefully, to act honorably, and to live thoughtfully in a complex world. May your engagement with this powerful text inspire meaningful reflection, dialogue, and a deeper understanding of what it means to truly live justly.

Persons of The Dialogue

Socrates, Crito.

SCENE: The Prison of Socrates.

Crito

Socrates: Why are you here so early, Crito? It must still be very early in the morning.

Crito: Yes, it is.

Socrates: Do you know exactly what time it is?

Crito: It's just starting to get light outside.

Socrates: I'm surprised the guard let you in at this hour.

Crito: He knows me well, Socrates. I visit often, and I've done him a few favors.

Socrates: Did you just get here?

Crito: No, I've been here for a while.

Socrates: Then why didn't you wake me up right away instead of sitting there silently?

Crito: Honestly, Socrates, I didn't want to disturb you. I know how troubled you must be, and I didn't want to add to it. But I was amazed at how peacefully you were sleeping. That's why I let you rest. I've always thought you had a calm nature, but I've never seen anyone handle something this serious so calmly and peacefully.

Socrates: Well, Crito, at my age, it wouldn't make sense to complain about dying. It's part of life.

Crito: True—but other men your age still worry when they're in situations like this.

Socrates: That's true. But you still haven't told me why you came so early today.

Crito: I came to give you some bad news. It may not upset you, but it's painful for all of us who care about you—especially me.

Socrates: What is it? Has the ship from Delos arrived? The one whose arrival means I must die?

Crito: Not yet, but people who just came from Sunium say they saw it there. So it will probably arrive today. That means tomorrow will be your last day, Socrates.

Socrates: Alright, Crito. If that's what the gods want, I accept it. But I believe there might be one more day.

Crito: Why do you think that?

Socrates: Let me explain. I'm supposed to die the day after the ship gets here, right?

Crito: Yes, that's what the officials said.

Socrates: Well, I don't think the ship will arrive until tomorrow. I say that because of a dream I had last night—actually, it was just before you let me sleep.

Crito: What kind of dream?

Socrates: I saw a woman—beautiful and glowing, wearing bright clothes. She called to me and said, "Socrates, in three days, you will reach fertile Phthia."

Crito: That's a strange dream, Socrates.

Socrates: Maybe, but I think the meaning is pretty clear.

Crito: Yes, I agree—it sounds very clear. But please, Socrates, I'm begging you again—listen to me and escape. If you die, I won't just lose a friend who can never be replaced. There's something else too—people who don't know us will think I didn't try to help you. They'll say I cared more about money than about saving your life. What could be more shameful than that? They won't believe that you refused to escape. They'll just assume I didn't try hard enough.

Socrates: Tell me, Crito, why should we care so much about what most people think? The people who really matter—the wise and good—will understand the truth about what's happening.

Crito: But Socrates, you can see for yourself that public opinion can be dangerous. What's happening to you right now shows that the crowd can do terrible things if they turn against someone.

Socrates: I wish that were true, Crito. If the majority really had the power to do the greatest harm, then they'd also have the power to do the greatest good—and that would be wonderful. But the truth is, they can do neither. They can't make a person wise or foolish. What they do happens mostly by chance, not through wisdom or understanding.

Crito: I won't argue with you about that. But tell me this, Socrates—aren't you at least thinking about me and your other friends? Are you afraid that if you escape, we might get in trouble with the authorities? Maybe they'll say we helped you escape and punish us by taking our money or worse? If that's what you're worried about, please don't be. We're ready to take that risk for you, even if it's dangerous. So please, listen to me and go along with the plan.

Socrates: I know that's one of your concerns, Crito—but it's not the only one.

Crito: You don't need to worry—there are people ready to help you escape, and it won't cost much. As for the officials, they're easy to satisfy with a small payment. I've got enough money, and you're welcome to use it. If that's not enough, our friends are ready to help. Simmias from Thebes even brought a large amount of money for this. Cebes and many others are ready to pitch in. So don't let money or fear for us hold you back. And don't say, like you did at your trial, that you wouldn't know what to do with yourself if you went somewhere else. You'll be welcomed in other places, not just in Athens. I have friends in Thessaly, and if you go there, they'll treat you with respect and protect you. No one there will cause you trouble.

I don't think it's right, Socrates, for you to let yourself die when you could easily avoid it. By doing nothing, you're helping your enemies destroy you. And think about your children—aren't you leaving them behind? You could raise them, teach them, and be there for them. Instead, you're walking away and leaving their future to chance. If things go badly for them, it won't be their fault—it'll be yours for not staying.

No one should have children if they aren't willing to stick around and take care of them. Right now, it seems like you're choosing the easy path instead of the brave and honorable one. That doesn't suit someone like you—someone who's always talked about living with virtue and doing the right thing.

Honestly, I'm ashamed—not just for you, but for us, your friends. People will think the whole situation happened because we were cowards. They'll say the trial could've gone differently, or that we gave up too easily in the end. And they'll blame us for this last, terrible mistake—letting you die when we could have saved you. The truth is, it wouldn't have been hard at all to help you escape.

Please, Socrates, think about how sad and shameful this all looks—for both of us. It's too late to keep discussing it. We need to act now, tonight. If we wait any longer, it'll be too late. I beg you, Socrates—listen to me this time. Do what I'm asking.

Socrates: Crito, I truly appreciate how much you care. Your passion is valuable—but only if it's based on the right reasons. If not, then the more passionate you are, the more danger there is. So we need to think carefully about whether I should really do what you're asking.

You know me. I've always lived by reason and by what makes the most sense after I've thought it through. This situation doesn't change that. I can't suddenly go against everything I've stood for. I still believe in the principles I've always followed—and unless we can come up with better ones, I can't just abandon them. Not even if the crowd had the power to lock me up again, take all my property, or even scare me with threats of death.

So, how should we figure this out? Should we go back to that old idea we've talked about—the one about how not all opinions matter? We used to say that some people's opinions are worth listening to, and others aren't. Was that just talk? Or does it still hold up now that I'm in danger?

I want to figure that out with your help, Crito. Has the situation changed the truth of that idea—or does it still stand? I think a lot of smart people agree that not every opinion is worth the same. And since you, Crito, aren't the one facing death right now, you can think more clearly. So tell me—am I right to say that only some opinions should be taken seriously?

Crito: Yes, I think you're right.

Socrates: So we should care about the opinions of good people, not bad ones?

Crito: Yes.

Socrates: And the thoughts of wise people are helpful, while the opinions of foolish people are not?

Crito: Absolutely.

Socrates: Let me ask you something, Crito. When someone is training their body, do they pay attention to everyone's opinions about how they should exercise, or just to the advice of one expert—their doctor or trainer?

Crito: Just the expert's opinion.

Socrates: So they should care more about that one person's praise or criticism, not about what everyone else says?

Crito: Exactly.

Socrates: That means they should eat, drink, and train the way that expert says is best, even if the rest of the world disagrees?

Crito: Yes, that's true.

Socrates: And if they ignore the expert and instead listen to the crowd, which has no real knowledge, won't that hurt them?

Crito: Definitely.

Socrates: And that harm—what part of them does it damage?

Crito: It harms their body.

Socrates: Right. And now let's think about something similar. When it comes to right and wrong, fair and unfair, good and bad— which is what we're really talking about here—should we listen to everyone's opinion, or just to the person who truly understands?

Crito: We should listen to the one who understands.

Socrates: Shouldn't we respect and fear that wise person's judgment more than the opinion of everyone else combined? And if we ignore that wise judgment, wouldn't we damage something important in ourselves? That part of us that becomes better through justice and worse through injustice?

Crito: Yes, Socrates. I agree.

Socrates: Now think about this: if we followed bad advice and destroyed what keeps us healthy, our body, would life still be worth living?

Crito: No, of course not.

Socrates: And if we destroyed the part of ourselves that's made better by justice—our soul, or character—would life be worth living then?

Crito: Certainly not.

Socrates: So that part of us is even more important than our body?

Crito: It definitely is.

Socrates: Then, my friend, we shouldn't worry about what the crowd thinks. We should care what the wise person says—and what's actually true. That's where your argument went wrong when you said we should care about what people think is just or unjust, good or bad. Someone might say, "But the public can kill us."

Crito: Yes, people would say that.

Socrates: And it's true. But even now, that old idea we've talked about still holds strong: what matters most isn't just living, but living well. Do you still agree with that?

Crito: Yes, I do.

Socrates: And living well means living justly and with honor?

Crito: That's right.

Socrates: Then let's ask ourselves: would it be right for me to escape without the city's permission? If we agree that it's the right thing to do, then we should go for it. But if it's not right, then we shouldn't do it—no matter what happens. Things like money, reputation, or even what happens to my kids shouldn't be the deciding factors. The crowd would bring someone back to life just as quickly as they would kill them—without really thinking it through. So since our reasoning so far seems solid, the only thing left to ask is this: is it right to escape? Or to accept help from others and pay them off in money or gratitude for helping me escape? Or is that wrong? If it's wrong, then whatever happens—death or anything else—shouldn't change what we decide.

Crito: I agree with you, Socrates. What should we do next?

Socrates: Let's work through it together. If you can prove I'm wrong, I'll gladly change my mind. But if not, please stop trying to convince me to escape. I know you mean well, and I appreciate that, but I can't go against what I believe is right. So now, listen to the first part of my argument and see what you think.

Crito: I'm listening.

Socrates: First, should we say that it's never right to do wrong? Or is it okay sometimes, but not other times? Or do we agree that doing wrong is always bad, like we said earlier?

We've spent years talking about this—have we really learned nothing? Have all our conversations meant nothing, and are we now like children who've learned no lessons at all? Or should we stick to what we've always believed: that doing wrong is always harmful to the one who does it?

What do you say?

Crito: I still believe that's true.

Socrates: Then we must never do wrong?

Crito: Yes.

Socrates: And if someone hurts us, we shouldn't hurt them back? Not even to get even?

Crito: That's right.

Socrates: So, Crito, can we ever do something evil?

Crito: No, Socrates.

Socrates: And what about doing something bad just because someone else did it to us first? That's what most people think is fair—but is that right?

Crito: No, it's not right.

Socrates: Because hurting someone else is still doing wrong?

Crito: Exactly.

Socrates: So we must never return harm for harm, no matter what has been done to us. But I want you to really think about whether you agree with this. Most people never believe this—and they probably never will. Those who agree with it and those who don't are on totally different paths. They don't understand each other at all.

So tell me: do you still agree with my first belief—that it's never right to hurt others, even if they hurt you first? Should we base everything else we say on that? Or do you disagree? I've always believed it, and I still do. But if you think differently, tell me now. If not, I'll move on to the next point.

Crito: No, I agree with you. Keep going.

Socrates: Alright. Here's the next question: Should a person always do what they believe is right? Or should they turn away from what's right?

Crito: They should always do what's right.

Socrates: So if all of this is true, what does it mean for us now? If I escape from prison, going against what the people of Athens have decided, would I be doing something wrong? Wouldn't I be hurting

140

the very people and values I should respect the most? Wouldn't I be turning my back on everything we've agreed is right? What do you think?

Crito: I'm not sure, Socrates. I really don't know.

Socrates: Okay, then let's think of it this way. Imagine I'm getting ready to escape—call it whatever you want—and the Laws of Athens come to me and ask, "Socrates, what are you doing? By escaping, aren't you trying to destroy us—the laws and the city itself? Do you really think a city can survive if people don't follow its laws and just do whatever they want?"

Now what would we say to that, Crito? Someone who knows how to speak well could easily argue that laws must be obeyed and that justice must be carried out. And what would we say back? "But the city hurt me—it gave me an unfair sentence!" Suppose I said that.

Crito: That's a fair point to bring up, Socrates.

Socrates: Then the Laws might ask, "Was that part of the deal, Socrates? Didn't you agree to accept whatever the city decided?" If I looked surprised, they'd continue: "Don't just sit there staring, Socrates—answer us. You always like asking questions, so now it's our turn. What reason do you have to say we treated you unfairly? Wasn't it because of us that you were born? Your father married your mother with our approval. You wouldn't even exist without us. Do you have anything bad to say about the laws that control marriage?"

I'd have to say, "No."

Then they might say, "Didn't we also guide your education and how you were raised? Weren't we the ones who made sure your father taught you music and sports like all good citizens?"

And again, I'd have to say, "Yes, that's true."

Then they might say, "So since we gave you life, raised you, and educated you, aren't you like our child, or even our servant? And if that's the case, you can't just treat us however you want. If a child or servant were to strike back at their father or master because they were punished, would that be right? No. So now that we're punishing you, do you think it's okay to destroy us in return—your city and its laws?

"Can you, who say you care so much about justice and virtue, really believe this is the right thing to do? Haven't you realized yet that your country deserves more respect than your parents or ancestors? That your country should be treated with the greatest care and honor—more than anyone else? If she's angry, she should be calmed with respect and reason. And if you can't change her mind, then you must obey her.

"If your country sends you to prison, you must go. If she says you must be punished, you must accept it. If she sends you to fight in a war, you must fight. No one can simply walk away or ignore what the city asks of them. They must either persuade the city to change—or follow its rules. And if it's wrong to hurt your parents, then it's even more wrong to hurt your country."

What would we say to all that, Crito? Are the Laws right or not?

Crito: I think they're right.

Socrates: Then the Laws would go on: "Socrates, think about this—if what we've said is true, and you escape, you're not just hurting us—you're breaking your promise. We gave you life, raised you, and shared with you all the rights and benefits of citizenship. And we also gave every Athenian the freedom to leave if they didn't like how things were run.

"If, once you grew up, you didn't like our system, you could have moved away. You were free to leave and take all your property with you. No law would've stopped you. You could've moved to another city or one of the colonies. But you stayed. You lived here, and by staying, you silently agreed to follow our laws.

"So if you run away now, you'll be breaking your agreement three times over. First, because you're disobeying the laws that gave you life, like disobeying your parents. Second, because we educated you. And third, because you chose to live here and accept how we do things. You never once tried to convince us that we were wrong. We didn't force you—we gave you a choice: follow the laws or try to change them. But you did neither.

"And now you plan to break the law in secret and sneak away? These are the charges you'll face, Socrates—especially because no one in Athens has benefited from our system more than you."

Then I might ask them, "Why me more than anyone else?" And the Laws would reply, "Socrates, of all our citizens, you've shown the most commitment to this city. You hardly ever left Athens—not for festivals or travel, unless it was for military service. You weren't interested in other cities or their governments. You clearly loved Athens.

"You even had children here, choosing to raise them under our laws. That shows how much you approved of our way of life. And during your trial, you had the chance to choose exile instead of death. The same city that won't let you escape now would've let you leave then. But you said you preferred death over exile.

"And now look—you've changed your mind. You're running from everything you claimed to believe. You're breaking the laws, the agreements, and the promises you made as a citizen. That's not something an honest man does. So answer us: didn't you agree to live by our rules, not just with your words, but through your actions?"

Crito, how could we answer that? Don't we have to admit it's true?

Crito: We really don't have a choice, Socrates.

Socrates: Then won't the laws say to me, "Socrates, you're breaking the promises and agreements you freely made with us—not because you were forced or tricked, but after seventy years of living here, thinking it over. All that time, you could've left if you didn't like how we do things. You could've moved to places you often praised, like Sparta or Crete, or anywhere else in Greece or even beyond.

"But you didn't. Out of all Athenians, you stayed here the most. You loved this city and its laws so much that you never even traveled—except for once, to the Isthmus, or when you were ordered to serve in the army. The disabled moved around more than you did. And now you want to run away and break your promises? Don't do it, Socrates. Don't make a joke of yourself by escaping the city like this.

"Think about the damage you'll cause. Your friends will likely be punished—maybe exiled, maybe stripped of their property. As for you, if you go to nearby cities like Thebes or Megara, both of which are well-governed, their leaders will see you as a threat. They'll treat you as someone who disrespects the law. People will believe the judges were right to convict you, thinking, 'If he runs from justice, he must've corrupted the youth just like they said.' You'll be viewed as dangerous.

"So what's the plan—avoid every city that's run with order and virtue? Will you just wander around from place to place, trying to survive? Or will you settle in Thessaly, where Crito's friends live and where anything goes? They'll probably enjoy the story of how you escaped in disguise, maybe in a goat skin or something silly like that. But what happens when they turn on you? When they say, 'You broke the most sacred laws of your homeland just to squeeze out a few more years of life.' If they're happy, they may not say it. But if they're upset with you, they'll throw your shame in your face.

"Yes, you might live—but what kind of life would that be? Always flattering others, always depending on people to feed you. You'd be a servant to everyone, doing nothing but eating and drinking far from home. And what happened to all those speeches about justice and virtue? What will you say then?

"You might say you're doing it for your children—to raise and teach them. But will you really help them by dragging them to Thessaly and taking away their right to be Athenian citizens? Is that the kind of help a father should give? Or do you think your friends will raise them better here if you're alive, even if you're gone? If they're really your friends, they'll take care of your children whether you're in Thessaly or in the afterlife.

"So listen to us—the laws that raised you. Don't put life and family first and justice last. Put justice first. That's the only way to be truly good and right—in this life and the next. You'll be happier, and so will those connected to you. But if you escape, you'll be doing wrong. You'll be returning harm for harm, breaking your promises, and hurting those you should protect—yourself, your friends, your city, and us. We'll be angry while you live, and when you die, the laws of the underworld will see you as an enemy because you tried to destroy us. So don't listen to Crito. Listen to us."

That, dear Crito, is the voice I hear inside me. It's like the sound of music stuck in my ears—I can't hear anything else. And I know no matter what you say now, it won't change my mind. Still, if you have anything left to say, go ahead.

Crito: I have nothing more to say, Socrates.

Socrates: Then leave me to do what I must. Let me follow the path that the gods have laid out for me.

The EndForeword

Conscience and Civic Duty:

The Moral Struggle of Socrates in Prison

Plato's Crito, written around 360 BCE, occupies a unique and intimate position among his dialogues. Unlike the ambitious scope of The Republic, with its expansive exploration of justice, the soul, and the ideal state, Crito narrows its philosophical lens, concentrating on a profoundly personal moment: Socrates' moral deliberation about escaping his imminent execution. Set in the early hours within an

Athenian prison cell, the dialogue captures an urgent conversation between Socrates and his close friend Crito, who desperately implores Socrates to flee and avoid the unjust sentence handed down by Athens.

For readers familiar with Plato's broader philosophical project, Crito provides a focused and dramatic illustration of principles previously discussed abstractly. Yet for readers new to Plato's works, this dialogue serves as a powerful introduction to some of the core questions of moral philosophy: What obligations do we have to the laws of our community? When is civil disobedience morally justified? And ultimately, how do we balance personal conscience with societal responsibility?

The dialogue is short, emotionally charged, and profoundly moving. It is set immediately after Socrates' sentencing, mere days before his scheduled execution by drinking hemlock, as vividly described later in the Phaedo. Socrates' friends, including Crito, are anguished, unable to accept the impending loss of their teacher and companion. Crito, in particular, struggles deeply with this injustice, driven by loyalty and love to save Socrates at all costs—even if it means breaking Athenian law.

Yet, as readers will discover, the seemingly straightforward choice to flee rather than die opens into a nuanced philosophical exploration of justice, citizenship, and integrity. Socrates, ever calm and rational, leads Crito—and by extension, all of us—through a rigorous examination of the ethical implications of his escape, forcing consideration not only of what is personally advantageous, but what is morally right and just. This introduction aims to guide readers through the central themes and arguments of the Crito, illuminating its significance both as an independent philosophical work and as a powerful complement to Plato's larger philosophical vision.

The Urgent Plea of Friendship: Crito's Appeal

The dialogue opens dramatically, with Crito entering Socrates' prison cell at dawn, visibly distressed and insistent upon Socrates' immediate escape. Crito, deeply troubled, presents several compelling reasons for Socrates to flee. First, he argues from personal and emotional grounds, urging Socrates to consider the pain and shame that his friends and family will suffer should he willingly accept death. Crito is not merely concerned about losing a friend; he also fears public judgment. He worries that others will accuse Socrates' companions of cowardice, believing they failed to save him due to greed, indifference, or fear.

Crito's second argument appeals to Socrates' self-interest. He notes that arrangements for escape are already in place—money is readily available, sympathetic friends abroad eagerly await him, and leaving Athens would grant Socrates additional years to continue his philosophical mission elsewhere. To Crito, this escape is not only feasible; it appears the rational and obvious choice. He sees Socrates' willingness to accept execution as absurdly stubborn, almost prideful, bordering on unjust itself.

These appeals set the stage for Socrates' characteristic method of careful, deliberate inquiry. Rather than responding hastily or emotionally, Socrates gently but firmly challenges Crito's assumptions, urging a deeper reflection on the true meaning of justice and moral obligation. For Plato, Crito's arguments represent the intuitive, emotional responses most of us might share: to act on friendship, fear of disgrace, personal preservation, and loyalty. But as readers soon discover, Socrates demands that decisions of such magnitude be governed not by sentiment or expedience, but by reason and moral principle.

The tension between emotion and reason, between loyalty and justice, becomes a central theme, inviting readers to question their own ethical instincts. What is the right action when personal loyalty conflicts with public responsibility? How should we weigh emotional attachments against moral duties? These pressing questions give the Crito its lasting power and resonance, engaging readers deeply in Socrates' personal dilemma.

Justice, Laws, and the Socratic Argument

Socrates' response to Crito forms the philosophical heart of the dialogue. Instead of immediately addressing the practicality or benefits of escape, Socrates redirects the conversation towards the nature of justice itself. He insists that the rightness of an action must be judged independently from its consequences or personal advantages. In his own words, Socrates argues famously: "One must never do wrong intentionally, even when one has been wronged."

This central assertion radically shifts the moral perspective. Rather than evaluating the escape based on personal outcomes, Socrates proposes considering it solely on ethical grounds: would escaping represent a violation of justice? To determine this, Socrates employs a unique rhetorical strategy, personifying the Laws of Athens, imagining them confronting him directly. In a compelling, imaginative passage, the Laws speak to Socrates, challenging him to consider his lifelong contract with Athens. Socrates has willingly lived under Athenian laws, benefiting from their protections, agreeing implicitly to abide by their judgments—even, tragically, when those judgments appear unjust.

Through this powerful metaphor, Socrates articulates the concept of a social contract—one of Plato's significant contributions to political philosophy. By living within a community and accepting its advantages, Socrates argues, citizens implicitly consent to abide by the laws governing that society. This consent is not conditional on always agreeing with individual judgments. Thus, even if the verdict against Socrates is unjust—and Plato clearly believes it to be—Socrates himself must still uphold his moral responsibility to the state by respecting its laws. To escape would constitute an act of injustice, undermining the authority and stability of the community to which he has dedicated his life.

This argument poses profound ethical questions still debated today: What does it mean to respect the law when it conflicts with personal morality? Is civil disobedience ever justified, and if so, under what conditions? Socrates does not deny the possibility of unjust laws, but he insists that violating one's moral commitment to justice is inherently damaging to the soul. By this reasoning, willingly accepting the consequences—even death—rather than betraying his moral obligations, preserves the integrity of his life's mission.

The Timeless Significance of Crito:

A Challenge for Modern Readers

While Crito is grounded firmly in the historical reality of Socrates' trial and imprisonment, its philosophical insights transcend the particularities of ancient Athens. Modern readers find in this short dialogue a powerful framework for reflecting on issues as relevant today as in Plato's time—civil disobedience, personal integrity, justice versus loyalty, and the role of law in a just society.

In an era marked by political turmoil, debates over unjust laws, and questions about civic responsibility, the dialogue's central questions are strikingly contemporary. Should citizens obey laws they believe to be unjust, or do they have a moral duty to resist? Under what conditions is civil disobedience ethically permissible? How can one balance loyalty to family, friends, and self with obligations to society and justice?

The enduring strength of Crito lies in Plato's ability to present these profound questions within a deeply human context, grounded in friendship, loyalty, love, and personal integrity. Socrates emerges not merely as an abstract philosopher but as a deeply relatable individual facing profound personal anguish. He confronts injustice not with resignation but with deliberate, reflective courage, guided by reason and moral conviction rather than emotion or convenience.

As you embark on your journey through this dialogue, consider not only the historical Socrates but your own beliefs, obligations, and decisions. The Crito is not merely a historical document—it is an invitation, as relevant today as ever, to reflect deeply upon the nature of justice, personal responsibility, and the ethical foundations of our lives.

Welcome to Plato's Crito, a dialogue that challenges us all to think carefully, to act honorably, and to live thoughtfully in a complex world. May your engagement with this powerful text inspire meaningful reflection, dialogue, and a deeper understanding of what it means to truly live justly.

Crito

Persons of The Dialogue:

Socrates, Crito.

SCENE: The Prison of Socrates.

Socrates: Why are you here so early, Crito? It must still be very early in the morning.

Crito: Yes, it is.

Socrates: Do you know exactly what time it is?

Crito: It's just starting to get light outside.

Socrates: I'm surprised the guard let you in at this hour.

Crito: He knows me well, Socrates. I visit often, and I've done him a few favors.

Socrates: Did you just get here?

Crito: No, I've been here for a while.

Socrates: Then why didn't you wake me up right away instead of sitting there silently?

Crito: Honestly, Socrates, I didn't want to disturb you. I know how troubled you must be, and I didn't want to add to it. But I was amazed at how peacefully you were sleeping. That's why I let you rest. I've always thought you had a calm nature, but I've never seen anyone handle something this serious so calmly and peacefully.

Socrates: Well, Crito, at my age, it wouldn't make sense to complain about dying. It's part of life.

Crito: True—but other men your age still worry when they're in situations like this.

Socrates: That's true. But you still haven't told me why you came so early today.

Crito: I came to give you some bad news. It may not upset you, but it's painful for all of us who care about you—especially me.

Socrates: What is it? Has the ship from Delos arrived? The one whose arrival means I must die?

Crito: Not yet, but people who just came from Sunium say they saw it there. So it will probably arrive today. That means tomorrow will be your last day, Socrates.

Socrates: Alright, Crito. If that's what the gods want, I accept it. But I believe there might be one more day.

Crito: Why do you think that?

Socrates: Let me explain. I'm supposed to die the day after the ship gets here, right?

Crito: Yes, that's what the officials said.

Socrates: Well, I don't think the ship will arrive until tomorrow. I say that because of a dream I had last night—actually, it was just before you let me sleep.

Crito: What kind of dream?

Socrates: I saw a woman—beautiful and glowing, wearing bright clothes. She called to me and said, "Socrates, in three days, you will reach fertile Phthia."

Crito: That's a strange dream, Socrates.

Socrates: Maybe, but I think the meaning is pretty clear.

Crito: Yes, I agree—it sounds very clear. But please, Socrates, I'm begging you again—listen to me and escape. If you die, I won't just lose a friend who can never be replaced. There's something else too— people who don't know us will think I didn't try to help you. They'll say I cared more about money than about saving your life. What could be more shameful than that? They won't believe that you refused to escape. They'll just assume I didn't try hard enough.

Socrates: Tell me, Crito, why should we care so much about what most people think? The people who really matter—the wise and good—will understand the truth about what's happening.

Crito: But Socrates, you can see for yourself that public opinion can be dangerous. What's happening to you right now shows that the crowd can do terrible things if they turn against someone.

Socrates: I wish that were true, Crito. If the majority really had the power to do the greatest harm, then they'd also have the power to do the greatest good—and that would be wonderful. But the truth is, they can do neither. They can't make a person wise or foolish. What they do happens mostly by chance, not through wisdom or understanding.

Crito: I won't argue with you about that. But tell me this, Socrates—aren't you at least thinking about me and your other friends? Are you afraid that if you escape, we might get in trouble with the authorities? Maybe they'll say we helped you escape and punish us by taking our money or worse? If that's what you're worried about, please don't be. We're ready to take that risk for you, even if it's dangerous. So please, listen to me and go along with the plan.

Socrates: I know that's one of your concerns, Crito—but it's not the only one.

Crito: You don't need to worry—there are people ready to help you escape, and it won't cost much. As for the officials, they're easy to satisfy with a small payment. I've got enough money, and you're welcome to use it. If that's not enough, our friends are ready to help. Simmias from Thebes even brought a large amount of money for this. Cebes and many others are ready to pitch in. So don't let money or fear for us hold you back. And don't say, like you did at your trial, that you wouldn't know what to do with yourself if you went somewhere else. You'll be welcomed in other places, not just in Athens. I have friends in Thessaly, and if you go there, they'll treat you with respect and protect you. No one there will cause you trouble.

I don't think it's right, Socrates, for you to let yourself die when you could easily avoid it. By doing nothing, you're helping your enemies destroy you. And think about your children—aren't you leaving them behind? You could raise them, teach them, and be there for them. Instead, you're walking away and leaving their future to chance. If things go badly for them, it won't be their fault—it'll be yours for not staying.

No one should have children if they aren't willing to stick around and take care of them. Right now, it seems like you're choosing the easy path instead of the brave and honorable one. That doesn't suit someone like you—someone who's always talked about living with virtue and doing the right thing.

Honestly, I'm ashamed—not just for you, but for us, your friends. People will think the whole situation happened because we were cowards. They'll say the trial could've gone differently, or that we gave up too easily in the end. And they'll blame us for this last, terrible mistake—letting you die when we could have saved you. The truth is, it wouldn't have been hard at all to help you escape.

Please, Socrates, think about how sad and shameful this all looks— for both of us. It's too late to keep discussing it. We need to act now, tonight. If we wait any longer, it'll be too late. I beg you, Socrates— listen to me this time. Do what I'm asking.

Socrates: Crito, I truly appreciate how much you care. Your passion is valuable—but only if it's based on the right reasons. If not, then the more passionate you are, the more danger there is. So we need to think carefully about whether I should really do what you're asking.

You know me. I've always lived by reason and by what makes the most sense after I've thought it through. This situation doesn't change that. I can't suddenly go against everything I've stood for. I still believe in the principles I've always followed—and unless we can come up with better ones, I can't just abandon them. Not even if the crowd had the power to lock me up again, take all my property, or even scare me with threats of death.

So, how should we figure this out? Should we go back to that old idea we've talked about—the one about how not all opinions matter? We used to say that some people's opinions are worth listening to, and others aren't. Was that just talk? Or does it still hold up now that I'm in danger?

I want to figure that out with your help, Crito. Has the situation changed the truth of that idea—or does it still stand? I think a lot of smart people agree that not every opinion is worth the same. And since you, Crito, aren't the one facing death right now, you can think more clearly. So tell me—am I right to say that only some opinions should be taken seriously?

Crito: Yes, I think you're right.

Socrates: So we should care about the opinions of good people, not bad ones?

Crito: Yes.

Socrates: And the thoughts of wise people are helpful, while the opinions of foolish people are not?

Crito: Absolutely.

Socrates: Let me ask you something, Crito. When someone is training their body, do they pay attention to everyone's opinions about how they should exercise, or just to the advice of one expert—their doctor or trainer?

Crito: Just the expert's opinion.

Socrates: So they should care more about that one person's praise or criticism, not about what everyone else says?

Crito: Exactly.

Socrates: That means they should eat, drink, and train the way that expert says is best, even if the rest of the world disagrees?

Crito: Yes, that's true.

Socrates: And if they ignore the expert and instead listen to the crowd, which has no real knowledge, won't that hurt them?

Crito: Definitely.

Socrates: And that harm—what part of them does it damage?

Crito: It harms their body.

Socrates: Right. And now let's think about something similar. When it comes to right and wrong, fair and unfair, good and bad—which is what we're really talking about here—should we listen to everyone's opinion, or just to the person who truly understands?

Crito: We should listen to the one who understands.

Socrates: Shouldn't we respect and fear that wise person's judgment more than the opinion of everyone else combined? And if we ignore that wise judgment, wouldn't we damage something important in ourselves? That part of us that becomes better through justice and worse through injustice?

Crito: Yes, Socrates. I agree.

Socrates: Now think about this: if we followed bad advice and destroyed what keeps us healthy, our body, would life still be worth living?

Crito: No, of course not.

Socrates: And if we destroyed the part of ourselves that's made better by justice—our soul, or character—would life be worth living then?

Crito: Certainly not.

Socrates: So that part of us is even more important than our body?

Crito: It definitely is.

Socrates: Then, my friend, we shouldn't worry about what the crowd thinks. We should care what the wise person says—and what's actually true. That's where your argument went wrong when you said we should care about what people think is just or unjust, good or bad. Someone might say, "But the public can kill us."

Crito: Yes, people would say that.

Socrates: And it's true. But even now, that old idea we've talked about still holds strong: what matters most isn't just living, but living well. Do you still agree with that?

Crito: Yes, I do.

Socrates: And living well means living justly and with honor?

Crito: That's right.

Socrates: Then let's ask ourselves: would it be right for me to escape without the city's permission? If we agree that it's the right thing to do, then we should go for it. But if it's not right, then we shouldn't do it—no matter what happens. Things like money, reputation, or even what happens to my kids shouldn't be the deciding factors. The crowd would bring someone back to life just as quickly as they would kill them—without really thinking it through. So since our reasoning so far seems solid, the only thing left to ask is this: is it right to escape? Or to accept help from others and pay them off in money or gratitude for helping me escape? Or is that wrong? If it's wrong, then whatever happens—death or anything else—shouldn't change what we decide.

Crito: I agree with you, Socrates. What should we do next?

Socrates: Let's work through it together. If you can prove I'm wrong, I'll gladly change my mind. But if not, please stop trying to convince me to escape. I know you mean well, and I appreciate that, but I can't go against what I believe is right. So now, listen to the first part of my argument and see what you think.

Crito: I'm listening.

Socrates: First, should we say that it's never right to do wrong? Or is it okay sometimes, but not other times? Or do we agree that doing wrong is always bad, like we said earlier?

We've spent years talking about this—have we really learned nothing? Have all our conversations meant nothing, and are we now like children who've learned no lessons at all? Or should we stick to what we've always believed: that doing wrong is always harmful to the one who does it?

What do you say?

Crito: I still believe that's true.

Socrates: Then we must never do wrong?

Crito: Yes.

Socrates: And if someone hurts us, we shouldn't hurt them back? Not even to get even?

Crito: That's right.

Socrates: So, Crito, can we ever do something evil?

Crito: No, Socrates.

Socrates: And what about doing something bad just because someone else did it to us first? That's what most people think is fair—but is that right?

Crito: No, it's not right.

Socrates: Because hurting someone else is still doing wrong?

Crito: Exactly.

Socrates: So we must never return harm for harm, no matter what has been done to us. But I want you to really think about whether you agree with this. Most people never believe this—and they probably never will. Those who agree with it and those who don't are on totally different paths. They don't understand each other at all.

So tell me: do you still agree with my first belief—that it's never right to hurt others, even if they hurt you first? Should we base everything else we say on that? Or do you disagree? I've always believed it, and I still do. But if you think differently, tell me now. If not, I'll move on to the next point.

Crito: No, I agree with you. Keep going.

Socrates: Alright. Here's the next question: Should a person always do what they believe is right? Or should they turn away from what's right?

Crito: They should always do what's right.

Socrates: So if all of this is true, what does it mean for us now? If I escape from prison, going against what the people of Athens have decided, would I be doing something wrong? Wouldn't I be hurting the very people and values I should respect the most? Wouldn't I be turning my back on everything we've agreed is right? What do you think?

Crito: I'm not sure, Socrates. I really don't know.

Socrates: Okay, then let's think of it this way. Imagine I'm getting ready to escape—call it whatever you want—and the Laws of Athens come to me and ask, "Socrates, what are you doing? By escaping, aren't you trying to destroy us—the laws and the city itself? Do you really think a city can survive if people don't follow its laws and just do whatever they want?"

Now what would we say to that, Crito? Someone who knows how to speak well could easily argue that laws must be obeyed and that justice must be carried out. And what would we say back? "But the city hurt me—it gave me an unfair sentence!" Suppose I said that.

Crito: That's a fair point to bring up, Socrates.

Socrates: Then the Laws might ask, "Was that part of the deal, Socrates? Didn't you agree to accept whatever the city decided?" If I looked surprised, they'd continue: "Don't just sit there staring, Socrates—answer us. You always like asking questions, so now it's our turn. What reason do you have to say we treated you unfairly? Wasn't it because of us that you were born? Your father married your mother with our approval. You wouldn't even exist without us. Do you have anything bad to say about the laws that control marriage?"

I'd have to say, "No."

Then they might say, "Didn't we also guide your education and how you were raised? Weren't we the ones who made sure your father taught you music and sports like all good citizens?"

And again, I'd have to say, "Yes, that's true."

Then they might say, "So since we gave you life, raised you, and educated you, aren't you like our child, or even our servant? And if that's the case, you can't just treat us however you want. If a child or servant were to strike back at their father or master because they were punished, would that be right? No. So now that we're punishing you, do you think it's okay to destroy us in return—your city and its laws?

"Can you, who say you care so much about justice and virtue, really believe this is the right thing to do? Haven't you realized yet that your country deserves more respect than your parents or ancestors? That your country should be treated with the greatest care and honor—more than anyone else? If she's angry, she should be calmed with respect and reason. And if you can't change her mind, then you must obey her.

"If your country sends you to prison, you must go. If she says you must be punished, you must accept it. If she sends you to fight in a war, you must fight. No one can simply walk away or ignore what the city asks of them. They must either persuade the city to change—or follow its rules. And if it's wrong to hurt your parents, then it's even more wrong to hurt your country."

What would we say to all that, Crito? Are the Laws right or not?

Crito: I think they're right.

Socrates: Then the Laws would go on: "Socrates, think about this—if what we've said is true, and you escape, you're not just hurting us—you're breaking your promise. We gave you life, raised you, and shared with you all the rights and benefits of citizenship. And we also gave every Athenian the freedom to leave if they didn't like how things were run.

"If, once you grew up, you didn't like our system, you could have moved away. You were free to leave and take all your property with you. No law would've stopped you. You could've moved to another city or one of the colonies. But you stayed. You lived here, and by staying, you silently agreed to follow our laws.

"So if you run away now, you'll be breaking your agreement three times over. First, because you're disobeying the laws that gave you life, like disobeying your parents. Second, because we educated you. And third, because you chose to live here and accept how we do things. You never once tried to convince us that we were wrong. We didn't force you—we gave you a choice: follow the laws or try to change them. But you did neither.

"And now you plan to break the law in secret and sneak away? These are the charges you'll face, Socrates—especially because no one in Athens has benefited from our system more than you."

Then I might ask them, "Why me more than anyone else?" And the Laws would reply, "Socrates, of all our citizens, you've shown the most commitment to this city. You hardly ever left Athens—not for festivals or travel, unless it was for military service. You weren't interested in other cities or their governments. You clearly loved Athens.

"You even had children here, choosing to raise them under our laws. That shows how much you approved of our way of life. And during your trial, you had the chance to choose exile instead of death. The same city that won't let you escape now would've let you leave then. But you said you preferred death over exile.

"And now look—you've changed your mind. You're running from everything you claimed to believe. You're breaking the laws, the agreements, and the promises you made as a citizen. That's not something an honest man does. So answer us: didn't you agree to live by our rules, not just with your words, but through your actions?"

Crito, how could we answer that? Don't we have to admit it's true?

Crito: We really don't have a choice, Socrates.

Socrates: Then won't the laws say to me, "Socrates, you're breaking the promises and agreements you freely made with us—not because you were forced or tricked, but after seventy years of living here, thinking it over. All that time, you could've left if you didn't like how we do things. You could've moved to places you often praised, like Sparta or Crete, or anywhere else in Greece or even beyond.

"But you didn't. Out of all Athenians, you stayed here the most. You loved this city and its laws so much that you never even traveled—except for once, to the Isthmus, or when you were ordered to serve in the army. The disabled moved around more than you did. And now you want to run away and break your promises? Don't do it, Socrates. Don't make a joke of yourself by escaping the city like this.

"Think about the damage you'll cause. Your friends will likely be punished—maybe exiled, maybe stripped of their property. As for you, if you go to nearby cities like Thebes or Megara, both of which are well-governed, their leaders will see you as a threat. They'll treat you as someone who disrespects the law. People will believe the judges were right to convict you, thinking, 'If he runs from justice, he must've corrupted the youth just like they said.' You'll be viewed as dangerous.

"So what's the plan—avoid every city that's run with order and virtue? Will you just wander around from place to place, trying to survive? Or will you settle in Thessaly, where Crito's friends live and where anything goes? They'll probably enjoy the story of how you escaped in disguise, maybe in a goat skin or something silly like that. But what happens when they turn on you? When they say, 'You broke the most sacred laws of your homeland just to squeeze out a few more years of life.' If they're happy, they may not say it. But if they're upset with you, they'll throw your shame in your face.

"Yes, you might live—but what kind of life would that be? Always flattering others, always depending on people to feed you. You'd be a servant to everyone, doing nothing but eating and drinking far from home. And what happened to all those speeches about justice and virtue? What will you say then?

"You might say you're doing it for your children—to raise and teach them. But will you really help them by dragging them to Thessaly and taking away their right to be Athenian citizens? Is that the kind of help a father should give? Or do you think your friends will raise them better here if you're alive, even if you're gone? If they're really your friends, they'll take care of your children whether you're in Thessaly or in the afterlife.

"So listen to us—the laws that raised you. Don't put life and family first and justice last. Put justice first. That's the only way to be truly good and right—in this life and the next. You'll be happier, and so will those connected to you. But if you escape, you'll be doing wrong. You'll be returning harm for harm, breaking your promises, and hurting those you should protect—yourself, your friends, your city, and us. We'll be angry while you live, and when you die, the laws of the underworld will see you as an enemy because you tried to destroy us. So don't listen to Crito. Listen to us."

That, dear Crito, is the voice I hear inside me. It's like the sound of music stuck in my ears—I can't hear anything else. And I know no matter what you say now, it won't change my mind. Still, if you have anything left to say, go ahead.

Crito: I have nothing more to say, Socrates.

Socrates: Then leave me to do what I must. Let me follow the path that the gods have laid out for me.

The End

Timaeus

Plato

Foreword

Exploring the Cosmos:
Plato's Vision of Nature, Creation, and the Universe

Plato's Timaeus is one of the most fascinating and enigmatic dialogues in the Western philosophical tradition. Written around 360 BCE, it has profoundly influenced philosophy, theology, science, and metaphysics for nearly 2,400 years. Unlike the deeply political and ethical concerns explored in The Republic, the Timaeus ventures into grand metaphysical territory, presenting an awe-inspiring vision of the cosmos, its creation, its structure, and the very nature of reality itself. It represents Plato at his most ambitious and speculative, weaving together philosophy, mathematics, astronomy, and myth to build a comprehensive cosmological framework.

For readers familiar with Plato's thought through works like The Republic, the Timaeus offers an intriguing expansion of his philosophical concerns into the natural world and its underlying order. But for those encountering Plato for the first time, the dialogue stands as a compelling entry point into his philosophy, addressing questions that remain strikingly relevant to contemporary readers: Where did the universe come from? Is there a purposeful order in nature, or is everything merely random chance? What is the relationship between physical reality and eternal truths? And perhaps most provocatively: what is humanity's place within this vast cosmic order?

At its core, the Timaeus seeks to offer a coherent explanation for the existence and nature of the cosmos, constructed through the narration of Timaeus, a philosopher from southern Italy renowned for his profound wisdom in mathematics and natural sciences. The dialogue itself unfolds dramatically as a continuation of the conversation begun in The Republic, where Socrates and his interlocutors discussed the nature of the just society. Now, Plato turns from human justice to cosmic order, subtly emphasizing a deeper philosophical unity: the principles governing morality and politics may also govern the cosmos at large.

The narrative setting is strikingly imaginative, marked by a calm yet intense intellectual atmosphere. Socrates gathers with his friends, including Timaeus, Critias, and Hermocrates, the day after the discussion recounted in The Republic. Socrates briefly recalls their previous conversation about the ideal city, expressing his wish to see it "come alive" through a vivid description. Critias responds by proposing to tell the story of ancient Atlantis—a legendary civilization whose story will eventually unfold in Plato's companion dialogue, the Critias. But first, Critias introduces Timaeus, who is tasked with explaining the origin and nature of the universe, thus preparing the philosophical groundwork for the Atlantis tale. What follows is one of the most detailed and intricate cosmological theories of the ancient world.

The Craftsman and the Cosmos: Plato's Theory of Creation and Order

Central to the Timaeus is the figure of the "Demiurge," a divine Craftsman who shapes the universe according to eternal, unchanging forms or patterns. Plato deliberately frames this creation not as a religious dogma but as a "likely story" (mythos eikos)—a rationally plausible myth designed to convey profound truths symbolically rather than literally. The Demiurge is not presented as an omnipotent deity creating from nothing, as in later monotheistic traditions, but rather as a supremely wise and benevolent craftsman bringing order from pre-existing chaotic materials. This depiction sets the Timaeus apart from purely theological or religious texts, emphasizing philosophical insight and rational coherence.

According to Timaeus, before creation, the cosmos was in a state of disorder, lacking coherent form. The Demiurge, motivated by pure goodness, imposed rational order upon this chaos by shaping matter into harmonious structures that reflect perfect mathematical proportions and geometrical forms. Plato's insistence that mathematics underpins the cosmos is revolutionary—asserting a deep connection between abstract mathematical principles and physical reality. This insight laid the groundwork for later Western scientific thought, influencing thinkers from Aristotle to Galileo and Newton.

Timaeus describes how the Demiurge fashions the cosmos as a living, ensouled being—a perfectly balanced, harmonious, spherical organism. Plato's vision here is radically holistic, suggesting that the universe itself possesses intelligence and purpose. The world-soul, an entity composed of mathematical proportions and relationships, permeates and animates the entire cosmos. This universal soul ensures harmony among celestial bodies, maintains order, and infuses the universe with rationality and purpose. Thus, Plato's cosmos is neither a mechanical clockwork nor mere lifeless matter; it is alive, vibrant, and deeply interconnected through mathematical and rational relationships.

Plato's cosmology in the Timaeus moves beyond mere astronomy or physics. It is fundamentally metaphysical and ethical, asserting that cosmic order mirrors moral order. The harmony of the universe provides a blueprint for human beings, guiding them toward virtue and wisdom. The cosmos becomes both a metaphor and a model: as above, so below—human societies and individual souls must emulate the universal balance and rational order instantiated by the Demiurge.

Humanity Within the Cosmos:
The Human Soul, Body, and Ethical Life

After establishing the cosmic order, Timaeus turns to humanity, discussing how humans fit into this grand scheme. Plato's treatment of humanity is both metaphysical and profoundly ethical. Humans, for Plato, occupy a unique and significant position. We are microcosms, smaller reflections of the greater cosmic structure, endowed with rational souls capable of comprehending the very principles underlying creation.

Plato describes the human soul as immortal and composed of the same rational structure as the cosmic soul. Souls originate among the stars, descend into material bodies, and undergo a cycle of rebirth—an idea elaborated in other dialogues such as the Phaedo and Republic. In Timaeus, Plato vividly illustrates the soul's embodiment, describing how it struggles against bodily passions, irrational appetites, and distractions from the senses. This duality between body and soul provides Plato's philosophical rationale for pursuing the philosophical life: through reason, reflection, and self-discipline, humans can restore their souls' original harmony, aligning themselves once more with cosmic order.

Plato also devotes significant attention to the physical constitution of human beings. He explores detailed explanations of human anatomy, physiology, senses, and even diseases. Though his explanations reflect ancient Greek medical knowledge, Plato's underlying philosophical aim remains evident. The human body is portrayed as intricately designed, mirroring the cosmos's order, and carefully arranged by the Demiurge to support the soul's intellectual and ethical functions.

Finally, the dialogue considers ethical and social implications derived from this cosmological framework. Plato's cosmos is fundamentally moral: the rational order governing nature also guides human conduct. The ideal human life, therefore, involves contemplation of eternal truths, moderation of bodily desires, and harmonious living within society. Ethical virtues like justice, wisdom, and temperance find their basis not in mere human convention, but in the fundamental structure of reality itself. The universe, Plato insists, is inherently ordered toward the good, and humans achieve true fulfillment by aligning their lives with this cosmic harmony.

The Enduring Influence and Relevance of the Timaeus

The impact of the Timaeus stretches far beyond ancient philosophy. Its influence resonates throughout Western history, inspiring religious thought, Renaissance humanism, scientific inquiry, and modern philosophical speculation. Early Christian and medieval theologians drew heavily on its cosmology, seeing in Plato's Demiurge a precursor to monotheistic ideas of a divine creator. Renaissance thinkers, fascinated by Plato's mathematics-based cosmology, sought to rediscover and apply these ideas to the burgeoning scientific revolution.

In modern times, the Timaeus continues to captivate philosophers, scientists, and general readers alike. Its questions about creation, the mathematical nature of reality, and humanity's place in the cosmos remain as provocative today as when Plato first penned them. Current discussions about the relationship between consciousness and the universe, the fine-tuning of physical constants, and debates over intelligent design find surprising resonance in Plato's ancient ideas. Even modern environmental ethics reflects echoes of Plato's view that the cosmos is an interconnected, living organism deserving respect and understanding.

Whether approached as philosophy, literature, or an early form of scientific speculation, the Timaeus challenges readers to confront profound mysteries. It invites us to think carefully about our relationship to the universe, the nature of reality, and our responsibilities as rational beings. Plato's profound vision of a harmonious cosmos—ordered, rational, and deeply purposeful—continues to inspire awe, contemplation, and philosophical reflection.

Welcome to Plato's Timaeus. As you embark on this remarkable journey through the cosmos, may its deep questions and rich imagery illuminate your understanding of nature, reality, and humanity's eternal quest for meaning within the universe.

Section 1

Socrates starts by giving a quick summary of the Republic. He mentions a few key ideas—how people are divided into different roles, how guardians are trained, and how property, women, and children are shared. But he doesn't talk about the second level of education or the rule of philosophers.

Now, he says he wants to see how this perfect society would act in a real-life challenge, like a major conflict. But he admits he can't come up with a good story himself, and he doubts that poets can either. Even though he says nothing bad about them, he points out that poets only imitate what they've seen. He's also unsure about Sophists, who may speak well but never settle down in one place, and so probably don't understand real cities or real leaders. That's why he turns to Timaeus, a man who is both a thinker and a statesman, as well as Critias and Hermocrates, who are also experienced and wise.

Hermocrates says, "We'll do our best. In fact, we've already been getting ready. On the way home, Critias told us an old story. Critias, would you please tell it again to Socrates?"

Critias answers, "I will—if Timaeus agrees."

"I do," says Timaeus.

Critias begins, "Socrates, this story comes from Solon, who was friends with my great-grandfather Dropidas. Solon told it to my grandfather, who told it to me. It's about ancient heroic deeds by the people of Athens, especially one event I'll tell to honor both you and the goddess. My grandfather was ninety years old when he told the story, and I was only ten. It happened during a festival called the Registration of Youth, where boys were awarded prizes for reciting things. Some recited poems by Solon, which were still popular at the time. Someone praised Solon, saying he wasn't just wise but also a great poet.

That made my grandfather smile. He said that if Solon had just had more time, he would've finished the amazing legend he brought back from Egypt. He might have become as famous as Homer and Hesiod.

'What was the legend about?' someone asked.

'It told the greatest story about Athens—its most glorious moment,' he said. 'But that memory faded because time passed and the people involved were gone.'

'Then tell us the whole story,' the other person said, 'and how Solon heard it.'

Critias explained that in Egypt, where the Nile splits into branches, there's a city called Sais. It's the birthplace of King Amasis and is protected by the goddess Neith, who is like Athena. The people there feel connected to Athens. When Solon visited, he was warmly welcomed. While speaking with the priests, he realized how little he and the Greeks really knew about the past.

To learn more, he shared the Greek myths he knew—like those about Phoroneus, Niobe, Deucalion, and Pyrrha—and tried to count how many generations had passed. But one of the older priests said, "Solon, you Greeks are always young. None of you are truly old."

"What do you mean?" Solon asked.

"You're young in your minds," the priest replied. "You have no ancient wisdom. That's because your people—and others—have been wiped out many times by natural disasters, like fire and floods. The Greek story of Phaethon, who drove the sun chariot and set the earth on fire, is a symbol of this. Every so often, disasters caused by changes in the sky destroy life on Earth.

"When fire destroys everything, people who live by rivers or the sea survive more often. When it's floods, people on high ground are safer. Egypt is safe from both. The Nile protects us from fire, and since we have little rain, we don't suffer from floods like other countries. But when floods do come, people elsewhere are washed away, and survivors start over without remembering the past.

"In Egypt, we keep written records in our temples. That's why we still remember what others have forgotten. The stories you've told us are childish in comparison. You remember only one great flood, but there were many. You don't even know about the amazing people you come from. Athens was once the greatest city on Earth, full of wise and noble people, but that history was lost because you didn't write it down.

"Solon was amazed and asked to hear more.

"Of course," the priest said. "It's good for you and for your city, and especially for the goddess who founded both of ours. According to our records, she founded Athens nine thousand years ago, and ours eight thousand. Many of your old laws are like ours. I'll summarize them, and you can read the details later in the temple books.

"In ancient Athens, people were divided into groups—priests, workers, farmers, hunters, and soldiers. Like in Egypt, your soldiers were set apart from others and carried shields and spears, a custom the goddess taught you first, then us.

"Your laws encouraged learning and using knowledge to help people. The land the goddess chose for you had the best weather and produced the wisest people. That's why it was the perfect place for her followers. You lived like children of the gods, better than anyone else. Many of your great deeds are still remembered. The most famous was defeating Atlantis.

"Atlantis was a massive island beyond the Pillars of Heracles. It was larger than Libya and Asia combined and led to other islands and even a huge ocean, while the Mediterranean was just a small bay. The Atlanteans ruled a huge empire that reached into Europe and North Africa, even as far as Egypt.

"But Athens stood up to them. When no one else would fight, your city faced them alone, risking everything to protect freedom. She defeated the invaders and gave liberty to many. Soon after, there were huge earthquakes and floods. Your brave warriors were swallowed by the ground, and Atlantis sank into the sea. That's why there are shallow waters in that part of the Atlantic."

Critias finishes, "That's the story Solon heard. Yesterday, as I listened to your speech, Socrates, I noticed how much your idea of a perfect city is like that ancient Athens. I didn't mention it right away— I needed to be sure I remembered correctly. I heard it as a child, but it's stuck in my mind, and I'm ready to tell you everything. Maybe your imaginary city is really the one Solon spoke of, and those ancient heroes are your citizens."

Socrates responds, "That's perfect, Critias. It fits well with our festival. And since the story is true, that makes it even better."

Critias adds, "Here's our plan for today: Timaeus will speak first about how the world began, all the way up to the creation of humans. Then I'll take those people, some of whom you've already taught, and present them as the long-lost citizens of Athens, just as the Egyptian story said. Like in Solon's law, we'll officially recognize them as citizens."

Socrates replies, "I see now that this will be quite a thoughtful gathering. Go ahead, Timaeus—say a prayer and begin."

TIMAEUS:

Whenever someone starts something important, they usually ask the gods for help. And if you're going to talk about how the universe began, it's even more important to do so. I hope what I say honors the gods, makes sense to you, and clearly shows what I mean.

First, we need to tell the difference between two things: something that always exists and never changes, and something that is always changing and never fully real. The first is understood by deep thinking, the second by opinion and senses. Everything that changes or is created must have been made by something. And if something is made using a perfect, eternal model, it turns out well. But if it's based on a copy or something already created, it doesn't turn out as well.

Now, is the world something that was made, or has it always existed? I believe it was made, because we can see and touch it. That means it's part of the physical world, and all physical things have a beginning. So, if it was made, there must be a cause—some maker. That maker is a perfect being, the ultimate creator. He looked at an eternal pattern and used it to shape the world. It would be wrong to say that the perfect model was made too—it's timeless. The world is just a copy of that perfect idea.

Because of this, anything we say about something unchanging and eternal can be completely true. But anything we say about something that changes—like the world—can only be probably true, not certain. So, since we're all just humans trying to understand the divine and the universe, we should accept that our understanding is only as good as it can be—not perfect, but close.

SOCRATES:

That's a great start, Timaeus. Please go on.

TIMAEUS:

Why did the Creator make the world? Because he is good. And someone good isn't jealous. Since he wasn't jealous, he wanted everything to be like himself—good and orderly. So, when he saw that the visible world was in chaos, he set it in order. And because he's the best, he wanted the world to be the most beautiful thing possible. He knew that intelligence is better than mindlessness, so he placed intelligence in the soul and the soul in the body. That's how he made the universe—a living, intelligent being, guided by a soul, with help from the divine.

What kind of creature did he model the universe after? The perfect creature—one that includes everything within it. The universe was made in its image and contains all visible beings.

Are there many universes or just one? Just one. If there were more than one, they would be parts of a bigger whole, and that bigger whole would be the real model. But since the model is already complete, the world must be one of a kind.

The universe, being visible and solid, must be made of fire (which we see) and earth (which we touch). But fire and earth are opposites, and you can't connect two extremes without something in the middle. One bridge isn't enough for solids; you need two. So between fire and earth, the Creator added air and water. He arranged these four elements in a balanced pattern:

fire : air = air : water

air : water = water : earth

This gave the universe harmony. Because all the elements worked together so well, the universe became a solid, visible heaven that could not fall apart unless the Creator himself chose to destroy it.

He used all the available materials to make the world whole. He didn't leave leftovers that could be used to make another world. He also made it so perfect that it wouldn't age or get sick, since aging and disease come from outside forces. The shape of the universe is a sphere—round in every direction and balanced around its center—because that shape holds everything equally and is the most complete.

The universe doesn't have eyes or ears because there's nothing outside it to see or hear. It doesn't eat or breathe, since nothing needs to come in or out. It doesn't have hands or feet, because there's nothing to grab or walk toward. Everything it does happens inside itself, using pure thought. It moves in a circle, turning in on itself—the most thoughtful kind of motion. It doesn't use any other kinds of movement, so it has no legs or parts for walking.

So, in short, God created a god-like universe—whole, balanced, needing nothing, and completely happy on its own. First, he made the soul to be the ruler of the body. Even though we usually talk about the body first, in truth, the soul came first.

To create the soul, God took some things that never change and some things that do. He blended these together to make something in between—a new kind of substance that combined both. This new thing had parts of sameness and difference in it. Once he had this blend, he divided it into portions based on specific number patterns—like 1, 2, 3, 4, 9, 8, and 27—and filled the spaces between them with numbers that fit in certain ratios. These ratios created musical harmonies, like

- 1, 4/3, 3/2, 2
- 2, 8/3, 3
- 4, 16/3, 6

and so on.

These numbers helped shape time, rhythm, and the structure of reality. Then he split the soul down the middle into two parts and joined them together like an X. He bent these into two circular paths—one inside the other—and they crossed at a point opposite where they met.

The outer circle was called the circle of sameness. The inner circle was called the circle of difference. The outer circle moved in one direction (horizontally to the right), and the inner one spun the other way (diagonally to the left).

The circle of sameness was left whole and put in charge. The circle of difference was split into seven uneven rings, each moving at different speeds. These became the orbits of the planets:

- The Sun, Mercury, and Venus moved at the same speed
- The Moon, Saturn, Mars, and Jupiter moved at different speeds

Each moved in perfect proportion, just as designed.

When the Creator made the soul, he placed the body inside it. The soul spread out from the center to the edges of the sky and began to move within itself in a steady, intelligent, and eternal way. The body of the heavens can be seen, but the soul is invisible. It's made with reason and balance, and it's considered the best creation because it was made by the highest power. The soul was made from three parts—the same, the different, and something in between. These were blended and arranged in a balanced way. As the soul moves within itself, whenever it comes into contact with something that truly exists—whether it's something simple or complex—it responds by recognizing how it is the same or different from something else. It can tell when, where, and how things are connected or affected, both in the physical world and in the world of unchanging truths.

When the soul is near the senses, and the "circle of difference" is moving correctly, it creates true beliefs and opinions. But when the soul focuses on thinking alone, and the "circle of sameness" flows smoothly, true understanding is formed.

When the Creator saw his universe, which he made in the image of the eternal gods, moving and alive, he was happy. Because the original model was eternal, he wanted the universe to last forever too—at least as much as possible. So, he created time as a copy of eternity. Time moves in a steady way using numbers, broken into days, months, and years. These divisions also created the ideas of past, present, and future. But these ideas only apply to things that change. They don't apply to what is eternal, because eternal things don't go through change. They don't grow old or young, and saying they "were" or "will be" is incorrect. Those words only make sense when talking about things that come and go—not things that always are.

So time was made as a reflection of eternity and was created alongside the heavens. If the heavens ever disappear, time would disappear with them.

The Creator made the sun, moon, and five other "wanderers" (the planets). These seven bodies were placed in seven separate paths, each part of the circle of difference. The moon was set in the orbit closest to Earth. The sun was placed in the next one. Venus (the morning star) and Mercury were placed in paths that move in the opposite direction of the sun but at equal speeds. That's why they sometimes catch up to each other or seem to fall behind.

All of these were made into living beings. They were given their roles and started to move—the ones closer to Earth moved faster, while the ones farther away moved slower, based on the way the "circle of difference" turns. But this motion was still influenced by the "circle of sameness." Because of this, the planets seemed to make spiral patterns in the sky. The ones that were actually slower looked like they were faster, and those that moved faster sometimes seemed slower.

The Creator placed a great fire in the second orbit from Earth, which became the sun. This light was meant to shine over the whole sky and help intelligent beings learn about numbers and time through watching the heavens move. Day and night began from the spinning of the sky. A month came from the moon's cycle, and a year came from the sun's path. Other time cycles, which are much longer and more complex, go unnoticed by most people. But there is a perfect time cycle—a complete year—when all these patterns line up again. That's why the stars were created: so the heavens could reflect the eternal world.

Up to this point, the universe had been shaped in a divine form, but it didn't yet include all living things. The Creator then made other kinds of life, based on eternal patterns that already existed. These included four main kinds: gods, birds, fish, and land animals.

The gods were created in the shape of a circle, the most perfect form, because it represents the whole universe. They were mostly made of fire so they would shine brightly. They were given wisdom to follow what is good and were placed throughout the heavens as shining symbols. These stars were given two types of movement: one was a circular motion in place, full of peaceful and unchanging thought; the other was a forward motion, controlled by the same balance.

This is how the fixed stars were created—divine, eternal beings that spin in the same spot. The planets, or "wandering stars," moved differently, just as explained earlier.

The Earth, which supports all life, was made to wrap around the central pole of the universe. It became the maker and guardian of night and day, and the first and oldest of the gods inside the sky.

It would be too much to explain every shape and movement of the stars, how they dance around each other, or where they appear and disappear, especially without a visual guide.

As for the other gods, we can only rely on stories passed down from ancient people, who said they were children of the gods. Since they claimed to know their ancestors, we must trust them, as is the usual custom.

According to these old stories, Oceanus and Tethys were children of Earth and Sky. Then came Phorcys, Cronos, and Rhea. After them came Zeus and Hera, along with their well-known brothers and children.

When all the stars and planets—both the ones we see and the ones we don't—had been created, the Creator spoke to them:

"Gods, children of gods, I made you. What I make cannot be destroyed—unless someone evil tries to break apart what is balanced and good. Though you are not naturally immortal, I will make sure you don't die by keeping you together myself. Listen: there are still three types of mortal beings that must be created. But if I make them myself, they'll be too much like the gods. So, I'm asking you to create them instead. I'll plant the seed of immortality in them, and your task is to join the mortal with the immortal. You must care for them while they live and welcome them back when they die."

After saying this, he took the leftover elements he had used for the soul of the universe. These weren't as pure as before—they had been mixed and weakened. From this blend, he created a number of souls equal to the number of stars and gave each soul its own star. Then, like placing a driver in a chariot, he set them there and showed them how the universe works. He explained what life would be like when they were born into human bodies.

These souls would enter the planets and become human—the most spiritual of all animals. Once placed in their bodies, which are always changing, the souls would experience feeling, then desire—made from both pleasure and pain—followed by emotions like fear and anger. If they could overcome these feelings, they would live a good life. If they were overcome by them, they would live badly. A soul that lived a good life would return to its home star and live there in peace. But a soul that lived badly would be reborn first as a woman, and if still unwise, as an animal. This would continue until reason regained control over the elements—fire, air, earth, and water—and the soul returned to its better self.

The Creator gave this rule to the souls to show he wasn't responsible for their future mistakes. Then he sent them down—some to Earth, some to the Moon, and some to the other planets. He told the younger gods to make human bodies for the souls, add what was needed, and protect them from all harm—except the harm they bring upon themselves.

After giving these instructions, the Creator remained in his divine form. His children, the younger gods, took the immortal soul and combined it with bits of earth, air, fire, and water from the physical world. These pieces were meant to return to the world later. They connected everything—not with unbreakable chains like their own bodies, but with tiny, invisible links. Each human body was built from all four elements, constantly taking things in and letting them out. Inside each body, the soul flowed like a river, moving wildly in all six directions: forward, backward, right, left, up, and down.

The wildness of these flows grew worse when the body touched things like burning heat, solid ground, rushing water, or powerful wind. These impacts caused the body to send signals to the soul—this is what we call sensations. These waves from inside and outside the body disrupted the soul's balance, twisting the soul's natural movement and throwing off the delicate patterns that help it think clearly. The soul's pathways, which are supposed to move smoothly, got bent and scrambled, making its thoughts confused and unstable.

It's like imagining someone standing on their head with their feet in the air—everything is reversed. That's what happens to the soul when its thinking gets confused by outside influences. It can mistake left for right, or up for down. It says something is the same when it isn't, or different when it's actually the same. These are false, foolish thoughts, and they don't help the soul understand anything. They seem strong, but in truth, they are being overpowered.

Because of all this confusion, the soul starts out without clear thinking. But as time goes on and the body stops growing so quickly, the soul slowly begins to move the right way again. Then it can start to understand truth and become wise. A soul that gets proper education becomes strong, healthy, and whole. But one that is left untrained moves through life broken and unsteady, and when it dies, it returns to the underworld having done nothing useful.

This comes later. Right now, we're focusing on how the soul and body were first made.

The gods placed the soul's two main circles—the ones that help it think—inside a round shape we call the head. This head became the ruler of the body. Then they attached the rest of the body to it as a vehicle. The arms and legs were added as tools, able to bend and stretch. The body was made to move forward, since the front was seen as the more important direction. The face was carefully made and filled with parts that would help the soul understand the world.

They created the eyes first. The gods filled them with a special kind of fire, like the light of day, and directed it through the pupils. When the light inside the eyes met the light outside, they blended and helped the soul sense movement and shape. But when it's dark, and this light doesn't meet anything similar, the eyes can't see, and we fall asleep.

When our eyelids close, the inner light is trapped, and our body settles down. Fewer dreams come. But if stronger motions remain inside us, they create dreams during sleep.

With this, we can understand how mirrors work. Light from inside the eyes and light from outside meet on the smooth surface. Since they bounce back in unusual ways, the right and left sides of the image are switched. A concave mirror flips top and bottom, but that isn't quite the same thing.

These are what we call second causes—things that help shape the world. Many people wrongly believe they are the main causes, but they're not. They don't think or plan. Someone who values reason knows that true causes are always thoughtful and invisible. These are the causes we should explore first. Only afterward should we think about causes that act randomly or through outside force.

I've explained how sight works, but now let's think about why the gods gave us eyes in the first place. Sight brings us our greatest blessings. If we couldn't see the sun, stars, or sky, we never would have had thoughts like the ones we're sharing now. Seeing the sky's movements gave us ideas of time and numbers, helped us ask questions, and led to philosophy—the greatest gift we've received. Even ordinary people benefit from sight in everyday ways.

So, God gave us eyes so we could watch the skies and learn from their order, then bring that same order into our own minds, which are often confused. He gave us speech and hearing for the same reason—not just for fun or pleasure, but to help us bring harmony into our thoughts through sound. Music and spoken words can guide our inner lives, making us calmer and more balanced.

So far, we've talked about what reason created. But not everything in the world comes from reason. Some things happen because they must—out of necessity. The universe is a mix of both: reason tries to guide necessity, making it produce good outcomes as much as possible.

Before the heavens existed, there was fire, air, water, and earth. People think they understand these, but they don't. Many say these are the basic building blocks of everything, but that's not quite right. They aren't even as clear as letters or sounds. I'm not trying to explain the very first source of things—that's beyond our current understanding. But I've followed a path of what seems most likely, and I'll keep going that way, hoping the divine will help us stay on course.

Earlier, I talked about two kinds of being: one that always stays the same and can't be seen, and one that constantly changes and can be seen. But now, there's a need to talk about a third kind—something I'll call the "space" or "container" where things are created and take shape.

It's not easy to describe this third type clearly, because the basic elements—fire, air, water, and earth—are constantly changing into each other. They're not stable enough to be given fixed names. So when we talk about fire or water, we're not talking about solid things, but more like changing qualities. It's similar to gold being shaped into different objects. If someone asks what they are, the safest answer is just to say "gold."

In the same way, there is a universal material out of which everything is formed. It doesn't have any particular form itself, but it takes on many shapes, each based on an eternal pattern. You could say this container is like a mother, the patterns are like a father, and the result is like a child.

This material that takes on all forms must be formless itself—like a scentless liquid that can take on any smell, or soft clay that can be molded into any shape. This "space" or "matter" isn't fire, water, air, or earth. It's something invisible, without shape, yet it somehow shares in the nature of things we can understand with reason. Generally speaking, we can say that when this formless space is heated, it becomes fire; when it's wet, it becomes water, and so on.

Let me ask something important: do the elements like fire have a true essence, or are they just what we can see and touch? I'd say this: if knowledge and belief are not the same, then real essences must exist. But if they are the same, then only the visible world is real. However, since belief and knowledge are clearly different—one learned through reason, the other through persuasion—it follows that real essences exist. Knowledge is logical, steady, and rare, while belief is emotional, changeable, and common.

So, just as there are two types of understanding, there are two types of reality: one that is eternal, invisible, and unchanging—known only through reason—and one that is created and always changing, which we experience through the senses. Then there's a third thing: space, which isn't destroyed, and which we understand only vaguely—not through the senses, but through a kind of unclear reasoning. It seems dreamlike but necessary, because everything needs to exist somewhere. Even if things are just copies of deeper truths, they still have to exist in space.

Real reason tells us that if two things—like a pattern and its copy—are truly different, they can't exist in the same thing at the same time. They have to be separate.

So here's the summary: before the universe was formed, there were three things—being (unchanging truth), becoming (change), and space (the container). This space, or "nurse of creation," was affected by fire and water and took on forms like air and earth. As it moved, the elements got sorted—heavier parts settled, lighter ones floated, like grain separated by wind. At first, all of this was messy and unshaped. But then God used numbers and shapes to bring order to it, turning something disorganized into something beautiful and good.

Now, let me explain how the world was made using an approach you may know from science. Fire, air, water, and earth are physical things—so they are solids. All solids are made from flat surfaces, and these surfaces are made from triangles. There are two main types of triangles: one with two equal sides (isosceles) and one with all sides different (scalene). These triangles are the basic building blocks of the elements.

Of all possible triangles, we'll pick two special ones:

- the isosceles triangle,
- and the right triangle where the longest side squared equals three times the shorter side squared.

We say these two are the ones used to build the elements.

I used to think all four elements could change into one another, but I was wrong. Three are made from the scalene triangle, and one from the isosceles triangle. So only three can transform into each other, while the fourth cannot.

Let's now talk about how the elements are built. From the scalene triangle, you get three perfect 3D shapes:

1. The tetrahedron (a pyramid with four faces),
2. The octahedron (eight faces),
3. The icosahedron (twenty faces).

From the isosceles triangle, you get the cube (six faces). There's also a fifth shape—the dodecahedron, which has twelve pentagon faces. God used this shape to model the twelve divisions of the zodiac.

Now let's match each shape to its element.

- The cube is the most stable—it stands firmly and is made of isosceles triangles. So it belongs to earth, the most solid and unmoving.
- The pyramid, or tetrahedron, is the sharpest and lightest, so it belongs to fire.
- The octahedron fits air, and
- The icosahedron, with its many faces, fits water, which is more

fluid and less able to resist.

These shapes are so tiny we can't see them alone. We only see them when many are packed together.

Their movements, sizes, and other qualities were set in order by God, who arranged them as best as he could within the limits of what was possible.

Here's what seems most likely: when earth is broken down by fire—either directly or through air or water—it doesn't turn into something else. It just breaks apart. Water, when broken by fire or air, changes: one part becomes fire, and the other two become air. When air is broken up, it turns into two parts fire. The reverse happens when things condense—two parts of fire combine to form one part of air, and two and a half parts of air make one part of water.

When fire breaks down something, it slices it apart using its sharp triangle-shaped particles. But once the fire fully mixes with the thing it's burning, the movement stops, because things that are alike don't attack each other. But when two different types of particles collide, they keep breaking each other apart until the smaller one either runs away to join its own kind or mixes into the stronger one. This pulling apart or joining together causes motion.

Movement needs something to push and something to be pushed. But this doesn't happen in something completely uniform—movement is caused by differences. So, why don't things stop moving once they've been sorted? Because everything in the universe is always being squeezed by spinning motions. Nature won't allow empty space, so lighter particles like fire and air are constantly being pushed into the gaps between heavier ones. Each one moves depending on how thick or light it is. That's why all the elements are always moving—rising, falling, or shifting to find their proper place. This imbalance keeps motion going at all times.

Now let's look at different types of fire. There's flame, light that doesn't burn, and the red glow of embers. There are also kinds of air, like clear aether and thick mist, and other unnamed kinds. Water comes in two types—liquid and fusible. The liquid has small, uneven parts and flows easily. Fusible water has larger, more even parts, and is thicker and heavier, but it melts when fire touches it and spreads across the ground. As it cools, fire turns into air, which escapes, pulling the remaining liquid particles together and making them solid again. This is how cooling and freezing happen.

Among the fusible types, gold is the heaviest and most beautiful. It hardens as it flows through rock and has a bright yellow color. A darker, denser form of gold is called adamant. Another form is copper, which is harder but lighter because the gaps between its parts are bigger. It also mixes with tiny amounts of earth, which show up as rust.

These are some ideas that philosophy explores when it turns away from eternal truths to playfully study how things are made in the world.

Water mixed with fire becomes liquid, which flows over the ground and feels soft because its base parts shift easily. If it loses the fire and air, it cools and hardens into ice, hail, frost, or snow. There are also watery substances called juices that flow through plants. Examples include:

- Wine, which warms both body and spirit
- Oils like olive oil or pitch, which are thick and smooth
- Honey, which softens the tongue and tastes sweet
- Plant acids, which bubble, sting, and can break down flesh

Some kinds of earth get filtered through water and turn into stone. In that process, water breaks apart and escapes as air, and the pressure pushes the earth together with any leftover water, turning it into solid rock. If the rock is made of even particles, it's clear and smooth. If not, it's rough and cloudy.

Earth becomes pottery when the water in it dries quickly. If moisture stays and the earth gets melted by fire, it cools into a black stone. When the earth is finer and salty, drying out the water makes soda and salt. Mixtures of earth and water that are very strong can't be broken down by water, only by fire. Loose earth can be washed away with water, but packed earth only melts with fire.

Water, when tightly held together, also needs fire to be broken up. If it's loosely held, then air or fire can split it—air fills the gaps, while fire slices through the parts. Thick air can't be broken unless fire reaches its tiny building blocks. Even when not thick, only fire can split it apart.

Mixtures of earth and water don't soften in water as long as the water fills their gaps. But when fire enters those gaps, it breaks the water apart, and the whole thing melts. These mixtures come in two types: some, like glass, contain more earth; others, like wax, contain more water.

Now that we've talked about things we can see and touch, let's move on to sensation. But to explain how we feel things, we also have to talk about the body and the soul. Since we can't explain both in full right now, let's just agree they exist so we can move on.

So what makes fire burn? Its sharp angles, tiny size, fast movement, and the way it's shaped—like a pyramid, which cuts more sharply than any other form.

Cold is felt when large, wet particles outside the body push against the smaller ones inside. That pressure causes shaking and discomfort, which is why we shiver. Something is considered hard if your skin gives way to it, and soft if it gives way to your skin. These ideas are relative. Materials with a wide, flat base feel firm and solid. Narrow-based ones feel soft and bendy.

Lightness and heaviness aren't really about being higher or lower. In a round universe, there is no true "up" or "down." What's above for one person might be below for someone on the other side of the world. Instead, heaviness depends on how tightly an element clings to its own kind. A small piece of earth can be pulled away more easily than a big one, but both want to return to other earth. The same is true when trying to move lighter elements downwards—they resist. Smoothness comes from even and tight parts, while roughness comes from jagged and uneven ones.

Pleasure and pain are the most important feelings in the whole body. When a part of the body moves easily, it can send signals quickly to the mind. If it doesn't move easily, it sends no signals. That's why bones and hair don't feel much, but eyes and ears do. Mild feelings, like soft touches or normal sights, aren't painful or pleasant. But when something hits the body hard or quickly—like a cut or burn—it causes pain. When the body is suddenly comforted or refreshed, we feel pleasure.

Now let's look at more specific senses, like taste. The tongue feels things through stretching or tightening. Rough or smooth particles create those feelings. Tiny earthy particles that melt or dry out the small veins on the tongue feel astringent if rough, harsh if slightly less rough, and bitter if very drying, like soda or lye. Milder versions of these are called salty—they have a strong flavor but not the bitterness.

Spicy or pungent tastes come from light, hot particles that rise into the head and cut through everything they touch. When things rot and break down, they create two kinds of particles. One is heavy and thick, boiling up into bitter-tasting bubbles. The other is cleaner and clearer, forming watery bubbles. Together, these make the sour or acidic taste.

But when the broken-down particles match what the tongue is made for, and fit well with its structure, they calm the tongue and create the taste we call sweet.

Smells don't fall into specific categories. They happen during the breakdown or transformation of one element into another. Pure air or pure water doesn't have any smell at all. Smells are like light vapors—

thicker than air but thinner than water. That's why when you breathe in and your nose is blocked, the air still passes through, but you don't smell anything. Smells don't have specific names; we just call them pleasant or unpleasant. They can be felt throughout the upper part of the body, from the head down to the stomach.

Hearing works when a sound hits the ear. The impact moves through the air, brain, and blood, all the way to the soul, starting from the head and reaching the liver. Fast-moving sounds are high-pitched, and slow ones are low-pitched. Smooth, steady sounds feel pleasant, while unsteady ones feel harsh. Loudness depends on how strong the sound is. I'll talk more about harmony in music later.

Colors are a kind of flame that shines off of objects. These flames contain tiny pieces that match up with our eyes. Some of the pieces are larger or smaller than what our eyes are built to receive. If the pieces are the right size, the object looks clear. If they're smaller, they make the eye expand and appear white; if larger, they make the eye contract and appear black. There's also a faster type of fire that pushes through the eye, causing tears. When the inner fire shoots out and mixes with the outer fire, it creates a reaction in the eye's moisture, which produces all kinds of colors. We call this "dazzling," and the object that causes it is "bright."

There's another kind of fire that blends softly with the eye's moisture and gives off the color red, like blood. When this brightness mixes with red and white, it creates a golden-brown shade we call auburn. But the exact math behind how mixed colors are formed is unclear—even guessing is hard. For example, red mixed with black and white gives purple. If you burn it and add more black, it turns into a brownish color called umber. Flame-color comes from mixing auburn and dull gray. Dull gray itself is made from white and black. Yellow is a mix of white and auburn. When white and brightness mix with strong black, you get deep blue. If deep blue blends with white, it becomes light blue. Mix flame-color with black, and you get green. Other colors can be guessed at in a similar way.

However, if someone tries to test all of this in a lab, they'd be missing the point—because only a divine power like God can truly mix and separate the basic parts of nature. Humans just aren't capable of that.

These are the necessary parts the Creator worked with when forming the universe. He used secondary causes like tools, but He Himself gave goodness to everything. There are two types of causes: the divine and the necessary. We should aim to understand the divine most of all, but we also need to understand the necessary, because without them, we can't fully understand the divine.

Now that we've covered the building blocks for our explanation, let's go back to where we started and finish the story properly.

In the beginning, everything was chaotic—there was no order or balance. The elements were scattered until the Creator organized them and made the world. He created the divine part Himself, but He let his children create the part that would die. He gave them the immortal soul, and they built a body for it. Then they created another soul—the mortal one—full of powerful feelings:

- Pleasure, which tempts us to do wrong
- Pain, which makes us avoid what's good
- Fear and overconfidence, which give bad advice
- Anger, which is hard to calm down
- Hope, which can easily be tricked

They mixed all of these with instincts and wild love, following nature's laws, and that's how humans were formed.

Because they didn't want the divine soul to be corrupted by these emotions, they placed the mortal soul lower down in the body, in the chest, away from the head. It was like dividing a house, with the men's and women's rooms kept separate. The chest was split into an upper and lower part. The upper section, between the lungs and the neck, is where courage and anger live. It's near the brain and helps support reason when controlling desires. The heart sits in this upper part and serves as the control center. Blood vessels connect to it, and through these, the soul sends instructions throughout the body. When strong emotions or danger appear, the heart speeds up. That's why the creators placed the lungs around it—they're soft, spongy, and bloodless so they can cool the body down using air and drink.

The part of the soul that craves food and drink was placed lower, between the lungs and belly. It was tied down in a kind of pen, like a wild beast, to keep it from bothering the higher part of the soul that makes wise decisions. The Creator knew this part wouldn't listen to reason. So, to help manage it, they made the liver to interact with it. The liver was designed to be bright, smooth, sweet, and sometimes bitter. That way, when thoughts from the mind reflected there, they could affect this lower part of the soul.

If something bad was felt, the liver would turn bitter and change color, causing pain. This happens when bile builds up, twisting the liver and closing its pathways. But when peaceful and gentle thoughts reach the liver, it relaxes, and the person feels calm and free. At night, when the body and mind rest, this quiet state can even bring dreams that seem to predict the future.

The creators wanted to help humans be as good as possible, so they gave the liver a small power of divination—a way to catch glimpses of the future. But this only works when people are sick or overwhelmed, not when they're healthy or awake. That's why some people are called prophets, though they're really just interpreters of what the unconscious soul picks up. Once someone dies, these signs disappear and make no sense anymore.

Nearby, on the left side of the body, is the spleen. It sits close to the liver and helps keep it clean, like a cloth wiping a mirror. Waste from the liver flows into the spleen, and since it's hollow, it swells up for a while. But when the body is cleansed, it shrinks back to normal.

We can only fully understand the soul through the word of God. Still, we can guess what seems most likely about both the soul and the body.

The creators of the human body knew that people would easily fall into overeating. So when they designed the stomach to hold food, they also made the intestines long and twisted. This slowed down how fast food passed through the body. That way, humans wouldn't spend all their time eating and drinking and forget about learning and higher thinking.

The bones and flesh were created starting from the marrow, which acts as a bridge between body and soul. God made the marrow using the most perfect basic building blocks—shapes that could form all four elements. He carefully mixed them in the right amounts, making different kinds of marrow to match the different types of souls. The part meant for the divine soul was shaped into a round form called the brain, which would be placed in the head.

The rest of the marrow was shaped into long, rounded strands to act like anchors for the mortal soul. Around these, God built the rest of the body, starting by wrapping the marrow in bone. Bone was made by filtering clean, fine earth, mixing it with marrow, and then hardening it by heating it in fire and cooling it in water. This made it strong and unable to dissolve.

God made a protective bone shell around the brain with a small opening and built the spine using jointed bones that stretched from the head down the back. Since bones are stiff and can damage the marrow if they get too hot or cold, God added muscles and tendons. Muscles help protect the body and keep it warm or cool as needed. They release sweat to cool us in summer and keep us warm in winter. To make muscle, God mixed earth with fire and water, adding a bit of sour and salty material to help the mix form soft, pulpy tissue. Tendons were made by blending bone and raw flesh, giving them a yellow color and a texture that was stickier than flesh but softer than bone.

God covered the bones that had more soul in them with a thin layer of flesh, and placed thicker flesh where there was less soul. Around the joints, he kept the flesh thin so the limbs could bend easily and so the brain could think clearly without distraction. On areas like the thighs and arms, where there isn't much soul, the flesh was laid on thicker. Some parts of the body, like the tongue, are made mostly of flesh and are very sensitive.

If it had been possible to combine hard bone and thick flesh with clear thinking, the gods would've given us heads full of muscle and tendons, and we'd live twice as long. But they believed a shorter, better life was more valuable than a longer, less thoughtful one. So they made the skull thin and placed tendons around the neck to connect the jaw to the face.

They shaped the mouth, with its teeth, tongue, and lips, to handle both practical needs like eating and higher needs like speaking—because food keeps us alive, and speech is one of our greatest gifts.

Still, they couldn't leave the head as bare bone. That would make it too hot or cold, or too numb to feel anything. So they covered it with skin, which formed with the help of the brain's natural fluids. The different seams (or sutures) in the skull came from the internal struggle between digestion and the movement of the soul.

When the head's skin was burned slightly by inner fire, some moisture leaked out. Part of it was watery, and part was thin and stretchy. The cold air outside hardened it into hair, which became a light covering to protect the head without getting in the way of thought. Nails were made from a mix of tendons, skin, and bone. The gods designed them knowing that one day women and animals, who would need such features, would be created from man.

The gods also gave other living things a nature similar to humans. That's how plants and trees came to be. They started out wild, but people eventually learned how to grow and use them. They are powered by the same type of passive life energy found between the chest and stomach—one that doesn't think or act on its own.

Once all these things were created to keep us alive, the gods carved out channels in the body, like irrigation systems in a garden. They cut two lines down the back, one on each side of the spine, surrounding the marrow of reproduction. They also wove together the veins in the head to link the brain with the rest of the body, so feelings and sensations could spread equally.

They next made the pathways for liquids in this way: heavier materials can hold lighter ones, but not the other way around. The stomach can hold food, but not air or fire. So God built a network of air and fire that sends moisture to the veins. Inside that, He added two smaller networks connected by cords. The inner parts were made of fire, the small nets of air. These led into the mouth: one part came from the lungs (the airways), the other from the stomach, running beside the lungs.

He split the upper air passage into two, both of which connected to the nose, so air could still flow even when the mouth was closed. This network extended through the body, letting fluids flow in and out of the smaller channels. Air passed through the skin, and heat followed it, moving in and out. These movements make up the process we call breathing. The goal of all this is to cool, water, and nourish the body, helping to digest food and drink and move it through the veins.

Now let's explain how breathing works. When we breathe out through the mouth and nose, we push out air, which leaves empty space behind. Air from the outside rushes in to fill the space. At the same time, the body pulls in air through the pores. The cycle goes back and forth.

Each element wants to return to its natural place. Since every living being has a fire inside, air that enters the body heats up as it touches this inner fire. Heated air moves out the same way it came in, toward the fire's location. When it exits and cools, it pushes outside air through the pores back into the lungs, which gets heated again and moves back out through the skin.

We can use the same idea to explain things like suction cups, swallowing, and objects being thrown. Sounds, too—sometimes harsh, sometimes pleasant—depend on how the vibrations match. Slower sounds catch up to faster ones and slowly blend in. That mix brings a feeling of joy, even to those who don't understand music. To the wise, it's even deeper—because it mirrors how the divine harmony works in the mortal world.

Lightning, magnets, and flowing rivers don't pull things because of magic, but because nature hates empty space. As things mix and break apart, they always move toward where they belong.

Back to breathing: the fire in our belly helps break down food. As it heats up and moves out, it pulls bits of digested food with it into the veins, spreading nourishment through the body. When fruits and plants are broken down inside us, their different colors mix. But red—the color of fire—is the strongest. That's why blood is red. Blood carries the nutrients the body needs, filling empty spaces and keeping everything alive.

The way we gain or lose weight depends on how much is taken out of or added to the body. New blood forms from food and is pulled to where it's needed. If more is taken away than added, we shrink and weaken. If more is added than removed, we grow stronger and larger.

Young animals are born with their tiny building blocks—these little shapes are fresh and closely locked together. Even though their whole structure is soft and delicate, made of new marrow and fed by milk, these shapes are sharper than those that come in as food later on. Because they are so sharp, they cut up the food. But as an animal grows, these tiny shapes wear out and lose their ability to break down food. Eventually, when the connections in the marrow start to fall apart, the bonds of the soul begin to loosen. If this happens naturally, the soul is set free with joy because natural death is seen as peaceful, while violent death causes pain.

Everyone can understand that diseases come from the disruption or imbalance of the elements that make up the body. This is the cause of many illnesses, but the worst ones come from a few key issues. In a healthy body, muscles and tissues form from blood, fibrous strands, and a thicker substance that comes from the fibers. This sticky substance not only holds the muscles to the bones but also feeds the bones and moistens the marrow. When all these processes happen in the right order, the body stays healthy.

However, when the flesh breaks down and goes back into the blood, the blood loses its normal color and gets mixed with air. It also takes on sour qualities because of acid and salt, which then create various types of phlegm and bile. Everything stops working as it should—each part fails to nourish the body and ends up fighting against itself, hurting the overall balance. The oldest tissues, which are hard to break down, begin to blacken from long exposure to heat and corrosion. This bitter substance then turns acidic. Mixed with blood, it can look red; mixed with dark matter, it takes on a greenish tint, and if it has an auburn tone when new flesh decays from heat, different medicines call these changes by different names. Doctors and philosophers have given names to these substances, such as bile, which comes in different varieties that match their colors. There is also a clear fluid called lymph or serum, which comes in two forms: a gentle whey from blood and a dark, bitter secretion. When heated and mixed with salt, this dark secretion becomes harmful and is known as acid phlegm. There's also white phlegm, which forms from soft, young tissue and appears bubbly when gathered. The water from tears and sweat is also considered part of fresh phlegm. When the blood is not restored properly by food and drink, these fluids can lead to diseases. The danger is lower if the basic structure of the body stays intact, because that creates a chance for recovery. But if the substance that binds the flesh to the bone becomes diseased and stops renewing itself properly, the flesh starts to wear away, leaving the muscles exposed and the flesh breaks down into the blood. This makes the diseases even worse.

There are even more serious illnesses that start earlier. For instance, if the bones don't get enough air because of thick flesh, they can rot, crumble, and mix into the food we digest, which then contaminates the flesh and returns to the blood. The most deadly disease is one that affects the marrow, reversing the normal course of the body. There is also a third group of diseases caused by excess wind, phlegm, or bile. When the lungs—the keepers of our breath—get blocked by mucus, some parts of the lungs don't get enough air while others get too much, leading to damage. This imbalance in air causes painful illnesses. The worst pain often comes from wind moving around the broad muscles of the shoulders, a condition we now call tetanus. These kinds of problems are hard to treat and are usually only eased by running a fever. If white phlegm is trapped in the body, it can be dangerous because of the bubbles trapped in it, though it is less dangerous if it can leave the body through the pores. It can, however, change the skin's appearance and cause various skin diseases. When white phlegm mixes with dark bile and interferes with the brain's activity during sleep, it might not cause much harm. But if it affects someone who is awake, it can lead to dangerous conditions like epilepsy, often known as the sacred disease. Acidic and salty phlegm is also the main cause of catarrh.

Inflammation starts with bile, which may be released through boils and swelling. If bile stays inside the body, especially when mixed with fresh blood, it disrupts the balance of thin and thick fibers that are needed for normal blood flow. When bile, which is like old blood or liquefied tissue, slowly trickles in, it thickens with the fibers and causes a cold feeling and shivering inside. But if it pours in quickly, its heat overpowers the fibers and reaches the spinal marrow. There, it burns the pathways of the soul and eventually disconnects the soul from the body. On the other hand, if the body, even though it is weakened, still manages to fight back, the excess bile gets expelled like an outcast from a troubled state, causing diarrhea, dysentery, and similar problems.

When the body is damaged by too much internal heat, it stays in a constant fever; if air is the culprit, the fever comes daily; if water is involved, the fever comes every other day; and if earth, which is very slow, is the cause, the fever lasts for three days and is hard to shake off.

There are also mental disorders, which fall into two groups: one is true madness, and the other is simple ignorance, both of which can be seen as types of disease. Overindulging in pleasures or suffering intense pain can overwhelm a person and dull their senses. If there is too much of the spirit around the spine, a person might feel excessive joy or pain and may even become partly insane for a long time. People might think that such a person is bad, but it's more accurate to say that extreme physical urges come from loose bones and problems in the body. This applies to vice in general. What we usually think of as a bad habit might actually be caused by a weak body and poor upbringing. Similarly, the soul can turn wicked because of constant physical pain. Bitter, salty, and other unpleasant fluids may build up and mix with the natural flow of the soul, affecting its three main centers. This can bring endless trouble, sadness, rash actions, cowardice, forgetfulness, and even dullness. When people suffer from these problems and are also surrounded by bad government and harmful ideas, and when they lack proper education, they are ultimately corrupted by forces beyond their control. In these cases, it is not the people who are to blame but the teachers and those who set the wrong examples. Nevertheless, we should always try to be virtuous and avoid vice, but that is a topic for another time.

Now, let's talk about how to keep the mind and body healthy—a more important subject. Good health means beauty, and beauty comes from balance. When the body and soul are in harmony, everything looks and works better. On the other hand, if an arm or leg is too long or too short, it not only looks bad but also doesn't work well, just as an imbalance between the body and the soul causes problems. A passionate and unruly soul can wear down a weak body, causing shocks and other issues. Stress from arguments or deep questions can trigger inflammations and mucus build-ups that doctors often misunderstand. Likewise, if the body is too burdensome for the soul, it can cloud thinking and heighten animal instincts. The key is to keep the two in balance. That is why scholars recommend exercise and why athletes benefit from music. Every part of the body needs proper exercise. A body functions best when its natural movement—like what we do in free gymnastics—is allowed to flow. It's not as beneficial when movement is forced by something else, like riding a horse or sailing, and it is least helpful if the body only moves in bits and pieces due to medicine. Such treatments should be used only in severe cases; minor illnesses should not be provoked by unnecessary drugs. Every disease has its own course, based on the natural life cycle, which in turn depends on the structure of these tiny building blocks. When they wear out, life cannot be extended. Those who try to prolong life with medicine often just multiply their illnesses.

When animals are young, their basic shapes are fresh and tightly arranged. Their bodies are soft and fragile because they're made of new marrow and fed with milk. These initial shapes are sharper than the ones that enter the body later with food, so they help break the food down. But over time, as these tiny structures wear out, they can no longer digest food as well. Eventually, when the connections in the marrow start to break, the soul's bonds weaken too. If this breakdown follows nature's course, the soul departs joyfully because a natural death is pleasant, unlike a violent one, which is painful.

Diseases often start when the elements in the body fall out of balance. In a well-ordered body, muscles and tissues form from blood, fibers, and a thicker substance that comes from separating the fibers. This sticky matter not only connects the muscles to the bones but also nourishes the bones and moistens the marrow. When everything is in order, the body stays healthy.

But if the flesh starts to break down and the nutrients go back into the blood, the blood loses its proper color, gets mixed with air, and takes on sour, salty qualities. These changes create various kinds of mucus and bile that disrupt the body's normal functions. Sometimes, the oldest tissues darken, become bitter, and then turn acidic. When this bitter substance mixes with blood, it can look red; if it mixes with dark tissues, it turns green; or it might show an auburn tint when new flesh decays due to internal heat. Physicians call these different substances "bile," naming each type for its color. There's also a watery part of the blood called lymph or serum: one form is like gentle whey, and another form, when mixed with salt under heat, becomes harmful acid phlegm. Additionally, white phlegm forms from soft, young tissue, bubbly on its own until it gathers enough to be seen. The water in tears and sweat also comes from fresh phlegm. These fluids can cause illness when the blood is not properly refreshed by food and drink. If the body's basic framework holds up, recovery is possible. But if the substance that keeps the flesh attached to the bones becomes diseased and stops renewing itself from the muscles and tendons, the flesh weakens, and the body falls apart further. Sometimes the bone itself doesn't get enough air because it's covered by too much flesh; it can decay, crumble, mix into food, and then contaminate the flesh and blood. The most dangerous condition affects the marrow, reversing the natural flow of the body.

There is also a group of diseases caused by imbalances in wind, mucus, or bile. When the lungs, which manage our breathing, become blocked by mucus—leaving some parts with no air and others with too much—those areas get damaged. This uneven air flow creates painful disorders. The worst pain comes from wind that stirs around the large shoulder muscles; we call this tetanus. Such cases are hard to treat and are usually only eased by fever. White mucus is dangerous if trapped, due to the air bubbles it contains, though if it can escape through the pores it's less harmful, even though it may change the skin's appearance and cause various skin diseases. If white mucus combines with dark bile and affects the brain while we sleep, it's not very serious. But if it disrupts a person while awake, it can lead to dangerous conditions known as epilepsy, or the "sacred disease." Acidic, salty mucus is the main cause of catarrh.

Inflammations start with bile, which can sometimes relieve itself by forming boils or swellings. However, if the bile stays and mixes with fresh blood, it disturbs the delicate balance of fine and coarse fibers needed for smooth blood flow. When bile drips in slowly, it thickens with fibers and causes a cold, shuddering feeling inside. But if it gushes in quickly, its heat overtakes the fibers, reaches the spinal marrow, and burns the nerve paths, breaking the connection between body and soul. On the other hand, if the body manages to resist, the bile is forced out like an exile, causing diarrhea, dysentery, and similar issues. A body damaged by internal fire suffers constant fever; if air is to blame, the fever comes every day; if water, it happens every other day; and if earth, the fever lasts for about three days and is hard to shake off.

Mental disorders can be divided into two types: true madness and simple ignorance. Extreme pleasure or pain can overwhelm a person and dull their senses. When too much of the inner life energy around the spine is present, a person may feel overwhelming joy or suffering and can become partly insane for long periods. Often, people blame the individual, but really it is the result of uncontrolled physical urges, like loose bones and weak tissue. This applies to bad habits in general, which might seem shameful but are usually the result of a weak body or poor upbringing. Similarly, the soul can be corrupted by constant physical pain. Unpleasant fluids can build up, mix with the natural flow of the soul, and disturb its normal functions. This can lead to trouble, sadness, impulsiveness, cowardice, forgetfulness, and a lack of clear thought. When these physical and mental problems combine with bad leadership and harmful ideas, and when proper guidance is missing, people become corrupted by forces beyond their control. In such cases, it is not the people themselves who are at fault but rather those who influence them. Still, we should strive for virtue and avoid vice, but that is a whole other topic.

Moving on from disease, it's time to talk about how to maintain a healthy mind and body—a higher subject. Good health is beautiful, and beauty comes from balance. The most pleasing shape is one where the body and soul fit together perfectly. If a leg or an arm is too long or too short, it is both ugly and useless. Similarly, if the body and soul are not in proper proportion, problems arise. An overactive soul can wear down a weak body, causing trembling and other harmful effects. Intense arguments or deep thinking can trigger inflammations and mucus build-ups that even doctors struggle to understand. Likewise, if the body is too dominant over the soul, it can cloud thinking and drive up basic desires. The only way to stay healthy is to keep both in balance. That's why scholars recommend exercise for both the body and the mind—physical training in gymnastics combined with the soothing power of music. Every part of the body needs regular exercise. The body moves best when it is naturally heated and cooled by the elements; however, if it's overworked when it's resting, it can break down. But natural movement helps create harmony and keeps conflicting forces apart. The best kind of movement is free, natural exercise, like gymnastics, because it most closely reflects the free movement of the mind. Riding or sailing, where the movement is controlled by something else, is not as beneficial. Medicine should only be used in the worst cases; minor issues usually resolve on their own. Every illness has its own life cycle that depends on the natural structure of these tiny building blocks. Once they are worn out, life cannot be stretched indefinitely. Trying to extend life with too much medicine only multiplies problems.

Let's leave behind the topic of the human body, our nature, and how we learn and grow. It's a big subject and deserves to be discussed on its own. But to sum it all up simply: we have three parts to our soul, and if we don't use any of them, that part becomes weak. If we do use them, they become strong. So, we should train and develop all three parts of the soul.

God placed the highest part of our soul—the divine part—in the head. This lifts us upward, like plants that grow toward their true home, not the earth. The head is closest to the heavens, where this divine part belongs. If someone focuses only on satisfying physical wants and feeds only the lower, mortal part of their soul, all their thoughts stay limited and earthly, and they become truly mortal in spirit. But if someone searches for truth and exercises the divine part of their soul through wise and noble thoughts, they grow closer to truth, happiness, and even a kind of immortality. They are strengthening the divine power inside them, which brings order to their life.

The only way one person can truly help another is by guiding them toward the right kind of nourishment and activity. The soul's motions are like the movements of the stars and planets. By studying these universal patterns, a person can return to their true nature.

And with that, we've completed our talk about the universe, bringing it all the way to the creation of human beings. But to make it complete, we should briefly talk about other living creatures—starting with women, who were thought to be men who had become weaker and less brave. When this change happened, the gods gave men a desire to join with women. They created two different living forms: one for men and one for women.

They connected the body's fluid channels with the life force in the spinal marrow. In men, this created a strong urge to release this life force into the woman's womb, which was like fertile soil where the seed could grow and be brought to life. If this desire is not satisfied, the man can feel overwhelmed by the force of this energy, and the woman may also suffer physical discomfort from the blocked pathways in her body. This continues until the two join together and create life.

Birds came from light-hearted, harmless men who focused too much on the stars and sky. Because they depended only on their eyes for knowledge of the heavens, they were transformed into birds, and their hair turned into feathers.

Wild animals came from people who had no interest in wisdom. They didn't look up to the sky or use their brains for thoughtful thinking. Instead, they followed their emotions. These people became more like the earth they were attached to. They leaned forward, walking on all fours, and their heads became oddly shaped. Some of them ended up with four legs, others with many more—the more legs, the less sense they had, as they became more like the earth. The most senseless creatures of all lost their limbs entirely and dragged their whole bodies along the ground.

The fourth kind of creatures were the ones living in water. These were made from the most ignorant and impure people, those who had completely turned away from knowledge. God placed them in the farthest places on Earth and made them breathe water instead of air.

These were the rules by which different types of animals were created and changed from one form to another.

And so, the world came to be filled with living creatures—some mortal, some divine. It became a complete and visible living being, a reflection of the eternal mind, a perfect and unique heavenly creation.

Section 2

The way nature appeared to a Greek philosopher in the 4th century BCE is hard for us to fully imagine today. To really see the world as they did, we'd have to add the stories and emotions of mythology and poetry, while also taking away the modern influence of science. Back then, a philosopher was both like a curious child and a deep thinker— he didn't know a lot by today's standards, but he had strong insights and often guessed truths far ahead of his time.

He had original ideas but was also easily fooled by simple mistakes. Sometimes he confused numbers with ideas or mixed up physical atoms with mathematical points. He relied more on theory than on observation and was quick to explain things in the sky using everyday examples from Earth. He accepted what nature showed him, but he didn't test things out for himself with experiments to prove or disprove his thoughts.

His knowledge was uneven. He understood some subjects like medicine and astronomy fairly well, but he had no idea about others, like chemistry, electricity, or physics. He often rejected myths, yet mythological ideas still shaped the way he saw the world. He tried to understand the basic truths behind things, but he treated these "truths" as real powers that controlled the world. He liked to reason from things he knew—like human experience—to things he didn't, like the universe, and then back again. In trying to organize the universe, he was also trying to organize his thoughts. But his thoughts and his view of the world often got mixed up.

You could compare him to a builder with a big dream but no proper tools—he had to dig with his hands. Or like a poet or musician who had big feelings to express but could only use a simple instrument like a flute or lyre.

The early creation stories by Hesiod and the Orphic poets were somewhere between myth and early science. These stories helped people start thinking about the world as a whole. They pushed the imagination back to a time before memory, and they encouraged people to notice how fire and water shape the earth. These myths were to ancient science what Homer's poems were to early history—they weren't accurate, but they got people thinking. They inspired thoughts of cities and civilizations that had existed for countless ages, and of customs and laws that were believed to have lasted for ten thousand years. Ancient Greeks understood that things like the Nile Delta formed slowly over time, but they believed history repeated itself instead of moving forward. This idea may have come from observing ancient cultures like Egypt, where traditions rarely changed.

Mythology gave the first philosophers many of their ideas, even if those ideas didn't originally come from nature. Concepts like love and hate became ways to explain attraction and repulsion in the natural world. Ideas of fate or justice symbolized the balance or chaos of nature. Chance was just a name for things they didn't understand. Even when they reinterpreted Homer and other poets, they believed their own explanations were the true meanings. They spoke about nature using poetic images, which to them weren't just symbols—they felt real. Poets like Hesiod and the Orphics imagined vague beings like Chaos, Night, and Aether, which were early attempts at understanding the forces behind everything. The gods themselves—especially Zeus, Apollo, Athena, and Poseidon—became more like universal ideas than individual characters. By the 6th century BCE, some thinkers were already moving toward belief in one single god who saw, heard, and knew everything.

With these ideas in mind, and perhaps with some bits of knowledge passed down from other cultures about health or astronomy, Greek philosophers started looking closely at nature. When one of them looked up at the bright blue sky, it struck him that everything in the universe might be connected. The noise of the senses faded, and the mind found peace in this new idea—a feeling that many generations had been trying to put into words. Their first attempts to describe this connection were usually based on a single element, like air or water, which they imagined getting more and more refined until it became almost spiritual.

Soon they turned inward and began exploring a world of ideas, which felt more powerful and lasting than anything they could see. The visible world seemed to fade in importance. At the same time, people began to split into two groups—those who saw change and motion as the truth of everything (like Heraclitus) and those who believed everything was still and unchanging (like Parmenides). Later, these would become the foundations for people who followed either Aristotle or Plato.

Like some modern thinkers who are accused of building theories first and only then looking for facts, these early philosophers were swept up by their ideas. They didn't test their beliefs or challenge each other using evidence. They were controlled by their thoughts instead of being in control of them. Some, like the followers of Heraclitus whom Plato mocked, couldn't even explain their own beliefs clearly. They behaved more like members of a strict religious group than like seekers of truth.

Still, just like myths, early philosophy was shaped by something real: the natural world. These thinkers weren't able to use modern scientific methods like testing or isolating variables, but they were inspired by what they saw. Simple, everyday facts—like the roundness of the sky, the life-giving power of water, the breath of air, the destructive nature of fire, the steady cycles of night and day, and the contrast between solid earth and invisible space—were always on their minds.

Their biggest strength—and also their biggest weakness—was reasoning by comparison. They could see similarities between things, but they struggled to see how those things were also different. They couldn't separate an example from an argument. In today's science, comparisons are only a starting point, and then you test them with experiments. Modern scientists filter out the false parts of an idea and keep only what's true. But in ancient times, philosophers didn't know how to do that. If a comparison popped into their heads, they followed it all the way to its conclusion, no matter how far off it was. They had no method to tell what was a coincidence and what was a real connection. They couldn't separate causes from results, and they were easily tricked by words that sounded similar but had different meanings.

The early philosophers depended heavily on comparisons to make sense of the world. Without this basic kind of thinking, they wouldn't have made any progress at all. If they hadn't compared one thing to another, natural events would have just passed by unnoticed—like beautiful sights or sounds ignored by an animal. Even superstitious beliefs among early people showed a step toward reasoning, because they tried to explain what they saw. Guessing strange causes was still better than not asking questions at all.

Thinking about the world as a living being—a giant person or animal—led to many mistaken ideas, but it also helped early thinkers imagine the universe as a whole. These big-picture ideas gave early philosophy a sense of unity and purpose, which actually became less common later, as knowledge split into more and more fields. Today, scientists often focus on just one subject and rarely think beyond it. This can limit their perspective, since focusing too much on one topic can narrow the mind.

Language also had a strong influence on early thinking. Because many Greek words had double meanings, early philosophers were sometimes led to confuse words with the things they described. They would ask, "If these are the same, why do they have different names? And if they're different, why the same name?" These kinds of questions were hard to answer when human knowledge was still very new. Modern thinkers are taught to focus on the things themselves, not just on the words used to describe them—but even today, that's a lesson we struggle to fully learn. Plato himself warned that we must pay attention to reality, not just to language, though even he sometimes fell into that trap.

Ancient thinkers were more influenced by words than we are now. They didn't have clear categories for colors or materials. Even basic elements like fire, water, air, and earth were loosely defined. All kinds of ideas were mixed together—experience, guesses, and theories based on nothing but imagination. Still, those early dreams and guesses often sparked more creative thinking and brought people closer to the truth than carefully collecting data ever could have at the time.

Another common mistake was the love of pure, abstract ideas. In Plato's later works, he seems to be pushing back against this. The early thinkers believed that the more abstract something was, the more true it had to be. They were constantly creating new ideas to link together other ideas. If there were two ideas, they would come up with a third one to include both. They believed that one was more perfect than two, and that two was more perfect than three. Words like "being," "unity," "essence," and "good" were almost sacred to them. But they didn't realize that these words were often empty—they had very little real meaning.

They didn't understand that the more general an idea is, the less specific and useful it becomes. In modern logic, we say that the more a word covers, the less it explains. Still, the idea of something being completely whole, still, or beyond physical things was powerful. It became the starting point for thinking itself. People didn't believe in these big ideas just because they wanted to generalize. They were driven by a kind of deep excitement—a hunger to understand more. Today, we know that "being" is just the most basic form of the verb "to be"—the simplest kind of concept—but to the early thinkers, it seemed full of divine meaning. They believed it explained everything.

So the world of the mind began to fill up with abstract concepts. A new, imaginary world was created to help explain the real one. But there was still a huge gap between these two worlds, and no one could truly bridge it.

The greatest tools the early philosophers had were numbers and shapes. These worked like abstract ideas, but they were also useful in everyday life. When compared with each other, numbers and shapes revealed surprising and mysterious patterns. They could be endlessly added, multiplied, or broken into smaller parts. Patterns like 1:2:4:8 or 1:3:9:27 seemed to unlock the secrets of nature. These were not empty ideas—they could grow and develop, and they made people feel that the universe had structure and purpose.

At that point, the outer world and the inner mind started to feel connected. The shapes and numbers people imagined in their minds also showed up in nature. It began to seem like math was the hidden truth behind everything else. Even things like law and ethics started to feel like they could be explained with numbers and geometry. These tools were so powerful and flexible that they gave a big boost to early human thought.

Another reason numbers were so important was that they worked. They could be tested and used everywhere. Even the simplest use of them—counting on your fingers—showed their truth. From these small beginnings, all science has grown. Numbers measured everything. They brought order to the chaos of nature. People saw numbers in music, in the stars, in the shapes of atoms, in the cycle of time, in how armies were organized, and even in how cities were structured. Without numbers, it was hard to imagine how the world or human life could function.

People even felt that music and numbers were deeply connected. There was harmony in the rhythm of music and in the motion of the planets. They imagined that if everything visible had numbers and shapes, maybe the invisible world was built the same way. Numbers seemed to reach into the unknown and connect with something eternal.

There are two more points worth noticing about how ancient thinkers used numbers. First, they often projected the number patterns they saw in their minds onto nature. If nature didn't seem to match, like when it came to fractions, they assumed nature must be wrong. They had spent so much time thinking about patterns like 1:2:4:8 or 3:4:5 that they believed these patterns were the key to the universe.

Second, they applied numbers and shapes not only to areas where they belonged—like astronomy and physics—but also to things like biology and psychology, where numbers don't play the same role. Back then, science wasn't divided into separate fields like it is now. It wasn't strange to believe that the same laws guiding the stars could also affect our bodies and minds. That's why astrology grew out of astronomy—because it seemed natural to think the stars had power over us.

Even Plato's idea that the same forces control both the heavens and the human body wasn't random. It made sense for his time and reflected how knowledge and thinking had developed up to that point.

When we look at the sky today, even if we're not scientists, we carry some basic scientific understanding. Most people know the Earth orbits the sun, not the other way around. They don't think the Earth is the center of everything, and they have a general idea about chemistry and similar sciences. But the world looked very different to early Greek philosophers. They didn't see the Earth through the lens of science. Instead, they thought of it as a flat surface tied to theories about one or more basic elements like fire or water.

To them, the universe seemed to be shaped by numbers and geometric forms. They believed the world was full of motion and stillness, with everything built out of combinations of shapes and sizes. Alongside these abstract ideas, they also had a rough idea of physical matter and drew from personal experiences with health and sickness. Their understanding of the world was naturally uneven—it was the first attempt to bring structure and meaning to what felt like a mess of random facts. It was like seeing the world in a dream—blurry, mysterious, and only partly understood.

Some modern thinkers, like Dr. Whewell, have criticized these early philosophers for using flawed methods, saying they had good ideas and plenty of facts but couldn't match them up properly. He contrasts their success in moral and political thinking with what he sees as failure in science. But this view misses the point. It's like judging people from the past by modern standards, forgetting how different their world was. Sure, the Greeks made mistakes. But the kind of science we use today hadn't been invented yet.

It's not fair to say they should have known more or done better. Given the tools and knowledge available to them, their progress was impressive. One of the biggest steps in astronomy was made by a forgotten Pythagorean who first suggested that the Earth moves around the sun. Another great insight was the idea that math could be used to understand both the stars and the smallest parts of matter.

The Greeks didn't have the tools to test or confirm many of their ideas, and they had very limited ways to observe the world. Plato, by encouraging people to use mathematics in science, may have helped more than Aristotle did with his collections of data. When modern scientists, influenced by thinkers like Bacon, dismiss ancient speculation, they often forget how difficult it was to make sense of the world back then.

We criticize ancient philosophers for getting caught up in language, but are we really free from that problem today? We complain that Greek science stopped progressing, but even modern science has gone through slow or unproductive periods—and likely will again. It's just as wrong to say Greek science failed as it would be to say Greek art wasn't great just because no one ever matched it later.

Another common criticism is that the Greeks made generalizations too soon. But this isn't quite right either. In fact, they didn't generalize much at all. It's more accurate to say they were refining and clarifying the ideas they already had, using what little experience they could gather. That's how all thinking about nature begins. A true scientific method takes hundreds of years to form, growing gradually through testing and discovery. At first, people treat nature like a person. Later, they form impressions. Eventually, they begin to understand nature through measurement and laws. This is how humanity moves from mythology to science.

Early science wasn't about discovering new facts in the way we think of it today. It was more about using observation to correct the first, often vague impressions people got from stories, everyday speech, or raw sensory experience. The most basic and important scientific idea is that nature follows consistent patterns. The Greeks described this in various ways—sometimes as fate, sometimes as necessity, sometimes as limits or balance. When something happened and they didn't know the cause, they called it chance. But they never believed nature followed rules that were constantly broken by random exceptions. That idea—popular in later times—doesn't match reality and doesn't really help us think clearly either.

Section 3

Plato's ideas about the soul are part metaphor and part literal explanation. But he doesn't clearly separate the two, and neither can we. There's no easy way to say, "This part is poetry, and that part is philosophy," because they blend together. Also, we shouldn't expect perfect consistency from Plato. He often shifts between different ways of thinking without always making it clear. To understand him, we have to look at the overall tone and purpose of his writing. Trying to force all his ideas into a neat, consistent system would actually stop us from understanding him properly.

Another challenge in this section of the Timaeus is that the usual order of thinking is flipped. Plato starts with big, abstract ideas and only later moves toward specific details. We start by talking about things that are right at the edge of human understanding, then suddenly drop into very basic physical ideas. There's no smooth path between the two. But abstract concepts don't mean much until they're connected to human experience or the natural world. Words like "God" or "the world" can feel empty unless we link them to something we understand. Even though we don't know much about them, the fact that they come first makes them feel important and powerful. As in many religions and philosophies, the things we know the least about often fascinate us the most.

There's not much use in trying to explain who or what Plato's "first God" really is. Some people have compared this figure to God the Father in Christianity, and some have seen "the world" as similar to Jesus, called "the firstborn of all creation" in the Bible. But Plato doesn't clearly say that God created the world out of nothing. His idea of matter is more like a blank, formless thing with no qualities at all. In fact, the Hebrew Bible's description of creation as a process over six days—with a chaotic beginning—is actually closer to Plato's version than people realize. Neither tradition claims matter has always existed in its current form. For Plato, the real act of creation wasn't about shaping physical stuff—it was about bringing ideas into reality.

In the Timaeus, Plato says that God took elements like sameness and difference, the limited and unlimited, and combined them to make "essence," which is the base of the soul of the universe. Then he added a body to that soul, made from the four elements. What this means is that God gave structure and variety to the universe by shaping how things behave and relate. Before creation, the elements were moving around in a messy, chaotic way. There was already an eternal "pattern" of the world, kind of like an ideal model. It wasn't God himself, but it also wasn't separate from him. This pattern was a world of thought that came before the physical one. It's a little like the "wisdom" of God mentioned in the Bible, or the idea of a perfect form held by earlier philosophers.

Plato strongly believed that the soul came before the body—both in people and in the universe. He described these deep ideas using symbols and stories, often in inconsistent ways, because even he admitted these matters were hard to explain clearly.

Compared to the Bible, Plato's version of creation seems less free or spontaneous. His Creator is limited by some kind of necessity—he can't do everything. Once the universe is finished, God retreats into his own nature. Plato seems more aware than the Hebrew prophets of how real and unavoidable evil is. He tries to distance God from anything bad by suggesting that lesser gods handled the parts of creation that involved imperfections. (Though in another work, the Laws, he explores different solutions to this problem.)

When Plato says the visible world is a copy of the invisible one, it's hard to make sense of what he means. How can something physical and constantly changing be a copy of something that doesn't change and has no physical features? This leads us back to old problems with his theory of "Forms" or "Ideas." Maybe we can imagine two worlds: one that mirrors the other, or one that's a blurry copy of a perfect original. But it's nearly impossible to imagine a perfect world with no qualities—something that has no size, no shape, no place. That kind of thing can't really be a model for the real world. In Plato, and even in later thinkers like Kant, these so-called "pure ideas" are more like what's left over when we strip away everything we can understand.

Another problem comes up when we ask what the "model" or "pattern" of the world has to do with the Creator. The pattern doesn't seem to be just a thought in God's mind. It's treated as something that exists on its own. But how can that be? Maybe Plato didn't think of subject (the thinker) and object (the thing being thought about) as separate. Maybe he just assumed creation happened the same way his theory of Ideas worked—and since that theory itself is unclear, the creation story can't be totally clear either.

It seems he was trying to say that creation wasn't physical, like building something with tools, but rather a mental or spiritual process. He beautifully writes that "the thought of God made the God that was to be." He also wanted to separate completely the invisible, unchanging world of ideas from the visible, changing world of physical things. In his view, the pattern or idea of the world came before the world itself, just like all other ideas come before the things we see. This pattern exists forever, just like the idea of "good," and it can be seen as separate from God's mind.

We could ask a lot more questions, but most of them wouldn't have clear answers. For example:

- How can matter exist without any form?
- How are the shapes or "essences" of things different from eternal ideas?
- How could motion exist before time?
- Where did chaos come from, if God didn't create it?
- How could there be a time when time didn't exist?
- How can something indivisible be split into parts?
- How can space be eternal if time is not?

- How can flat shapes form solid objects?

The truth is, we can't always follow Plato's reasoning all the way through. What seems confusing to us may not have seemed that way to him. He might have said that only God—or a person truly loved by God—can know how everything began. Faith often overlooks the gaps that logic can't fill.

To really understand Plato, we need to use our imagination and try to see things the way he did. We shouldn't expect everything to make perfect sense. A lot of what he says about knowledge uses images and symbols. We have to mentally translate them to more modern ideas before they make sense to us. And since Plato presents his ideas in so many different ways across his dialogues, we can't always use one to explain another—like using Timaeus to explain Phaedrus, Philebus, or Parmenides.

Plato's idea of the world's soul can be thought of as a kind of mathematical spirit that gives life and order to the universe. He imagined that everything in the cosmos moves in patterns, like numbers and shapes, similar to a dream where everything is made of math. These patterns follow consistent rules, much like the laws of nature we understand today. They exist in space but not in time, and they help create time itself. Plato believed that thinking is the same as understanding truth or law, and this doesn't necessarily mean human thought—it could be a universal principle.

Opposite to this orderly principle is the idea of "the other," representing randomness, disorder, and chance. This chaotic element is only partly shaped by mathematical rules. The orderly part keeps the chaotic part in check to some extent, like how the fixed stars influence the wandering planets. Similarly, in humans, there's a principle of order that helps maintain our physical health. However, some disorder remains, coming from the original chaos, leading to problems and illnesses.

Plato described "essence" as something made from both sameness and difference, and from this combination, along with the other two, the world's soul was created. This concept is complex and blends modern ideas together. The "same" refers to the unchanging, like the fixed stars, representing order and stability. The "other" is the changing part, the leftover chaos that can't be fully organized, causing errors and unpredictability. When Plato talks about "essence," he seems to mean a mix of understanding and intelligence. By combining sameness and difference, the idea of intelligence emerges, creating a new existence—the intelligible world.

The creator divided this mixture in specific proportions and reassembled it. He then split it into two strips, forming inner and outer circles that move uniformly around a center—the outer with fixed stars, the inner with wandering stars. The world's soul spread from the center to the edges. The creator gave it a body, starting with fire and earth, then adding air and water, because solid bodies like the world need two connecting elements. The world was shaped as a globe, using all available materials.

The soul of the world and the human soul were divided according to a series of numbers: 1, 2, 3, 4, 9, 8, 27. These numbers come from two Pythagorean sequences: 1, 2, 4, 8 and 1, 3, 9, 27. The number 1 represents a point; 2 and 3 represent lines; 4 and 8, 9 and 27 represent squares and cubes of 2 and 3, respectively. This series likely represents the musical scale, the arrangement of celestial bodies, and possibly the "music of the spheres" mentioned in Plato's Republic. Plato noted that solid bodies are always connected by two middle terms, meaning that between fire and earth, two elements—air and water—are introduced, similar to how two mean proportionals connect two cube numbers. His language is vague, so it's unclear if he meant more than this.

Returning to the main point: Why did the creator make the world? Like humans, he must have had a purpose—to spread his own goodness. Here, "goodness" means law, order, and harmony, not kindness or love in the modern sense. Ancient myths and even Hebrew prophets spoke of a jealous God, and Greeks imagined a force that punished human success. But Plato preferred to think of God as a creator of order, like a father who lives through his children and desires as much good and friendship among them as possible. However, since some evil remains in matter that he can't eliminate, he distances himself from it, leaving it alone so he isn't responsible for its faults and sufferings.

Plato believed that between perfect, unchanging ideas and the changing world we see around us, there are two things in the middle— time and space. He thought of time as just a moving image or shadow of eternity. Eternity always exists, without a past or future. Time, on the other hand, is described as having a past and future, but it isn't truly real—it's more like a way we picture eternity. This idea is very deep and was just as hard to understand for early thinkers as it is for people today. In fact, it might even be harder now, because we can better see the effects of this idea.

Many of the same problems people have with Kant's view of time and space come up here too. If time isn't real, then everything that happens in time—like our thoughts and feelings—is also not real. There would be no true connection between cause and effect. Still, we also feel that real knowledge doesn't rely on time. Truth isn't something that belongs only to the past or future it's always true, no matter when. Someone who could see all of time at once would see a universe that never changes. Math and logic always stay the same, even as people are born and die, like the changing leaves on trees. Math laws never fade.

Plato even imagined that time, like space, could be pictured as something stretched out. He got rid of the idea of "up and down" in space and of "before and after" in time. Without numbers to divide it, time becomes unclear, like the constant change the philosopher Heraclitus talked about. Through thinking like this, Plato's people reached their idea of eternity—not through religion, like the Hebrews, but through thinking about the world itself. They didn't see that these big ideas were shaped by how people think and feel. Saint Augustine, inspired by Plato, said, "God created the world not in time, but along with time," without realizing how far that idea might go.

The ideas of time and motion were full of contradictions that confused Greek thinkers. They tried to rise above them. These issues became more common as older philosophies faded, and Plato was very familiar with them. One philosopher, Parmenides, reacted by saying that true being doesn't change, move, begin, or end. It always is, one and the same, and couldn't have come from something else. His idea of eternity was mostly built by saying what it is not. Some types of philosophy—like Buddhism and early Greek or Christian thought—show how people can find meaning even in ideas that seem to be only negative. At times, ideas that seem like empty light have still inspired and guided people. It's as if the human mind needs something beyond not just our senses, but beyond even our normal knowledge—something we call Mind, Truth, Being, God, or the eternal. These things can't be described completely with words. Eternity isn't just endless time—it's the most real, most certain thing we can barely understand. Parmenides was deeply serious about this, even if the idea itself was hard to grasp.

Plato said space is like a container or a kind of nurse that holds everything that's born. He thought about the four basic elements—earth, air, fire, and water—and imagined a kind of substance they were all made from. He didn't think they should be seen as totally separate. From this, he started to think about what we now call "matter," a concept that later became important in Aristotle's philosophy. But besides the stuff things are made of, there's also the space where they exist. This space isn't something we can sense directly or clearly understand with reason. It exists in a strange way—when it's full, it's nowhere; when it's empty, it's nothing. That's why Plato said we can only grasp it with a kind of weak or fake reason. Even though it's hard to notice, space keeps coming back as the background where everything happens. It didn't have the solid meaning it has today in science or math. In fact, the Greek words Plato used weren't as abstract as our word "space." No Greek thinker would have talked about "space" the same way we do now.

Still, Plato seemed more open to the idea that time is unreal than that space is unreal. He thought space had to exist because everything needs somewhere to be. Today, we might think that time could still exist even if space didn't. Plato admitted that we can't clearly know space—it's like a dream, grasped only through a poor kind of reasoning, not through our senses. It's not as clear as ideas, but it stays around, even if everything in it disappears. So it made sense for Plato to think of space as eternal. It's also important to note that when Plato thought of space and matter, he didn't yet have the ideas of weight or size the way we do now.

Plato believed that God, following an eternal plan, used goodness to create three things—the same, the different, and the essence. These match three ideas from another one of Plato's works: the limited, the unlimited, and the mix of the two. From these, God made the outer stars and the inner planets, arranged using musical numbers. He also created time as a moving image of eternity, and space as something that exists by necessity and is very similar to matter. The matter used to form the world wasn't completely empty; it already had tiny bits of the four elements—fire, air, earth, and water. Even in the chaos before creation, those elements had their proper places. Plato didn't try to explain that chaos in detail. He called these the "elements," but they weren't truly basic yet—not even like letters in a word. The real building blocks, for him, were two triangles: one is a single type of isosceles triangle, and the other is a special scalene triangle that's half of an equilateral triangle. By combining these triangles in different sizes, the surfaces of the four elements were formed.

People back then already knew that there were only five regular solid shapes. Plato used the triangle surfaces to build the first four of these five solids. He may have overlooked the fact that he was only combining surfaces and hadn't shown how they form full 3D shapes.

The first shape is a pyramid, made from four equilateral triangles or 24 scalene ones. Each corner of the pyramid has an angle just a bit bigger than an obtuse angle. The second shape is made from eight equilateral triangles and forms a solid called an octahedron. The third shape, the icosahedron, has 20 triangle faces and 120 scalene triangle pieces. The fourth solid, the cube, is formed by putting four isosceles triangles into a square, and then six squares into a cube. The fifth shape, the dodecahedron, is different—it can't be made from those two triangles, but each of its faces can be built from 30 different triangles. Plato probably pointed this one out because it was the last regular solid, looked like a sphere, and maybe because it had 12 faces with 30 triangles each, making 360 triangles total—matching the number of degrees in a circle or days in a year. That's why he thought God used it to shape the whole universe. For Plato, earth was made of cubes, fire from pyramids, air from octahedrons, and water from icosahedrons. The more sides the shape had, the more stable it was.

The elements—fire, air, water, and earth—are thought to change into one another, but it's important to understand that these changes aren't real physical ones. Instead, Plato is talking about how their shapes, which are imaginary geometric figures, can be taken apart and put back together again. It's like rearranging the pieces of a house of cards—we're working with the flat surfaces, not the actual building blocks. Still, Plato might believe that these shapes are simply forms pressed into matter that already exists.

It's interesting that Plato says each of these shapes could be a world on its own. But overall, he leans toward the idea that all the shapes belong to one single world, not five separate ones. He jokes that believing in countless worlds, like the philosopher Democritus did, is something only a vague and clueless person would do.

Plato explains that the icosahedron (a shape with 20 triangle faces, which stands for water) can be broken down into parts that match two octahedrons (which stand for air) and a pyramid (which stands for fire). So when water breaks apart, it turns into two parts air and one part fire.

And since an octahedron can be split into two pyramids, air breaks down into two parts fire.

These changes happen when a stronger element overpowers a weaker one. The process goes like this: first, bits of the elements separate from the larger group; next, they break down into their triangle shapes; and finally, they combine again into new forms. Plato asks, why doesn't everything stay still once the elements are in place? He answers that while similar pieces are pulled toward each other, the spinning of the universe squeezes them and pushes them out of place again. This constant imbalance is what keeps everything moving.

Whenever elements clash, the weaker one has two options: either it escapes to join its own kind, or it changes into the stronger one—becoming heavier or lighter depending on which one is stronger. Fire, air, and water can change into each other because they're made from the same type of triangle shapes. Earth is different. Its triangles are unique, so it can break down, but it can't turn into something else. Among the changeable elements, fire is the lightest and can only turn into something heavier. Water is the heaviest and can only turn into something lighter. Air, however, can go either way.

No single piece of an element is big enough for us to see. We only see them when many pieces are grouped together. Differences between types of fire, air, or water come not from the shape of their triangles, but from their size. Plato seems to base his ideas on things he observed, like how fire changes air, water, and earth, and how water can affect earth. He believed the elements were always cycling between forms because of these imbalances. And this never-ending movement doesn't allow for any empty space, as shown in his unusual explanation of how breathing works.

Plato also talks about what makes things feel heavy or light. He doesn't believe it's about being "above" or "below," because in a round world, those directions don't really exist. Instead, he says things are pulled toward other things that are like them—fire moves toward fire, air to air, water to water, and earth to earth. He believed there were two types of attraction: first, similar elements pulling each other together, and second, smaller bits being pulled toward larger ones. If he had focused more on that second idea, he might have come close to discovering gravity. But he didn't notice that water is attracted to both water and earth, which doesn't match his theory. It shows how even the most obvious facts can be missed when they don't fit someone's beliefs.

Here's a summary of Plato's ideas about the physical world:

1. When the world was created, the big groups of each element were already in their proper places.
2. There are four elements, each made from different combinations of triangle shapes forming solid figures.
3. Fire, air, and water can change into each other, but earth cannot change in the same way.
4. The different types of each element come from different sizes of the same triangle shapes.
5. Similar things are drawn to each other, and smaller bits are pulled toward larger ones.
6. There's no such thing as empty space—particles are always moving and pushing each other in a cycle.

Like the atomists, Plato thought that what makes the elements different are the shapes they're made of. But he doesn't explain how flat shapes turn into 3D solids. And he mocks Democritus for thinking there are endless worlds, insisting instead that the universe is limited.

Section 4

Plato's ideas about astronomy are based on two main concepts: "the same" and "the other." According to him, these two were combined by God when creating the world. The soul of the universe, which includes "the same," "the other," and "essence," stretches from the center of the heavens outward. Instead of just saying the universe has a soul, Plato's view is that the entire universe is a soul—one guided by a divine mind, though it still contains a leftover part of matter or evil that even God couldn't remove. Plato never explains where this leftover evil came from.

In Plato's thinking, creating the world meant bringing order to it. The first part of creating this order was dividing the sky into two paths: an inner circle and an outer circle. One represents what can be divided or changed, and the other represents what stays the same. These circles correspond to the movements of the planets and the stars beyond them, all of which revolve around Earth at the center.

It's hard for us to understand how something can be at rest and moving at the same time, or how something indivisible can exist in space. But Plato's description is so imaginative that it's more like a poetic story than a scientific explanation. He even said that the idea of planets moving randomly (or "wandering stars") was false—he believed everything in the sky moved in circles.

Plato thought the stars were homes for human souls. Souls come from the stars and return there after death. He believed the fixed stars were the most perfect because they move in place, going around the same spot. To someone who can see all of time at once, the stars would seem completely still. They only appear to move so we can track time. So, even though the stars are always moving, we can think of them as resting while space—or the soul of the world—spins.

Plato said the entire universe rotates around a center every 24 hours, but the paths of the fixed stars and the planets go in different directions. The inner and outer circles cross paths, meeting again on the opposite side. One moves in a circle from left to right along the edge of a shape called a parallelogram, while the other moves diagonally from right to left. This means the outer circle moves like the equator, and the inner like the ecliptic, which is the path of the sun. Because the inner circle is controlled by the outer one, it turns into a spiral.

The outer motion stays whole, but the inner one is divided into seven paths, with distances based on ratios of two and three. The sun moves in the opposite direction from Mercury and Venus, but just as fast. The other planets—the moon, Saturn, Mars, and Jupiter—move at different speeds. The order of speed goes like this: Moon (1), Sun (2), Venus (3), Mercury (4), Mars (8), Jupiter (9), Saturn (27). These numbers match a pattern used by Pythagorean thinkers and are similar to the way the soul of the world was originally divided.

Plato was curious about why Mercury, Venus, and the Sun sometimes seem to pass each other. He didn't know they were all within Earth's orbit. Instead, he said they move in opposite directions, but that explanation doesn't really match what we see in the sky.

All the planets, including the sun, are carried around the sky by the daily motion of the fixed stars. But they also have their own diagonal movement, which explains why the sun seems to take longer or shorter paths in different seasons. The fixed stars move in two ways: they travel around their orbit and also spin in place. Plato called the second type "the movement of thought." Because of this spinning motion, the fixed stars were seen as more perfect than the wandering planets—even though in one of his other works, he rejected calling them "wandering" altogether.

Plato called the 24-hour rotation of the universe the most perfect and intelligent motion. But he also talked about a "great year," or "annus magnus," when the cycles of all the planets line up perfectly at one moment. That moment would be represented by a perfect number—like 6, because $1 + 2 + 3 = 6$. While this idea doesn't directly contradict the daily rotation, it does seem to clash with it. It's also hard to understand how the complex paths of the stars and their appearances and disappearances would work if the whole sky spun around Earth every day. In trying to find perfect math in the sky, Plato mixed real observations with his dreams of ideal order. He even said that the way the planets seem to wander is just an illusion—and that some simple math could fix our mistaken view.

Now we come to a major question: Did Plato believe the Earth moves, or does it stay still? He once wrote that the Earth—our "nurse"—was made to be the creator of night and day, held or spinning around a cosmic axis. But there's confusion here. The Greek word used could mean either "fixed" or "spinning," so it's unclear what Plato meant.

Also, does calling the Earth the "maker of day and night" mean it's active, or just passively involved while the sky moves around it? Aristotle later said Plato believed Earth rotated, but there are reasons to question that. If Earth moved exactly with the sky and the sun every 24 hours, we wouldn't get day and night—everything would seem frozen. But Plato never clearly says that Earth moves like that. He also doesn't explain the connection between Earth's motion and the rest of the sky. Still, if Plato did think the Earth spins once per day while the sky does the same, it's hard to believe he didn't notice the problem it would cause.

Even though Plato sometimes missed obvious things, it wouldn't be fair to say he couldn't understand simple logic or didn't grasp how shapes and motion are connected. Earlier philosophers, especially the Pythagoreans, had already discussed causes of day and night, so this question must have crossed Plato's mind. Yet, it's also possible that he just didn't make that final leap to explain it clearly.

Mr. Grote suggested that the word "revolving" was meant literally, and that rotation is implied by Earth being tied to the universe's axis. But even if Plato didn't see how Earth's spin could cancel out the sun's motion, he also might not have seen a problem with saying the axis spins while Earth stays still. And there's no real proof the axis spins at all. Mr. Grote compares some writings of Aristotle that seem to treat the word as meaning "spinning," but that debate isn't very important here.

Looking at all of Plato's works, it seems more likely that he thought the Earth didn't move. In one dialogue, Earth is described as the world's center but not as moving. In another, people seem to be watching the sky from Earth. In yet another, the goddess Hestia stays still while the other gods move around—she likely symbolizes Earth. Plato also stayed quiet about Earth's movement in many places where you'd expect him to bring it up. If he believed Earth spun, he probably would have said so clearly.

Even if the Earth doesn't move, Plato's words—calling it the "maker of day and night"—still make sense. Day and night happen not just because the sky spins, but also because Earth stays put while everything else moves. Something that can stay perfectly still while everything else moves is still playing an active role.

We shouldn't rely too much on Aristotle's interpretation, especially since he often misquoted or misunderstood Plato. In this case, Aristotle's comment was vague, and it's unlikely he was even thinking about the daily spinning of the sky.

After looking at all the arguments, we're left with no clear answer. Some thinkers, both ancient and modern, say Plato believed the Earth stayed still. Others, like Aristotle and Mr. Grote, think Plato believed it rotated. Either way, Plato never explained how Earth's motion relates to the changing lengths of day and night during the year. His descriptions of Earth and the heavens are often unclear or poetic, so we might never know what he really believed—if he even had a firm view at all.

Section 5

Plato imagined the soul of the universe to be like the soul of a person. He often described the world using human qualities, even when discussing big, ideal concepts. He believed the stars and planets had thoughts, and that the forces of sameness and difference existed not only in people's minds but also throughout the universe. The human soul, according to Plato, was made from leftover parts used to create the world's soul. These leftovers were much weaker—diluted three times over—to show how much less powerful human souls are compared to the divine.

The human soul, like the universe's soul, is created before the body. Mind comes first, then the soul, and finally the body. Even within the body, the parts closest to the soul—like the spinal cord—form before things like bones and flesh. The brain, which holds the divine part of the soul, is almost shaped like a globe. This round shape reflects the form of the gods, who Plato believed were the stars, and also the shape of the universe.

Still, Plato's explanation of the soul has some contradictions. He includes the idea of "necessity," or outside forces, which seems to limit human freedom. Unlike Kant, who tried to show that people have free will beyond space and time, Plato admits that humans are affected by outside causes. This leaves little room for true freedom. For example, he says our desires come from our body's nature, but they can also be made worse by poor education or bad laws—suggesting they could be improved with better ones.

He seems to sense that people with a higher nature don't choose evil on purpose. At the same time, he also says that bad behavior comes from the body, which is the opposite view. In this work and in others, he says crime and wrongdoing are like sicknesses—they come from the same causes as physical illnesses. If you look at both sides of his thinking, Plato's beliefs seem to mix idealism (striving for perfect ideas) with fatalism (the belief that everything is set in motion by outside forces), much like the philosopher Spinoza.

Plato splits the human soul into three parts, kind of like the charioteer and horses from one of his other stories. First, there's the immortal part, which lives in the brain and is like the soul of the universe. This part thinks, understands, and leads the other parts. Second, there's a mortal part that stands with reason against lower desires. It's found in the heart, where emotions like courage and anger live. Plato thought this area was like a command center, where veins meet and send out orders from the mind to the rest of the body. Finally, there's the lowest part of the soul—the part that craves and desires. It takes instructions from the higher part of the soul, but only indirectly. These messages are passed through the liver, which shows signs of reason's approval or warnings like a kind of mirror.

Plato pictured the liver as shiny and smooth, filled with both sweetness and bitterness. Reason uses these to send rewards and punishments. Ancient beliefs also said the liver could show the future. Plato includes this idea but makes it clear that any messages received in this way need to be interpreted by reason. True guidance doesn't come from wild feelings or mystical experiences—it comes from thoughtful understanding. He believed people are only "inspired" when they're under the influence of some illness or possession. He agreed with the saying that only a sane person can truly judge their own actions. You can see this same dry humor in Plato's comment that we should trust what the ancient people said about the gods just because tradition says so.

The part of the soul that seeks pleasure and comfort lives in the belly. Plato describes it like a wild animal locked up far from the "council chamber," which is the head. This separation is to keep selfish desires from getting in the way of reason and decision-making. Even though he says the soul comes before the body, it's clear that he builds the soul's structure to match the body: the thinking part in the head, the emotional part in the heart, and the desiring part in the belly.

The big difference between the human soul and the soul of the universe is that the human one is trapped in and expressed through matter, while the world's soul actually surrounds and moves through matter. A person breathes air inside their body, but the universe's soul is like the air or aether that surrounds everything.

Plato also talks about pleasure and pain. He says they come from sudden changes in how we feel. Pleasure is when something is quickly fixed or restored, and pain is when something suddenly goes wrong or is damaged. We become aware of our senses mostly when something unusual happens. For example, sight doesn't usually bring pain or pleasure, but hunger and eating do—because they're not constant, and they bring noticeable changes.

Section 6

Plato's ideas about the human body and health can't really be compared to modern or even ancient medical science. Instead, we can understand them better by looking at how they fit into his larger beliefs about the universe.

One big idea in Plato's view of nature is continuity—that everything is connected. He saw the world as one whole system where the elements—earth, air, fire, and water—change into each other. In the same way, the human body is treated as one connected thing. To Plato, things like blood, flesh, and muscle aren't separate materials but parts that blend into each other. He didn't focus on how complex the body really is. In his view, diseases happen when the natural balance between the four elements is upset. When the body parts form in the wrong order, that leads to sickness.

Plato believed the human body contained heat, air, and blood flowing everywhere. He described a sort of "net" of fire and air that surrounds most of the body. Inside this outer net, he imagined two smaller ones—one near the stomach and one near the lungs. The lung passage splits into two paths: one to the nose and one to the mouth. During breathing, air moves through the skin's pores into and out of this outer net, while the two smaller nets shift back and forth. This explanation is symbolic, not literal. When he mentions a "fountain of fire," he's describing body heat and blood flow. So, this part is part guesswork and part observation.

Plato had a unique idea about breathing. He believed it was caused by air moving in and out of the body on its own, not by any physical effort. Air entered and left through the mouth, nose, and skin. When we breathe out through our mouth or nose, it creates a small vacuum, which pulls in more air through the skin. When we breathe in through our mouth or nose, the outgoing air pushes other air out through the skin. He said the inner fire in our bodies pushes the air outward, and the need to fill empty space pulls it inward.

This theory is based on three ideas Plato often used to explain nature: first, empty space (a vacuum) can't exist; second, similar things are attracted to each other; and third, tiny particles can mix depending on how thick or thin they are. These ideas explain how fire and air move through the flesh.

His theory of digestion is linked to his view of breathing. He thought digestion happened because the body's inner fire entered the stomach during breathing and broke down food. As the fire returned to its place, it carried the digested food with it, turning it into blood and refilling the veins. Plato didn't explain how waste is separated from blood.

He didn't know much about the body's structure. For example, he didn't understand that nerves carry signals; instead, he thought movement and feeling came from bones and veins. He didn't know the difference between veins and arteries. He thought the air tubes that lead to the lungs were arteries and believed lungs were empty and had no blood. He also thought the spinal cord created reproductive cells. He often confused body parts with body functions. For instance, he treated the fire and air net as an organ. He misunderstood breathing, thinking it was just about air balancing itself, and he had no real understanding of how digestion worked.

Aside from basic body parts like the spleen, liver, stomach, lungs, bones, and muscles, his knowledge of anatomy wasn't accurate. Most of what he said came from his ideas about the universe. He believed the human body was a small version of the larger world. Just as the universe is made of the four elements, so is the body. Both have motion, intelligence, and balance. To the tiny parts of blood inside us, the body is like a little world.

Plato said the body was first created using all four elements. Bones were made from smooth earth. Liquids flowed throughout. A network of fire and air filled the veins. Childhood was like the early, chaotic stage of the world. Fevers with repeating patterns matched the density of the elements inside us. He believed the brain and spinal cord were made from the finest triangle shapes, linking body and soul.

Health, he said, could only be maintained by following the movements of the stars, which were responsible for life and growth. The sharpest triangle shapes were found in young people, making their bodies stronger. As people age, these shapes get duller, eventually falling apart—leading to aging and death.

Plato didn't support using purging or strong medicines, like some doctors did. He thought only in rare cases should they be used. He believed disease is natural to living beings and is often made worse by drugs. Instead of using medicine, he trusted in nature and believed diet and exercise were more helpful—especially for older people. He even joked that a warm bath might help a tired farmer more than a doctor's advice.

If Plato seems too critical of medicine, many modern doctors might actually agree with him. Even today, people are careful with medicines and don't like the idea of strong treatments unless absolutely necessary. In some ways, Plato seems to have guessed how future medicine would shift toward more natural healing.

Just like in another one of his works where he says you can't heal the body without healing the soul, Plato here also says body and soul are deeply connected. A weakness in one causes problems in the other. He may have even sensed that one day, medicine would take this connection more seriously—and that the mind could affect the body in powerful ways we're only beginning to understand.

Section 7

In Plato's view of how we sense the world, he doesn't describe the eyes, ears, and other parts of the body as tools like we do today. Instead, he thinks of the senses as open paths that let things from the outside world reach the mind. The eye is a kind of opening where vision flows through, and the ear is a similar opening where sound vibrations pass. But he doesn't seem to fully understand that the physical structures of the eye and ear actually cause sight and hearing.

Plato explains sight as involving three main parts: the light inside the eye, the light from the sun, and the light coming from whatever you're looking at. Vision happens when all three meet. If the light coming from the object matches the light from your eyes, the object looks see-through. If the light from the object is too strong and pushes back the eye's light, it looks black. If it's too weak and is pushed away, it looks white. Other colors are created by how light moves and interacts with the moisture in the eye. For example, a bright flash causes both light and moisture to burst from the eye, creating a bright color. A softer light mixing with that moisture produces red. All colors come from mixing brightness and red with white and black. Plato admits he doesn't know the exact amounts needed to create each color—he believes only the gods understand that. Still, he does recognize how colors relate to each other and to light, which is a decent starting point for a theory of color. He didn't see colors the way we do now, separated by tools like prisms or paint. Instead, he saw them as nature presents them—blended and often unclear.

Plato also believed smells couldn't be sorted into different types. He thought things that are changing form—like vapors or scents— don't have clear qualities. He did make a clever observation that smells must be heavier than air but lighter than water, since air can get through a blocked nose but smells can't.

Taste, according to him, is caused by how things affect the tongue through squeezing or stretching its surface. Rough or harsh particles cause unpleasant reactions, while smoother, more agreeable ones feel pleasant. Some tastes are sharp or irritating, and others are calming. Plato believed the tongue sends these taste signals all the way to the heart. He was aware that sensations travel through the body, though he sometimes mixed up the feelings themselves with the body parts involved.

Plato said hearing works like a quick strike or impact that travels through the ear, down through the air, the brain, and the blood, until it reaches the soul. Sounds that move faster seem high-pitched, and slower ones seem deeper. Loud sounds come from bigger waves, while softer sounds come from smaller ones. When two different sounds move at different speeds and clash, they create noise. But when the faster sound slows down and matches the slower one, it becomes music.

Some feelings come from inside us, but stronger ones happen when our body hits or is hit by something from the outside. Plato noticed that the parts of our body that feel the most—like the head and elbows—are less protected by flesh. He thought if our heads were more padded, we might live longer, but we wouldn't sense things as quickly. The tongue, on the other hand, is one of the most sensitive parts, but that's because it was made for a special job and doesn't need to protect the bone or the life-giving marrow like other parts do.

Section 8

Now let's look at how close Plato's ideas came to discoveries made in modern science. Today, scientists often focus on how wrong or strange ancient ideas were. They point out how old thinkers guessed wildly, confused facts with opinions, or ignored things that seem obvious to us. But they often forget that early science wasn't a free or clear search for truth. It was more like a natural development where people were still learning how to think scientifically. Their minds were shaped by the world around them, and they didn't yet have the tools to resist false impressions. Many people today also forget that ancient ideas helped build the path toward modern knowledge. They overlook how impressive it was for early thinkers to form any big ideas at all—like imagining how the body or the world worked as a whole.

The mistakes early scientists made were often just part of how people thought in those times. Their creativity was real, and they weren't always rushing to draw conclusions like some people claim. As time went on, people became more open to learning from experience. At first, they understood everything vaguely—like in a dream. But later, they learned to look closely, test things, sort them into categories, and connect causes to effects. You need broad ideas to understand smaller facts. You can't study the world until you have some way of imagining it.

To truly understand ancient science, we need to look at it as a full picture. Some early thinkers already believed in ideas that sound modern, such as:

1. The nebular theory (that stars and planets come from clouds of dust and gas).
2. The idea that sea creatures slowly turned into land animals, and humans developed from animals—this was suggested by Anaximander in the 6th century BCE.
3. The belief, held by Philolaus and the early Pythagoreans, that Earth was just one of many moving bodies in space, orbiting a central fire or the sun.
4. The idea of "similar particles" from Anaxagoras, which hints at early chemistry.
5. The understanding that plants had male and female parts, like animals.
6. The discovery that musical notes depended on the length and tension of strings and could be explained through numbers.
7. The belief that math rules applied to the whole universe, and

that even differences in quality came from shape and number.

8. The idea that matter can't be destroyed—only changed.

Each of these ideas alone might seem like lucky guesses. But when you put them together, they show real progress and even a surprisingly deep understanding of nature.

We also shouldn't judge ancient thinkers too harshly for making broad guesses or using unclear language. Even today, modern science and philosophy fall into the same traps. We still mix up thoughts and physical things. For example, people have confused mathematical points with physical atoms. Some ideas like "life energy" or "phlogiston" were made up to explain things we didn't understand. Illness, like sin, has sometimes been seen as a kind of evil force instead of a natural problem. The mental traps that philosopher Francis Bacon called "idols" are still common today. They're part of how the human brain works, and the more we fall under their spell, the less we realize it. We can spot these problems in ancient thinkers, but we often miss them in ourselves.

These thoughts help us appreciate Plato's scientific ideas in the Timaeus. Instead of judging how much he actually knew, we should ask how his thinking influenced later science. Some of his ideas may seem outdated now, but they helped shape how people searched for knowledge. Some were even ahead of their time and are still part of science or philosophy today. Others fall in between—he wasn't exactly right, but he wasn't totally off, either.

One major idea from Plato is that everything in nature has a purpose. This belief—that the world has order and design—is called the teleological view. Today, people still debate whether everything happens just because of natural laws or if some things seem designed. Even if we accept that nature runs on fixed rules, it still makes sense to describe parts of the world as having a kind of "mind" or plan behind them. Plato's way of describing the world has lasted all the way into modern religious thinking. His idea that there are main causes (like design or purpose) and secondary ones (like physical forces) helped build a bridge between science and religion.

Plato also came very close to modern ideas about how we sense qualities in the world. He believed God truly understood the original nature of things, while humans could only guess. We still say similar things today—we admit that human thinking is limited. However, unlike Plato, we now use experiments to test our knowledge of nature. Ancient philosophers, including Plato, didn't experiment. In fact, Plato seemed to think doing so would be disrespectful. He even wrote that someone who tried to test colors would be forgetting the difference between humans and gods.

He thought some things—like colors—couldn't be tested because they were too unclear or mixed. That's probably why he said they couldn't be properly studied. (Compare this to Anaxagoras, who once argued that snow should be black because it's made of water, and water looks black.)

One of the most impressive ideas from ancient times was the belief that mathematics lies at the heart of everything in nature. The ancients believed that numbers and shapes were not just important for science and math, but for understanding the world itself. Even in the human body, Plato saw patterns of number and shape. He wasn't wrong to think this way, but he didn't realize how little these ideas could actually explain.

Still, it's worth noting that what might seem like the most imaginative of ancient ideas—like thinking the universe is made up of numbers—turned out to be one of the most insightful guesses. The Pythagoreans' and Plato's ideas about musical scales even helped Kepler develop his theory of how the planets move. They believed the planets moved in perfect circles, which we now know isn't true, but that mistake helped people begin to understand the heavens. In fact, astronomy has often advanced more through big, bold theories than through slow, cautious steps.

Even so, these big theories were still based on observation. The ancients were most confident about numbers because they saw them working consistently in everyday life. Once they saw how numbers explained a few things, they applied them to everything—from tiny atoms to giant stars, from the body to the whole universe. Today, modern chemistry often explains different qualities using amounts and measurements, which is a bit like returning to Plato's triangles or Democritus' atoms. Just because the ancients couldn't prove their ideas doesn't mean they weren't on to something. Maybe they sensed truths they couldn't yet fully understand, just like animals sometimes act on instincts.

The Timaeus also includes some ideas that come surprisingly close to modern science. One example is the idea of balance. Plato says that nature hates empty space—what we now call a vacuum. Whenever something moves out of its place, other things rush in to fill the gap, trying to keep everything equal. These thoughts weren't based on experiments but were early reflections on how nature seems to work.

Modern science talks a lot about growth, connection, and development. Plato saw this as the core of all knowledge. He believed everything in the world is part of a single system, shaped by the same world-soul acting on the same matter. He would likely agree with the idea that all living things came from one original substance, like today's idea of cells or protoplasm. But for Plato, mind and intelligence—not a person, but a guiding force—came first and shaped everything. He doesn't explain how this mind works, saying it's beyond what humans can understand or describe.

Plato also seemed to hint at two important scientific ideas: gravity and the circulation of blood.

1. Gravity

Plato thought that objects are drawn not just to bigger objects, but also to similar ones. He believed things like earth, water, and air each had a natural place, and that fire rose above air. To him, when air rises or fire shoots upward, it's because they're trying to return to their own kind. However, he didn't realize that a simpler explanation—like objects having weight and being pulled by gravity—would make more sense. Still, he wasn't entirely wrong. His idea that things are drawn to what they are like has something in common with what we now know about chemical attraction and the way substances interact over time.

2. Circulation of Blood

Plato knew that blood is always moving and that it has both liquid and solid parts. He even noticed that when blood stops moving, like in medical cupping, it dies or separates. But he didn't know how blood flows through the body—that it leaves the heart through arteries and returns through veins. The full discovery of blood circulation came much later.

Studying the Timaeus more closely leads to a few final thoughts. These include how it connects to Plato's other works, what it says about God and creation, and its views on morality.

a. Connection to Plato's Other Writings

The Timaeus is more imaginative and less scientific than most of Plato's other works. It guesses at how the world works—astronomy, biology, and medicine—but always admits these are just likely stories, not facts. The speaker in the dialogue is Timaeus, a Pythagorean, which makes it unclear how much of this actually reflects Plato's personal beliefs. While some ideas from the Timaeus appear in other dialogues, there's no strong link between them. You might be able to connect parts of it with ideas from the Republic, Phaedrus, Laws, or Philebus, but doing that assumes Plato wanted all his ideas to fit into one system. There's no real reason to believe that was his plan.

There is a shared spirit across his writings—like the idea that thought comes before physical things, or that the mind is more important than the senses—but he doesn't always say things in the same way. He's still working out his ideas, which means he's often unsure or trying different explanations. And when he talks about the start or end of the world, he often uses myths. These aren't hard truths to him—they're more like stories he uses to explore big ideas. He was still influenced by mythology and hadn't yet pushed past it into clearer, more scientific thinking.

So instead of forcing his ideas into a complete system or using other dialogues to explain the Timaeus, it's better to accept its uncertainties. We can use our own imagination, shaped by the dialogue itself, to explore its meaning. But we shouldn't expect other works—or later philosophers—to solve all its mysteries.

We can better understand the Timaeus by comparing it with earlier philosophies. Ancient science wasn't created all at once—it developed over generations, especially among the Ionian and Pythagorean thinkers. Plato didn't just observe the sky and describe what he saw. Instead, he built on the work of others, adding ideas from deep within his own thinking.

Socrates had already talked about a divine creator who made the world in the best way possible. He criticized shallow explanations for natural events, like those based only on wind or water, and instead saw clear signs of intelligence and goodness in the design of both humans and nature. In his dialogue Phaedo, Socrates mocks basic physical explanations but praises the idea that a greater force—the "Best"—is behind everything.

Plato followed his teacher's thinking and supported the idea that everything was made for the best. However, he added that this perfection was limited by matter, which isn't always easy to shape. Before Socrates, the philosopher Anaxagoras had connected "Chaos" (a shapeless beginning) with "Mind" (a guiding force). Plato took that idea and added his own twist: he introduced the concept of a pattern or design, which "Mind" uses to shape the world.

Both Plato and Anaxagoras talked about a circular motion, but Plato imagined this movement in a more spiritual way. Unlike

Anaxagoras, who thought the sun and stars were just glowing rocks, Plato believed they were living beings. The Pythagoreans, another group of early thinkers, believed the world was made out of numbers, which they used to form shapes. Plato borrowed these ideas but added more advanced geometry to them.

The Atomists, another school of thought, believed that everything was made of tiny, invisible particles. Plato didn't name them directly, and he seemed to dislike their approach, but he did have a similar idea: his world was made up of tiny triangles instead of atoms.

Plato preferred the Pythagoreans because they believed in number relationships that matched the distances between planets. He likely agreed with some Pythagoreans who, like him, thought Earth was at the center of the universe. It's unclear whether Plato got his "circles of the Same and the Other" idea from someone else, but the concept of four elements came from Empedocles. The way elements fit into one another in the Timaeus is similar to ideas from Heraclitus and other early Ionian thinkers.

Plato took ideas from many sources, blending and reshaping them into something new. Unlike the later Neoplatonists, who mixed philosophies without changing them much, Plato made borrowed ideas part of his own original thinking.

However, Plato avoided some early views. He didn't believe, like the Eleatics did, that the physical world is just an illusion or a collection of opposites. He didn't think the world was in constant chaos. Instead, he believed it changed within set limits, controlled by what he called the principle of sameness.

Unlike the Eleatics, who said that true being could only exist outside the world of appearances, Plato accepted that the world we see is real and lasting—though still dependent on a creator. He didn't agree with the belief that empty space (the void) had to exist. Instead, he followed the idea that nature "hates a vacuum," meaning that space always gets filled. This idea also shows up in another one of his works, where he denies that "nothingness" is real.

Even though Plato disagreed with some early philosophers, he still respected their ideas. He admired the deep thinking of Parmenides, even while offering a different view.

Some scholars think there's a strong connection between the Timaeus and the ideas of Philolaus, a Pythagorean philosopher who lived in Thebes during the late 5th century BCE. Philolaus is mentioned in Plato's Phaedo as the teacher of two students who later followed Socrates. There's not much known about him, though ancient writers claim that Plato bought some of his writings. This story likely isn't true and just reflects how similar some of their ideas seem.

Fragments of Philolaus's work have survived, mostly through later writers like Stobaeus and Boethius. These fragments remind us of the Timaeus, as well as parts of Plato's Phaedrus and Philebus. For example, when Philolaus says everything is either limited, unlimited, or a mix of both, it echoes ideas from the Philebus. When he talks about the center of the world, we hear a connection to the Phaedrus. His division of the universe into an orderly part (with stars and planets) and a chaotic part (between the Earth and Moon) is similar to Plato's idea of the Same and the Other.

Philolaus also denied that "up" and "down" existed in space and said everything should be understood in relation to a center. He described the world as one unified thing that could not be destroyed from the inside or outside—just like Plato in the Timaeus. He believed in ten heavenly bodies: the sun, moon, Earth, counter-Earth, and others—all orbiting around a central fire, which was hidden from view by the counter-Earth. Plato never mentioned the counter-Earth or central fire; instead, he made Earth the center of his universe.

Philolaus believed certain numbers had special powers, especially the number 10. He talked a lot about odd and even numbers, as later Pythagoreans did. But Plato avoided this kind of number mysticism.

While he often used numbers to express ideas, he didn't treat them as magical or sacred. Both he and Philolaus believed that the movements of the universe followed musical ratios, although some scholars say their musical scales didn't actually match.

The truth is, we don't know enough about early Pythagorean thinking to be sure how much of what Philolaus wrote truly reflects their views. Because of that, it's hard to say whether the fragments we have are genuine or not. But one thing is clear: even if there are some similarities, these fragments don't tell us much about the Timaeus, and any likeness between them has probably been overstated.

Plato's description of people and the universe is sometimes unclear and hard to separate from storytelling. Even he probably didn't know where the myths ended and the philosophy began. He couldn't fully explain how the world of perfect ideas connects to the world we experience. These two are supposed to be copies of each other, yet they seem totally different.

This contrast appears in many forms: one vs. many, limited vs. unlimited, unchanging vs. changing, what we can understand with our minds vs. what we experience with our senses. We see it in the difference between the fixed stars and the moving planets, or between a creator's order and the chaos before creation. Sometimes these opposites seem completely different in kind; other times they're just different in degree. Like Aristotle's idea of matter and form, Plato's opposites are tied together. If you try to separate them, they lose meaning. The idea with no details is no different from chaos. "Pure being" and "nothing" start to look the same.

Even though Plato often says one side (the world of ideas) is real and the other (our world) is just appearance, he doesn't fully explain how they relate. That's why, when we read only short parts of his writings or try to draw logical conclusions, we often get confused.

The same kind of confusion shows up in his thinking about free will and destiny, or about what happens to the soul after death.

Sometimes God seems to be part of the world, and sometimes he seems to exist far beyond it. Plato slides from one viewpoint to another without clearly separating what is objective (external reality) and what is subjective (thought or experience). He shifts from talking about reason to the soul, from eternity to time, without always making it clear.

These contradictions might be softened by using careful language, but they can't be completely erased. Times of major intellectual change are always full of mixed ideas. Creative thinking and clear thinking don't always go together. Plato himself said that repeating something important more than once is worthwhile—and this is one of those cases.

What many people overlook is that part of the confusion in Plato's ideas comes from how he blended different philosophies. He brought these ideas together and tried to connect them, but he didn't completely sort them out. They became part of how he thought, and he couldn't step outside of them to judge them clearly. He believed he understood them, but they also shaped him. In his later years, he admitted they still felt unclear.

Plato gave new meanings to the words of older thinkers like Parmenides and Heraclitus, but sometimes their ideas went further than his. In those moments, not only does the world we see seem to disappear, but the theory of perfect forms also seems to fall apart. The truth is, many of these early philosophers were closer to each other— and to Plato—than they realized. They all had something in common: they were skeptical of the senses, believed in the power of numbers and measurements, and had a feeling that deeper ideas existed behind the physical world.

Plato's philosophy still carried the energy of argument and debate, which had developed through years of questioning and discussion. He couldn't fully connect the early natural causes of the world with Socrates' focus on moral and purposeful causes. He never gave a clear answer about how numbers relate to universal ideas, or how those ideas connect to the highest idea of all—goodness. He got these ideas from different sources: the Pythagoreans (who focused on numbers), Socrates (who focused on ethics), and the Megarians (who focused on logic). Because each helped explain the world in a different way, Plato didn't want to drop any of them—even though he couldn't combine them into a single system.

Although Plato was an idealist, he was still Greek in mindset, not mystical or overly spiritual like some Eastern philosophers. He wasn't trying to escape the material world or lose himself in the soul of the universe. That's why, in the Timaeus, we see his love for the heavens. To him, nature—even though it includes some evil—is still beautiful and divine. He sets aside mythology and shows the world using mathematical shapes and patterns. This mix of math and nature is what makes the Timaeus stand apart from Plato's other writings and shows its connection to Pythagorean ideas.

In the Timaeus, Plato also clearly says that God is good. God created everything out of goodness and wanted everything else to be good too. God isn't jealous or selfish. He's the very idea of goodness, and in this story, he becomes a person who speaks and acts. Still, this personal side of God mostly appears during creation. God, like the craftsman in the Republic, works by following a perfect model. But Plato doesn't explain where that model comes from. In modern terms, he splits God's mind into two parts: the thinker and the idea being thought about.

Once the first creation is done, lesser gods take over, and the supreme God steps back to his original state. In another dialogue, The Statesman, Plato also describes God as stepping away after setting the universe in motion. This idea—that God is distant—became common in Greek thinking. As people moved from mythology to reason, they still saw purpose in the world but no longer imagined God walking among them. Plato wrestled with this tension: he tried to explain how a good God could allow evil, and in another work, he criticizes people who say the gods don't care about humans.

Creation, in Plato's view, is about bringing order to a chaotic state. Anaxagoras had said that everything was once in confusion, and then mind stepped in to organize it. That's basically how the Timaeus starts. Plato didn't picture chaos as a mix of different things but as one single shapeless thing, which made it easier for later thinkers to link his story with the biblical idea of creation. Even when Plato talks about "mind" or "intelligence," he doesn't go much deeper than describing it as a kind of perfect spinning motion. Like Anaxagoras, Plato starts with the idea of a wise creator, but then he ends up using simple, old-fashioned science to explain how the world works.

The Timaeus also touches on morality, but it's not always easy to figure out. Plato, like many of us, struggled with how to balance human freedom with the fact that people are shaped by nature and surroundings. Sometimes he focused more on free will, and other times on natural causes.

In the Republic, he says people choose their own path before they are born, but once they're alive, they're shaped by that choice. In the Statesman, he says humans only survive because of divine help. And in the Timaeus, the main God assigns lesser gods to protect people from everything except the evils they bring on themselves. So, according to this view, all human suffering is self-inflicted.

However, Plato isn't always consistent. Earlier, it seemed like he believed all wrongdoing was involuntary. But in the Timaeus, he also says that bad behavior can come from a weak body—and yet he also tells people to choose virtue. He admits that good or bad laws and systems shape our behavior, and since individuals can't create laws for themselves, actions shaped by them are more involuntary than voluntary. Like many thinkers, Plato couldn't avoid some contradictions.

He got the idea from Socrates that vice is a kind of ignorance. Later, he saw that people's actions also depend on their physical health and makeup. This idea—that free will is shaped by physical causes—still comes up in modern debates.

The Timaeus also shares a bit with Stoic philosophy, which came later. Plato says people should study the heavens and try to bring their lives into balance with the order of nature. He believed we should match the steady parts of our soul with the steady patterns in the universe. To him, morality is about living by natural law—feeling that you're part of the greater order is one of the strongest forces for good. This is what he means when he says the soul should "move with the same in unchanging thought." He doesn't fully explain how daily habits or opinions affect people, or how the soul sends commands to the body—but as he often says, those might be topics for another time.

It's easy, especially with help from Aristotle and later thinkers, to find flaws in the Timaeus. We can point out where Plato misunderstood biology or used strange logic. Still, despite all its weaknesses, the Timaeus remains one of the most powerful attempts in ancient times to explain the universe as a whole.

***

There's one last part of the Timaeus that's worth talking about—its mythological and geographical side. It's amazing that just a few pages from one of Plato's dialogues turned into a massive legend that spread far beyond Greece. Like the story of Troy or the tale of the Ten Lost Tribes of Israel, it became famous partly because it seemed to connect with something people believed might be historically true. Like the legend of King Arthur, it crossed borders and languages. It even inspired explorers during the 1400s and 1500s, long before they knew what lay across the ocean. The idea of Atlantis fit perfectly with a popular belief—that a great, ancient civilization must have existed somewhere in the past, giving birth to all the arts and knowledge we have today.

Atlantis could be placed anywhere—north, south, east, or west. People imagined it near the Strait of Gibraltar, in Sweden, in the Holy

Land, or in the mythical Islands of the Blessed. It didn't matter whether Plato's description matched the actual location. The legend was so flexible that it adapted to wherever people wanted to find it. It became a kind of floating fantasy, an island seen only by those who believed in it. Some writers in France and Sweden loved diving deep into this myth, collecting tons of information, but often missing the point entirely.

A French writer, M. Martin, wrote a detailed study of how people have viewed the story of Atlantis throughout history. It's a strange and interesting chapter in the history of ideas. Atlantis was clearly a myth, but it kept people fascinated. Even in ancient times, opinions were split. Thinkers like Strabo and Longinus didn't believe the story any more than we believe in Gulliver's Travels or Robinson Crusoe. But plenty of other writers, both ancient and modern, believed wild theories about it.

The Neoplatonists, loyal to Plato, tried to explain the story as both symbolic and historical, similar to someone today claiming that The Iliad is both Christian allegory and literal truth. During the Middle Ages, the story faded but came back when America was discovered. It influenced books like Utopia by Sir Thomas More and New Atlantis by Francis Bacon. But these writers probably didn't believe it was real—they just used it as a creative idea.

The story was especially popular in the 1600s and 1700s, when people were imagining perfect societies and wanted to escape the boring present by dreaming of better times in the past or future. Later versions of Atlantis included pieces from Norse mythology, the Bible, stories from missionaries, and reports from explorers.

These different views of Atlantis only really matter because they show how easily people can be misled by myths. That lesson still applies today. The human mind is always at risk of falling for new versions of old illusions.

If we clear away the confusion built up over time, we're left with a couple of real questions worth asking:

1. Did Plato get the story of Atlantis from Egypt?

There's no record of the Atlantis story in any older source. Homer, Pindar, and Herodotus never mention it. Even Aristotle doesn't bring it up, and no later writers quote anything older than Plato that includes it. There's also no evidence from ancient Egyptian texts or monuments linking Egypt to Greece before the 800s or 900s BCE.

Proclus, who lived about 900 years after Plato, claimed that there were stones in Egypt with the story of Atlantis written on them. That's probably false. Similar claims have been made about monuments left by the Canaanites, which also have no evidence. Even if true, these stories would only show that people later tried to link Atlantis to Egypt, long after Plato's time.

It's possible that during the Alexandrian period—when Egypt had lost its own history and began borrowing from others—some monuments were created to reflect famous myths. The earliest known person to mention the story after Plato was Crantor, a Stoic philosopher. But since he lived just one generation after Plato, he probably got the story from him.

2. Could Plato have made up the story himself?

It's more likely that Plato invented the Atlantis story than that it came from Solon's trip to Egypt, as he claims. Plato was perfectly capable of creating believable stories. He even admits in another dialogue that he could easily make up Egyptian tales. When he writes, "It helps if the story is true," he might be hinting that it's not.

The part about Solon visiting Egypt sounds like fiction. Even if he did go there, he probably couldn't have spoken with priests or read temple records. Plato fills the story with small, convincing details that make it feel real. For example, he says Critias heard the story as a boy from his grandfather, who had heard it from Solon himself. This long memory chain feels carefully constructed to earn the reader's trust.

The famous quote—"You Greeks are always children; none of you has old knowledge"—sounds more like Plato complimenting his fellow Athenians than a genuine quote from an Egyptian. When the Egyptian priest says, "Later we'll go over the documents in more detail," it's likely just a literary trick to make the tale seem more real.

Could a war between Athens and Atlantis really have happened, as Plato hints? Where did Egypt get that story from? The whole legend boils down to a war between two great powers, ending with both being destroyed. How did that become a poem by Solon? Historian George Grote said it's possible that Solon began a poem about Egypt, but there's no proof.

Why didn't any trace of that poem survive? And if Plato knew the full story, why did he stop telling it almost as soon as he began? These questions suggest that the entire Atlantis tale is a clever fiction, not a lost piece of ancient history.

While M. Martin's deep research and learning are impressive, it's hard to believe that an Egyptian priest actually told the Atlantis story to Solon, or that Solon wrote a poem about it that later vanished. It's much more likely that the Island of Atlantis—and the earlier version of Athens that fought it—existed only in Plato's imagination. Martin believes that Plato would have been horrified if he had known how many wild ideas his story would later inspire. But more likely, Plato would have been amused—especially if he saw that even Martin believed Solon brought the story from Egypt and made it into a poem.

Martin can also be gently criticized for quoting ancient sources without considering how reliable they are. Some of the authors he cites don't carry much weight, and mixing them together without careful judgment weakens his argument.

Another interesting question Martin brings up is whether Plato's Atlantis influenced early explorers. He thinks there wasn't a real connection. But it's very possible that the discovery of the New World was encouraged by a deep hope, similar to the belief in a coming savior.

This hope was supported by old stories and traditions, like the famous lines of Seneca, and by the powerful voice of Plato. So even if Atlantis didn't directly guide the explorers, the legend may have helped keep the dream of discovery alive.

Plato's Timaeus—like his Protagoras and parts of the Phaedrus and Republic—was translated into Latin by Cicero. About a quarter of it survives in different handwritten copies. These versions mostly match, so they probably came from one original. Cicero's translation is faithful and shows his skill in dealing with Plato's complicated Greek. He also refers to the Timaeus in his book On the Nature of the Gods, where, writing as the Epicurean Velleius, he criticizes it harshly.

Proclus, a philosopher from the Alexandrian era, wrote a huge commentary on the Timaeus. His explanation is about thirty times longer than the actual text. Thomas Taylor, a translator who admired Proclus and was a kind of modern-day Neoplatonist, brought it into English. But the commentary isn't very useful. Proclus doesn't explain passages clearly or understand the text as a whole. He forces meanings onto Plato's words based on later thinkers like Porphyry, Iamblichus, and Plotinus. His writing is full of confused logic and spiritual ideas that don't match what Plato actually said.

Even though Proclus's work doesn't help much in understanding Plato, it does show what philosophy had become during that time—lots of words without much meaning. It shows how people kept patching up old ideas instead of thinking clearly, and how speech replaced true understanding. If someone wants to study how philosophy declined in the later Greek world, Proclus's Timaeus commentary is a good place to start.

A much clearer and simpler work is the short text called Timaeus Locrus. It's a summary of the Timaeus, leaving out the introduction and adding a few small touches. It doesn't mention Plato or the original source. It's written in a Greek dialect called Doric and uses some unusual words. While we don't know when it was written, its plain style avoids mystical ideas and focuses on giving a clean outline of Plato's thoughts. Sometimes it simplifies Plato's language, and other times it adds a little flair. But overall, it does a good job of keeping the meaning and spirit of the original.

From the rich garden of the Timaeus, like from Plato's other works, we can still pick a few lasting ideas to reflect on. One of the most memorable scenes is the talk between Solon and the Egyptian priest, where Egypt's long memory is compared to the youthfulness of Greece. That's where we get the famous line: "O Solon, Solon, you Greeks are always children; none of you is truly old." It reminds us of Hegel's comment that Greek history began with the youth Achilles and ended with the youth Alexander.

Plato uses many clever tricks to make his story feel true. He even adds a bit of playful irony. For example: "We can't know the origin of the other gods, so we'll trust the stories of the ancients who say they were children of the gods. They should know their own ancestors! Even if they can't give solid proof, they're talking about their own families, so we should respect tradition and believe them."

Or take this amusing explanation: "Our creators knew that humans would eventually turn into women and other animals, and that some of those animals would need claws. So, when they first made people, they built the beginning of nails into their fingers."

But not all the passages are playful—some are deeply thoughtful. In one, Plato imagines how the soul responds to reality: when it touches something real, it tries to understand what it is, how it connects to other things, what affects it, and when and how it changes. He says that when the soul uses reason and pays close attention to both the changing world and unchanging truths, it can form true beliefs and opinions. And when the soul focuses only on pure reason, it reaches real knowledge and understanding.

Another powerful idea is that God gave us sight so we could look at the stars and learn from them. By studying their steady paths, we could better guide our own thoughts and actions. In other words, learning about the universe helps bring order and reason into our own lives.

There are other important thoughts too. Like this one: "Someone who ignores learning will walk through life crippled and return to the afterlife broken and useless." Or this: "The creator of the universe is beyond human understanding—and even if we could understand him, we couldn't explain him to others." And again: "Why did the Creator make the world? Because he is good. And someone good isn't jealous. So, he wanted everything to be as good as possible. That's the true reason for creation."

This last quote captures the heart of the Timaeus, just like the Republic centers on the idea of the Good. One describes a personal God, the other a more abstract principle—but both mean the same thing for Plato: a higher, divine truth. And when he adds a small line like "as we should believe, according to the wise," Plato might be smiling behind the words.

✳✳✳

Characters

Characters in the Conversation: Socrates, Critias, Timaeus, Hermocrates

Timaeus

SOCRATES: One, two, three... but Timaeus, where's the fourth person who was with us yesterday and supposed to speak today?

TIMAEUS: He's sick, Socrates. He really wanted to be here but couldn't make it.

SOCRATES: In that case, you and the other two will have to take his place.

TIMAEUS: Of course. You treated us well yesterday, so it's only fair that we return the favor today.

SOCRATES: Do you remember the topics I asked you to speak about?

TIMAEUS: We remember some, but you're here to remind us if we forget anything. Or better yet, if it's not too much trouble, could you go over everything briefly? That would help us remember the details better.

SOCRATES: Sure, I'll do that. The main topic of yesterday's discussion was the ideal city—what kind of structure and citizens would make it the best it could be.

TIMAEUS: Yes, Socrates, and we really liked what you said about it.

SOCRATES: Didn't we start by separating farmers and workers from the group that defends the city?

TIMAEUS: Yes.

SOCRATES: Then we gave each person just one job, based on what they're naturally good at. We talked about the warriors, who protect the city both from enemies outside and from threats inside. They shouldn't have any other job. They should be kind to the people they protect, because they're like their family, but strong and fierce when fighting enemies.

TIMAEUS: Exactly.

SOCRATES: We also said, if I remember correctly, that these guardians needed a special mix of personality traits—they had to be both brave and thoughtful. That way, they could be gentle with their friends and tough with their enemies.

TIMAEUS: That's right.

SOCRATES: And we discussed their education. They should learn physical training, music, and other important knowledge that fits their role.

TIMAEUS: Yes, we did.

SOCRATES: And because of their training and responsibilities, they shouldn't own gold, silver, or any private property. Instead, they'd live like hired soldiers, getting paid just enough to live simply. They'd share everything and live together, always working to become better and more virtuous people.

TIMAEUS: We said that too.

SOCRATES: We didn't forget about the women either. We said their nature should be shaped to match the men's, and they should share the same duties—both in everyday life and in war.

TIMAEUS: That's what we agreed on.

SOCRATES: What about children? Or rather, that unusual idea we had—how could we forget? All the wives and children were to be shared in common. No one would know who their real child was. People would think of each other as one big family. Those around the same age would be siblings, the older ones would be seen as parents and grandparents, and the younger ones as children and grandchildren.

TIMAEUS: Yes, that part's definitely memorable.

SOCRATES: We also said that, to make sure the best children were born, the top leaders—men and women—would secretly plan the pairings using something like a lottery. That way, the best people would match with others like them. No one would complain because they'd think it was just chance.

TIMAEUS: I remember that.

SOCRATES: And we said the good children would be raised properly, while the children of the less worthy would be quietly placed among the lower citizens. As they all grew up, the rulers would watch closely—lifting up those who proved themselves and replacing any unworthy leaders with better ones from below.

TIMAEUS: That's right.

SOCRATES: So, have I covered everything we discussed yesterday, Timaeus? Or is there anything I missed?

TIMAEUS: No, Socrates. That was everything—just as you said.

SOCRATES: Before we go any further, I want to say how I feel about the city we imagined yesterday. It's like seeing a beautiful animal, either painted or resting, and wishing you could see it in action—running, fighting, doing what it was made to do. That's how I feel about our city. Cities always face struggles, and I'd love to hear someone describe ours going to war, acting with courage, and proving that all its training and values actually work in real life.

Now, Critias and Hermocrates, I know I couldn't describe this properly myself. And I'm not surprised—I'm more surprised that poets, both past and present, haven't done much better. I don't mean to insult them, but they're imitators. They write best about things they know from their own lives. If something's outside their experience, it's hard for them to describe it well, especially in poetry. The Sophists have a lot of fancy words and clever ideas, but since they wander from city to city and don't really live the life of statesmen or philosophers, they probably don't understand what those people actually do—especially in war or peace talks.

That's why I think people like you are the best suited to talk about these things. You've lived in strong cities, and you've studied philosophy. For example, Timaeus is from Locris in Italy—a city known for its great laws. He's respected, wealthy, and has held high office, and I believe he's mastered all areas of philosophy. Everyone in Athens knows Critias is wise and experienced. And as for Hermocrates, many have told me he's thoughtful and well-educated.

So, when I saw that you wanted me to describe how a city should be built, I agreed—knowing that you'd be the perfect people to take the story forward. I imagined you would tell how our city behaves in a real challenge, like war, and you would make the story come alive. I've finished my part, and now it's your turn. Yesterday, you promised to entertain me today with a story in return for mine. Well, here I am—eager and ready for your promised tale.

HERMOCRATES: And we're ready too, Socrates, just like Timaeus said. There's no reason to back out now. Yesterday, while we were heading to Critias's house, we talked it over. He told us an old story that I think you'll find interesting. Critias, why don't you tell it to Socrates so he can decide if it fits what he asked for?

CRITIAS: I will, if Timaeus agrees.

TIMAEUS: I agree completely.

CRITIAS: Then listen, Socrates. This might sound strange, but the story is true. It was passed down by Solon, one of the wisest of the seven sages. He was a close friend and relative of my great-grandfather, Dropides. Solon told the story to my grandfather, Critias, who then told it to us. He said that long ago, Athens did amazing things—great deeds that were forgotten over time because of disasters and the passing of generations. But one story stands out as greater than the rest. I'll share it now as a way to honor you, and also as a tribute to the goddess on her special day.

SOCRATES: That sounds good. So what was this ancient story about Athens that Solon claimed was true?

CRITIAS: It's a very old tale I heard from my grandfather when he was almost ninety and I was about ten. It was during the festival called the Registration of Youth, where boys recited poems for prizes. Many of us performed poems by Solon, which were still popular back then. One of the boys said Solon wasn't just wise—he was also a great poet. The old man smiled and said, "Yes, Amynander. If Solon had focused only on poetry and had finished the story he brought back from Egypt, instead of being pulled into political trouble at home, he might've been as famous as Homer or Hesiod."

Amynander asked, "What was the story about?"

"It was about the greatest achievement Athens ever had," he said, "something that should've been the most well-known, but it was forgotten because of how much time had passed and because those involved died without passing it on."

"Please tell us," Amynander said. "What was the story and how did Solon learn it?"

Critias continued: Solon went to Egypt and visited a city in the Nile Delta called Sais. This city honored a goddess called Neith, whom the Greeks know as Athena. The people there respected the Athenians and even said they were related. Solon was welcomed warmly and spoke with the priests who were experts in ancient history. He quickly realized that neither he nor any other Greek knew much about the deep past.

To get them talking, Solon started telling stories about the oldest Greek legends—like Phoroneus, who was thought to be the first man, and Niobe, and the survival of Deucalion and Pyrrha after the flood. He even tried to calculate how long ago those events happened.

One of the priests, who was very old, said, "Solon, Solon, you Greeks are always like children. None of you have truly ancient knowledge."

Solon asked what he meant.

The priest explained, "Your minds are young. You have no old traditions or ancient science because, time after time, human life has been wiped out by disasters—especially floods and fires. There's a myth you have about Phaethon, the son of the sun god, who tried to drive his father's chariot and burned the world. That story represents a real event—huge destruction caused by the stars shifting and setting the world on fire. These disasters happen in cycles, and mountain people are hit hardest, while those living near rivers survive more easily. Here in Egypt, the Nile protects us from destruction, which is why we have the oldest stories."

He continued, "When there's a massive flood, your cities are wiped out. Only shepherds in the mountains survive, and because they can't read or write, they pass down nothing. That's why you forget your own history. Every time your culture starts to grow, another disaster hits, and you start over like children. The stories you told earlier, Solon, are just fairy tales. You only remember one flood, but there were many. You also don't know that Athens used to be home to the greatest and most noble people who ever lived. You and your city come from the few survivors of that lost civilization—but the memory of it was wiped out."

"There was a time, long before the great flood, when Athens was the most powerful and best-governed city on earth. It did amazing things, and had a government better than anything we've ever known. Solon was amazed and begged the priest to tell him more about these ancient Athenians."

The priest agreed. "Yes, Solon," he said, "we'll tell you everything—for your sake, your city's sake, and for the sake of the goddess we both worship. She built your city a thousand years before ours. According to our sacred records, our city is 8,000 years old—and your city is 9,000 years old. I'll give you a brief version of your ancestors' laws and their greatest achievements. Later, if you want, we can go through the full details in our temple records."

"If you compare your old laws to ours," he said, "you'll see they're very similar. We have priests who live separately, just like you did. Our craftsmen work by themselves, not mixed with other classes. We have shepherds, hunters, farmers—and warriors, who do only military work, just like your old city. Even the weapons are the same—spears and shields—which the goddess gave to us first in Asia and to you first in your land."

"As for knowledge," he added, "our laws encourage the study of the natural world, prophecy, medicine, and everything needed for human life. Your city learned these things from the goddess when she founded it, choosing your land because the climate would help raise wise people. She loved both wisdom and war, so she picked the place most likely to grow people like her. And that's where you lived—with laws like ours, or even better—and you were better than all other people in every kind of virtue, just like children of the gods should be."

We have many amazing stories about your city in our records. But one stands out above the rest for its greatness and bravery. These records speak of a powerful empire that, without being provoked, tried to conquer all of Europe and Asia. But your city stopped it.

This powerful empire came from across the Atlantic Ocean. Back then, the Atlantic could be sailed. In front of the strait you call the Pillars of Heracles, there was a large island—bigger than both Libya and Asia combined. From that island, people could travel to other islands, and eventually to a huge continent that surrounded the real ocean. The sea inside the Pillars of Heracles was just a bay with a narrow entrance. The other sea, though, was a real ocean, and the land surrounding it could truly be called a vast continent.

The island was called Atlantis. It was home to a strong empire that ruled the entire island, several other islands, and parts of the continent. The rulers of Atlantis also took over lands as far as Egypt in Africa and as far as Tyrrhenia in Europe.

This massive power tried to conquer our lands and yours, and everything inside the straits. That's when your city, Athens, stood out. It showed amazing courage and strength and led the Greek cities in battle. When the others gave up, Athens stood alone, faced extreme danger, and still managed to win. It freed not only its own people but also helped save others from slavery.

But then, terrible earthquakes and floods happened. In just one day and night, your brave soldiers vanished into the earth, and Atlantis sank into the sea. Now that part of the ocean is full of mud and can't be crossed, because the island's collapse caused the seabed to rise.

That, Socrates, is the story the old man Critias heard from Solon and told us. When you spoke yesterday about your city and its people, I remembered this tale. I was amazed by how closely your description matched Solon's story. But I didn't speak then because it had been so long, and I needed time to remember the details. That's why I quickly agreed to your request. In stories like this, the hardest part is finding one that fits—and we already had the perfect one.

So, like Hermocrates mentioned, after leaving yesterday, I told the story to my friends. Then, later that night, I remembered most of it clearly. Childhood memories really do stick with us. I may forget what we talked about yesterday, but I'm sure I'll always remember this old tale. I listened to it so closely as a child, asking the old man to repeat it again and again, and his words are still fixed in my mind.

When morning came, I shared it with my friends so they could also take part in today's conversation. Now, Socrates, I'm ready to tell you the full story—not just the highlights, but all the details. We're going to take the city and people you imagined yesterday and place them in real history. We'll say they were the ancient Athenians the priest spoke of. Everything will match up. Let's divide the story among us, and each of us will do our part as best we can. So, tell me, Socrates—does this story work for our purpose, or should we look for a different one?

SOCRATES: What other story could be better, Critias? This one fits perfectly with the festival we're celebrating, and the best part is— it's a true story, not a made-up one. There's no reason to change it. Please, go ahead and tell it, and may everything go well. As for me, after giving yesterday's talk, I'll now enjoy listening.

CRITIAS: Then let me explain how we've planned our talk. Timaeus, who knows the most about astronomy and the universe, will speak first. He'll start with the creation of the world and go on to how humans were made. After that, it'll be my turn. I'll describe the people he created—some of whom have received the kind of excellent education you described—and I'll place them into the story as the ancient Athenians the priest mentioned. From then on, we'll treat them as real citizens of Athens and speak of them as our fellow countrymen.

SOCRATES: It sounds like I'm going to enjoy a wonderful feast of ideas. Timaeus, I think it's your turn to speak now—after you say a proper prayer to the gods.

TIMAEUS: Socrates, every thoughtful person knows it's important to call on the gods at the start of any big or small task. And since we're about to talk about the creation of the universe—how it began or how it might have always existed—we need to pray to the gods and goddesses. We ask that our words be respectful and aligned with the truth. So let this be our prayer, and I also remind myself to speak clearly, in a way that's easy to understand and stays true to what I want to share.

First, let's ask a basic question: What is something that always exists and never changes? And what is something that is always changing and never stays the same? Things that are understood through thinking and reason stay the same. But things we understand through our senses and opinions are always changing—they are constantly forming and disappearing and never truly "are."

Everything that is created must have a cause. Nothing can come into being without something that made it. So, whenever a creator uses something perfect and unchanging as a model, the result will also be beautiful and well-made. But if the creator copies something that was already created, the result won't be perfect.

Now, was the world always here, or was it created at some point? Since the world can be seen and touched, and it has a physical form, it must have been created. And, as we said, anything created must have a cause.

But the true maker of the universe is extremely hard to discover. And even if we found him, explaining him to everyone would be impossible.

Still, there's another question to consider: When the creator made the world, did he base it on something unchanging, or on something already made? If the world is truly beautiful, and the creator is truly good, then he must have looked to something perfect and eternal when making it. Because something good and beautiful must come from a good and unchanging source.

So the world, made by this good creator, is a copy of something that is perfect and unchanging. And just like that model, the world is something we can understand with our mind and reason.

It's important that everything starts off in the right way. When talking about the original model and the copy, we should use the right kind of words. If we're talking about something eternal and unchanging, our words should be strong and solid too. But when we're describing a copy or an imitation, it's enough for the words to be likely or close to the truth. Just as "being" is to "becoming," truth is to belief.

So, Socrates, if we can't explain everything perfectly about the gods or how the universe began, don't be surprised. It's enough if our story is just as believable as any other. After all, both you and I are just human, and we should accept the version that sounds the most likely and not push beyond that.

SOCRATES: That's well said, Timaeus. We'll do just as you suggest. That was a wonderful introduction—now let's hear the main story.

TIMAEUS: All right. Let me tell you why the creator made the world. He was good, and someone who is truly good isn't jealous. Because he wanted everything to be as good as possible, he decided to create the world. This, according to wise people, is the true reason why the universe exists: God wanted everything to be good and nothing to be bad, as much as possible.

When he saw that the world was moving in a chaotic and messy way, he brought order out of that mess, because order is always better than disorder.

The creator realized that intelligent beings were more beautiful than unintelligent ones, and that intelligence can't exist without a soul. So when he made the universe, he put intelligence inside a soul, and that soul inside a body—so the world itself would be a living creature, full of mind and purpose. So, we can say that by the care and wisdom of God, the world became a living being, with both soul and intelligence.

Now let's move to the next question: What kind of creature did the creator model the world after? It wouldn't make sense to copy just a small part of nature. That would be like making something incomplete. Instead, he made the world as a complete image of the whole— something that includes all other animals and living beings, just as this universe includes all living things we can see.

The original perfect being included all living things within it, so the world was designed to be one large, complete creature containing all others.

Should we say there is one world or many? There must be only one. If the world is a copy of that perfect original, it should also be one of a kind. If there were two or more, we'd need something bigger that included them both—and that would be the true copy instead.

So, to match the perfect model, the creator made just one world— one perfect, created heaven that exists alone.

Now, anything that's made has to be physical, which means it must be something you can see and touch. But you can't see anything without fire, and you can't touch anything without solidity, which comes from earth. So God used fire and earth to create the body of the universe.

But you can't just combine two things and expect them to hold together without something in between. There has to be a third element that connects them. The best way to do this is through balance—through proportion. When three things are in the right ratio, they blend together perfectly. For example, when one thing is to the second as the second is to the third, they form a strong bond. If the world had no depth, only one middle element would be needed. But since it's solid, and solids need three parts, God added air and water between fire and earth.

He placed air and water in between, balanced so that as fire relates to air, air relates to water, and water to earth. In this way, he created a visible and touchable world held together in harmony.

So the body of the world was made from these four elements: fire, air, water, and earth. Because they were balanced through proportion, the world became united, friendly to itself, and impossible for anything except its creator to tear apart.

The Creator used all of the four elements—fire, water, air, and earth—to make the world. He left none of them out because he wanted the world to be complete, with nothing missing. First, he wanted the world to be perfect and made of perfect parts. Second, he wanted it to be the only world, with no leftover pieces that could form another. He also wanted it to be free from aging and sickness. He knew that outside forces like heat and cold could harm living things, causing them to get sick or grow old. To prevent this, he made the world one complete whole, strong enough to resist those outside forces.

He gave the world the most fitting and natural shape—the shape of a sphere. Since this world was meant to include all living things, the round shape was best because it includes all other shapes. He made it perfectly round, the same in every direction, like a ball turned on a lathe. This shape was the most balanced and beautiful. The surface was smooth all over, since it didn't need eyes, ears, or even lungs—there was nothing outside it to see, hear, or breathe. It didn't need a mouth or stomach either, because nothing went in or came out. It was designed to be self-sufficient—feeding itself with its own waste and needing nothing from outside.

Since it didn't need to fight or gather anything, it had no hands. It didn't need to walk either, so it had no legs or feet. Instead, it moved in circles, which was the best motion for something intelligent. Of all the seven kinds of movement, this circular one was the most fitting. It didn't go up, down, or sideways. It just turned gently in place. That's why the universe was made round and smooth, without limbs, and able to move in a perfect loop.

This was the Creator's plan for the living universe, which he called a god. He gave it a smooth, balanced body made out of the most perfect materials. He placed the soul at the center of it, spreading it through the whole body and even wrapping it around the outside. This made the universe one, complete, and able to understand itself, needing no one else. In this way, the Creator made the world into a blessed living god.

Even though we're describing the soul after the body, the Creator actually made the soul first. He would never let something younger rule over something older. It's just the way we usually talk, since we're used to thinking randomly. In truth, the soul came first, was better, and was made to lead, while the body was made to follow.

The Creator made the soul from a mix of three things: one part was unchanging and eternal, another part came from the changing physical world, and the third was something in between. He blended these three together—the same, the different, and the essence of being—into one balanced whole. Then he divided this mix into parts, each still holding the same three ingredients. He made seven main parts with special mathematical relationships: 1, 2, 3, 4, 9, 8, and 27. These numbers had important ratios and meanings. He then filled in the spaces between these with more fractions to create perfect harmony. One of the important leftover fractions was the ratio 256 to 243.

He shaped this soul mixture into two long strips, bent them into circles like the letter X, and joined them at the middle. One of these circles spun in one direction, and the other spun in the opposite direction. He called the outer spinning circle "the same" and the inner one "the different." The outer one turned to the right, the inner one to the left. The outer stayed whole, while the inner was divided into seven uneven rings—these would be the paths of the sun, moon, and planets. Some moved at the same speed, others moved faster or slower, but they were all in proportion.

When the Creator had shaped the soul like this, he placed the body of the universe inside it. He joined them at the center, so the soul stretched through and around the entire universe. The soul turned within itself, beginning a life that would last forever—wise, steady, and always moving. The body could be seen, but the soul could not. The soul was full of reason and harmony and was the most perfect thing ever created.

Since the soul was made of the same, the different, and the essence of being, and was carefully divided and balanced, it could recognize patterns. When the soul came into contact with something that existed—whether it was whole or in parts—it reacted by identifying what was the same, what was different, how things were connected, what caused them, and in what way, how, and when those things occurred, both in the changing world and in the unchanging one.

When reason worked together with the circle of the different, helping the soul understand the physical world, it formed beliefs and opinions that could be trusted. But when reason joined with the circle of the same, focusing on pure ideas, it led to true understanding and knowledge. If anyone says that something other than the soul holds both these powers, they would be wrong.

When the Creator saw the living world he had made—an image of the eternal gods—he was filled with joy. Wanting to make it even more like the original, he tried to make it last forever. But since only eternal things can truly last forever, and a created thing can't be exactly like that, he came up with a solution: he created time as a moving version of eternity. While eternity never changes, time moves in measured steps, and that's how the heavens were arranged. Before this, there were no days, nights, months, or years. These all began when the universe was created.

Time includes past and future, but we often mistakenly use those words when talking about eternal things. We say things like "he was" or "he will be," but really, for something eternal, only "he is" is correct. Time affects things that move and change. Eternal things stay the same and don't get older or younger. Time mimics eternity by spinning in a steady cycle. Even when we talk about what has happened or will happen, or things that don't exist, our words don't always match what's real. But maybe that's a conversation for another time.

So, time and the heavens were created together. The Creator wanted them to start and end together, if they were ever to end. He shaped the heavens to match the eternal world as closely as possible. While the eternal world simply is, the heavens were made to be "has been," "is," and "will be." That was God's purpose in making time.

He also made the sun, moon, and five planets to help measure time. After creating their physical forms, he placed them in seven orbits. The moon was placed closest to Earth. The sun came next. Venus and Mercury were also placed nearby, and even though they move as fast as the sun, they go in the opposite direction. That's why they seem to pass each other in the sky.

Explaining exactly where and why the other stars were placed would take too long now. That can be saved for another time.

Once the stars were all set in motion the right way, they became living beings. Each star had a body and was held in place by invisible forces. They learned their paths, moving in a slanted motion that was guided by another steady rotation. Some moved faster in smaller orbits, while others were slower in larger ones. But because everything spun together, it sometimes looked like the slow ones were passing the fast ones, even though that wasn't true. This was because their spiral paths made it look that way.

To help living things measure this movement, the Creator lit the sun in the second orbit, so it would shine across the sky. That way, people could learn numbers and time from the regular spinning of the stars.

That's how day and night were created, based on the smartest and most regular rotation. A month happens when the moon finishes its circle and catches up to the sun. A year happens when the sun completes its own orbit.

Most people don't notice the paths of the other planets, so they don't name or count their cycles. Because of that, they don't really understand that these complex paths also form part of time. Still, if you watch carefully, you'll see that all eight orbits eventually line up again— this perfect alignment marks the complete and perfect year.

This is also why some stars seem to reverse their motion—they were made that way so the created sky could be as close as possible to the eternal world.

Up to the creation of time, the universe was shaped to match the eternal one. But it was still incomplete because it didn't yet have all kinds of living creatures. So, the Creator continued, modeling his work after the eternal example.

The perfect eternal creature had four types of life, so the Creator made four in our world too: the heavenly gods, the birds in the air, the water creatures, and the land animals.

The gods of the heavens were mostly made from fire so they would shine the brightest and look the most beautiful. They were shaped like circles to match the universe and followed the highest kind of motion. He spread them all around the edge of the sky, decorating the whole heavens.

Each star had two kinds of movement: one where it stayed in place and always thought the same thoughts, and another where it moved forward under the control of the heavens' regular spin. They didn't have the other five types of movement, so they could stay perfect. These fixed stars were made to be eternal, divine beings, always staying in the same place and moving the same way.

The other stars that seem to move backward were created the way we talked about earlier. The Earth, which cares for us, spins slowly around a central axis stretched through the universe. It's the maker of day and night, and the oldest of the gods in the sky.

Trying to explain how all the stars move—how they line up, cross paths, hide and reappear—would be impossible without showing a model. Some stars disappear and come back, scaring people or giving signs of the future to those who can't read the sky. It's too hard to explain all that now, so let's finish our talk about the visible gods here.

As for the other gods, we can't say where they came from. We have to rely on old traditions passed down from people who said they were children of the gods. Since they claimed to speak of their own ancestors, we follow custom and believe them.

According to them, Earth and Heaven had two children: Oceanus and Tethys. From them came Phorcys, Cronos, Rhea, and others. Cronos and Rhea then gave birth to Zeus, Hera, and their siblings, along with their children—many of the gods we know.

When all the gods had been created—both the ones we can see in the sky and those who are hidden—the creator of the universe spoke to them like this:

"Gods, children of gods, I made you, and I am both your maker and your father. What I have created cannot be destroyed—unless I choose it. Anything that is put together can be taken apart, but only someone evil would want to ruin something beautiful and good. So while you're not completely immortal, you also won't die or fall apart, because I've given you a stronger bond—my will.

Now listen. There are still three types of mortal creatures that need to be created. Without them, the universe wouldn't be complete. But if I made them myself and gave them life, they'd be equal to you gods. To keep them mortal, I want you to make these creatures, using the power you've seen me use. I'll give each one a divine, immortal part— the soul—which will guide those who want to live justly and follow your lead. I'll begin this task and then hand it over to you. Your job is to connect the mortal with the immortal. Give these living creatures bodies, help them grow, feed them, and welcome them back in death."

Then he took what was left from the mixture he used to create the soul of the universe. It wasn't as pure this time—more diluted. He mixed it again and divided it into a number of souls equal to the number of stars. Each soul was placed in its own star like a chariot. He showed them how the universe works and explained their destiny. Their first birth would be equal for all of them—none would be treated unfairly. They would be placed into bodies suited to their time and would be the most spiritual of all creatures. The higher kind would later be called humans.

When these souls entered their bodies, which constantly change by gaining and losing parts, they needed some shared abilities. First, they had to feel sensations caused by strong physical experiences. Second, they needed emotions like love, pleasure, pain, fear, and anger. If they could control these feelings, they would live good lives. If not, they would live badly. Those who lived well would return to their home star and live a blessed life. Those who failed would be reborn as women, and if they still did wrong, they would eventually turn into animals that reflected their bad nature. They would go through many lives until they learned to follow reason and returned to their original, better state.

After setting all this in place so he wouldn't be blamed for any future wrongs, the creator planted these souls into the earth, the moon, and other places in time. Then he gave the younger gods the task of forming their physical bodies and adding anything else the souls would need. He told them to guide these creatures in the best and wisest ways and protect them from all harm except what they bring upon themselves.

Once the creator finished, he returned to his own way of being. The younger gods obeyed and, copying their father, created mortal bodies. They borrowed bits of fire, earth, water, and air from the world and promised to return them later. They used tiny, invisible links to build each body and attached the soul to these ever-changing forms.

Because the body is always changing—taking things in and pushing things out—the soul was constantly being moved around. The body didn't move in an orderly way but was pulled in all directions, reacting to anything it touched—fire, earth, water, or air. These reactions reached the soul and were called "sensations," a name we still use. These sensations stirred the soul, making it shake violently and stopping its calm inner movement. This disrupted its natural balance and twisted the soul's structure. The soul became confused, turning upside down, spinning backward, or swaying at odd angles. It couldn't tell left from right or truth from falsehood.

In this state, if the soul encountered something familiar or unfamiliar, it often got confused and misjudged it. These mistakes caused the soul to become foolish. Even when it thought it was in control, it was actually being controlled by these wild sensations.

Because of all this, the soul in a human body starts off lacking intelligence. But as the person grows and the chaos settles, the soul gradually returns to its natural shape. When this happens, it can understand truth again and begins to think clearly. If this soul is combined with good learning and guidance, the person becomes wise and whole. But without education, the person stays broken, never living up to their full potential, and eventually returns to the next world in that poor state.

Now, to understand more clearly how the soul and body were made, we need to go deeper. The gods, following the round shape of the universe, put the soul in a round body—which we call the head. This was the most important and divine part, meant to rule over everything else in us. So the gods gave it a body to carry it around. They gave it a long shape with four flexible limbs—arms and legs—so it could move through the world and carry the head safely above all. That's how legs and hands came to be.

And because the front of the body was seen as more noble and suited for leadership, they made humans walk mostly forward. This is also why our front side looks different from the rest of our body.

In the head, they placed the face and added the organs that would help the soul carry out its work. They made sure the face, which gives direction and awareness, was placed at the front, where it could guide everything. The first organ they created was the eye, meant to give us the gift of sight. They used a gentle kind of fire—not the kind that burns, but one that glows softly. This fire was similar to the light we see every day. They connected this inner fire with a matching fire inside us and made it flow outward through the eyes in a smooth, steady stream. This flow filled the eye, especially the center, allowing only the pure light to pass through and blocking everything else.

When daylight surrounds this stream from our eyes, the outer light meets the inner light. Since they are the same kind of light, they mix together and form a connection. This connection happens where the light from inside meets the object outside. The vision stream reacts in a similar way across its entire length, passing movements from what it touches to our whole body until it reaches the soul. That's how we see.

But when night comes and the outside light goes away, the vision stream doesn't meet anything similar. It becomes weak and fades, unable to keep going in the cold, dark air. So, we can't see, and we feel like sleeping. Our eyelids, which the gods designed to protect our sight, close and keep the inner fire in. This helps calm the body's motions.

When everything inside us becomes balanced, we fall into deep rest. If there are still strong movements in the body, they create dreams that reflect them. We remember these dreams when we wake up.

It's also easy now to understand how mirrors work. The images we see in mirrors or shiny surfaces come from the joining of the inner light from our eyes and the outer light reflecting off our face. When these lights meet on a smooth surface, they create images. The reason things appear flipped in mirrors—like right becoming left—is that the lights cross paths in an unusual way. But when the mirror is shaped in certain ways, like being curved, the direction of the light can change, making things appear as they truly are—or even upside down if the mirror is vertical and concave. In that case, the light from below moves up, and the light from above moves down, flipping the image.

These things—like fire heating and freezing, or water expanding and shrinking—are often mistaken by most people as the main causes of everything. But really, they are just tools used by a higher power. They don't have reason or understanding. Only the soul, which is invisible, can think and plan. Fire, water, earth, and air are all physical and can't think. So, anyone who loves wisdom should focus first on causes that come from intelligence, and then look at causes that are just reactions without thought. We need to understand both kinds, but also recognize the difference: some causes are smart and aim for good, while others are blind and work by chance without meaning.

We've talked enough about how the body helps the eyes do their job. Now, let's think about the deeper reason we were given sight. I believe vision is one of the greatest gifts we have. Without it, we wouldn't have seen the stars, the sun, or the sky. Without those things, we wouldn't have started wondering about the world. Seeing day and night, the changing seasons, and the movement of the heavens helped us create numbers and understand time. That curiosity gave birth to philosophy, which is the greatest gift the gods have ever given us. So, sight doesn't just help us get around—it helps us think.

Even an ordinary person would be devastated if they lost their sight. But for now, I'll just say this: the gods gave us vision so we could study the patterns in the sky and match them with our own thoughts, trying to make our minds as steady as the stars. By doing that, we learn to follow truth and reason, copying the perfect order of the universe in our own lives.

The same goes for speech and hearing. The gods gave them to us for similar reasons. Speech helps us understand each other and share knowledge. Music, when it matches the natural flow of the voice and ear, isn't just for fun. It's meant to bring balance. Harmony, which moves in ways like our soul does, was given to us to heal our inner confusion—not to entertain, as many people now believe. It helps our soul become more ordered and peaceful. Rhythm was given for the same reason: to fix the wild and clumsy ways people often act.

So far, we've mostly talked about how intelligence plays a role in the universe. But now we need to include another factor: necessity. Everything in creation comes from a mix of reason and necessity. Reason is the ruler, and it convinced necessity to shape most things as perfectly as possible. So in the beginning, when reason took control, the universe was formed. But to fully explain how this happened, we need to understand the other side too—how change and unpredictability play a part.

To do that, we should look again at the elements: fire, water, air, and earth—how they were before the world began. No one has clearly explained how they came to be. People talk about them like we understand them, calling them the building blocks of everything. But really, we don't even understand them well enough to compare them to letters, let alone words. So, I won't try to explain the ultimate beginning of everything—not now. It's too difficult, especially using the way we've been talking so far.

I won't pretend to know the exact truth, but I'll try to offer the most reasonable explanation I can. I'll return to the beginning again and try to describe how things came to be.

This time, we need to add one more category to our thinking. Before, we only had two: one was the unchanging, perfect pattern, and the other was its copy—visible and changing. But now, we need to add a third: a kind of space that holds everything, like a background or a container. It's not easy to describe, but it's like the mother of all creation, a place where everything is shaped.

To explain this clearly, we first need to understand fire, water, air, and earth. What are they really? How do we know one is fire and not water—or any of the others? This is a hard question. But we must try to figure it out if we want to understand the world better.

First, let's look at how everything changes. What we call water can turn into stone or earth when it becomes dense. When it's heated and spread out, it turns into vapor or air. Air can catch fire and become flame. Fire, when cooled and put out, becomes air again. That air, when compressed, turns into clouds or mist. Compress it more, and it becomes water again. Water then becomes earth or stone once more. This shows that things don't stay in one form—they keep changing in a cycle.

Since everything is always changing, how can anyone say for sure that a thing is truly one thing and not another? We really can't. So it's better to talk about them differently. Instead of calling something "this" or "that"—like saying "this is fire" or "that is water"—we should say "something like fire" or "something of that nature." These words help us understand their changing nature. None of these elements stay the same long enough to be fixed with names like "this" or "that."

Instead, we should only use words like "such" or "of this kind" to describe their nature. Fire should be called something that always has that kind of behavior. The only thing we should call "this" or "that" is the space where things appear, grow, and disappear. But things like "hot," "white," or any mixed quality shouldn't be fixed with names, because they keep changing.

Here's another way to understand it: imagine someone shaping gold into different forms. They might turn it into a triangle or a square or something else. If you ask what it is, the best answer is simply "gold." The shapes aren't really separate things, since they're always changing. The same idea works for the space that holds all things—it stays the same even as things come and go inside it.

This space takes on different shapes depending on what enters it, but it never becomes those things itself. It just receives their impressions and changes how it looks because of them. These forms are like copies of real things, shaped after true patterns in a mysterious way. We'll talk more about how that works later.

For now, we need to think about three things: one, the thing that's being created; two, the space where it's created; and three, the true pattern it's copied from. You could say the space is like a mother, the pattern is like a father, and the created thing is like their child.

If something is going to take on all kinds of shapes, the space it fills needs to have no shape of its own. That way, it's ready to take on any form. It's like when people make perfume—they use a base with no smell so it can absorb any scent. Or when shaping clay, they make the surface smooth first, so it can take any pattern. In the same way, the space that holds all things must be formless, so it can receive everything.

This "mother space" isn't air, earth, fire, water, or any mix of those. It's something invisible, without shape, but able to hold all things. Somehow, it connects with the world of true knowledge, even though we can't fully understand it. We can say parts of it become fire, water, earth, or air depending on what it receives.

Now let's think more carefully: is there such a thing as fire or other elements that exist by themselves? Or is it only what we see and feel through our senses that is real? Is the world of ideas and invisible patterns real, or just something we made up? We can't ignore these questions or be too sure of the answer. But let me try to say something meaningful in just a few words.

Here's what I believe: if true knowledge and opinion are two different things, then there must be real, invisible ideas that we don't sense with our bodies but only know through the mind. But if opinion and knowledge are the same, then only what we see and feel with our senses is real.

However, I believe opinion and knowledge are not the same. They come from different places and act differently. Knowledge is taught, and it's always backed by reason. Opinion comes from being convinced, and doesn't always have reason behind it. Knowledge stays firm, but opinion can be changed. Everyone has opinions, but only a few people—and the gods—have true knowledge.

So we must admit that there is one kind of being that never changes, is never created, and never destroyed. It doesn't take anything in or send anything out. It's invisible and can only be understood by the mind. There's another kind that is similar but seen with the senses. This one is created, always moving, appearing and disappearing. It's known through our senses and opinions.

Then there's a third kind—space. It always exists, can't be destroyed, and holds everything created. We don't see it with our senses, but we know it in a strange way, like a dream. We think that everything must be somewhere, in some space, and anything that isn't, doesn't really exist. But even when we think about space and reality, it feels like we're dreaming. We can't fully wake up to see the truth.

Images or copies of real things don't have their own realness. They are always just shadows of something else, and they only exist because they're held in space. But reason tells us that if something is truly real, it can't be inside something else and still be itself. Two different things can't be one and two at the same time.

So here's what I believe: real being, space, and change all existed before the world began. The "mother" space was filled with fire, water, earth, and air in all kinds of unstable and unbalanced ways. It moved wildly and made the elements move too. As this space shook, it separated the elements—some were heavy and stayed together, others were light and scattered.

Before everything was arranged into the world we know, the elements didn't have order or balance. They were just random pieces, not yet shaped by reason. But when the world started to come together, God gave shape and number to everything and made them beautiful and good—even though they started out messy and imperfect. That's what we must believe: God made the best out of what wasn't good.

Now I'll try to explain how these elements were created, using a new and unusual kind of reasoning. I think you'll be able to follow, because your education has prepared you for it.

First, fire, water, earth, and air are all physical. Every physical thing has shape and takes up space. All solid shapes are made up of flat surfaces, and these surfaces are made from triangles. There are two kinds of triangles: one is made of equal sides with one right angle, and the other has different side lengths, still with one right angle.

We believe that these two triangles are the building blocks of the elements. Only a god could know what comes before these triangles, but we can use what we know. Next, we need to find the four most beautiful solid shapes, which can break down and turn into one another. These are the shapes of fire, earth, water, and air. Once we figure them out, we'll understand what these elements really are.

Of the two triangles, the one with equal sides makes only one shape. The one with different sides can make many, even infinitely many, different shapes. So we must choose the most beautiful one. If someone finds a better one, they'll have made a great discovery. But we believe the best is the triangle that, when two are put together, forms a perfect equilateral triangle. The reason for this would take too long to explain here, but it works well.

So, we choose two triangles—one with equal sides and one special kind of triangle with unequal sides, where the square of the longer side is three times the square of the shorter one. These are the triangles from which fire and the other elements are formed.

Now it's time to explain something that was unclear earlier. It was a mistake to think that all four elements—earth, air, fire, and water—could turn into each other in any way. That idea isn't correct. From the triangles we chose before, four kinds of shapes are formed. Three of these come from one kind of triangle (the one with unequal sides), and one shape comes from the isosceles triangle (the one with two equal sides). Because of this, not all of them can change into each other easily. Many small shapes can combine to form a few large ones, or large ones can break into smaller ones—but only for the three shapes that come from the same triangle type. These three can switch between each other because they come from the same triangle. When large shapes break apart, they become many small shapes, and when small ones are combined, they make a bigger shape of a different kind.

Now let's look at what each of these shapes is made of. The simplest one is built from the triangle where the longest side is twice the shortest. When two of these triangles are joined along their longest side, and this is repeated three times, six triangles together form one equilateral triangle. Then, four of these equilateral triangles can join to make one corner of a solid shape. When you combine several of these corners, you get the first 3D form that fits perfectly into a circle.

The second shape is made from the same basic triangles. When eight equilateral triangles come together, they make one solid corner, and six of these corners build the second 3D body.

The third shape is more complex—it uses 120 triangles to make twelve solid corners, each made up of five flat equilateral triangles. In total, it has twenty triangular faces.

These three shapes all come from the triangle with unequal sides. The triangle with equal sides makes a different shape. Four of those triangles join at their right angles to make a square. Six squares together form eight solid corners, each made from three right angles. This creates a cube, which has six square faces.

There is also a fifth shape that God used to shape the universe, but its purpose is not discussed here.

Now, if someone carefully thinks about this and asks whether there are an unlimited number of worlds or just a specific number, it would be wrong to say there are endless worlds. That idea shows confusion. It's smarter to ask whether there is only one world or maybe five. That's a more thoughtful question. Based on reasoning, I believe there is just one world. Others might think differently depending on their point of view. But for now, let's continue and connect each of the four shapes to one of the elements.

Let's assign the cube to earth. Earth is the most solid and stable of all elements. It doesn't move easily, and it can hold its shape. That fits the cube, which has the strongest and most stable base. The triangle with equal sides, which the cube is made from, is more stable than the triangle with unequal sides. And a square is a more stable base than a triangle. That's why giving the cube to earth makes sense.

Next, we give the least mobile of the remaining shapes to water. The most mobile goes to fire, and the one in between goes to air. Fire also gets the smallest shape, water gets the biggest, and air is in the middle. Fire's shape is the sharpest and most pointed, so it moves and cuts through other things easily. Air's shape is also sharp, but less so than fire. Water's shape is softer, and earth's is the most stable.

The shape for fire is the pyramid, or tetrahedron—it's made of four triangles. That's the smallest and sharpest, so it makes sense to assign it to fire. Then comes air, then water, based on how large and pointed their shapes are. These shapes are so small that we can't see a single one by itself. But when many of them gather, we can see them as fire, air, water, or earth. God carefully arranged the sizes, movements, and other qualities of these elements in perfect balance, as much as was possible.

Here's what likely happens with the elements: earth, when broken down by fire, gets scattered around until the pieces come back together and form earth again. It can never become something else. But when water is broken down, it can turn partly into air and partly into fire. A piece of air, if split, can become two parts of fire.

Also, if a small amount of fire is trapped inside a larger amount of air or water or earth, and everything is moving, the fire might be destroyed and broken apart. Then two pieces of fire might combine to make one piece of air. If air is broken into tiny parts, two and a half pieces of it can become one piece of water.

Think about it this way: if fire attacks another element and cuts it with its sharp points, it will keep doing so until the other element gives in and joins the fire. Then the two combine and stop fighting. One element can't change another if they are the same kind and in the same condition. But when a weaker element tries to resist a stronger one, it keeps breaking apart.

Sometimes, when a few small pieces are trapped inside larger ones and are being destroyed, they will stop fighting only when they agree to become part of the stronger one. So fire turns into air, and air turns into water. If different kinds of particles attack each other, the weaker ones will keep breaking until they either escape to rejoin their own kind or become part of the stronger one. Then they stop fighting and stay there, becoming one.

Because of these constant changes and the movement of space itself, everything shifts around. As space shakes, the different types of elements move to the right places. When something starts to resemble a different element, it gets pushed toward where that element belongs.

This is how the basic, pure elements are formed. The more specific versions of them—like different types of fire or air—come from variations in the size and shape of the original triangles. Not all triangles were the same size at first. Some were bigger, some smaller, and that's why there are different types of each element. These mixtures lead to endless variations, and anyone who wants to understand nature should pay close attention to these differences.

To understand what comes next, we first need to get a clear idea of what motion and stillness really are. This was talked about a little earlier, but there's more to explain. Motion doesn't happen in things that are perfectly even or unchanging. It's hard—even impossible—to imagine something moving on its own without something else pushing it. Likewise, there can't be a mover unless there's something that can be moved. So, motion needs both a mover and something to move. And those two can't be exactly the same or perfectly uniform. That's why stillness belongs to things that are uniform, and motion comes from things that are uneven or unbalanced.

This lack of uniformity comes from inequality. We already explained where that comes from. Now we need to understand why elements—like fire, air, water, and earth—keep flowing through each other and moving around instead of staying in one place.

All four elements move within the spinning motion of the universe. This spin is round, like a circle, and pulls things inward, squeezing them together so that nothing is left empty. Because of this compression, fire can pass through anything most easily because it's the lightest, followed by air, which is the next lightest. Water and earth also move through things, but not as easily. The easier something moves, the smaller its particles are. The bigger the particles, the more empty space they leave behind. Smaller particles get pushed into these spaces when things are squeezed together.

So, smaller particles slip between the larger ones. This causes everything to move around—up and down, side to side—until each element finds the place it belongs. As their size changes, their position in space changes too. This imbalance keeps everything in constant motion.

Next, let's look at the different types of fire. First, there's actual flame. Second, there's the kind of light that comes from fire but doesn't burn—it only helps us see. Third, there's the leftover heat in glowing embers after the fire goes out.

Air also comes in different forms. The clearest and lightest part is called aether. The thickest and darkest parts are fog and darkness. There are other kinds of air too, caused by differences in the shapes of the tiny building blocks.

Water can be divided into two main types: liquid and molten (or fusible). Liquid water is made of small, uneven particles. That's why it moves so easily and can be moved by other things. Molten water is made of bigger, more equal particles, so it's heavier and more solid. But when fire enters and breaks apart these particles, it loses its balance, becomes more fluid, and spreads across the ground, pushed by the air. This breaking down of solids is called melting, and the spreading is called flowing.

When fire leaves the molten material, it doesn't disappear into nothing—it enters the surrounding air. That air pushes back, forcing the melted material to come back together and become solid again. This process is called cooling, and the return to solid form is called freezing.

The densest and most tightly packed molten substance is gold. Gold forms when water filters through rock and becomes solid. It shines and has a yellow color. A very hard and dense type of gold that turns black is called adamant.

There's another material similar to gold, made of tiny bits of earth and gold-like stuff. It's harder than gold because of the earth in it and lighter because of the empty space inside. When this bright, dense kind of water becomes solid, we call it copper. When the earth and copper parts grow old and separate, the leftover earth becomes rust.

Other similar changes can be figured out with careful thinking. Sometimes it's good to take a break from deep thinking about eternal truths and instead enjoy studying the likely truths about how things are formed. It's a relaxing and useful activity.

Let's keep going with that. When water mixes with fire, it becomes soft and liquid because of how easily it moves and rolls on the ground. It's called soft because its base is weaker than that of solid earth. If the fire and air leave it, the water becomes more balanced and tightens into itself. If it tightens a lot, it turns into hail in the air or ice on the ground. If it only partially hardens, it becomes snow in the air or frost on the ground.

Some types of water mix with each other and pass through plants. These are called juices or saps. Most of them don't have names, but four are clearly known because they act like fire.

First is wine, which warms both the body and the soul. Second is the oily kind—like oil, pitch, and castor juice—which shines and reflects light because it's smooth. Third is the sweet kind, like honey, which makes the mouth feel normal again after being tight. Fourth is a foamy, sour liquid that burns the skin—it's called "opos," a type of plant acid.

Now let's talk about earth. When water runs through it and breaks it apart, the water changes into air and rises. But there's no empty space, so the rising air pushes nearby air out of the way. That surrounding air then presses down on the earth and squeezes it tight. When the earth gets packed tightly with the leftover water, it turns into stone. Clear and balanced pieces of earth make nicer, more transparent stone. Uneven pieces make rougher, lower-quality stone.

If all the water is burned out quickly by fire, the leftover material becomes brittle and turns into pottery. If a little water stays, the heated earth cools and becomes a black-colored stone.

Something similar happens with salt-like earth materials that mix heavily with water. When the water leaves, they turn into partly solid substances that can dissolve in water. One becomes soda, used for cleaning oil and dirt. The other becomes salt, which adds flavor and was once thought to be sacred.

Earth mixed with water doesn't usually dissolve in water, only in fire. That's because fire and air have tiny particles that can pass through earth without breaking it. But water particles are bigger and can break it apart. So, loose earth is dissolved by water. Hardened earth can only be broken down by fire.

Water, if tightly held together, can only be broken by fire. If it's held more loosely, it can be broken by either fire or air—air enters the gaps, and fire breaks the structure itself. Strongly packed air can only be broken by fire that reaches deep into its smallest parts.

When a solid mix of earth and water is tightly packed, the water inside fills all the small spaces. If more water tries to enter, there's no room, so it flows around the outside without dissolving it. But fire can enter the water's spaces and break it down, just like water breaks earth or fire breaks air. Fire is the only thing that can melt these mixed materials and make them liquid.

There are two kinds of these materials. Some, like glass and meltable stones, have more earth than water. Others, like wax and incense, have more water than earth.

I've described how different kinds of physical matter exist, how they change form, and how they affect each other. Now I want to explain how these changes relate to feelings and sensations. To do this, we first need to talk about physical things we can sense—like heat or cold—and the parts of our bodies that respond to them, like flesh and the part of the soul that feels pain or pleasure. But it's hard to explain the feelings without first explaining the body, and hard to explain the body without understanding feelings. So, we have to start somewhere. For now, let's assume that both the body and soul exist so we can focus on how these reactions happen.

Let's begin with a simple question: what does it mean when we say fire is hot? We can understand this by thinking about how fire cuts or burns our bodies. Fire feels sharp because its particles are tiny, move fast, and have pointed shapes. These sharp edges poke and slice into us, creating the feeling we call heat. Fire's shape—often thought of as pyramid-like—is perfect for cutting into things, which is why it creates that intense, sharp feeling of heat.

Now let's look at the opposite—cold. Cold happens when larger, heavier particles of moisture push into our bodies. These bigger particles push out the smaller ones but don't take their place. Instead, they squeeze our inner moisture into a tight, still state. When something is pressed together like this, it loses its balance and starts to fight back. That struggle creates the feeling we call shivering or trembling, and this reaction is what we call cold.

We also call things hard or soft based on how they react to touch. If something doesn't give way when you press it, it's hard. If it does give way, it's soft. A soft object usually has a small base, while hard things sit on wide, solid bases like squares, making them more stable. The tighter and denser something is, the more it resists being pushed in, which also makes it hard.

Next, let's think about what we call "light" and "heavy," and the idea of "above" and "below." It's wrong to think of the universe as having a true top and bottom, like two opposite sides. The universe is shaped like a sphere, and the center is the same distance from all sides. So, there is no true "up" or "down" in space—only the center and the outer edge. Every point on the edge is equally far from the center. That means if someone stood on the opposite side of the globe from where they started, they might call what was once "below" now "above." In a round universe, using words like "above" and "below" doesn't really make sense.

But we do still use those words, and here's why: imagine someone standing in the part of the universe where fire naturally collects. If they used a scale to lift different amounts of fire upward toward the air—something fire doesn't usually mix with—the smaller amounts would move more easily than the larger ones. When two things are pulled in the same way, the smaller one will respond faster. That's why we say the smaller one is "light" and moves "up," and the bigger one is "heavy" and moves "down."

We do the same thing here on Earth. When we lift chunks of earth or soil into the air—away from where they naturally belong—the smaller bits move more easily, so we call them light. The heavier ones resist, so we call them heavy. But in different places in the universe, what's light or heavy can change, because the main groupings of elements are in different places. What's light in one place might be heavy in another, and what's "down" in one place might be "up" in another.

What really matters is this: things naturally want to move toward other things that are like them. So when something moves toward its own kind, we say it's heavy and moving down. When it moves away from its kind, we say it's light and moving up. These are the real reasons behind how we describe weight and direction.

As for what's smooth or rough, that's easy to understand. Roughness comes from hard materials with uneven surfaces. Smoothness happens when the surface is even and tightly packed.

Now we come to something even more important—the cause of pleasure and pain. These feelings happen in the body when we experience certain sensations. Let's think about how this works.

Some materials move easily when touched. When you press them, the movement spreads through them in a circle, reaching all the parts and finally signaling the brain. That's how we sense something. But in materials that are stiff or don't move easily, that motion doesn't spread. The sensation doesn't get passed on, so the person doesn't feel anything. This happens with things like bones or hair, which are more solid. The sensations that reach us best—like sight and sound—come through body parts filled with air and fire, which are more responsive.

Now let's talk about pleasure and pain. If something touches us in a harsh or unnatural way, and it happens suddenly, we feel pain. If something harsh stops suddenly and we return to a normal state, we feel pleasure. But if the return is slow and gentle, we might not even notice it—and the same goes for a slow build-up to pain.

Some sensations, like seeing, are felt clearly but don't cause pleasure or pain. That's because our eyes naturally connect with light. When something enters the eye, it doesn't hurt, and when it goes away, we don't feel joy either. We just see more or less clearly depending on how the eye reacts to the object.

But things made of larger particles resist being moved. When they do move, they affect the entire body, leading to pleasure or pain. If they're pushed out of their natural state, we feel pain. If they return to normal, we feel pleasure.

When something is slowly drained from the body, we usually don't feel it. But when it rushes back in, we notice it, and this often brings pleasure—like when we smell a nice perfume. On the other hand, when something hurts us suddenly, like a burn or a cut, and takes a long time to heal, it causes a lot of pain. This is because our body is being forced out of its natural balance and struggles to return.

Now that we've talked about how the whole body reacts to things and what causes those reactions, let's move on to how specific parts of the body respond and what causes those feelings.

Let's start with the tongue, which we didn't fully cover earlier when discussing different kinds of liquids. Like many other body reactions, the tongue senses things through expansions and contractions. But in this case, there's also more to do with texture—how rough or smooth something is. When solid particles from what we eat or drink get into the small veins of the tongue and reach the soft, moist flesh near the heart, they dissolve and affect the veins. If they're rough and dry things out, we call them "astringent." If they're only slightly rough, we call them "harsh."

Some substances clean the tongue's surface. If they clean too harshly and even damage the flesh—like strong soaps or chemicals—they taste bitter. If the cleaning effect is gentler, and they don't have that strong, bitter bite, we call them salty. Salty things don't have the unpleasant roughness of bitterness, so we often find them more pleasant.

Things that heat up in the mouth, and in return heat the mouth itself, are light enough to rise up to the head and seem to cut through everything they touch. These are called "pungent" tastes. If these pungent particles are decayed or fermented just right and match the shapes of air and earth inside us, they make everything spin and swirl inside the tongue's tiny channels. This swirling motion creates small pockets of air surrounded by a wet coating. When those bubbles are made of clean water, they're see-through and called bubbles. When they're full of muddy liquid that's bubbling and foamy, the liquid is said to be boiling. This sharp, sour reaction is what we call "acid."

Now for the opposite kind of taste—sweetness. When particles mix well with the moisture in the mouth and feel smooth to the tongue, they help relax any tight parts and tighten the parts that are too loose. They return everything to its natural balance, and that calming effect feels pleasant to everyone. That feeling is what we call sweetness.

Now let's look at the sense of smell. Smell doesn't come in many kinds. None of the four basic elements—earth, air, fire, or water—

have a smell on their own. That's because the nose's veins are too small for heavy elements like earth and water to enter, and too wide to hold onto light ones like air and fire. So, we only smell things when something is breaking down or changing—like something decaying, melting, or evaporating. These smells come from a mix between water and air. Mist happens when air turns into water. Vapor happens when water turns into air. That means smells are thicker than air but thinner than water.

You can prove this for yourself. Try to smell something while breathing in sharply through a stuffy nose—only air goes in, not the smell. That's why smells don't have many clear types or names. We mostly just call them good or bad, based on how they make us feel. Some smells irritate us and upset the body, especially the area between the chest and the belly. Others have a calming effect and help the body return to a more balanced, pleasant state.

Let's now talk about hearing. Sound is caused when something hits the air and creates a wave. This wave travels through the air, into the ear, through the brain, and down through the blood until it reaches the soul. Hearing happens when that wave shakes us from the head down to the liver. A fast-moving sound feels sharp or high-pitched. A slow one feels low or deep. If the sound is smooth and even, we call it pleasant. If it's uneven, it sounds rough. A strong sound is loud; a weak one is quiet. I'll talk more about how different sounds combine into music later.

Now let's talk about color, which is another thing we sense. Color is like a flame that comes from objects and touches our eyes. The small particles that hit our eyes come in different sizes. Some are bigger than our visual rays, some smaller, and some just the right size.

If the particles are the same size as the parts of our eyes, we can't see them—they're invisible, like clear glass. If they're larger, they squeeze and tighten our visual ray, and if they're smaller, they stretch it out. This is similar to how hot and cold affect our skin or how sour and spicy things affect the tongue.

White makes our vision stretch, and black makes it tighten. Bright, flashing light happens when a strong kind of fire enters the eye and melts the surface slightly, making us cry. The inner fire of the eye meets the outer fire of the light, and they mix together to form different colors.

One kind of fire enters gently without flashing. When this kind of fire mixes with the eye's moisture, it makes a color like blood—we call that red. When red mixes with white and a bright shine, the result is a golden-brown color called auburn. If red mixes with black and white, we get purple. When the mixture is heated and black is more fully blended, we get a darker color called umber.

Flame color comes from mixing auburn with grayish brown. Pale yellow comes from mixing white with auburn. When bright white light hits full black, it can create deep blue. If blue mixes with white, we get light blue. If flame color mixes with black, we get greenish colors like leek green.

These are just a few of the colors made by mixing other colors in different ways. But anyone trying to explain exactly how each color is formed, using experiments alone, will run into trouble. Human minds aren't equipped to fully understand or recreate the work of the divine. Only a god could perfectly combine and separate things this way. People can try, but we'll never fully succeed.

So now we've laid out the basic materials—different causes and effects—that will help us understand the rest of the world. These causes are like the wood a builder uses. Before we continue, let's quickly go back to where we started and then try to bring everything together with a fitting conclusion to this story.

As I mentioned earlier, everything was once in chaos. Then God brought order by giving everything its proper balance and harmony—

both in itself and in relation to everything else. Before this, nothing had any real shape or proportion. Things like fire, water, and the other elements didn't even deserve to have names yet. God was the first to organize them, and from them, He built the universe as one living being that contained every other living thing—both mortal and immortal.

God personally created the divine part, but He gave His children the task of creating the mortal parts. Following His example, they took the immortal soul He gave them and built a body to carry it. Inside this body, they placed another kind of soul—a mortal one—that would be affected by strong feelings. These included pleasure (which tempts us to do wrong), pain (which keeps us from doing right), and emotions like anger, fear, and hope, which can all mislead us. Along with those, they added instincts and intense desires, mixing them all according to certain laws—and that's how humans were made.

To keep the divine part of the soul as pure as possible, they gave the mortal part a separate home in the body. They placed the neck in between like a barrier, separating the head from the chest. The mortal soul was placed in the chest. Since this soul had two sides—one strong and brave, the other more basic and wild—they split the chest into two parts, like separate rooms in a house. A dividing wall, the diaphragm, was placed between them.

The stronger side of the mortal soul, the part full of courage and drive, was put closer to the head—between the diaphragm and the neck—so that reason could keep it in check. This part was meant to support reason by helping calm down wild desires when they wouldn't listen on their own.

The heart, where all the blood flows and where the veins come together, was placed in this upper chest area to act like a guard. Whenever reason detected danger or trouble—either from outside or from the body's own desires—it could signal the heart. Then the whole body would be ready to follow those commands and defend itself.

Since excitement and fear cause the heart to heat up and beat quickly, the gods placed the lungs next to it. The lungs are soft and full of air pockets, like a sponge, so they could take in breath and drinks to cool the heart and ease the heat. They wrapped the lungs around the heart to act as a cushion. That way, when emotions ran high, the heart could press against something soft, which would calm it down and make it more ready to work with reason instead of against it.

The lower part of the soul—the part that craves food, drink, and other bodily needs—was placed between the diaphragm and the belly. This part of the body was designed like a feeding stall or manger, to keep that wild, animal-like desire full and calm. The gods tied this part down low and far from the brain, so it wouldn't interfere with the quiet, rational thinking happening up top.

Knowing that this lower part wouldn't understand reason and would constantly chase illusions, the gods gave it the liver to help keep it in check. The liver was made smooth, solid, shiny, and sweet, but with a little bitterness too. The idea was that when the mind created thoughts or images, they would reflect onto the liver like in a mirror. If a bad or scary thought came, it would stir up the bitter part of the liver and send it through the whole organ, making it twist, shrivel, and hurt. That would scare the desires into calming down. But if the thought was peaceful, it would use the liver's sweet side to smooth everything out, relax the organ, and make that part of the soul feel happy and restful. In this peaceful state, people could even dream and get hints about the future—because the lower soul doesn't have reason, but it can still receive visions.

This is why the gods gave us prophecy not through our intelligence, but through our less rational parts. No one receives true inspiration while completely in their right mind. The person must either be dreaming or in a trance, disconnected from normal thinking. And to understand what those visions mean, the person has to return to their senses first. That's why there are interpreters, sometimes called prophets, who help explain dreams and inspired messages—they translate the confusing signs into real meaning. So, the true prophet is not the person who sees the vision, but the one who can explain it.

The liver gives us these visions most clearly while we're alive. After death, it becomes dark and unclear, and its messages are too mixed up to understand. Next to it, on the left side, is the spleen. It was designed to keep the liver clean and bright, like a cloth that wipes down a mirror. When the body gets unhealthy, the spleen absorbs the waste and grows swollen. When the body gets better, the spleen shrinks back to normal.

Now, about the soul—what's divine and what's mortal, where they are, and why they're separated—if God agrees with what we've said, then we can trust we're close to the truth. Even if we can't be completely sure, it's still a reasonable explanation and worth exploring further.

Next, let's look at how the rest of the body was made.

The gods knew humans would overeat and overdrink, driven by greed. To keep us from dying quickly because of this, they created the lower belly—a special area to hold all the extra food and drink. They made the intestines twist and turn so food wouldn't pass through too fast and make us constantly hungry. Without this, our cravings might have kept us from ever focusing on higher things like music or wisdom, which are the most divine parts of life.

As for bones, flesh, and the rest of the body's structure, everything started with the marrow. The marrow connects the soul to the body—it's like the root of human life. To make the marrow, God took the finest, straightest building blocks of the elements—those that made up fire, water, air, and earth—and mixed them in perfect balance. This special mixture became the "seed" of the human race. Into this seed, God planted the soul.

He shaped the marrow in different forms depending on the type of soul it would carry. The part meant to hold the divine soul was made completely round and was called the brain. When the body was finished, this part would be placed in the head. The part meant to carry the mortal soul was made longer and round, and also called marrow. Around all these, God began shaping the rest of the body, first wrapping the marrow in a strong outer layer—the bones.

God made bone in this way: He took clean, fine earth, mixed it with marrow, and shaped it. Then, He heated it in fire, cooled it in water, and repeated this process several times. This made the material strong, so it wouldn't break down in either fire or water. From this, He shaped a round shell of bone to protect the brain, leaving only a small opening. He also created the bones of the neck and spine by stacking them like gears from the head down the back. This hard shell was meant to protect the body's core, so He added joints using a different type of material that allowed movement.

But since bone by itself is too stiff and could easily crack with heat or cold, He added muscles and flesh. Muscles helped connect everything, especially around the spine, so the body could bend and move. Flesh gave protection against the cold in winter and heat in summer. It also cushioned the body from impacts, like padding, and helped keep it cool by releasing moisture in the summer or warm by holding heat in the winter. To make flesh, God blended earth, water, and fire, adding a touch of sour and salty mix to make it soft and moist.

He created muscles by combining bone with firmer flesh, giving them a yellow color. Muscles were firmer than flesh but softer than bone. He wrapped bones and marrow with muscles, then covered everything with flesh. The more sensitive bones were given a thin covering of flesh, while less sensitive ones were wrapped in thicker layers. Around joints, He used just enough flesh to avoid making movement hard or dulling the body's sensitivity or thinking.

Places like the thighs, arms, and hips, which don't have joints, were packed with more flesh because they have less awareness. On the other hand, bones connected to more active and aware parts of the soul had less flesh. The tongue is an exception—it's made of flesh for sensing taste. But overall, mixing thick flesh and bone with high sensitivity wasn't possible. If it had been, the head would have had both strong protection and sharp awareness. Humans might have lived longer and healthier lives. But the creators chose to give us shorter but better lives instead of long but worse ones. That's why the head has a thin bone covering, without extra muscle or joints, so it could stay sharp and aware, even though it's more fragile.

God placed muscles at the bottom of the head in a ring around the neck, connecting them to the jaw and spreading them through the body to link all the limbs. He made the mouth with lips, teeth, and a tongue to serve two needs—eating, which is necessary for life, and speaking, which expresses thought and is the highest purpose. The mouth lets food in and lets speech out, like a river flowing from the mind.

The head couldn't be left bare because of the cold and heat, but it also couldn't be buried under too much flesh, which would dull its senses. So, the flesh was partly dried out, leaving behind a thick layer— this became the skin. It grew with help from the brain's moisture and formed a covering over the head. Where the bones of the skull join together (the sutures), the moisture rose and sealed the skin, creating a knot at the top of the head. The number of these sutures depended on how much the soul's energy and the body's nourishment pushed against each other—more conflict meant more sutures.

Then, divine fire poked holes through the skin, and moisture leaked out. The purer part escaped, but the thicker part stayed under the skin. Since it was too slow to evaporate, it curled under the skin and took root. That's how hair was formed—it's like fine, leathery threads. The cold air compressed and hardened it as it separated from the skin. Hair was placed on the head as a light cover to protect the brain from heat and cold without blocking our senses.

Where the bones, skin, and muscles came together at the fingers, a tough layer formed. It was made from all three parts, dried out into one solid surface. God allowed this to happen because He knew that men would someday give rise to women and animals, and some of those animals would need claws or nails. So, He added the beginnings of nails at the ends of our limbs. That's why skin, hair, and nails grow at the outer tips of the body.

Now that all the parts of the body were in place, God had to fix one more problem. Since human life is made of breath and fire, people would eventually break down and die. To slow this down, the gods created another kind of creature by mixing human nature with other forms. This gave us plants and trees and all the crops we now grow. At first, only wild plants existed; cultivated ones came later.

Anything that has life is a living being. Plants are living things too, even though they don't have thought or reason. They have a different kind of soul that lives between the stomach and the belly. This soul doesn't think or make choices—it only feels pleasure, pain, and desires. It doesn't notice or reflect on anything. It stays in one place and doesn't move by itself, but it still counts as alive because it grows and responds to what's around it.

After the higher powers made all living things that would serve as food for us, they designed our bodies like gardens, cutting channels through them so fluids could flow like water through pipes. First, they made two hidden veins running down the back where the skin and flesh meet. These veins went along the spine on both the left and right sides, wrapping around the area where the body produces life. This helped nutrients flow smoothly from the top of the body to the rest, spreading nourishment evenly.

Next, they split the veins in the head and crisscrossed them. Veins from the right side went to the left and vice versa. This helped hold the head in place, since there were no sinews (tough tissues) at the top of the skull, and it allowed feelings and sensations to travel across the whole body.

Now about the body's internal "water system." It helps to understand that smaller particles can pass through larger ones, but not the other way around. Fire, having the smallest parts, can move through earth, water, and air without being stopped. Our stomach is similar—it can hold food and drink, but it can't trap fire or air because their particles are too small.

So, the gods designed a special system using fire and air to move moisture from the stomach into the veins. They created a net-like structure made of fire, with two smaller spinning sections made of air at the front. One of these was connected to the lungs through the windpipe, and the other led into the stomach. The airways from the nose also joined this system, so that even when the mouth wasn't in use, breathing through the nose could still help.

This system allowed air to flow in and out of the body. The fire bound within the body moved with the air, helping to break down food and push nutrients into the veins. This movement of air in and out is what we call breathing.

Breathing works like this: since there's no such thing as empty space, when you breathe out, you push the air around you, and that air pushes other air until it circles back to replace what you breathed out. This cycle—air moving in and out—is why we have constant breath.

Inside the body, the hottest part is around the veins and blood. It's like a built-in fire. When this heat moves toward the skin or the mouth, it pulls in cooler air from the opposite direction. This back-and-forth flow is what creates the rhythm of breathing in and out.

This same idea helps explain how suction cups work, how we drink, how balls roll, and even how lightning and static electricity happen. There's no magical "pulling"—it's all about pressure, movement, and how objects replace one another when pushed.

So, the main idea is that the fire inside helps cut and digest food. As you breathe, fire and air rise together and break the food into smaller parts, which then get pushed into the veins and carried throughout the body. This keeps everything nourished.

All the different kinds of fruits, plants, and vegetables we eat get mixed with each other and create all sorts of colors. The color red appears the most because fire cuts into wet substances and leaves a red mark. That's why blood—which is the liquid moving through our veins—is red. It feeds the flesh and fills up every part of our body.

The way our bodies fill up with food and get rid of waste follows the same rule as everything else in nature—similar things are pulled toward each other. The elements around us constantly wear us down and take away parts of us, sending similar pieces to match what's already there. Even our blood, which is spread throughout our bodies like stars in the sky, moves in a way that mirrors how the whole universe moves. Every little part inside us tries to return to where it belongs. If more is lost than is replaced, we shrink or get weaker. But if more is added than is taken away, we grow and become stronger.

When we're young, the body is made of new, fresh shapes—tiny triangles that fit together tightly, like the wooden base of a brand-new boat. Everything is soft and delicate because it's freshly made from marrow and fed by milk. When we eat and drink, the food is broken into triangles that are older and weaker than the young ones in our bodies. These weaker triangles get broken down by the stronger ones, which helps us grow as the body absorbs more and more matching pieces.

But over time, those strong inner triangles get damaged from repeated use. They can't break down food anymore and instead get broken down themselves by the new material. This is how all living things start to age and slowly fall apart. When the connections holding our body together finally break under the strain of life, the soul is gently released, happy to leave. A natural death like this feels peaceful. But if death is caused by injury or illness, it's painful and rough. Death from old age, though, is calm and even pleasant because it happens the way nature intended.

It's easy to see where illness begins. Our bodies are made of four basic elements—earth, fire, water, and air. If any of these go out of balance, or one of them ends up in the wrong place, or even changes to the wrong version of itself, sickness happens. If something cool becomes hot, or light becomes heavy, or wet becomes dry, our balance is thrown off. A body stays healthy only when things are added or taken away in the right way and amount. If this balance is broken, the result is sickness and all kinds of problems.

There's another way to understand illness by looking at how things inside us are built. Marrow, bones, muscles, and tendons are made from those same four elements. Blood is too, in a different way. Most diseases start when these things are built out of order. Normally, blood should turn into fibers, fibers into clots, clots into flesh and tendons. The sticky, rich material from the flesh not only connects it to the bones but also helps bones grow around the marrow. Since bones are dense, they release pure, smooth particles that drip like dew into the marrow and nourish it.

When this process happens in the right order, we stay healthy. But when it goes backward, illness begins. Rotting flesh sends waste back into the bloodstream. This adds too much of the wrong kinds of blood, which mix with air and carry bitterness, acid, salt, and strange colors. This causes bile, serum, and phlegm. These infected fluids no longer nourish the body. Instead, they spread everywhere, out of control, attacking the body's natural balance and breaking it down.

The oldest and hardest parts of the flesh become black and bitter. They damage the healthy parts still left. Sometimes the bitterness turns sour. Sometimes it mixes with blood and turns red or greenish. When the burning inside the body breaks down fresh flesh, it mixes in more colors like brown or yellow. All these problems—whether black, red, green, or sour—are often just called "bile," though there are different types based on color.

Now, some types of serum (the watery part of blood) are harmless. But others, made from bad bile and salt, are dangerous and are known as acid phlegm. When soft flesh breaks down in the presence of air, it can create tiny bubbles of foam. Alone, they're too small to see, but together they look white. This is known as white phlegm. The leftover liquid from this process turns into sweat, tears, and other fluids the body releases to stay clean.

All of this becomes a problem when blood is no longer refreshed in a natural way—by food and drink—but instead comes from harmful sources. When parts of the flesh fall apart due to sickness, it's not so bad if the base structure is still okay. Then recovery is still possible. But if the part that connects the flesh to the bones gets sick—if it stops feeding the bones and holding things together—then it dries out and becomes rough and salty. The flesh crumbles away from the bones, and the sinews are left exposed and soaked in salty fluid. Some of this damaged flesh gets back into the bloodstream and makes everything worse.

If all that sounds bad, it gets even worse when the bones can't breathe properly through the dense flesh. They grow moldy, hot, and infected. They stop receiving nutrients. The natural order is flipped around. Bone starts turning into food, food into flesh, flesh into blood—and the whole system breaks down. But the very worst happens when the marrow itself goes wrong—either there's too much or too little. That's when the body loses all control, and the most deadly diseases appear.

Some diseases come from three main sources: wind, phlegm, and bile. When the lungs, which send air throughout the body, get blocked by mucus, the air can't flow evenly. Some parts don't get enough air and start to rot, while others get too much and swell, causing damage. This trapped air can move through the body and settle in the area around the chest, creating painful diseases and heavy sweating.

Sometimes, gases form inside the body and can't escape, which causes pain just like when outside air gets stuck. The worst pain happens when these gases reach the tendons and veins in the shoulders, causing swelling that twists and pulls the tendons. This results in conditions like tetanus, where the body locks up. These illnesses are hard to treat, but sometimes a fever helps the body fight them.

White phlegm is harmful when it stays inside the body, especially because of air bubbles. If it can connect to the outside air, it's not as dangerous. Instead, it causes skin problems like leprosy. But when white phlegm mixes with black bile and spreads through the brain—the most important part of us—it can cause serious illness. If this happens during sleep, it's not as bad. But when it attacks someone who's awake, it's harder to heal and is called a "sacred disease" because it affects such an important area.

Another type of phlegm, which is sour and salty, causes illnesses like colds and congestion. These take many forms depending on where the phlegm goes in the body.

Inflammation, or swelling in the body, is usually caused by heat and burning from bile. If bile escapes the body, it boils and causes swelling. But if it gets stuck, especially when mixed with healthy blood, it causes even more inflammation. The bile upsets the balance of fibers in the blood, which normally keep the blood from getting too thin or too thick. If the bile comes in slowly, the fibers make it solid and cold, causing chills. But if the bile floods in with heat and overwhelms the fibers, it can reach the marrow, burn the body's deepest parts, and release the soul, leading to death.

If the bile isn't that strong, the body might survive. Then, the bile is pushed into the lower or upper stomach and exits the body through diarrhea or dysentery. These diseases show how the body fights back when it's in trouble.

Different kinds of fever come from different imbalances in the elements. Too much fire causes constant heat and fever. Too much air leads to daily fevers. If water is the problem, fevers show up every third day. When the issue is earth, which moves the slowest, fevers come every four days and are the hardest to get rid of.

Just like the body can become sick, the mind can also suffer from illness, which shows up as either madness or ignorance. When someone is in extreme pain or joy, they lose control and can't think or act clearly. Their emotions take over, and they can't use reason.

Sometimes people are overwhelmed by physical desires—like someone who has too much seed near their spine. Their body is full of intense urges and pleasures, which make their mind confused. Even though they seem to act badly on purpose, it's really a disease caused by the body. People think they're just being immoral, but in truth, they're sick.

This shows how strong emotions—especially from love and desire—can confuse the soul. The body's moisture and looseness can stir up these feelings, making it hard to control them. People aren't bad by choice. They're made that way through poor health and poor teaching, which they didn't choose. So we shouldn't blame them, but instead try to help through better education and care.

Pain works the same way. Harmful substances like bitter phlegm or bile move through the body and mix with the soul's natural movements. When these toxic substances reach any of the soul's main areas, they cause things like anger, sadness, fear, forgetfulness, and stupidity. If people grow up with bad governments or harmful messages, and they never get proper teaching, then they become bad through no fault of their own. In those cases, it's the teachers, not the students, who are at fault.

Even though we can't always avoid these problems, we should still try to improve ourselves through learning and practice, so we can avoid vice and grow in virtue.

It's also important to talk about how to keep the mind and body healthy. Goodness is always connected to beauty, and beauty comes from balance. A healthy person must have a balanced relationship between mind and body. We can notice small imbalances, like a leg that's too long, but we often miss the most important ones—when the mind and body are out of sync.

For example, a strong soul in a weak body, or a small soul in a big body, throws everything off. When they don't match, it's not only unattractive but also harmful. The person may struggle with simple tasks, feel pain, or fall into harmful behavior. A powerful soul in a weak body can wear the body out, especially if that person focuses too much on study or argument. On the other hand, a strong body with a weak soul can lead to a dull and ignorant mind because the physical desires take over.

The best way to avoid these extremes is to make sure the soul and body work together. Don't move the body without involving the soul, and don't engage the soul without giving the body activity. For example, a mathematician or scholar should also exercise, and an athlete should also study and reflect.

Each part of us should be cared for in a balanced way, just like the universe keeps its balance. Our bodies are affected by heating, cooling, drying, and moistening. If someone lets their body stay still for too long, it becomes vulnerable. But if they keep it moving gently and regularly, they protect it from harm.

The best kind of movement is the kind we create ourselves, like walking or stretching. That's closest to how thought and the universe move. The second-best is gentle motion, like traveling by boat. The least effective is medical treatment that forces movement, like using strong drugs. Unless an illness is truly dangerous, medicine often makes it worse. Every body, like every life, has a natural limit. The shapes that make us were designed to last only a certain time. If we try to stretch that time with drugs, we may do more harm than good.

So it's better to manage health with routine and care—not with harsh medicines. We should live in a way that helps the body heal itself rather than forcing it to fight back.

Let's stop talking about the body for now and focus on how people can train themselves to live with reason. The most important part of this is making sure that the part of us doing the training is the best and most suited for the job. Going deep into this would take a lot of time, but here's a quick summary.

I've said before that we have three parts in our soul, and each one needs movement to stay strong. If any part of the soul stops moving, it becomes weak. The part that gets regular use becomes stronger. So, it's important to keep all parts of the soul balanced and active.

We should remember that the highest part of our soul is a gift from the gods. It lives in the head and is the part that connects us to the heavens. It pulls us upward, because we're not just from Earth—we have a higher origin. That's why our bodies were made to stand upright, with our heads pointing toward the sky.

When someone spends all their energy chasing desires like power or pleasure, their thoughts become focused only on mortal things. They act like they're fully human but forget the divine part of themselves. But someone who loves wisdom and truth, and uses their mind more than anything else, starts to think in an immortal way. If they reach real truth, their thoughts become godlike. And as much as it's possible for humans, they begin to live like an immortal being. By constantly growing this divine part inside themselves, they find real happiness.

To take care of something, you must give it the right kind of movement and nourishment. The divine part of us thrives when we think deeply and try to understand how the universe moves. If we do this, we can repair the confusion in our minds that we're born with. By learning how the universe works, we bring our thinking in line with it, and we restore our natural state. That's how people can reach the best life possible—one that reflects the life the gods intended for us.

Now that we've talked about the universe and how humans were created, we can briefly look at how other animals came to be. This will help bring everything together more completely.

The idea is that some people who lived badly in their first lives—cowards or those who acted unfairly—were reborn as women. This is also when sexual desire was created. The gods gave men and women different reproductive systems so they could have children.

In men, the pathway that carries liquid from the lungs to the bladder was designed to reach the spinal marrow—what we've called the source of seed. This seed has life, and once it connects to breath, it creates a strong urge to reproduce. That's why the male reproductive organ can sometimes act on its own, not listening to reason, and trying to take control.

The same thing happens in women. Their womb, or uterus, acts like a living creature inside them. When it stays empty for too long, it becomes restless and upset. It moves around the body, blocking the breath and causing all kinds of illnesses. When the man and woman finally come together and the seed is planted like a seed in soil, small living beings begin to form inside the womb. They grow until they are ready to be born, and that's how new life begins.

That's how the female sex was created. Birds came from people who were light-hearted and innocent. They looked up at the sky often, hoping to learn through sight alone. Because of this, they were transformed into birds and grew feathers instead of hair.

Land animals came from people who never thought about the heavens or philosophy. They followed only their instincts and the feelings in their chest. Because of this, they were drawn toward the ground. Their bodies changed so that they walked on all fours, with their heads facing downward. Their skulls became long or oddly shaped because their thinking had been neglected.

The most foolish of all became creatures that crawl, like snakes. Since they no longer needed legs, they were made without them and lived flat on the ground.

Sea creatures were made from the most ignorant and disobedient souls. These souls had done so much wrong that they were no longer allowed to breathe air. Instead, they were given the sea as their home and had to breathe in muddy water. That's how fish, oysters, and other sea animals came to be. They were sent far away, as punishment for their deep ignorance.

These are the rules that still govern how souls can move between different types of animals, changing based on how wise or foolish they become.

And with that, we've finished talking about how the universe was formed. It's now filled with all kinds of life—both mortal and immortal—and it has become a living, visible being. The world is like a god we can see: the greatest, the best, the most beautiful, and complete. It is the one and only heaven, perfectly made.

The End

Gorgias

Plato

Foreword

Plato's Gorgias is one of the most penetrating and provocative dialogues in the history of Western philosophy, offering a powerful critique of rhetoric, power, morality, and the nature of the good life. Set in dramatic conversation between Socrates and several prominent Athenian figures—Gorgias, Polus, and Callicles—this dialogue presents an intellectual contest that explores some of the most fundamental questions of human existence: What is justice? Is it better to suffer wrong or to commit it? Can power without virtue lead to happiness? What is the purpose of speech, persuasion, and public life? Though the dialogue is ancient, its relevance remains undiminished, as it probes the ethical underpinnings of politics, media, law, and education—domains that continue to dominate modern public life.

Written during the early-middle period of Plato's philosophical career, Gorgias marks a transition from his earlier Socratic dialogues, which focus on elenchus (refutation through questioning), toward more developed metaphysical and ethical positions. Here, Plato presents Socrates not only as a relentless questioner but as a philosopher who begins to articulate a vision of the just soul and the morally ordered life. The dialogue pits this vision against the pragmatic, relativistic, and power-centered views of his interlocutors, exposing the tensions between appearance and reality, persuasion and truth, might and right. Through this clash, Plato's Gorgias presents not only a powerful philosophical argument but a dramatic, literary work that showcases his mastery of style, character, and intellectual drama.

This introduction provides a comprehensive framework for engaging deeply with Plato's Gorgias. By exploring its historical context, examining its central arguments and philosophical themes, and considering its literary structure and enduring influence, readers will be equipped to approach the dialogue with both appreciation and critical insight. Whether read as a critique of sophistry, a defense of ethical living, or a meditation on the soul's ultimate destiny, Gorgias remains an indispensable text for anyone seeking to understand not only Plato's thought but the enduring philosophical challenges of power, persuasion, and justice in human life.

Historical Context and the Figure of Gorgias

To appreciate Gorgias, it is essential to understand the historical and intellectual context of its composition. Plato likely wrote the dialogue around 380 BCE, during a period of political instability and moral reflection in Athens following the Peloponnesian War (431–404 BCE). The war had devastated the Athenian empire and led to the rise of oligarchic factions, widespread corruption, and a loss of civic confidence in democratic institutions. The execution of Socrates in 399 BCE, on charges of impiety and corrupting the youth, further marked a turning point in Athenian intellectual life. It was against this backdrop of disillusionment with traditional politics, and in the wake of his mentor's death, that Plato developed his vision of philosophy as the path to truth and justice, in contrast to the sophistry and rhetoric that he believed had corrupted Athenian public life.

The character of Gorgias in the dialogue represents one of the most prominent and influential sophists of the 5th century BCE. A native of Leontini in Sicily, Gorgias was renowned for his rhetorical skill, elaborate prose style, and theoretical reflections on the power of speech. In his extant works—such as the Encomium of Helen—he defends the ability of rhetoric to shape belief, move emotions, and construct realities. For Gorgias, rhetoric is a technê, a craft or art, capable of achieving practical success in the law courts and political assemblies. His approach reflects the broader sophistic movement of the time, which emphasized relativism, pragmatic knowledge, and the power of persuasion over philosophical inquiry into truth.

In Plato's dialogue, Gorgias is portrayed as a courteous but evasive interlocutor. He initially asserts that rhetoric is the art of persuasion, especially in matters of justice, but under Socrates' persistent questioning, he is led to concede that rhetoric can also be used unjustly and without true knowledge. While Gorgias attempts to maintain a neutral stance about the moral use of rhetoric, Socrates forces the issue: can a craft that produces persuasion without knowledge be considered good or even legitimate? This line of inquiry opens the way for deeper philosophical investigations into the relationship between speech and truth, power and morality, and the nature of the human soul.

Power, Justice, and the Soul: The Philosophical Core

At the heart of Gorgias lies a powerful philosophical confrontation between two fundamentally opposed views of life. On one side stands Socrates, who champions the life of justice, self-discipline, and philosophical reflection. On the other stand Polus and Callicles, two ambitious and politically-minded young men who argue that the pursuit of power, success, and gratification is the natural and desirable goal of human existence. Through their arguments, Plato presents a series of increasingly radical and provocative claims, culminating in Socrates' defense of the idea that it is better to suffer injustice than to commit it, and that the unjust soul is ultimately more wretched than the victim of injustice.

Polus, stepping in after Gorgias' retreat, defends rhetoric as a means of achieving power and success, dismissing Socrates' moral objections. He argues that those who can escape punishment through clever speech are happier and more successful than those who submit to justice. Socrates dismantles this view by appealing to the nature of punishment as a form of moral cure. Just as a sick body benefits from painful medical treatment, the diseased soul benefits from punishment because it restores moral order. Therefore, those who commit injustice and evade punishment are not truly happy—they remain corrupted and sick in soul. This redefinition of punishment as therapy rather than retribution marks a profound philosophical innovation in Plato's moral psychology.

The most intense confrontation comes with Callicles, whose arguments represent the most explicit rejection of conventional morality. Callicles asserts that nature—not law or custom—defines justice. In nature, the strong dominate the weak, and true virtue lies in the assertion of power and pleasure by those who are superior. For Callicles, laws and moral norms are artificial constraints invented by the weak to restrain the strong. He advocates a life of hedonism and domination, celebrating unrestrained desire and political ambition as the path to fulfillment. Socrates counters with a sustained critique of this view, arguing that such a life leads to disorder, dissatisfaction, and spiritual ruin. He insists that a just and ordered soul, governed by reason and discipline, is the true condition for happiness.

Socrates' closing myth in Gorgias—concerning the judgment of souls after death—provides a powerful allegorical conclusion to the dialogue. Drawing on Orphic and Pythagorean traditions, Plato presents a vision of cosmic justice in which every soul is held accountable for its actions, stripped of earthly reputation and judged according to its true moral state. This eschatological framework reinforces the dialogue's central thesis: the state of the soul matters more than appearances, reputation, or worldly power. Socrates warns that those who pursue pleasure and power at the expense of justice will face eternal consequences, while those who practice philosophy and virtue will attain purification and ultimate fulfillment.

Literary Form, Enduring Legacy, and Contemporary Relevance

Plato's Gorgias is not merely a philosophical treatise—it is also a dramatic and literary masterpiece. The dialogue's structure is carefully composed, moving from the relatively calm and courteous exchange with Gorgias to the increasingly confrontational and emotionally charged arguments with Polus and Callicles. This dramatic progression mirrors the unfolding philosophical depth of the dialogue, as the stakes move from a discussion of rhetoric to a debate about the very meaning of life, virtue, and the soul's destiny. Plato's skill in character development, rhetorical pacing, and dramatic irony lends the dialogue a vitality and realism that continue to captivate readers across millennia.

The influence of Gorgias has been profound and far-reaching. In antiquity, it shaped early conceptions of philosophy as a moral and spiritual discipline distinct from sophistry and rhetorical performance. In the Middle Ages and Renaissance, its critiques of hedonism and political ambition informed Christian moral thought and humanist ethics. In the modern era, philosophers such as Nietzsche, Arendt, Foucault, and Habermas have engaged with the issues it raises—especially concerning the relationship between truth, power, and speech. Contemporary political theory, media criticism, and ethics continue to wrestle with the problems of persuasion versus truth, image versus reality, and strength versus justice.

For modern readers, Gorgias remains strikingly relevant. In an age saturated by rhetoric—whether in politics, media, advertising, or digital discourse—Plato's questions about the ethical use of speech, the manipulation of belief, and the temptation of power are more pressing than ever. The dialogue invites us to consider whether our public discourse serves truth or merely manipulates opinion; whether our political institutions cultivate justice or reward dominance; and whether we ourselves live in pursuit of appearances or cultivate the integrity of the soul.

Ultimately, Gorgias offers a timeless meditation on the ethical foundations of life in community. It challenges us to reflect not only on what we believe but on how we live, what we value, and what kind of human beings we aspire to become. By confronting the seductive power of rhetoric, the ambition of unchecked desire, and the illusions of worldly success, Plato calls us—through Socrates' voice—to turn inward, examine our lives, and pursue the well-being of the soul as the highest form of happiness. In doing so, Gorgias affirms philosophy's enduring mission: to speak truth in the face of power, to live justly in the midst of corruption, and to seek wisdom in a world too often driven by ignorance and illusion.

Characters

Characters: Callicles, Socrates, Chaerephon, Gorgias, Polus

Scene: Callicles' house

Gorgias

Callicles: They say a wise man might be late to a fight, but never to a feast.

Socrates: So are we late to a feast?

Callicles: Yes, and a really good one. Gorgias just gave us a great show.

Socrates: That's not my fault, Callicles. It's Chaerephon's. He made us stay too long in the marketplace.

Chaerephon: Don't worry, Socrates. Since I caused the delay, I'll fix it too. Gorgias is my friend, and I'll ask him to give the show again—either now or later if you prefer.

Callicles: Wait, does Socrates want to hear Gorgias?

Chaerephon: Yes, that's why we came.

Callicles: Come inside, then. Gorgias is staying here with me. He'll show you.

Socrates: That sounds good, but will he also answer questions? I want to know what kind of skill he teaches and what it's all about. He can save the full show for another time if he wants.

Callicles: Just ask him, Socrates. He said earlier that anyone here could ask him anything, and he'd answer.

Socrates: That's lucky! Chaerephon, can you ask him for me?

Chaerephon: What should I ask?

Socrates: Ask who he is.

Chaerephon: What do you mean?

Socrates: I mean ask him the kind of question that would get the answer "a shoemaker" if he made shoes. Get it?

Chaerephon: Got it. I'll ask. Gorgias, is it true, like Callicles said, that you'll answer any question?

Gorgias: That's true, Chaerephon. I said so just a moment ago. And honestly, it's been years since anyone asked me something new.

Chaerephon: Then you must be really good at answering.

Gorgias: You can test me and see.

Polus: Or you can test me instead, Chaerephon. Gorgias has been talking for a while—he might be tired.

Chaerephon: So, Polus, do you think you can answer better than Gorgias?

Polus: Does it matter, as long as I answer well enough?

Chaerephon: Not at all—you can answer if you want.

Polus: Go ahead, ask.

Chaerephon: Here's the question: if Gorgias had the same skill as his brother Herodicus, what would we call him? Wouldn't we give him the same title as his brother?

Polus: Of course.

Chaerephon: So, we'd call him a doctor?

Polus: Yes.

Chaerephon: And if he had the talent of the artist Aristophon, or his brother Polygnotus, what then?

Polus: Then he'd be a painter, obviously.

Chaerephon: So what do we call him now? What is his actual skill?

Polus: Chaerephon, there are lots of skills that people learn through experience. Experience helps guide our actions wisely, while inexperience leads to random results. Everyone gets good at different things, and the best people are good at the most important ones. Gorgias is one of those best people, and his skill is one of the greatest.

Socrates: Gorgias, it seems Polus is great at making speeches, but he hasn't really answered the question Chaerephon asked.

Gorgias: What do you mean, Socrates?

Socrates: He didn't actually say what Gorgias' skill is.

Gorgias: Then why don't you ask him yourself?

Socrates: I'd rather ask you, if you're willing to answer. From what Polus said, it sounds like he's more focused on public speaking than careful discussion.

Polus: What makes you say that?

Socrates: Because when Chaerephon asked what Gorgias' skill was, you gave a long speech about how great it is. But you never actually said what it is.

Polus: Didn't I say it was the finest skill?

Socrates: Sure, but that wasn't the question. No one asked how good it was—we asked what it was, and what Gorgias should be called. So could you give a short, clear answer like you did at first? Or better yet—Gorgias, let me ask you directly: what do you call yourself, and what is your skill?

Gorgias: My skill is rhetoric, Socrates.

Socrates: Then I should call you a rhetorician?

Gorgias: Yes, and a good one too, as I proudly claim—like a line from Homer.

Socrates: I'd like to call you that.

Gorgias: Then please do.

Socrates: And do you teach other people to become rhetoricians too?

Gorgias: Yes, that's exactly what I do—not just here in Athens, but everywhere I go.

Socrates: Will you keep answering my questions this way, like we're doing now? We can save the long speeches Polus was giving for another time. Will you stick to short answers like you promised?

Gorgias: Some answers naturally take longer, but I'll try to keep them short. Part of my skill is being able to speak briefly when needed.

Socrates: That's perfect, Gorgias. Let's keep it short for now, and you can show off the longer version another time.

Gorgias: Alright, I will answer—and you'll probably say you've never heard anyone say so much with so few words.

Socrates: Excellent. Since you say you're a rhetorician and that you train others to be the same, let me ask you: what exactly does rhetoric deal with? Like, if I asked what weaving is about, you'd say it's about making clothes, right?

Gorgias: Right.

Socrates: And music deals with creating melodies?

Gorgias: Yes.

Socrates: Wow, Gorgias, I admire how short and clear your answers are.

Gorgias: Thanks, Socrates. I think I'm pretty good at that.

Socrates: Glad to hear it. So tell me, what is rhetoric about?

Gorgias: It's about speech.

Socrates: What kind of speech? Like the kind that teaches sick people how to get better?

Gorgias: No.

Socrates: So rhetoric doesn't deal with all types of speech?

Gorgias: Definitely not.

Socrates: But rhetoric helps people speak well, right?

Gorgias: Yes.

Socrates: And it helps them understand what they're talking about?

Gorgias: Of course.

Socrates: But doesn't the skill of medicine also help people understand and talk about illnesses?

Gorgias: Yes, it does.

Socrates: Then medicine also involves speech?

Gorgias: Yes.

Socrates: And doesn't physical training involve speech about health and fitness?

Gorgias: That's true.

Socrates: The same goes for other skills, too—they all include some kind of speech related to what they deal with.

Gorgias: Clearly.

Socrates: Then why, if you say rhetoric is the skill of speech, don't we also call medicine, fitness training, and other skills types of rhetoric?

Gorgias: Because, Socrates, those other skills involve using your hands to do things. Rhetoric doesn't use hands at all—it works entirely through speech. That's why I say rhetoric is focused on speaking.

Socrates: I'm not sure I totally get that, but maybe I will soon. Just answer me this—do you agree that there are many different arts or skills?

Gorgias: Yes.

Socrates: And most skills involve doing things, not talking much. For example, painting or sculpting—you don't need to talk much to do those jobs. I guess you'd say those aren't part of rhetoric?

Gorgias: You've understood me perfectly.

Socrates: But then there are other skills that rely almost completely on talking—like math, calculation, geometry, or even playing board games. In some of these, speaking and doing are pretty much the same. But mostly, these skills work through speech. So would you say rhetoric is one of those kinds of skills?

Gorgias: Exactly.

Socrates: Still, I don't think you really mean to call all of those things rhetoric, even though you said that rhetoric is the kind of skill that works only through speech. Someone who wanted to be difficult might say, "So you think math is rhetoric too?" But I know you don't really believe that—no more than you'd say geometry is rhetoric.

Gorgias: You're absolutely right, Socrates.

Socrates: Great. Now let's go further. Since rhetoric is one of the skills that works mostly by using speech—and since other skills also use speech—what makes rhetoric special? What kind of speech does it focus on? Let's say someone asked me, "What is math?" I'd say it's a skill that uses speech. Then they'd ask, "Speech about what?" And I'd say, "About odd and even numbers and how many there are."

If they asked, "What about calculation?" I'd say it also uses speech—but about comparing numbers and figuring out how they relate to each other. If they asked, "What's astronomy?" I'd say it uses speech to talk about the movement of stars, the sun, and the moon, and how fast or slow they move.

Gorgias: That's right, Socrates.

Socrates: So now it's your turn, Gorgias. Tell me clearly: Rhetoric is a skill that works through speech—right?

Gorgias: Right.

Socrates: Speech about what, exactly? What kind of things does rhetoric talk about?

Gorgias: About the most important and valuable things in human life.

Socrates: That sounds nice, Gorgias, but it's still unclear. What exactly are the most important and valuable things in life? You've probably heard the song people sing at parties—you know, the one that lists life's blessings: first is health, second is beauty, and third, according to the song, is wealth honestly earned.

Gorgias: Yes, I know the song. But what are you getting at?

Socrates: Here's what I mean—imagine that the people who create the things praised in that song—like the doctor, the fitness trainer, and the person who makes money—came up to talk to you. First, the doctor might say, "Socrates, Gorgias is wrong. My job is what truly helps people the most." If I ask, "Who are you?" he'll say, "I'm a doctor." And if I ask, "Are you saying your work gives people the greatest good?" he'll say, "Yes, because health is the greatest good. What's more important than that, Socrates?"

Next, the trainer might speak up: "Socrates, I'd be surprised if Gorgias can prove that his work helps people more than mine does." I'd ask, "And who are you?" and he'll reply, "I'm a fitness trainer, and my job is to help people become strong and healthy."

Then comes the money-maker, who'll probably laugh at them all. He'll say, "Think about it, Socrates—can Gorgias or anyone else offer something better than money?" Then you and I might ask, "So, do you create wealth?" and he'll answer, "Yes, I do." "And who are you?" we'll say, and he'll reply, "I'm a money-maker." "And you think wealth is the greatest good for people?" "Of course," he'll say.

Then we'll tell him, "But Gorgias says his skill gives something even better than money." And the money-maker will surely respond, "What could that possibly be? Let Gorgias explain."

So now, Gorgias, imagine all of us—those people and me—asking you: What is this greatest good that you say comes from your work? What do you create?

Gorgias: That good, Socrates, is personal freedom—being in control of your own life—and the power to lead others in society.

Socrates: And what exactly gives people that kind of power?

Gorgias: What's more powerful than speech that can convince judges in court, or lawmakers in council, or everyday people in a public meeting? If you can speak like that, you'll control the doctor, the trainer, and the money-maker. They'll work for you. The money they make won't be for themselves, but for you—the one who can persuade the crowd.

Socrates: I think you've explained clearly what you believe rhetoric is. If I understand you right, you're saying rhetoric is all about persuasion—and that's its only job. That's the main goal. Are there any other results of rhetoric besides persuasion?

Gorgias: No, Socrates. That's exactly what I meant—persuasion is the main purpose of rhetoric.

Socrates: Then listen, Gorgias. I really think I'm someone who truly wants to learn and understand, and I believe you're the same way.

Gorgias: What are you getting at, Socrates?

Socrates: I'll tell you. Even though you've said what rhetoric is, I still don't fully understand what kind of persuasion it gives or what it deals with. I have a guess, but I'm going to ask anyway—not just for you, but so our conversation stays clear and helps us find the truth.

Think about this: if someone asked me, "What kind of artist is Zeuxis?" and I answered, "He paints figures," it would be fair to ask, "What kind of figures? Where do we see them?"

Gorgias: Yes, that would be fair.

Socrates: And the reason they'd ask is because other painters also paint different kinds of figures, right?

Gorgias: That's right.

Socrates: But if Zeuxis were the only one painting that kind of figure, then "He paints figures" would be enough of an answer?

Gorgias: Exactly.

Socrates: So I want to understand rhetoric in the same way. Is rhetoric the only skill that uses persuasion, or do other skills persuade too? For example, don't teachers persuade people to believe what they teach?

Gorgias: They do, Socrates. No doubt about it.

Socrates: Like we said before—doesn't the math teacher help us understand numbers?

Gorgias: Of course.

Socrates: And so they persuade us about numbers?

Gorgias: Yes.

Socrates: Then math, like rhetoric, also persuades?

Gorgias: That's clear.

Socrates: And if someone asked what kind of persuasion math gives, we'd say it's about odd and even numbers and how many of each there are. And we could explain the kind of persuasion that other skills give too—what they're about and how they work.

Gorgias: Very true.

Socrates: So rhetoric isn't the only skill that uses persuasion?

Gorgias: That's right.

Socrates: Since we now agree that other skills also persuade, just like painting is one of many that create images, I think it's fair to ask: What kind of persuasion does rhetoric give, and what is it about?

Gorgias: I would say that rhetoric is the art of persuasion used in courts and public meetings—where people talk about what's fair or unfair.

Socrates: That's what I figured you meant. But don't be surprised if I ask more questions that seem obvious. I'm not trying to argue with you—I just want our talk to stay clear and build step by step. I want you to explain your own ideas in your own way, however you see them.

Gorgias: I think you're doing exactly the right thing, Socrates.

Socrates: Alright, then let me ask something else. You'd agree there's such a thing as "learning," right?

Gorgias: Yes.

Socrates: And there's also something called "believing"?

Gorgias: Yes.

Socrates: Are learning and believing the same thing?

Gorgias: No, I don't think they are, Socrates.

Socrates: I agree. And here's how we can tell: If someone asked, "Gorgias, can people believe things that are false as well as things that are true?"—you'd say yes, right?

Gorgias: Yes.

Socrates: But can knowledge be false?

Gorgias: No.

Socrates: Exactly—and that proves knowledge and belief are not the same.

Gorgias: That's very true.

Socrates: And yet people who learn something and people who just believe something are both persuaded, right?

Gorgias: Yes, they are.

Socrates: So we could say there are two types of persuasion—one that leads to belief without real knowledge, and one that leads to actual knowledge?

Gorgias: That makes sense.

Socrates: Then which kind of persuasion does rhetoric create—especially in courts and public meetings when talking about justice and injustice? Does it lead to true knowledge, or just belief without real understanding?

Gorgias: Clearly, Socrates, rhetoric only creates belief—it doesn't teach true knowledge.

Socrates: So then, rhetoric is a kind of skill that makes people believe something about what's right and wrong, but it doesn't actually teach them what's truly right or wrong?

Gorgias: That's correct.

Socrates: And a public speaker doesn't teach the courts or the crowds what's truly just or unjust. He just gets them to believe his version of it, since it's impossible to truly teach such deep topics to a large group in a short time.

Gorgias: Exactly.

Socrates: Okay, let's figure out what rhetoric really is, because I'm not completely sure what it means. Let's say there's a public vote to choose a doctor, a shipbuilder, or any other expert. Do you think the public speaker would be the one they ask for advice?

No way. People choose the person with the most skill. And when a city needs walls built or a harbor made, they don't ask the speaker, but the builder. When it's time to choose generals or decide how to fight a battle, they ask the soldiers, not the speakers. Would you agree with that, Gorgias? Since you say you teach rhetoric and train others, I want to learn what this skill really does from you.

Also, I want to help others here understand too. Some of these young men might want to become your students, but they're probably too shy to ask questions. So when I question you, imagine that they are the ones asking through me. They might say, "Gorgias, what will we learn from you? Will you teach us only how to speak about right and wrong, or about the other things Socrates just mentioned too?" What would you say to them?

Gorgias: I like the way you're guiding this, Socrates. I'll do my best to explain all of what rhetoric is. You must have heard how the Athenians built their docks and walls and designed the harbor—those were planned with the help of leaders like Themistocles and Pericles, not just the builders.

Socrates: That's what the stories say about Themistocles, and I actually heard Pericles speak when he explained the idea for the middle wall.

Gorgias: And you'll notice, Socrates, that in these kinds of situations, it's the public speakers who lead the way and get people to agree. They are the ones who succeed in getting their plans chosen.

Socrates: Yes, that's exactly what I was thinking about when I asked what rhetoric really is. It seems like a powerful and impressive skill.

Gorgias: It truly is, Socrates. Rhetoric controls all the other arts. Let me give you an example. I've gone with my brother Herodicus, who is a doctor, to visit sick patients. Sometimes the patient refuses to take the medicine or treatment the doctor offers. But I've been able to talk them into it using only the power of speech.

I say, if a speaker and a doctor went to a city and had to compete for the role of official state doctor, the speaker would win—he could convince the people, even without medical knowledge. He could beat out any expert because he can speak more persuasively than anyone else, and about anything. That's how strong rhetoric is.

But, Socrates, rhetoric should be used responsibly, just like any other skill. A speaker shouldn't misuse his power, just like a fighter or athlete shouldn't go around hurting friends or innocent people just because they can. For example, a trained boxer who hits his parent or friend isn't proof that boxing is bad. The coach who trained him shouldn't be blamed either. The skill was meant for self-defense, not for attacking the wrong people.

It's the same with rhetoric. The speaker can talk about anything and convince almost anyone, but that doesn't mean he should use it to steal credit from doctors or other experts. He should use it properly and fairly. If someone becomes a public speaker and uses their skills to do harm, it's not the teacher's fault. The teacher gave the knowledge for good reasons, but the student chose to use it badly. So it's the speaker himself who deserves blame, punishment, or even exile—not the person who taught him.

Socrates: Gorgias, you've been in a lot of debates, just like I have. So I'm sure you've noticed how these discussions often don't go the way they should. Instead of both sides learning something, they end up arguing. One person says the other is wrong or unclear, and then they both get defensive. Soon it's more about personal attacks than about the actual topic. It becomes so unpleasant that everyone regrets even listening to the conversation.

Why am I saying this? Because I feel like you just said something that doesn't really match what you said earlier about rhetoric. And I'm a little hesitant to point it out because I don't want you to think I'm just trying to argue with you or show you up. That's not my goal—I really just want to understand the truth.

So let me ask you this: Are you the kind of person who wants to find the truth, even if it means being proven wrong? That's the kind of person I am. I actually feel happy when someone shows me I'm wrong, because I learn something. It's more helpful to me to be corrected than to correct someone else. It's like being sick—getting cured is better than curing someone else. And I believe that having the wrong idea about important things is one of the worst things that can happen to a person.

So if you feel the same way, let's keep going. If not, we can stop here.

Gorgias: I do feel the same way, Socrates. But maybe we should think about the people listening. Before you arrived, I had already spoken for a while. If we keep going, the conversation might take a long time, and some people might want to leave.

Chaerephon: Gorgias, Socrates—you hear the audience clapping. That shows they want you to keep talking. And I personally hope nothing pulls me away from this amazing conversation.

Callicles: By the gods, Chaerephon, I've been to a lot of discussions, but I don't think I've ever enjoyed one as much as this. You two could talk all day, and I'd love every minute.

Socrates: Then I'll gladly continue—if Gorgias agrees.

Gorgias: After all this, Socrates, I'd be ashamed to say no—especially since I promised to answer anyone who had questions. So, go ahead and ask me anything you like.

Socrates: Thanks, Gorgias. Here's what I find surprising about what you've said. Maybe you're right and I just misunderstood, but I want to be sure. You said you can turn anyone who studies with you into a skilled speaker, right?

Gorgias: Yes, that's correct.

Socrates: Do you mean that you teach people to speak persuasively to crowds about any topic—not by teaching the subject, but just by convincing them?

Gorgias: Exactly.

Socrates: You even said that a speaker trained by you can persuade people more effectively than a doctor can, even when it's about health?

Gorgias: Yes, but only with people who don't know much—ordinary folks.

Socrates: So you mean with people who are ignorant, not with experts?

Gorgias: Right.

Socrates: But that means someone who doesn't actually know about health could still convince the public better than someone who does?

Gorgias: Yes, in that situation.

Socrates: So this would be true with other skills too—someone could appear to know more than the expert just by being better at persuading people?

Gorgias: That's right, Socrates. Isn't it amazing? You don't need to learn all those other skills. Just study rhetoric and you'll seem just as smart as those who did.

Socrates: Whether that's a good or bad thing is something we can talk about later. But first, let me ask you this: does a person trained in rhetoric know what's really right and wrong, good and bad, just and unjust? Or can he only convince people he knows—without really knowing himself? And what about your students—do they need to already know right and wrong before they study with you? Or will you teach them those things too?

Because if they come in not knowing what justice is, and you don't teach them, then all you're really doing is helping them fool others into thinking they know. They'll appear to be good people without truly being good. Or do you only teach rhetoric to people who already know what justice and goodness are? Please explain this, Gorgias—I really want to understand what rhetoric can do.

Gorgias: Well, Socrates, I suppose if the student doesn't already know those things, then I would have to teach them, too.

Socrates: That's a good answer. So anyone who becomes a speaker through you must either already know what's just and unjust or be taught that by you.

Gorgias: Yes, exactly.

Socrates: Okay. Let's take this further. Someone who learns carpentry is called a carpenter, right?

Gorgias: Right.

Socrates: And someone who learns music is a musician?

Gorgias: Yes.

Socrates: And someone who learns medicine is a doctor. In general, when someone learns something, we call them by the name of that skill?

Gorgias: Yes, of course.

Socrates: So, someone who learns what is just becomes a just person?

Gorgias: Definitely.

Socrates: And a just person will act in just ways?

Gorgias: Yes.

Socrates: And someone who is just will always want to do what's right?

Gorgias: That follows.

Socrates: Then a just person would never choose to do something unjust?

Gorgias: Certainly not.

Socrates: So, based on our discussion, a trained speaker—your student—must be a just person?

Gorgias: Yes.

Socrates: And therefore, he would never willingly do anything unjust?

Gorgias: That's right.

Socrates: But earlier, didn't you say that if a speaker uses his skill in a bad way, like unfairly persuading people, then that's his own fault—not the teacher's?

Gorgias: Yes, I did say that.

Socrates: But now we're saying that a true speaker, trained properly, would never do anything unjust at all?

Gorgias: That's what we're saying now.

Socrates: And in the beginning, didn't you say that rhetoric deals with things like justice and injustice—not with numbers like arithmetic does?

Gorgias: Yes, that's what I said.

Socrates: When I first heard you say that rhetoric always deals with justice, I thought it couldn't possibly be used for anything unfair. But then, soon after, you said a speaker could use rhetoric in the wrong way—and that surprised me because it didn't match what you said before. I thought if you, like me, believed it's good to be proven wrong when you're mistaken, we should keep going with the conversation. Otherwise, I was fine with stopping. But as we've kept talking, it's turned out that a true speaker can't actually do anything unjust or unfair on purpose. Honestly, Gorgias, we're going to need a lot more discussion before we fully figure all this out.

Polus: Socrates, do you really believe what you're saying about rhetoric? Come on—just because Gorgias felt too embarrassed to deny that a speaker knows about justice, goodness, and honor, and said he could teach those things if a student didn't already know them... you're acting like that proves something. But really, it only created a contradiction—something you love to point out. And you pushed the conversation that way with tricky questions. Do you seriously think there's any truth in what just happened? I mean, who would ever admit they don't know or can't teach what justice is? It's kind of rude to steer the conversation like that.

Socrates: Polus, my friend, we keep people like you and our children around us so that when we stumble—whether in our actions or our words—they can help us back up again. So if you think Gorgias or I have slipped up here, it's your job to correct us. And I promise, I'll take back anything you prove wrong—if you agree to one small thing.

Polus: What's that?

Socrates: That you don't give another long speech like you did before.

Polus: What? So I'm not allowed to talk as much as I want?

Socrates: Imagine this—you come to Athens, which is the freest city in Greece, and suddenly you're the one person who's not allowed to speak? That would be pretty unfair. But now imagine me—I have to sit through your long speeches without getting real answers to my questions, and I'm not even allowed to leave. Isn't that unfair, too? So, if you really care about the conversation and want to help us figure things out, then go ahead—take back anything you want, and join the discussion properly. Ask and answer, just like Gorgias and I have been doing. Argue, respond, and let others challenge you too. You say you know what Gorgias knows, right?

Polus: Of course.

Socrates: And, like him, you're open to any questions and ready to give answers?

Polus: Yes, absolutely.

Socrates: So, will you ask the question, or answer?

Polus: I'll ask. You say Gorgias couldn't answer it, so let me try. Tell me, Socrates: what is rhetoric?

Socrates: Are you asking what kind of skill it is?

Polus: Yes.

Socrates: Well, to be honest, Polus, I don't think it's a real skill at all.

Polus: Then what is it?

Socrates: It's something you've written about yourself, calling it an art—but I'd say it's really just a kind of practice or technique.

Polus: You think it's just a practice?

Socrates: Yes, that's how it seems to me—but you may see it differently.

Polus: A practice of what?

Socrates: A practice of creating pleasure or enjoyment.

Polus: But if it gives people pleasure, doesn't that make it a good thing?

Socrates: Hold on, Polus. You're jumping ahead. You're asking whether it's good before we've even settled on what it is.

Polus: Didn't you just say rhetoric was a kind of practice?

Socrates: Yes—but since you're eager to please others, will you do me a small favor?

Polus: Sure, what is it?

Socrates: Ask me this: what kind of skill is cooking?

Polus: Alright—what kind of skill is cooking?

Socrates: It's not a real skill either.

Polus: Then what is it?

Socrates: It's a kind of practice.

Polus: A practice of what? Please explain.

Socrates: It's the practice of creating pleasure and enjoyment, just like I said about rhetoric.

Polus: So, are you saying cooking and rhetoric are the same?

Socrates: Not exactly—but they're both parts of the same general thing.

Polus: What thing?

Socrates: I hesitate to say, because the truth might sound rude. I don't want Gorgias to think I'm mocking his profession. I don't even know if this is the kind of rhetoric he means—because from what he said earlier, I still don't really know what he thinks of his own skill. But the kind of rhetoric I'm talking about is part of something that isn't very respectable.

Gorgias: Part of what, Socrates? Say what you really mean—don't worry about me.

Socrates: Alright then, Gorgias. I think rhetoric, along with some other things, is not a real skill, but more like a way of being clever and manipulating people. I call the whole group of these things "flattery." It's not about truth or learning—it's about knowing how to get people to like what you say. Flattery has several branches. One is cooking—it may look like a skill, but it's just a way to make food seem enjoyable. Another is rhetoric. Then there's dressing up or styling, and also trickery in arguments, which some call sophistry. So there are four types in this group.

Now, Polus may ask—which part of flattery is rhetoric? He didn't realize I hadn't answered his earlier question yet when he went on to ask if I thought rhetoric was a good thing. But I can't say if it's good or bad until I've clearly said what it is. That wouldn't make sense.

So go ahead, Polus—ask me what part of flattery rhetoric belongs to, and I'll answer.

Polus: Okay, I'll ask. What part of flattery is rhetoric?

Socrates: Will you be able to follow my answer? In my view, rhetoric is like a shadow or fake version of a part of politics.

Polus: And is that noble or not?

Socrates: Not noble, if you want a direct answer—because I believe anything harmful is not noble. But I'm not sure you fully understood what I meant earlier.

Gorgias: Honestly, Socrates, I'm not sure I understand either.

Socrates: I'm not surprised, Gorgias, that you're confused—I haven't fully explained myself yet. And our friend Polus, true to his name, tends to run off like a young colt when things get tricky.

Gorgias: Don't worry about him. Just explain what you meant when you said that rhetoric is a fake version of part of politics.

Socrates: Alright, I'll try to explain what I think rhetoric really is. And if I'm wrong, Polus can challenge me. Let's start with this: we all agree that people have both bodies and souls, right?

Gorgias: Of course.

Socrates: And both the body and the soul can be in good condition?

Gorgias: Yes.

Socrates: But sometimes things only look good, when they really aren't. For example, someone might seem healthy, but a doctor or fitness expert could tell they're not.

Gorgias: That's true.

Socrates: And this doesn't only apply to the body—it's the same with the soul. Someone can seem to be good or virtuous, but not actually be that way.

Gorgias: Certainly.

Socrates: Okay, now let me make it clearer. Just like the body and soul are two things, there are two types of care or guidance—one for the body and one for the soul. The body has two major helpers: medicine and physical training. And for the soul, we have politics, which also splits into two parts: making laws (which is like training for the soul) and justice (which is like medicine for the soul).

These four—lawmaking, justice, medicine, and fitness—are true arts that aim at helping people live their best lives. But then comes flattery, which is just guessing what people like. It imitates those real arts but only tries to make people feel good, not actually do what's best for them.

Cooking pretends to be medicine. It claims to know what's best for the body, but it really just aims to make food taste good. If a cook and a doctor had to convince a group of kids—or adults who think like kids—about who knows best about food, the cook would win. The doctor would starve. Why? Because people love what tastes good more than what is good.

Polus, this is why I say cooking is a form of flattery. It's not a real art. It doesn't explain anything or give real reasons—it just works by habit and experience. That's why I don't call it a skill. I only consider something a skill if it's based on reason and understanding.

So, cooking is a fake version of medicine. In the same way, personal styling (like makeup and dressing up) is a fake version of physical training. It tricks people into thinking they look healthy and strong, when really they're just covering things up with paint, colors, and clothes. It hides true beauty, which should come from taking care of the body.

I won't go on too long. But just like in geometry, I'll give you a quick comparison:

Styling is to fitness as cooking is to medicine.

Also:

Styling is to fitness as sophistry is to lawmaking.

And:

Cooking is to medicine as rhetoric is to justice.

This shows the difference between a real art and a fake version. Sophists and rhetoricians are often confused for each other. They're so similar, even they might not know what they really are. Other people are confused about them too.

If our bodies were the ones deciding between cookery and medicine, and they chose based on what felt good instead of what was good, everything would fall apart. Like the saying you know well, Polus—"Chaos would return." Everything would get mixed up: health, taste, real skills, and fake ones.

So now you've heard my view. Rhetoric is to the soul what cooking is to the body. I know I've made a long speech, even though I told you not to. But I had to, because you didn't understand my short answer earlier. If you don't understand my long one either, then you can go on at length too. But if you do understand, then I hope you'll keep it brief, just like I'll do in return.

Now, you can respond however you want.

Polus: Are you serious? You really think rhetoric is just flattery?

Socrates: No, I said it's part of flattery. If you already forgot, Polus, and you're still this young—what will happen when you get old?

Polus: But don't people respect good public speakers in society? Do they really think of them as flatterers?

Socrates: Is that a question—or are you about to give a speech?

Polus: I'm asking a question.

Socrates: Then my answer is this: no, they aren't respected. They're not truly valued at all.

Polus: What? Aren't they extremely powerful in their cities?

Socrates: Not if you believe, as you said earlier, that real power is something good for the person who has it.

Polus: That's exactly what I believe!

Socrates: Well then, I think these speakers have the least power of all.

Polus: What? But aren't they like tyrants? They can kill, steal, and exile anyone they want!

Socrates: Polus, I honestly can't tell if you're giving your own opinion or asking me a question.

Polus: I'm asking a question.

Socrates: Then you've asked two things at once. Let me break them down.

Polus: How are there two?

Socrates: You said public speakers are like tyrants—they can kill, rob, or exile whoever they want. That's two separate claims.

Polus: Yes, that's what I said.

Socrates: So let me answer both. I still say that public speakers and tyrants have the least real power. They don't actually do what they want—only what they think is best.

Polus: But isn't that real power?

Socrates: You already said that power is only good if it benefits the person who has it, right?

Polus: Yes—that's what I said and still believe.

Socrates: Then you've already gone against yourself.

POLUS: Yes, I do.

SOCRATES: So would you say that if a foolish person does what they think is best, then that's a good thing? Would you call that real power?

POLUS: No, I wouldn't.

SOCRATES: Then to prove me wrong, you have to show that a speaker or public persuader isn't foolish—and that their skill is a real art, not just flattery. Only then will you have defeated my point. But if you can't, then these speakers and rulers who act however they want won't really have anything to be proud of—because you already said that power is a good thing, and doing things without wisdom is bad.

POLUS: Yes, I admit that.

SOCRATES: So how can these speakers or rulers truly have great power in their cities unless you can prove me wrong and show that they really do what they want?

POLUS: This guy—

SOCRATES: I'm saying they don't really do what they want. Prove me wrong.

POLUS: Didn't you say they do what they think is best?

SOCRATES: I still say that.

POLUS: Then they must be doing what they want, right?

SOCRATES: No, I don't agree.

POLUS: But they do what they think is best?

SOCRATES: Yes.

POLUS: That's ridiculous, Socrates.

SOCRATES: Be respectful, Polus. Speak in your usual polite style. If you have a question, ask it. If you think I'm wrong, prove it—or just give your own answer.

POLUS: Fine, I'll answer so I can understand what you mean.

SOCRATES: Do you think people want the actions they take, or do they want the results of those actions? Like when someone drinks medicine because a doctor told them to, do they want the painful drink, or do they want to get healthy?

POLUS: Obviously, they want to get healthy.

SOCRATES: And when people travel or do business, they don't really want the risks or the hard work. They do it for the money they hope to earn, right?

POLUS: Of course.

SOCRATES: So isn't this always true? When someone does something to get something else, what they really want is the result— not the action itself?

POLUS: Yes, that's right.

SOCRATES: And aren't all things either good, bad, or in-between?

POLUS: Definitely.

SOCRATES: Things like wisdom, health, and wealth—you'd call those good, right? And their opposites would be bad?

POLUS: Yes.

SOCRATES: And things that aren't really good or bad, like sitting, walking, sailing, or objects like wood and stone—those are neutral?

POLUS: Exactly.

SOCRATES: So do we do these neutral things to get the good things? Or do we do good things for the sake of the neutral ones?

POLUS: We do the neutral things for the good ones.

SOCRATES: So when we walk or stand, we do it because we believe it's the better thing to do at that moment?

POLUS: Yes.

SOCRATES: And when someone kills, exiles, or takes from someone, they do it because they think it benefits them?

POLUS: That's true.

SOCRATES: So people do all of these things because they believe it will lead to something good?

POLUS: Yes.

SOCRATES: And we agreed that when people do something for the sake of something else, what they really want is the result—not the action?

POLUS: Yes, that's very true.

SOCRATES: So when someone kills, exiles, or takes from another, they don't actually want to do those things by themselves. They only want the benefits they believe those actions will bring. But if those actions don't bring any real benefit, then they don't actually want them. Because people only want what's good for them, right? Not what's neutral or harmful. Why aren't you saying anything, Polus? Am I wrong?

POLUS: No, you're right.

SOCRATES: So then, if someone—whether a ruler or a speaker—kills or exiles someone, or takes their stuff, thinking it will help them when it actually won't, then they're only doing what they think is best?

POLUS: Yes.

SOCRATES: But are they doing what they really want if they're doing something that's bad? Why don't you answer?

POLUS: I guess not.

SOCRATES: And if great power is truly a good thing, as you say, then would someone like that have great power in their city?

POLUS: No, they wouldn't.

SOCRATES: So I was right when I said someone might do what seems good to them in their city, but still not have real power or do what they really want?

POLUS: As if you wouldn't love to have the power to do whatever you thought was best in your city. Don't tell me you wouldn't be jealous of someone who could kill, steal, or lock people up whenever they wanted. Oh, sure.

SOCRATES: Are we talking about doing those things fairly or unfairly?

POLUS: Either way. Isn't that still something to admire?

SOCRATES: Stop it, Polus.

POLUS: Why? Why should I stop?

SOCRATES: Because we shouldn't admire people who don't deserve admiration. We should feel sorry for them instead.

POLUS: Wait—are you saying those kinds of people are to be pitied?

SOCRATES: Yes, absolutely.

POLUS: So you're saying someone who kills whoever he wants— even if he does it fairly—is miserable and deserves pity?

SOCRATES: No, not exactly. I'm just saying he isn't someone to admire.

POLUS: Didn't you say earlier that he was miserable?

SOCRATES: Yes, but only if he killed someone unfairly. In that case, yes, he's both miserable and deserves pity. But even if he killed someone fairly, he still shouldn't be admired.

POLUS: But you'd agree that someone who is killed unfairly is miserable and deserves pity?

SOCRATES: Not as much as the one who killed him unfairly. And not even as much as someone who is fairly punished.

POLUS: How can that be true, Socrates?

SOCRATES: It makes sense if you believe that doing something wrong is the worst kind of evil.

POLUS: But is doing wrong really the worst? Isn't it worse to have something wrong done to you?

SOCRATES: No, I don't think so.

POLUS: So you'd rather suffer injustice than commit it?

SOCRATES: I wouldn't want either to happen, but if I had to choose, I'd rather be treated unfairly than treat someone else unfairly.

POLUS: So you wouldn't want to be a tyrant?

SOCRATES: Not if you mean the kind of tyrant I'm thinking of.

POLUS: I mean the kind of person who can do whatever they want in a city—like killing, banishing people, and doing anything else they feel like.

SOCRATES: Alright, my friend, let's imagine this. After I've spoken, I want you to answer. Let's say I walk into the marketplace with a dagger hidden under my cloak. I turn to you and say, "Polus, I now have great power. I can kill anyone I want in this crowd. If I think someone should die, I just stab them and they're gone. Or if I want to hurt someone or rip their clothes, I can do it instantly. That's how powerful I am in this city!" Then I show you the dagger. You'd probably reply, "Socrates, anyone could do that. Anyone could set fire to houses, destroy the docks and ships, or ruin anything they wanted. But does just doing what you want really count as great power?"

POLUS: No, not that kind of action.

SOCRATES: So why do you think that kind of power is bad?

POLUS: Because the person doing it would surely be punished.

SOCRATES: And punishment is bad?

POLUS: Definitely.

SOCRATES: So let's go back to something we agreed on—real power is good if it brings benefit. But if it causes harm, then it's actually bad and not real power at all. Now, let's look at it another way: things like killing, banishing, or taking someone's belongings—do you agree these things can sometimes be good, but other times bad?

POLUS: Yes, I agree.

SOCRATES: So we both see eye to eye on that?

POLUS: Yes.

SOCRATES: Then tell me—how do you decide when these things are good and when they're not? What rule do you use?

POLUS: Honestly, Socrates, I'd rather hear your answer.

SOCRATES: Okay, Polus. If you want my view, here it is: I think these things are good when they are fair and just, and bad when they're unfair and unjust.

POLUS: Socrates, you're hard to argue with, but don't you think even a child could prove you wrong?

SOCRATES: Then I'd thank that child, just like I'd thank you, for helping me realize I was wrong. I'd be glad to be corrected. So go ahead and help your friend—prove me wrong if you can.

POLUS: I don't even have to look far or go back in time to find an example. There are things that happened just a few days ago that show how people who do wrong can still be happy.

SOCRATES: What things are you talking about?

POLUS: You've heard of Archelaus, son of Perdiccas? He rules Macedonia now, right?

SOCRATES: I've heard of him, yes.

POLUS: Do you think he's happy or miserable?

SOCRATES: I can't say, Polus. I've never met him.

POLUS: Can't you just tell, without meeting someone, whether they're happy?

SOCRATES: No, I really can't.

POLUS: So you're telling me you don't even know if the great king is happy?

SOCRATES: That's correct. I don't know whether he's educated or just.

POLUS: Are you saying that happiness depends only on those things?

SOCRATES: Yes, that's exactly what I believe. People who are kind and good are happy. People who are unjust and evil are miserable.

POLUS: Then by your thinking, Archelaus is miserable?

SOCRATES: Yes—if he's unjust, then he's miserable.

POLUS: I can't deny that he's unjust. He didn't have any right to the throne. His mother was a slave of Alcetas, Perdiccas's brother. That means Archelaus was born a slave. If he wanted to do the right thing, he would have stayed a slave—and according to you, that would have made him happy. But instead, he did terrible things to get power. First, he invited his uncle Alcetas and cousin Alexander, who was close to his age, by pretending he'd give the throne back. He treated them kindly and got them drunk. Then he secretly loaded them into a wagon, killed them both, and got them out of the way. And even after doing all this, he didn't feel bad or realize he was miserable. Want to know how he showed his guilt? He had a younger brother—just seven years old—the rightful heir to the throne. But instead of raising him and returning the crown, Archelaus had him thrown into a well and drowned. He told the boy's mother, Cleopatra, that he fell in while chasing a goose. So here you have a man who's committed terrible crimes. If anyone is miserable in Macedonia, it's him. And I bet there are plenty of Athenians—including you—who would rather be anyone else in Macedonia than Archelaus.

SOCRATES: At first, I said you were better at speaking than reasoning, Polus. And now, I suppose this is the kind of argument you think even a child could use to prove me wrong—because I said an unjust person isn't happy. But honestly, I don't see how your argument proves anything. I don't accept any part of what you just said.

POLUS: That's only because you don't want to agree with me. Deep down, you must think the same way I do.

SOCRATES: No, my friend. It's not about wanting or not wanting to agree. It's that you're using the kind of argument a lawyer might use in court. In trials, people think they win by getting a lot of well-known witnesses to back them up, while the other side may have no one. But that kind of "proof" doesn't help when we're trying to find the truth. A crowd of impressive-sounding people could still all be wrong.

And in this argument, most people—Athenians and foreigners alike—would probably agree with you. You could bring in Nicias, the son of Niceratus, and all his famous brothers who donated tripods to the god Dionysus. Or you could bring Aristocrates, son of Scellius, who made that famous gift to Delphi. You could even bring in the whole family of Pericles. They would all agree with you.

But I wouldn't. I'm alone in this. You haven't convinced me, even though you have many so-called "witnesses" against me trying to take away the truth, which I value like an inheritance. To me, nothing important has been proven unless I can make you accept what I say— and the same goes for you. It doesn't matter what the rest of the world thinks.

There are two kinds of arguments: yours, which is popular and appeals to the crowd, and mine, which is different. Let's compare them and see how they differ. What we're arguing about is something big—what it means to be happy or miserable. And knowing this is valuable; not knowing it is shameful. What could be more important than understanding that?

So let's go back to what you believe. You think someone who's unjust and does wrong can still be happy—like Archelaus, whom you believe is both unjust and happy. Is that right?

POLUS: Yes, that's my view.

SOCRATES: I say that's impossible. So that's one thing we disagree on. Now let me ask—do you also think he would still be happy if he were caught and punished?

POLUS: No way. If he were punished, he'd be totally miserable.

SOCRATES: So, to you, an unjust person is happy only if they don't get punished?

POLUS: Exactly.

SOCRATES: I disagree. I think anyone who does wrong is miserable no matter what—but even more miserable if they never face consequences. If they do get punished, they're still miserable, but a little less so, because justice has been served.

POLUS: That's a pretty strange belief, Socrates.

SOCRATES: I'll try to get you to agree with me, Polus—because I do consider you a friend. Let's be clear about what we're disagreeing on: I said doing wrong is worse than suffering it, right?

POLUS: That's right.

SOCRATES: And you said the opposite?

POLUS: Yes.

SOCRATES: I also said that people who do wrong are miserable, and you said I was wrong?

POLUS: I sure did.

SOCRATES: You also said that if someone does wrong and isn't punished, they're happy?

POLUS: Yes, I said that.

SOCRATES: I say that person is actually the most miserable, and the one who gets punished is better off. Are you going to try to prove me wrong again?

POLUS: That one's even harder to argue with, Socrates.

SOCRATES: It's more than hard—it's impossible. Because how can anyone argue against the truth?

POLUS: What do you mean? Imagine someone tries to take over a city unfairly, gets caught, and is tortured—his eyes burned out, his body ruined. He sees his wife and kids suffer too, and finally he's executed horribly. Are you saying that person is better off than someone who succeeds in becoming a tyrant, lives how he wants, and is admired by everyone? Is that what you call an idea that can't be disproven?

SOCRATES: There you go again, Polus, trying to scare me with terrible stories instead of truly proving me wrong. A moment ago, you were just trying to gather witnesses. Now, let me double-check something you said. You described someone making an unjust attempt to become a tyrant, right?

POLUS: Yes, I said that.

SOCRATES: Then here's what I think. Neither person—the one who fails and suffers, or the one who gets away with it—is actually happy. They're both miserable. But the one who succeeds in becoming a tyrant is worse off.

POLUS: You're joking, right? That's ridiculous. Laughing at that is the only way to respond.

SOCRATES: So now laughing counts as a way to prove someone wrong? That's a new one, Polus. Instead of answering, you just laugh?

POLUS: But Socrates, don't you think you've been proven wrong when you say something no one in their right mind would agree with? Ask the people around us!

SOCRATES: Polus, I'm not a public speaker. Just last year, when it was my turn to lead the assembly and count the votes, I couldn't even manage that—I got laughed at. So don't expect me to take a vote from the crowd now. Besides, if the only argument you have is what most people think, then let me take a turn.

I'll use a kind of proof that really matters: I'm going to rely on just one person—you, the person I'm talking to. I don't care what the crowd thinks. So will you answer my questions and let your words be tested?

Because I believe deep down that you, and I, and every person, really do think it's worse to do wrong than to suffer it. And it's worse to get away with wrongdoing than to be punished for it.

POLUS: I don't think so. I don't think anyone believes that—not you, not me, not anyone. Would you really rather suffer injustice than commit it?

SOCRATES: Yes—and you would too. Everyone would.

POLUS: No way. Not me, not you, not anyone else.

SOCRATES: But will you still answer my questions?

POLUS: Of course. I'm interested to hear what you'll say.

SOCRATES: Tell me this, Polus, and you'll understand. Let's start from the beginning: which do you think is worse—doing something unjust, or having something unjust done to you?

POLUS: I'd say it's worse to suffer injustice.

SOCRATES: And which one is more shameful?

POLUS: Doing injustice.

SOCRATES: And isn't something more shameful also more wrong?

POLUS: Not always.

SOCRATES: So just to be clear, you're saying that what's shameful isn't always bad, and what's honorable isn't always good?

POLUS: That's right.

SOCRATES: Let me ask you another question. When you say something is beautiful—like a body, a color, a shape, a sound, or even a law—don't you call it beautiful because it's useful or brings some kind of pleasure? For example, don't we say a body is beautiful when it's helpful or nice to look at?

POLUS: Yes, I don't think there's any other reason.

SOCRATES: And shapes or colors—aren't they beautiful because they're useful, pleasing to look at, or both?

POLUS: Yes, that's true.

SOCRATES: The same with music and sounds—they're beautiful because they sound good or serve a purpose?

POLUS: That's how I see it.

SOCRATES: And laws or rules—we only call them beautiful if they help people or make them happy?

POLUS: Right.

SOCRATES: And wouldn't the same thing apply to knowledge?

POLUS: Absolutely. I really like how you're measuring beauty based on usefulness and pleasure.

SOCRATES: So then, we can also measure ugliness or shame by the opposite: by how harmful or painful something is?

POLUS: Yes, that makes sense.

SOCRATES: So, if we compare two beautiful things, the one that brings more pleasure or is more useful is more beautiful, right?

POLUS: Exactly.

SOCRATES: And if we compare two shameful things, the one that causes more pain or more harm is more shameful?

POLUS: Yes.

SOCRATES: Now, let's go back to what you said earlier. You said it's worse to suffer injustice, but more shameful to do it, right?

POLUS: That's what I said.

SOCRATES: Then if doing wrong is more shameful, it must also be more painful or more harmful—or both. Wouldn't that follow?

POLUS: It would.

SOCRATES: Let's test that. Do people who commit injustice suffer more pain than those who are treated unjustly?

POLUS: No, definitely not.

SOCRATES: So then, they don't feel more pain?

POLUS: No.

SOCRATES: And if they don't feel more pain, then the only way their action is worse is because it causes more harm?

POLUS: Yes.

SOCRATES: So doing injustice causes more harm than suffering it?

POLUS: That's clear now.

SOCRATES: And earlier, you agreed that doing wrong is more shameful than suffering it?

POLUS: I did.

SOCRATES: And now we've shown it's actually more harmful too?

POLUS: That's true.

SOCRATES: So let me ask you—would you rather experience something that causes more harm and shame, or something that causes less?

POLUS: Of course I'd choose the lesser.

SOCRATES: Would anyone prefer the greater evil over the lesser one?

POLUS: No, not if we look at it this way.

SOCRATES: Then I was right to say that neither you, nor I, nor anyone would rather do injustice than suffer it—because doing it is worse.

POLUS: That's the conclusion.

SOCRATES: You see, Polus, how different our types of reasoning are? Everyone else might agree with you, but if I can get you to agree with me, that's all I need. I don't care what the crowd thinks.

Let's move on to the next point. You said earlier that the worst thing for a guilty person is to be punished. I say it's actually worse to not be punished. Let's think it through. Would you agree that being punished justly means being corrected when you've done wrong?

POLUS: Yes, I'd say that.

SOCRATES: And wouldn't you also agree that anything just is also honorable, as long as it's truly just?

POLUS: Yes, I think so.

SOCRATES: Let's consider something else: whenever someone does something, isn't there always someone or something that it's done to?

POLUS: I'd say yes.

SOCRATES: And whatever is done to that person or thing—won't the effect match the action? For example, if someone hits another, someone else must be hit?

POLUS: Right.

SOCRATES: And if the person hits hard or fast, the one being hit experiences it the same way—hard or fast?

POLUS: That's true.

SOCRATES: So the pain felt by the one hit is the same as the strength of the hit?

POLUS: Yes.

SOCRATES: And if someone sets something on fire, there must be something that gets burned?

POLUS: Definitely.

SOCRATES: And if the burning is extreme or painful, the thing being burned will feel it that way?

POLUS: Absolutely.

SOCRATES: And if someone cuts something, the same rule applies—something has to be cut, right?

POLUS: Yes.

SOCRATES: And if the cut is deep or painful, the injury is just as serious?

POLUS: That's obvious.

SOCRATES: So, would you agree that whatever someone does to another, the result matches the action?

POLUS: I agree.

SOCRATES: Since we agree on that, let me ask you this: Is being punished something you do, or something you experience?

POLUS: It's something you experience, Socrates. No doubt about it.

SOCRATES: And if someone suffers, then there must be someone causing it?

POLUS: Yes—the person punishing them.

SOCRATES: And when someone punishes fairly, they're doing what's just?

POLUS: Yes.

SOCRATES: So, if their action is just, then they're acting rightly?

POLUS: That's correct.

SOCRATES: And the person being punished is suffering something just?

POLUS: That's clear.

SOCRATES: And we already agreed that what is just is also honorable?

POLUS: Yes.

SOCRATES: So the one punishing is doing something honorable, and the one being punished is experiencing something honorable?

POLUS: That's true.

SOCRATES: And if something is honorable, it must also be either helpful or pleasant?

POLUS: Yes, that follows.

SOCRATES: So the person being punished is going through something good?

POLUS: Yes, that's true.

SOCRATES: Then they're actually being helped?

POLUS: Yes.

SOCRATES: Just to be sure—when I say someone is "helped," I mean their soul is improved through fair punishment. Is that what you mean too?

POLUS: Yes, definitely.

SOCRATES: So someone who is punished fairly is freed from the wrong in their soul?

POLUS: Yes.

SOCRATES: And that would mean they're freed from the greatest kind of harm, right? Let's think about this: when it comes to someone's money, isn't poverty the worst harm?

POLUS: There's nothing worse in that area.

SOCRATES: And in terms of the body, wouldn't sickness, weakness, and deformity be the worst things?

POLUS: That's right.

SOCRATES: So wouldn't the soul also have its own kind of evil?

POLUS: Of course.

SOCRATES: And wouldn't those be things like injustice, ignorance, and cowardice?

POLUS: Definitely.

SOCRATES: So, in wealth, health, and character, we have three main types of harm—poverty, disease, and moral failure?

POLUS: That's true.

SOCRATES: And of the three, isn't the one involving the soul—moral failure—the most shameful?

POLUS: By far.

SOCRATES: And if it's the most shameful, isn't it also the worst?

POLUS: What do you mean by that?

SOCRATES: I mean that we've already agreed that something is more shameful if it causes more pain, more harm, or both.

POLUS: Yes, that's right.

SOCRATES: And we agreed that injustice and other flaws in the soul are the most shameful?

POLUS: We did.

SOCRATES: So they must be the most painful or the most harmful—or both?

POLUS: That makes sense.

SOCRATES: So being unjust, reckless, cowardly, or ignorant is worse than being poor or sick?

POLUS: I'm not so sure about the pain part, Socrates. That doesn't seem to follow.

SOCRATES: Even if it's not more painful, it's clearly more shameful. And shame, in this case, must come from how deeply harmful it is.

POLUS: That's true.

SOCRATES: So the things that damage the soul—like injustice and lack of self-control—are the worst evils?

POLUS: That's clear.

SOCRATES: Now let's talk about how we deal with these evils. What helps people escape poverty? Isn't it the ability to earn money?

POLUS: Yes.

SOCRATES: And what helps us recover from sickness?

POLUS: Medicine.

SOCRATES: And what cures injustice and moral failure? If you're not sure, ask yourself this—where do we take someone who's sick?

POLUS: To a doctor.

SOCRATES: And where do we take someone who's done something wrong or lacks self-control?

POLUS: To a judge.

SOCRATES: And the judge's job is to punish them, right?

POLUS: Yes.

SOCRATES: And when the judge punishes fairly, he does so according to justice?

POLUS: Clearly.

SOCRATES: So then, making money saves a person from being poor, medicine saves them from sickness, and justice saves them from selfishness and wrongdoing?

POLUS: That's clear.

SOCRATES: Out of those three—money-making, medicine, and justice—which one is the best?

POLUS: Could you list them again?

SOCRATES: Sure—making money, practicing medicine, and applying justice.

POLUS: Justice is definitely better than the other two.

SOCRATES: And if justice is the best, then it must bring the most pleasure, or the most benefit, or both?

POLUS: Yes.

SOCRATES: But when someone is getting medical treatment, is it enjoyable? Are people happy when they're being healed?

POLUS: I don't think so.

SOCRATES: So healing isn't pleasant, but it is helpful?

POLUS: Yes, it helps.

SOCRATES: It helps because the person is being cured of something bad, right? That's the benefit—they're getting better?

POLUS: Exactly.

SOCRATES: Now, who's better off physically—someone who was never sick, or someone who got sick and then healed?

POLUS: Clearly, the one who never got sick.

SOCRATES: Right, because true happiness doesn't come from escaping something bad—it comes from never having to deal with it at all.

POLUS: That's true.

SOCRATES: Now think about this: if two people have an illness, and one of them gets healed and the other doesn't, who is worse off?

POLUS: The one who stays sick, obviously.

SOCRATES: And didn't we say that punishment is what cures the worst sickness—the sickness of the soul, which is vice?

POLUS: Yes.

SOCRATES: And justice is what punishes us, making us better people. It's like medicine for the soul, right?

POLUS: That's right.

SOCRATES: So the happiest person is the one who never had vice or injustice in their soul, since that's the worst kind of sickness.

POLUS: Yes, clearly.

SOCRATES: And the second happiest is the one who had vice but was cured of it?

POLUS: True.

SOCRATES: That would be the person who accepts criticism, correction, and punishment?

POLUS: Yes.

SOCRATES: So the worst life belongs to the person who was unjust and never corrected—who never got better?

POLUS: Definitely.

SOCRATES: In other words, the worst off is someone who commits serious crimes and never gets punished—someone like Archelaus, or other powerful rulers and persuasive speakers you mentioned?

POLUS: That's true.

SOCRATES: Isn't that like someone who has a terrible disease but refuses to see a doctor because they're afraid of getting hurt—like a kid who avoids getting burned or cut in treatment? Isn't that the same idea?

POLUS: Yes, exactly.

SOCRATES: That kind of person clearly doesn't understand what health means. And if our earlier points are correct, then people who try to avoid justice are doing the same thing. They think justice is painful, so they run from it—but they don't understand the benefit it brings. They don't realize how much worse it is to live with a damaged, corrupt, and unjust soul than with a sick body. That's why they do everything they can to avoid punishment. They gather money, build friendships, and become great at persuasion. But if we're right, Polus, do you see where this leads—or should I explain the result?

POLUS: Please go on.

SOCRATES: Isn't it true that injustice—doing wrong—is the worst evil?

POLUS: Without a doubt.

SOCRATES: And getting punished is what cures that evil?

POLUS: Yes.

SOCRATES: So not being punished means keeping that evil inside?

POLUS: Exactly.

SOCRATES: So doing wrong is bad—but doing wrong and escaping punishment is even worse?

POLUS: That's true.

SOCRATES: And wasn't that what we were debating earlier? You said Archelaus was happy because he was a great criminal who didn't get punished. I said no—he's actually the most miserable kind of person. I said anyone who does wrong and doesn't get punished is more miserable than someone who suffers injustice. That was my argument, right?

POLUS: Yes.

SOCRATES: And now we've proven it to be true?

POLUS: Certainly.

SOCRATES: Then, Polus, if all that's correct, what good is rhetoric? If we accept this, then every person should do all they can not to do wrong—because doing wrong brings the greatest harm.

POLUS: True.

SOCRATES: So, if someone does something wrong—or someone they care about does—then they should go straight to the judge to be punished. Just like you'd run to a doctor if you were sick, you should run to justice if your soul is sick with wrongdoing. Otherwise, the problem becomes permanent, like a disease that turns into cancer. Wouldn't you agree this must follow, Polus, if everything else we've said is true?

POLUS: There's really only one answer to that, Socrates.

SOCRATES: Then it seems rhetoric isn't meant to help someone escape punishment—for themselves, their family, or even their country. Instead, it should help someone confess wrongdoing. First and foremost, you should be willing to accuse yourself, and then your loved ones, if necessary. You should shine a light on injustice instead of hiding it, so people can be punished and healed from it. Even if it's painful, like a surgery or burn, you have to be brave and go through it to become better. If someone deserves a beating, let them be beaten. If they deserve prison, let them be locked up. If they deserve a fine, exile, or even death, they should accept it. And rhetoric should be used not to defend the guilty, but to make the truth known—so that justice can free them from wrongdoing, which is the worst thing of all. That, Polus, is when rhetoric would actually be helpful. Would you agree?

POLUS: Socrates, what you're saying sounds very strange to me, though I suppose it fits with everything else you've said so far.

SOCRATES: But if we haven't proven anything wrong up to now, then this must be the conclusion, right?

POLUS: Yes, it has to be.

SOCRATES: Now let's look at the opposite. If it were right to hurt others—even people who aren't your enemies—unless it's to protect yourself, then sure, you should avoid being punished. And if your enemy hurts someone else, then you should try your best to protect him from being caught or judged. If he does go to court, you should help him get away with it. If he stole money, help him keep it and use it, even if it's unfair. If he deserves death, help him live forever in his evil. And if that's not possible, at least let him live as long as he can. That's when rhetoric becomes useful—to help people avoid the consequences of their actions. But for someone who wants to live a just life and not do wrong, it's pretty useless—at least based on everything we've said so far.

CALLICLES: Hey Chaerephon, is Socrates being serious right now, or is he just joking?

CHAEREPHON: I'd say, Callicles, he's completely serious. But you can ask him yourself.

CALLICLES: By the gods, I will. Socrates, are you actually serious, or are you just playing around? Because if you really mean what you're saying, then our entire way of living is completely backward. It seems like everything we do is the exact opposite of what we should be doing.

SOCRATES: Callicles, if people didn't share at least some feelings and understanding with one another—even if they vary from person to person—I don't think we could ever communicate at all. I'm bringing this up because I think you and I actually have something in common. We're both passionate, both lovers. I love Alcibiades, the son of Cleinias, and I love philosophy. You love the people of Athens, and you love Demus, the son of Pyrilampes.

And I've noticed something—you're clever, but you never go against what your favorites say. Whenever the Athenian public disagrees with you, you change your position. And when Demus, that handsome young man, says something, you switch your view to match his too. It's like you can't say no to your loves. If anyone pointed out how odd your opinions sound sometimes, I bet you'd say, "I'm just saying what my favorites say—I can't help it." And you'd only stop talking if they stop.

Well, you should know that I'm doing the same thing. My words are just an echo of someone I love too—philosophy. But unlike your other love, Alcibiades, who says one thing today and something else tomorrow, philosophy is always consistent. She's the one guiding my words right now. So if you want to prove me wrong, you'll have to argue against her. You'll have to prove that doing wrong and getting away with it isn't the worst thing.

But if you can't disprove what she teaches, then I swear, Callicles, you'll never be at peace with yourself. Your life will always be full of inner conflict. Honestly, I'd rather have my music sound bad, or have the whole world hate me, than to be in conflict with myself. I'd rather be in harmony inside, even if everything else falls apart.

CALLICLES: Socrates, you're always making speeches and stretching the argument too far. You're doing it again now because Polus ended up making the same mistake he accused Gorgias of making. When you asked Gorgias if he'd teach justice to someone who wanted to learn public speaking but didn't know what justice was, Gorgias, wanting to please the crowd, said "yes." That answer forced him to contradict himself, which is exactly the kind of trap you love to set. Polus laughed at you for it, and rightly so. But now, Polus has fallen into the same trap.

He shouldn't have agreed with you that doing wrong is more shameful than suffering it. That's what allowed you to catch him. He didn't really believe it—he just didn't want to say the unpopular thing, so he stayed quiet. The truth is, Socrates, even though you say you're chasing after truth, you're actually using arguments that rely on popular beliefs—what most people think is right, not what actually is right by nature. What's natural and what society teaches are often totally different. So when someone is too shy to say what they really think, they end up contradicting themselves. And you're clever enough to take advantage of that. You ask questions based on one standard—nature—when the other person is speaking from the rules of society. And when they switch to nature, you switch back to convention. That's what happened when you and Polus were arguing about doing and suffering injustice. He was talking about what society sees as shameful, and you flipped the conversation to what nature says.

According to nature, suffering injustice is worse, because it's more harmful. But society teaches that doing injustice is worse. Being treated unfairly is seen as weak, something fit for slaves—people who can't fight back or protect their loved ones. They might as well be dead. You see, the people who make laws are the majority—and they're weak. They make laws that benefit themselves, and they try to scare the stronger people who could overpower them. They call it unfair and shameful for someone to want more than others. But that's because they know they're not strong enough to take more themselves. They praise equality not because it's good, but because they can't do better. So society says it's wrong to want more than others—but nature says it's right for the strong and capable to have more than the weak.

Just look at the real world. Why did Xerxes invade Greece? Or his father attack the Scythians? These powerful rulers didn't follow society's made-up rules—they followed the natural law: that the strong should rule over the weak. That's true for people, animals, cities, and even entire nations. What we call "laws" are just tricks we use to tame the strongest people—like lion cubs trained from childhood to accept equality, as if that's fair or noble. But if one of these people ever realized their power, they'd break free of all those lies. They'd throw off the fake rules we use to control them and rise up. That's when we'd finally see what justice really is—when the strong rule and take what's theirs.

I think this is what Pindar meant when he said, "Law is king over all, both people and gods." He meant that true law—the law of nature—makes strength into justice. Like when Heracles took the cattle of Geryon. He didn't buy them or ask for them. He just took them by force, because he was stronger. That's natural justice. The things of the weak rightly belong to the strong.

And if you, Socrates, would give up this endless talk of philosophy and aim higher, you'd understand. Philosophy is fine in small amounts, especially for young people. But too much of it ruins a person. Even someone smart, if they stay stuck in philosophy as they get older, ends up knowing nothing useful. He doesn't understand how his own city works, doesn't know how to talk to others, and has no idea what people want or enjoy. These people are clueless about real life. When they finally try to get involved in politics or anything practical, they look just as silly as politicians would look if they tried to do philosophy.

Like Euripides said, people spend their time doing what they're best at—and avoid what they're bad at. And then they pretend the thing they're best at is the most important, because that makes them feel good about themselves. The real answer is to balance things. Philosophy is great for education, and there's nothing wrong with studying it while you're young. But if an older person is still stuck in it, it becomes ridiculous.

It's like a child learning to talk. When a baby lisps, it's cute because it's natural. But if an older child still lisps carefully, it sounds awful—like they've never been allowed to speak freely. Same with adults: if a grown man still talks like a child or plays like one, he looks ridiculous and weak. I feel the same way about people who study philosophy their whole lives. When I see a young person doing it, I respect them. But when an adult can't let it go, I want to knock some sense into them.

Because even someone naturally smart becomes soft and weak if they avoid real life. They run from the city square, where great people make names for themselves, and hide in corners whispering with a few young admirers. They never speak up boldly in public like a real man. And Socrates, I say this to you with good intentions. I feel like Zethus talking to Amphion in that play by Euripides. I think you're ignoring the things you should be focused on. You have a great mind, but you act like a child. You can't even defend yourself in court, or give solid advice to help someone else.

Socrates, don't take this the wrong way—I'm saying it because I care—but aren't you even a little embarrassed to be so helpless? And I don't just mean you; I'm talking about anyone who studies philosophy too much. Imagine if someone falsely accused you or someone like you of a crime and dragged you to prison. You'd be totally lost. You wouldn't know what to say or do. And if you had to stand trial—even if your accuser wasn't very smart—you'd probably be sentenced to death just because you wouldn't know how to defend yourself.

So I have to ask, what's the point of studying something that turns a smart man into someone who can't protect himself or anyone else? What good is a skill if it leaves you powerless in the worst moments of your life, letting your enemies take everything from you, while you stand there speechless and stripped of your rights? You'd be like someone anyone could hit without consequence.

So, take my advice, Socrates. Stop spending your time trying to win arguments.

Learn something practical, something that earns respect. Leave all these tiny, confusing details to others—whether you call them nonsense or foolishness. All they'll do is make you poor. Stop copying these clever word-twisters and instead follow the path of someone successful and respected—someone with real influence and stability.

SOCRATES: Callicles, if my soul were made of gold, wouldn't I be happy to find a perfect tool to test its purity—something I could use to see if my soul was being trained the right way? And if that test showed me that my soul was in good shape, I'd know I was on the right track.

CALLICLES: What are you trying to say, Socrates?

SOCRATES: I think I've found that test—and it's you.

CALLICLES: Why me?

SOCRATES: Because if someone as sharp and honest as you agrees with my ideas, then I know those ideas must be true. To really test whether the soul is good or bad, we need three things: knowledge, kindness, and the courage to speak honestly. You have all three. Most people I meet either aren't smart enough or don't care enough to tell me the truth. Gorgias and Polus are wise and kind, but they're too polite—they hold back. They got so caught up trying to sound proper that they ended up contradicting themselves, one after the other, right in front of everyone.

But you're different. You've had a great education—many Athenians would agree. And you're my friend. I know this because I once overheard you, Tisander, Andron, and Nausicydes talking about philosophy. You were discussing how far one should go with it, and you all agreed not to take it too far. You warned each other that becoming too wise might end up ruining your lives without you realizing it. Now that you're giving me the same advice, I believe you're truly looking out for me.

And you've also proven you're not shy about saying what you really think—your last speech made that very clear. So here's my point: if we agree about something, then we don't need to test it any further. Your agreement can't come from ignorance, from being too polite, or from trying to fool me—because you're smart, bold, and my friend. So if you and I both agree on something, we can trust it's true.

And there's no better question to ask than the one I'm exploring, even if you criticize me for it: what kind of person should someone be? What should they focus on in life? How far should they go in learning and action, whether they're young or old? Believe me, if I make mistakes, it's not because I want to—it's because I don't know better. That's why I need your help. Don't stop advising me until I really understand how to live the right way. And if I say I agree with something and then don't live by it, call me a fool and say I'm not worth teaching anymore.

So tell me again—what do you and Pindar mean by "natural justice"? Do you mean that the strong should take from the weak, that the better should rule over the worse, and that those who are more noble should get more than others? Is that what you meant?

CALLICLES: Yes, that's exactly what I said—and I still believe it.

SOCRATES: When you say "better," do you mean the same thing as "superior"? I wasn't sure earlier. You seemed to say that "superior" means "stronger," and that the weak should obey the strong. Like when you said big cities have the right to conquer smaller ones because they're stronger. So are you saying that the better, the stronger, and the superior are all the same? Or do you think someone can be better without being stronger, or superior without being better? I really want to understand—are those three words just one and the same?

CALLICLES: I'll say it clearly—they're all the same.

SOCRATES: So if a group of people is stronger than one person, then by nature they are superior to that person?

CALLICLES: Yes, of course.

SOCRATES: And the laws those many people create are the laws of the superior?

CALLICLES: Yes.

SOCRATES: Then those laws must also be the laws of the better group, since the superior are also the better, according to you?

CALLICLES: That's right.

SOCRATES: So the laws they make must be naturally good?

CALLICLES: Yes.

SOCRATES: But didn't you just say earlier that most people believe justice means equality? And that doing wrong is more shameful than suffering it? Isn't that what you said?

CALLICLES: Yes, that's what most people believe.

SOCRATES: Then it seems that both society and nature agree: doing wrong is more shameful than suffering wrong, and justice means equality. So you must have been mistaken earlier when you accused me of switching back and forth between nature and custom, claiming they're opposed, and saying I was being dishonest by doing that.

CALLICLES: You never stop twisting things, Socrates. Aren't you ashamed? You're too old to be playing games with words and laughing at someone's phrasing. Didn't I already say that by "superior," I meant "better"? Do you really think I meant that a random group of slaves or useless people, just because they're strong, suddenly get to make laws?

SOCRATES: Ah, so that's what you meant, my wise friend?

CALLICLES: Of course.

SOCRATES: I thought so, which is why I kept asking what you meant by "superior." I wanted to make sure. Because surely, you don't think two people are better than one just because they're stronger—or that your slaves are better than you because of their strength. So please, let's start over. Tell me clearly: who are the "better" people, if not simply the stronger ones? And go easy on me with your teaching—or I might have to run for cover!

CALLICLES: You're being sarcastic.

SOCRATES: No, Callicles, I swear by Zethus—the same hero you were just quoting when you were teasing me—I'm not joking. Just tell me clearly: when you say "the better," who exactly do you mean?

CALLICLES: I mean people who are more excellent.

SOCRATES: But you're not actually explaining anything. What do you mean by "better" or "superior"? Do you mean the wiser person? Or who?

CALLICLES: Yes, I mean the wiser.

SOCRATES: So, you believe one wise person is better than ten thousand fools, and that he should rule over them and get more than they do. That's what you're saying, right? Don't worry—I'm not twisting your words—I just want to make sure that's really what you mean.

CALLICLES: Yes, that's exactly what I believe. I think it's only fair that the wiser and better rule over the weaker and get more than them.

SOCRATES: Okay, let's test that. Let's say we're all together like we are now, and we've got a bunch of food and drinks to share. Some of us are stronger, some weaker, and one of us is a doctor who understands food and health better than anyone else. Maybe he's stronger than some of us and weaker than others. But since he's the most knowledgeable, doesn't that make him the best and the most qualified to decide what food is best?

CALLICLES: Sure.

SOCRATES: So then, should he eat the most food and drink just because he's wiser? Or should he just be in charge of dividing it fairly? And what if he ends up getting less than everyone else because he's also the weakest? Isn't it possible the best person ends up with the smallest share?

CALLICLES: You're just talking nonsense now—food and doctors aren't what I meant at all.

SOCRATES: Fine. But you said the wiser person is better, right? Yes or no?

CALLICLES: Yes.

SOCRATES: And the better person deserves a bigger share?

CALLICLES: Yes—but not when it comes to food and drink.

SOCRATES: Got it. Then what about clothes? Should the best weaver have the biggest and nicest coats?

CALLICLES: Come on—forget about coats.

SOCRATES: Okay, shoes then. Should the best shoemaker wear the most shoes and the biggest ones?

CALLICLES: You're being ridiculous again.

SOCRATES: So maybe the best farmer should get the most seeds to plant in his own land?

CALLICLES: You're repeating yourself, Socrates. You always go off on the same silly examples.

SOCRATES: Yes, and always about the same issue.

CALLICLES: Yeah, by the gods, you always talk about shoemakers, tailors, cooks, and doctors—as if that helps your argument.

SOCRATES: Then why won't you tell me clearly: what kind of skill or wisdom makes someone deserve more? If you won't accept my examples, give me one of your own.

CALLICLES: I've already said what I meant. I'm not talking about cooks or cobblers. I mean those wise and strong people who know how to lead a city—people with courage who follow through on their plans and don't give up out of fear.

SOCRATES: See, Callicles, the difference between you and me is this: you say I keep repeating myself, but I say you keep changing your definitions. First you said the better person is the stronger, then you said the wiser, and now it's someone who's both wise and brave. Please, just tell me clearly once and for all—who do you believe is better and superior, and in what way?

CALLICLES: I've told you already. I mean people who are both wise and courageous when it comes to leading a state. They should rule, and justice means they should get more than everyone else.

SOCRATES: Should they also get more than themselves?

CALLICLES: What do you mean?

SOCRATES: I mean, should a person rule over themselves? Or do you think ruling others is all that matters?

CALLICLES: What do you mean by "ruling over yourself"?

SOCRATES: It's simple. I mean being in control of your own desires and emotions—being disciplined and not letting your wants take over.

CALLICLES: Oh, you mean those foolish people who call themselves "self-controlled"?

SOCRATES: Yes, that's exactly who I mean.

CALLICLES: Well, they are fools. How can someone be happy if they're a slave to rules or restraint? Real happiness comes when you let your desires grow as much as they want, and then you have the guts and smarts to satisfy them completely. That's what I call true justice and real greatness.

But most people can't handle that. They're too weak to satisfy their own cravings, so they shame the strong and call self-control and justice "good" to cover up their own failures. They praise restraint because they can't have what they want. And they try to chain down the ones who can.

Imagine someone who could be a king or take power—what could be worse for him than to be "self-controlled"? He could have anything he wants, but instead he lets fear, custom, and public opinion boss him around. Isn't it sad if someone like that—who could give more to his friends than to his enemies—is stopped by some fake idea of justice?

You say you care about truth, Socrates. Well here it is: the truth is that pleasure, indulgence, and freedom—if you have the power to support them—are what bring real happiness and excellence. Everything else—self-control, fairness, all that stuff—is just made-up nonsense by weak people who can't live that way.

SOCRATES: Callicles, I admire how boldly you're speaking. Most people think the way you do but won't admit it. Please keep going—I want the truth about how we should live to come out clearly. So just to confirm: you're saying that in a fully developed person, desires shouldn't be controlled, but allowed to grow as much as possible—and then that person should satisfy them in every way possible. And you call that "virtue"?

CALLICLES: Yes, that's exactly what I believe.

SOCRATES: Then you'd say that people who need nothing—who have no desires—aren't really happy?

CALLICLES: Of course not. If that were true, then stones or dead people would be the happiest of all!

SOCRATES: But if what you're saying is true, Callicles, then life sounds like something awful. I think Euripides might've been right when he said, "Who knows if living is actually dying, and dying is living?" I once heard a philosopher claim that we're actually dead right now, and that our body is like a tomb for our soul. He said that the part of the soul that deals with desires is easily shaken and pulled around by words and emotions.

There was also this clever person—probably a Sicilian or Italian— who made a pun and said the soul is like a jar because it's so full of belief and imagination. He called people without wisdom "uninitiated," and said their souls were like jars full of holes—they can never be filled up, no matter how much you pour into them. He said these people are the most miserable in the afterlife, because they're stuck trying to fill a leaky jar using a leaky spoon. He claimed both the jar and the spoon are like the soul of a person who has no self-control, no memory, and no faith in anything.

That may sound strange, but it helps explain the point I'm trying to make: instead of chasing a life of endless cravings, you should choose a life that's calm, balanced, and meets your real needs. Have I convinced you that self-controlled people are happier than those who are ruled by their desires? Or are you still holding on to your opinion no matter what stories I tell?

CALLICLES: No, Socrates, I'm still not convinced.

SOCRATES: Okay, here's another example from the same school of thought. Imagine this: two men both have a bunch of barrels. One man's barrels are sturdy and full—some with wine, others with honey, milk, and so on. The streams that fill them are small and take hard work to reach, but once the barrels are full, he doesn't have to worry anymore.

The second man's barrels are leaky and broken. He can also get liquid, but it's not easy—and no matter how much he pours in, it just keeps leaking out. He has to keep refilling them constantly, day and night, or else he suffers.

Now, which life sounds better to you: the one where the person's needs are full and stable, or the one where the person is always chasing satisfaction but never gets there?

CALLICLES: The first man might be full, but then he has no more pleasure. Like I said earlier, that's basically the life of a rock. He doesn't feel joy or pain anymore—pleasure comes from the constant rush of new experiences.

SOCRATES: But if you keep pouring more and more in, won't the waste just increase? The holes have to be huge for all that liquid to drain out.

CALLICLES: That's true.

SOCRATES: So the life you're describing isn't like a stone or a dead man. It's more like a sea bird that's always starving and always eating.

CALLICLES: Exactly.

SOCRATES: And always thirsty and drinking too?

CALLICLES: Yes, that's right—always chasing desires and living happily by satisfying them.

SOCRATES: That's great—keep going and don't hold back. So let me ask: do you think constant itching and scratching would also count as happiness? What if someone spent their life just scratching an itch—would that count?

CALLICLES: You're such a strange person, Socrates. You sound like a guy trying to win over a crowd with silly talk.

SOCRATES: That's why I scared Polus and Gorgias—they were too polite to say what they really thought. But you're not afraid, and I know you won't shy away from the truth. So answer me.

CALLICLES: Fine. Even someone who just scratched themselves all the time would live a pleasant life.

SOCRATES: And if it's pleasant, then it's happy?

CALLICLES: Sure.

SOCRATES: What if the itch wasn't just on the head? Want me to keep going with this? Because, Callicles, I want you to think carefully before you answer questions that might lead you somewhere uncomfortable—like saying that someone who lives a shameful or miserable life is actually happy, as long as they get what they want.

CALLICLES: Aren't you embarrassed to bring up things like that, Socrates?

SOCRATES: Should I be? I'm not the one who said pleasure equals happiness no matter where it comes from. That was your idea—no difference between good or bad pleasures. So I'm asking: do you really believe all pleasure is good? Or do you think some pleasures are not good?

CALLICLES: To keep my argument consistent, I'll say all pleasure is good.

SOCRATES: But now you're going against what you really believe, and that ruins our whole search for truth.

CALLICLES: You're doing the same thing, Socrates.

SOCRATES: Maybe we both are. But even so, I ask you again: do you seriously believe that all pleasure, no matter what kind, is good? Because if you do, then all the disturbing consequences I mentioned would have to follow.

CALLICLES: That's just your opinion, Socrates.

SOCRATES: And are you being serious about what you're saying?

CALLICLES: I am.

SOCRATES: Then let's keep going with the discussion.

CALLICLES: Let's do it.

SOCRATES: Great. First, let me ask: would you say there's such a thing as knowledge?

CALLICLES: Yes.

SOCRATES: And didn't you just say a moment ago that some courage comes from knowledge?

CALLICLES: I did.

SOCRATES: So courage and knowledge are different things, right?

CALLICLES: Yes, they are.

SOCRATES: Would you say that pleasure and knowledge are the same thing?

CALLICLES: Of course not.

SOCRATES: And courage—is that the same as pleasure?

CALLICLES: No.

SOCRATES: Then let's be clear: Callicles says pleasure and good are the same, but knowledge and courage are not the same as each other, or as the good.

CALLICLES: And what does Socrates have to say about that? Do you agree?

SOCRATES: I don't agree—and you won't either once you see the truth. Tell me this: you admit that good and bad luck are opposites?

CALLICLES: Yes.

SOCRATES: And opposites can't happen at the same time, just like health and sickness—you can't have both or neither at the same moment?

CALLICLES: What do you mean?

SOCRATES: Let's take a simple example. Imagine someone has a problem with their eyes—like an infection called ophthalmia.

CALLICLES: Okay, sure.

SOCRATES: But that person can't have healthy eyes and infected eyes at the same time, right?

CALLICLES: Of course not.

SOCRATES: And when the infection goes away, he doesn't lose his healthy eyes too, does he? He doesn't get rid of both at once?

CALLICLES: No, definitely not.

SOCRATES: That would be weird and make no sense.

CALLICLES: Very weird.

SOCRATES: So he goes back and forth between being sick and being healthy, right?

CALLICLES: Yes.

SOCRATES: And it's the same with strength and weakness?

CALLICLES: Right.

SOCRATES: Or being fast and being slow?

CALLICLES: Yes, the same.

SOCRATES: So a person also goes back and forth between being happy and unhappy, just like with other opposites?

CALLICLES: That's true.

SOCRATES: So if something can exist and not exist in a person at the same time, then it can't be either fully good or fully bad. Do you agree? Please think before answering.

CALLICLES: Yes, I agree.

SOCRATES: Let's go back to something we said earlier. You said hunger, by itself, is painful, right?

CALLICLES: Yes, I did. But I also said that eating when you're hungry is pleasant.

SOCRATES: I know. But hunger alone—just being hungry—is painful, isn't it?

CALLICLES: Yes.

SOCRATES: And thirst is painful too?

CALLICLES: Very much so.

SOCRATES: Then we can agree that all needs or desires are painful?

CALLICLES: Yes, I agree.

SOCRATES: Okay. Now, drinking when you're thirsty is pleasant, right?

CALLICLES: Yes.

SOCRATES: And in what you just said, being "thirsty" means you're in pain?

CALLICLES: That's right.

SOCRATES: And "drinking" means you're getting pleasure and relief from the pain?

CALLICLES: Yes.

SOCRATES: So drinking brings pleasure?

CALLICLES: Of course.

SOCRATES: But you're still thirsty when you drink?

CALLICLES: Yes.

SOCRATES: So you're in pain while you're getting pleasure?

CALLICLES: Yes.

SOCRATES: Then don't you see what this means? When someone says, "I'm thirsty and I'm drinking," it means pain and pleasure are happening at the same time, to the same person, in the same moment. Whether it's the body or soul doesn't matter. Isn't that true?

CALLICLES: Yes, that makes sense.

SOCRATES: But earlier you said a person can't have good and bad luck at the same time.

CALLICLES: I did.

SOCRATES: Yet you also said a person can feel pain and pleasure at the same time.

CALLICLES: Clearly, yes.

SOCRATES: So pleasure can't be the same as good luck, and pain can't be the same as bad luck. That means "good" isn't the same as "pleasant," right?

CALLICLES: I honestly don't understand what you're getting at, Socrates.

SOCRATES: Oh, you understand, Callicles. You're just pretending not to.

CALLICLES: Fine, fine. Keep going and stop wasting time. Then we'll see how smart you think you are.

SOCRATES: Okay then—when someone stops being thirsty, does he also stop enjoying the drink at the same time?

CALLICLES: I don't follow what you're asking.

GORGIAS: Come on, Callicles, just answer. We'd really like to hear where this goes.

CALLICLES: Alright, Gorgias. But I still say Socrates is always wasting time with these small, ridiculous questions.

GORGIAS: What does it matter? Your reputation isn't on the line. Let Socrates ask his questions however he wants.

CALLICLES: Okay, Socrates. Go ahead with your silly little questions—just because Gorgias asked me to.

SOCRATES: I admire you, Callicles. You seem to have learned the deep truths of life before learning the simpler ones—I didn't think that was possible! But let's get back to the point: Doesn't someone stop feeling thirsty and stop enjoying the drink at the same time?

CALLICLES: Yes.

SOCRATES: And the same goes for hunger or any other desire— they end along with the pleasure of satisfying them?

CALLICLES: That's true.

SOCRATES: So the pain and the pleasure both stop at the same time?

CALLICLES: Yes.

SOCRATES: But you also agreed that good and bad things don't stop at the same time. You still believe that, right?

CALLICLES: Yes, I still believe that. But where are you going with this?

SOCRATES: Well, the conclusion is this: pleasure isn't the same as good, and pain isn't the same as bad. They may stop at the same moment, but good and bad do not—because they're different. So how can pleasure and goodness be the same thing? They can't.

Let me ask you in another way. When we say someone is good, we mean that they have goodness in them—just like someone beautiful has beauty in them, right?

CALLICLES: Yes.

SOCRATES: And you wouldn't call foolish or cowardly people "good," right? You said earlier that wise and brave people are the good ones.

CALLICLES: That's correct.

SOCRATES: But haven't you ever seen a foolish child feeling happy?

CALLICLES: Yes, I have.

SOCRATES: And a foolish grown-up too?

CALLICLES: Yes, of course. But what are you getting at?

SOCRATES: Nothing too deep, just keep answering me.

CALLICLES: Alright, go on.

SOCRATES: Have you ever seen a smart person feeling happy or sad?

CALLICLES: Yes.

SOCRATES: Who feels more happiness and sadness—wise people or foolish ones?

CALLICLES: I'd say they're about the same in that way.

SOCRATES: Okay. And have you ever seen a coward in battle?

CALLICLES: Definitely.

SOCRATES: And who was happier when the enemy ran away— the brave or the coward?

CALLICLES: Probably both were very happy. Maybe equally.

SOCRATES: So cowards feel joy too?

CALLICLES: Yes, a lot of it.

SOCRATES: And so do foolish people?

CALLICLES: Yes.

SOCRATES: Now, when the enemy is approaching, do only cowards feel scared, or do brave people feel it too?

CALLICLES: Both feel fear.

SOCRATES: But do cowards feel it more?

CALLICLES: I'd say so.

SOCRATES: And do they also feel more joy when the danger is over?

CALLICLES: I think that's true.

SOCRATES: So both the brave and the cowards, and the wise and the foolish, all feel joy and pain—but the cowards and fools feel them more strongly?

CALLICLES: Yes.

SOCRATES: But we agree that brave and wise people are good, and cowards and fools are bad?

CALLICLES: Yes.

SOCRATES: Then both good and bad people feel pleasure and pain, but the bad feel both more intensely?

CALLICLES: Right.

SOCRATES: Then are the bad just as good and bad as the good people? Or are they maybe even more good and bad—since they experience more pleasure and pain?

CALLICLES: I don't really get what you're trying to say.

SOCRATES: Don't you remember agreeing earlier that good people are good because good things are with them, and bad people are bad because bad things are with them—and that pleasure is good and pain is bad?

CALLICLES: Yes, I remember.

SOCRATES: So people who feel pleasure have good things with them?

CALLICLES: Yes.

SOCRATES: And people who feel pain have bad things with them?

CALLICLES: That's right.

SOCRATES: And you'd still say that people are bad because evil is present in them?

CALLICLES: Yes.

SOCRATES: So then, people who are feeling pleasure are good, and people in pain are bad?

CALLICLES: Yes.

SOCRATES: And you believe that how good or bad a person is depends on how much pleasure or pain they feel?

CALLICLES: Yes.

SOCRATES: But we just said the brave and wise—who are good—have about the same or even less pleasure and pain than cowards and fools, who are bad. So what follows from that?

CALLICLES: I'm not sure what you're getting at.

SOCRATES: Well, if good equals pleasure and bad equals pain, then the bad people would actually be more good and bad than the good ones—because they feel both pleasure and pain more. Doesn't that follow from your earlier claim?

CALLICLES: Socrates, I've been answering your questions honestly, but now I feel like you're just twisting everything. If someone gives you an inch, you take a mile like a child who won't let go of a toy. Do you really think I—or anyone—believes all pleasures are good?

SOCRATES: Oh, Callicles, that's not fair. Now you're treating me like I'm playing a game. At first, I thought you were being genuine, like a true friend. But I guess I was wrong. Still, I'll try to make the best of it and work with what you've given me. So now I'll take it as agreed that some pleasures are good and some are bad?

CALLICLES: Yes.

SOCRATES: The good ones help us, and the bad ones harm us?

CALLICLES: Exactly.

SOCRATES: So the good ones bring benefit, and the bad ones bring harm?

CALLICLES: Yes.

SOCRATES: For example, pleasures from eating and drinking—if they lead to better health or help the body, then they're good. If they hurt the body, they're bad?

CALLICLES: That's correct.

SOCRATES: And the same goes for pain? Some pains help us, like a tough workout, and some harm us?

CALLICLES: Yes.

SOCRATES: So we should seek out the good pleasures and pains?

CALLICLES: Definitely.

SOCRATES: But not the bad ones?

CALLICLES: Clearly not.

SOCRATES: Because, remember, Polus and I agreed that everything we do should aim at the good. Will you agree with us on that? That we act for the sake of what's good—not the other way around? Will you join us and make it three votes for that idea?

CALLICLES: Alright, I will.

SOCRATES: Then pleasure, like everything else, should be pursued for the sake of what is truly good—not the other way around, right?

CALLICLES: Yes, of course.

SOCRATES: But can anyone just figure out which pleasures are good or bad? Or does it take some kind of skill or knowledge?

CALLICLES: It takes skill.

SOCRATES: Let me remind you of something I said to Gorgias and Polus. I said that some activities are only focused on creating pleasure and don't think about whether something is good or bad. Other activities actually care about what's good or harmful. For example, I said cooking isn't really an art—it's just experience. It aims at making food taste good, but it doesn't care about whether it's actually good for you. Medicine, on the other hand, is a true art. It studies the body, follows reason, and aims to improve health. Cooking doesn't do that—it just goes by trial and error, repeating what brought pleasure before. Please, Callicles, don't take this as a joke. Don't answer carelessly or say things you don't believe. We're talking about how a person should live. What could be more serious than that? Should we follow the life you recommend—being bold, speaking in public, using rhetoric, and chasing power? Or should we live a life of philosophy? But before we compare the two, maybe we should first agree that these are really two different ways of living. Do you follow?

CALLICLES: No, I don't quite get it.

SOCRATES: Let me try again. You and I have agreed that pleasure and good are not the same. They're different things. So the way we try to gain pleasure isn't the same as the way we try to gain what's truly good. Do you agree?

CALLICLES: I do.

SOCRATES: Then do you agree with me that cooking is just a skill based on experience—not a real art like medicine? Medicine works with knowledge and logic, while cooking just repeats what tastes good, without thinking about what's healthy or harmful. Have I proven this?

CALLICLES: Yes, I think you have.

SOCRATES: Now, aren't there also things that deal with the soul in the same way? Some activities try to improve the soul and do what's truly good for it. Others only care about what makes us feel good right now, even if it's not helpful. In my view, that kind of thing is called flattery. It only aims to please, whether it helps or not. It doesn't care about what's truly right or wrong. Do you agree with that?

CALLICLES: Yes, I agree—if only to finish the argument and do Gorgias a favor.

SOCRATES: Would you say this is true for one soul or for many?

CALLICLES: It's true for everyone.

SOCRATES: So it's possible for someone to entertain a whole crowd and not actually care about what's good for them?

CALLICLES: Yes.

SOCRATES: Can you name the activities that only aim to please people? Or maybe it's easier if I ask, and you just answer. For example—what about flute-playing? Isn't that something that's just for fun?

CALLICLES: Yes, definitely.

SOCRATES: And isn't the same true for playing the lyre at festivals?

CALLICLES: Yes.

SOCRATES: What about singing and dancing? Do you think someone like Cinesias, who sings, cares about making people better— or just about entertaining them?

CALLICLES: No doubt—he only cares about entertaining them.

SOCRATES: What about his father, Meles the harp-player? Was he trying to help people, or even give them pleasure? Or was his music just painful?

CALLICLES: His music was awful.

SOCRATES: So, you'd agree that harp-playing and similar performances are really just about giving pleasure?

CALLICLES: Yes, that's how I see it.

SOCRATES: Now think about Tragedy—those serious plays. Do you think they try to help people be better, or do they just try to please the audience?

CALLICLES: No question—they're all about pleasing the crowd.

SOCRATES: And wouldn't you say that kind of performance fits our earlier description of flattery?

CALLICLES: Definitely.

SOCRATES: Let's imagine we remove all the music and rhythm from a poem—what's left?

CALLICLES: Just speech.

SOCRATES: And it's speech meant for a crowd?

CALLICLES: Right.

SOCRATES: So poetry is basically a kind of public speaking—a kind of rhetoric?

CALLICLES: That's true.

SOCRATES: Then the poets in the theaters are really public speakers too?

CALLICLES: Yes.

SOCRATES: So now we've identified a kind of public speaking aimed at men, women, kids, slaves, and freemen alike. And it's the kind we called flattery, right?

CALLICLES: Exactly.

SOCRATES: What about another kind of public speaking—like what happens in the Athenian assembly? Do you think those speakers are always focused on what's best for the people? Or are they like the others—just trying to make the crowd happy and win approval, without really helping anyone?

CALLICLES: Well, I think some truly care about the public good. But others are just like you said.

SOCRATES: That's fine. Then let's say there are two types of public speaking: one is shallow flattery, and the other is noble. The noble kind tries to help people become better, saying what's right even if it's not popular. Do you know of any speaker, past or present, who actually made people better through his speeches?

CALLICLES: I can't think of any current ones.

SOCRATES: How about anyone from the past? Someone who made the people of Athens better from the moment he started speaking?

CALLICLES: Haven't you heard of Themistocles, Cimon, Miltiades, and Pericles? You even heard Pericles speak yourself.

SOCRATES: Yes, Callicles, they were great—if true greatness is just about giving people what they want. But if we now agree that not all desires are good, and that true virtue means helping people become better by satisfying only the right desires, can you name one of those men who made that distinction?

CALLICLES: No, I can't.

SOCRATES: Still, Callicles, if you really think about it, you might find someone like the kind of person I'm describing. Let's calmly look at the question. Wouldn't a truly good person, someone who always speaks with a goal of doing what's best, speak according to a clear standard, not just say things randomly? Think about other skilled people—like painters, builders, or shipwrights. They don't just throw things together; they work toward a goal, fitting each part carefully with the others until the whole thing makes sense. The same is true for doctors and trainers. They bring order and balance to the body, right?

CALLICLES: Yes, I agree with that.

SOCRATES: So a house where everything is in order is good, and one filled with chaos is bad?

CALLICLES: Yes.

SOCRATES: The same goes for a ship?

CALLICLES: Yes.

SOCRATES: And also the body?

CALLICLES: Yes.

SOCRATES: What about the soul? Is a good soul one that's full of disorder, or one that's balanced and well-ordered?

CALLICLES: I guess it's the second one.

SOCRATES: What do we call it when the body is in good order?

CALLICLES: I suppose you mean health and strength.

SOCRATES: Exactly. Now what would you call it when the soul is well-ordered and in harmony? Can you name it, like we did with the body?

CALLICLES: Why don't you tell me?

SOCRATES: Alright, I'll try. Tell me if you agree or not. We call the body "healthy" when its parts are in balance, and that's how we get physical health and strength. Do you agree?

CALLICLES: Yes.

SOCRATES: In the same way, we call a soul "lawful" or "disciplined" when its thoughts and actions are in order. And from that come justice and self-control. Do you agree?

CALLICLES: Okay, I agree.

SOCRATES: Then a truly skilled speaker—an honest one—will aim for this kind of order in the souls of the people he speaks to. In everything he says or does, whether he gives or takes away, his goal will be to add justice and remove injustice, to grow self-control and reduce selfishness. His purpose will be to build virtue and remove vice. Do you agree?

CALLICLES: Yes, that makes sense.

SOCRATES: Now what good would it do to give a sick body the most delicious food and drink if it only makes things worse? That could be just as bad as giving it nothing—or even worse. Isn't that true?

CALLICLES: I won't argue with that.

SOCRATES: If someone is in bad health, life itself becomes bad too. Do you agree?

CALLICLES: Yes.

SOCRATES: When someone's healthy, doctors usually let them eat when they're hungry and drink when they're thirsty. But when they're sick, doctors don't let them give in to those desires. You admit that, right?

CALLICLES: Yes.

SOCRATES: Then shouldn't the same thing apply to the soul? If someone's soul is unhealthy—foolish, greedy, unjust, or unholy—then their desires need to be kept in check. They should be stopped from doing things that would harm them even more.

CALLICLES: Yes.

SOCRATES: That kind of discipline is good for the soul, isn't it?

CALLICLES: Definitely.

SOCRATES: So to control those desires is really to correct or heal the soul?

CALLICLES: Yes.

SOCRATES: Then discipline or correction is better for the soul than letting it run wild, which you said earlier was best?

CALLICLES: I don't really understand what you're saying, Socrates. Maybe ask someone else.

SOCRATES: So this is a man who refuses to be helped or corrected—even though that's exactly what the argument says he needs!

CALLICLES: I'm not listening to any of this. I've only been answering out of politeness to Gorgias.

SOCRATES: So what should we do—just quit now?

CALLICLES: Do whatever you want.

SOCRATES: Well, people say that a story should have a proper ending, not just stop halfway. I wouldn't want to leave this discussion without finishing it. Let's wrap it up.

CALLICLES: You're so pushy, Socrates. I wish you'd take a break or argue with someone else.

SOCRATES: Who else is willing? I want to see this through.

CALLICLES: Can't you finish without me—just talk to yourself or answer your own questions?

SOCRATES: Then like the old saying goes, "Two were talking before, but now one will do." It looks like I'm on my own. Still, I think we should all care about discovering what's true or false here, because truth helps everyone. So I'll keep going on my own. But if anyone thinks I'm wrong, please jump in and correct me. I don't claim to have all the answers—I'm just trying to learn like everyone else. If someone proves me wrong, I'll be glad to agree with them. I'm assuming we want to finish this properly. But if not, we can stop now.

GORGIAS: No, Socrates—I think we should continue until the end. I'm sure everyone else feels the same. I really want to hear what else you have to say.

SOCRATES: I would've preferred to continue with Callicles, and then I could've responded to his words just like Amphion replied to Zethus in the old play. But since he won't continue, I hope he'll at least listen—and speak up if he thinks I'm wrong. If he does point out a mistake, I won't get upset like he does. Instead, I'll be grateful and think of him as one of my greatest teachers.

CALLICLES: Go ahead. Forget about me and keep talking.

SOCRATES: Okay, listen while I sum things up. Are pleasure and goodness the same thing? No, they're not—we both agree on that. And should we chase after pleasure because it's good, or chase good things because they're pleasant? We agreed that we go after pleasure because it's good. Something is pleasant when it makes us feel good, and something is good when it makes us better, right?

CALLICLES: Yes, that sounds right.

SOCRATES: And we only become good when we have some kind of virtue, just like everything else becomes good when it gets the right kind of order and purpose. I believe that's true. Would you agree that the goodness of anything—like a body, a soul, or a tool—comes from the right structure or arrangement?

CALLICLES: Yes, I agree with that.

SOCRATES: And when something has that right structure, it's considered good. So a soul with its own inner order is better than one that's messy or disorganized?

CALLICLES: Yes, absolutely.

SOCRATES: And when a soul is orderly, we say it's self-controlled, right?

CALLICLES: Of course.

SOCRATES: Then a self-controlled, or temperate, soul is a good one?

CALLICLES: I can't say anything else.

SOCRATES: If that's true, then a soul that's the opposite—disorganized and reckless—is a bad soul.

CALLICLES: That follows.

SOCRATES: And wouldn't a self-controlled person act rightly toward both gods and people? Because if he didn't, he wouldn't really be self-controlled.

CALLICLES: That's true.

SOCRATES: So he'd be just in dealing with others, and respectful toward the gods. And someone who acts justly and respectfully is himself a just and respectful person?

CALLICLES: Yes.

SOCRATES: And wouldn't he also be brave? Because someone who is truly self-controlled will only avoid or go after things he should, whether it's people or pleasures or pains. He'll endure hardships when he must. That means a temperate man is also just, brave, and respectful. So he must be truly good—and someone who is good will do well in life. And doing well brings happiness, while doing badly brings misery. That miserable person is the one you admire—the reckless, selfish man who lives for pleasure.

But I say if someone really wants to be happy, they need to work on being self-controlled and avoid being reckless at all costs. If they can, they should live in a way that never needs punishment. But if they or someone close to them—whether a friend or even a whole city—does wrong and deserves punishment, then it must be accepted, because justice is necessary to fix the soul. This is what I believe everyone should aim for, both as individuals and as a society. We should live with self-control and fairness if we want to be happy—not give in to every craving and live like a thief. People like that are no friends to gods or humans. They can't connect with others or form real friendships.

Philosophers say that connection, friendship, balance, self-control, and justice hold everything together—from the heavens to the earth, and from gods to people. That's why the universe is called "Cosmos," which means "order," not chaos. But even though you're a philosopher, Callicles, it seems you've never really noticed that fairness—like in geometry—is powerful for both gods and people. You chase after excess and inequality instead, ignoring what geometry teaches.

So we're left with this: either we reject the idea that happiness comes from justice and self-control and misery from vice, or we accept it—and if we do, all the things I said before must be true too. Like when I said a man should call himself and others out when they do wrong and use rhetoric not to avoid punishment, but to help seek justice. That's true. And what Polus admitted earlier out of embarrassment—that doing wrong is worse than suffering it—is also true. And Gorgias was right when he said a good speaker should understand justice.

Now that all of this has been laid out, let's talk about what you said to mock me. You said I can't help myself or my friends if we're in danger. That I'm like an outlaw, weak and powerless—someone who can be slapped, robbed, banished, or even killed. You said that's the worst kind of shame. But I've said this before, and I'll say it again: it's not the worst thing to be slapped unfairly, or robbed, or even killed. The real disgrace is to do those things—to hurt or steal from others. That's worse for the person doing it than the one suffering.

These beliefs we've talked about are, I believe, now locked in place like iron. And unless someone really clever can break them, they'll stay unshaken. My position is still this: I may not know everything, but no one has ever convinced me otherwise without sounding foolish. And if what I'm saying is true—that the greatest evil is to do injustice—and even worse than that is doing wrong and not being punished, then what kind of protection do we really need?

Surely, the best kind of defense is the one that keeps us from the worst evil. And the worst kind of failure is to not be able to protect ourselves or those we care about from these great evils. Wouldn't you agree?

CALLICLES: Yes, you're right.

SOCRATES: So, if the worst evil is doing wrong and the lesser evil is suffering wrong, how can we avoid both? Is it enough to just want to avoid them, or do we need the ability too?

CALLICLES: We need the ability. That's obvious.

SOCRATES: And what about not doing wrong—do we just need the will, or do we also need skill and practice? Can someone avoid being unjust just by wanting to, or do they need to work at it?

CALLICLES: We already agreed—no one does wrong on purpose.

SOCRATES: Then it seems that we need both the skill and training to avoid doing wrong.

CALLICLES: That's right.

SOCRATES: And what skill helps us avoid being treated unjustly—even if it can't protect us entirely, at least as much as possible? I believe it's the skill of either being in power, like a ruler or a tyrant, or being close to those who are in charge. Do you agree?

CALLICLES: That's well said. I like it when you speak clearly.

SOCRATES: Tell me this—do you agree that people are most connected with those who are most like them?

CALLICLES: Yes, I do.

SOCRATES: But if a ruler is rude and uneducated, he'll fear those who are more virtuous than him and will never be truly friends with them.

CALLICLES: That's true.

SOCRATES: And he won't be close to those who are far below him either, because he'll look down on them and never treat them as real friends.

CALLICLES: That's also true.

SOCRATES: Then let's look at it this way, Callicles. If a tyrant is to have any real friend, that friend has to be just like him—same character, same likes and dislikes, and willing to serve him completely. That kind of person would have power and would be safe from harm, right?

CALLICLES: Right.

SOCRATES: So, if a young man wants to grow powerful and untouchable, the best thing he can do is start early, copying his leader's feelings—being happy or sad at the same things—and become as much like him as possible?

CALLICLES: Yes.

SOCRATES: That's how, according to you and your friends, someone becomes great and avoids being hurt?

CALLICLES: Exactly.

SOCRATES: But would he also avoid doing wrong? Isn't it more likely that, by being like the unjust leader and gaining his favor, he'll end up doing a lot of harm and never be punished for it?

CALLICLES: That's true.

SOCRATES: And by copying the tyrant and gaining that power, won't he ruin his own soul, becoming deeply corrupt—and wouldn't that be the worst thing that could happen to him?

CALLICLES: You always flip everything around, Socrates. Don't you get that if someone copies the tyrant, he can kill anyone who doesn't and take their stuff?

SOCRATES: Oh, Callicles, I've heard that argument from you and others many times. But will you listen to my side? Yes, the bad man might kill the good and honest man.

CALLICLES: And isn't that the most upsetting part?

SOCRATES: Not for someone wise. Should our whole focus in life really be on staying alive as long as possible and learning any skill that protects us from harm—like rhetoric, which you told me to study so I could win in court?

CALLICLES: Of course! That's great advice.

SOCRATES: Then what do you think of swimming? Is that a very impressive skill?

CALLICLES: No, not really.

SOCRATES: But swimming saves lives, doesn't it? And sometimes, you need it. If you think swimming's too simple, think about piloting a ship. A pilot saves not just lives but property too—just like a speaker might in court. But he doesn't boast about it. All he asks for is a small payment when he sails people safely to port, even though he's saved their lives, families, and belongings. And once he does, he just walks calmly along the shore—not acting like a hero.

He knows he didn't really improve them—he just got them there alive. If someone was sick in body or soul before the trip, they're still sick afterward. And if it's bad to save someone physically broken, how much worse to save someone whose soul is deeply damaged? Life isn't worth much for someone like that, even if they escape drowning, or jail, or anything else.

That's why the pilot, even though he saves lives, doesn't act full of himself—just like the engineer, who sometimes saves entire cities. Why do people look down on him? If he bragged like you, he could talk endlessly about how everyone should become engineers, since their work is so powerful. But people still laugh at them, call them "just engineers," and wouldn't let their children marry into their families. Why? Because you say you're better born or more important?

But if being "better" just means keeping yourself and your family safe, then criticizing engineers, doctors, or others who save lives makes no sense.

Listen, Callicles. Maybe what's noble and good isn't just about surviving. Maybe a real man doesn't worry about how long he lives. He knows, like many say, that no one can escape fate. Instead, he tries to spend his life in the best way possible.

You, for example, need to figure out how to become more like the people of Athens if you want to gain their approval and power in the city. But I ask, is that really good for either of us?

I wouldn't risk the most important things in life just to win public favor, like those women who supposedly bring the moon down with magic, only to destroy themselves.

And if you think someone can teach you to gain power in Athens without acting like the people there—whether they're right or wrong— you're fooling yourself. To really be accepted, you have to be naturally like them, not just a copy.

So whoever makes you the most like the people is the one who can make you a true leader or speaker—because people love hearing someone speak their own language and share their mindset.

But maybe you don't agree. What do you say?

CALLICLES: Somehow, Socrates, your words always sound wise. Still, like most people, I'm not totally convinced.

SOCRATES: That's because, deep down, your loyalty to the people of Athens is getting in the way of truly hearing me. But if we keep going and think more carefully, you might change your mind.

So let's remember something: we said everything—bodies, souls, anything—can be trained in two ways. One way aims to give pleasure, the other aims to bring out the highest good. The first gives in to desires, the second resists them. Do you agree we said that?

CALLICLES: Yes, that's right.

SOCRATES: And we also said the first path—the one focused on pleasure—is just flattery. Isn't that what we agreed?

CALLICLES: Sure, let's say we did.

SOCRATES: And the second path—the one that aims to improve what's being helped, body or soul—is the better one?

CALLICLES: That's true.

SOCRATES: So shouldn't that also be the goal when dealing with the city and its people? We should try to make them as good as we can, right? Because we've already agreed that giving people other things—like money or power—does no good unless their minds are kind and noble.

Shall we agree on that?

CALLICLES: Sure, if you want.

SOCRATES: Now imagine, Callicles, that you and I wanted to take on a public project—maybe building walls, docks, or huge temples. Shouldn't we first ask ourselves whether we actually know how to build and who taught us?

Wouldn't that be necessary?

CALLICLES: Yes, that's true.

SOCRATES: Let's think about it like this. If you and I wanted to build public buildings—like city walls or temples—shouldn't we first ask if we know anything about construction? And not just whether we've studied it, but also if we've actually built anything ourselves. If we've built strong and impressive houses for ourselves or our friends, with or without help, then maybe we'd have reason to believe we could handle bigger projects. But if we haven't, or if our buildings have been poorly made, wouldn't it be foolish to try something even bigger?

CALLICLES: That makes sense.

SOCRATES: And wouldn't the same be true for anything else? Imagine if you and I were doctors and wanted to treat the whole city. Shouldn't we first ask: Have we ever healed anyone? Do we even know what we're doing? If neither of us had helped anyone get better, not even once, how silly would it be for us to claim we could take care of an entire city's health? It would be like a beginner potter trying to make a huge jar on his first try.

CALLICLES: True.

SOCRATES: So now, since you've started getting involved in politics and criticize me for not doing the same, let's ask each other a few questions. Tell me, Callicles—have you ever helped make a single person better? Has any citizen or stranger, slave or free person, ever gone from being unjust or foolish to being noble and good because of you? Can you name anyone whose character you've improved through your conversations?

CALLICLES: You're just trying to argue again, Socrates.

SOCRATES: I'm not doing this just to argue. I really want to understand how you think a city should be led. When you enter politics, do you have any other goal besides helping the people become better citizens? Haven't we already agreed that's what a good public leader should do? I believe we have. So, let me bring up the names you mentioned earlier—Pericles, Cimon, Miltiades, and Themistocles. Do you still believe they were good leaders?

CALLICLES: Yes, I do.

SOCRATES: Then, if they were truly good, they must have helped the people become better, not worse, right?

CALLICLES: That follows.

SOCRATES: So the people of Athens must have been better at the end of Pericles' career than at the beginning?

CALLICLES: Probably.

SOCRATES: No, not "probably." If Pericles made the people better, it has to be definitely true.

CALLICLES: Alright, fine.

SOCRATES: But here's what I've heard—and you probably have too—that Pericles was the first to start paying the people for public service. That made them lazy and greedy for money and praise.

CALLICLES: That's just what the Sparta-loving critics say.

SOCRATES: But here's something you and I both know: at first, when Pericles began leading, people respected him. But later, near the end of his life, the same people charged him with theft and almost sentenced him to death. They must have believed he had done something wrong.

CALLICLES: How does that show he was a bad leader?

SOCRATES: Well, think about it. If someone is given animals that don't bite or kick and later turns them into violent beasts, would you call that person a good caretaker?

CALLICLES: No.

SOCRATES: And isn't a human being also a kind of animal?

CALLICLES: Yes.

SOCRATES: And wasn't Pericles like a shepherd or caretaker for the people?

CALLICLES: Yes.

SOCRATES: Then if he was a good leader, shouldn't his people have become more just and kind, not worse?

CALLICLES: That's true.

SOCRATES: But they became more aggressive and even turned against him. That's not something he would have wanted.

CALLICLES: Do you want me to agree with that?

SOCRATES: Yes—if you think it's true.

CALLICLES: Alright, I agree.

SOCRATES: Then we must say that Pericles didn't actually make the people better, and therefore he wasn't a good leader.

CALLICLES: That's what you think.

SOCRATES: No, that's what your answers show. Let's look at Cimon next. Didn't the people exile him so they wouldn't have to hear him for ten years? And the same thing happened to Themistocles. Miltiades, who led at Marathon, was almost executed and only barely saved. If they were really good leaders like you claim, these things wouldn't have happened to them. A great charioteer doesn't lose control of his horses after becoming more experienced. Right?

CALLICLES: Right.

SOCRATES: So that supports what I said earlier—that no one has ever really led Athens well. You said that was true of current politicians, but not of those older ones. Yet they turned out to be just as flawed. If they had really used the true art of leadership or rhetoric, they wouldn't have lost the people's trust.

CALLICLES: Still, I don't think any modern person can compare with what they achieved.

SOCRATES: My friend, I'm not saying those leaders didn't serve the city. I think they were better at meeting the people's desires than today's leaders. But when it comes to improving the people—not just giving them what they want, but using their power to make the citizens better—I don't see that they were any better than the politicians we have now. Sure, they were good at building ships, docks, and city walls. But you and I keep going in circles, misunderstanding each other.

I think we've already agreed more than once that when it comes to both the body and the soul, there are two kinds of work: one kind just gives what's wanted, like food or drink or clothes; the other kind actually cares for the body's health, like medicine or exercise. The people who bake bread or cook meals or make shoes—yes, they serve the body. But the real caretakers are doctors and trainers, who know what the body truly needs, not just what it craves. The others don't really understand what's good or bad for the body.

Now, the same thing applies to the soul. You seemed to agree before, but now you keep bringing up how the city has had "great" citizens. And when I ask who, you list politicians the way someone might list cooks or bakers—people who please the public but don't really make them better.

If someone said, "Look at these trainers," and then named a baker or a wine merchant, you'd probably laugh. They might feed people well, but in the end those people end up sick, and they don't even realize who made them sick. They blame the doctor who tries to help, not the ones who caused the problem. That's what you're doing now—you praise the leaders who gave the people what they wanted, without realizing they made the city worse in the long run. These leaders built harbors and walls and brought in money, but they didn't leave room for justice or self-control.

When things eventually go bad, the people will blame whoever's currently in charge—maybe even you or Alcibiades—but they'll still praise those past leaders who caused the mess in the first place. People always talk like this about politicians. When one gets punished, everyone cries out, "How unfair, after all they've done for the city!" But that's just not true. No real statesman ever gets unfairly punished by the city they served well.

It's like what we see with teachers of virtue, the sophists. They say they teach people to be good, but then complain when their students cheat them or show no gratitude. Isn't it strange? If someone becomes just and good, how can they act unjustly? If they do, then they weren't really made good at all.

You're forcing me to talk like a street-corner speaker, Callicles, because you won't engage.

CALLICLES: Can't you talk without someone responding?

SOCRATES: I can, clearly, since I've been doing most of the talking. But I'm asking you—don't you think it's strange to say someone became good, and then blame them for still being bad?

CALLICLES: Yeah, it does seem odd.

SOCRATES: Don't our so-called educators say this kind of thing?

CALLICLES: Sure, but they're just useless people.

SOCRATES: Then what about leaders who say they've improved the city but also say the people are terrible? Isn't that just as ridiculous? Honestly, sophists and public speakers are basically the same. You think speech-making is noble and philosophy is useless, but really, philosophy is better. Legislation is greater than legal practice, and physical training is greater than medicine. Yet only sophists and speakers complain that their students didn't become better, while still claiming they helped them. Doesn't that sound wrong?

CALLICLES: Yes, it does.

SOCRATES: If their teaching really worked, they'd be the only teachers who could confidently let their students decide what to pay—because those students would truly be better people. A running coach might get cheated out of his pay, but that's because speed doesn't make someone honest. Only injustice makes someone cheat.

CALLICLES: That's true.

SOCRATES: So the one who removes injustice can safely trust his students to pay him fairly, because he's made them just. Right?

CALLICLES: Yes.

SOCRATES: That's why it's okay for people like builders or engineers to take money for their services?

CALLICLES: Exactly.

SOCRATES: But when it's about how to become your best self or how to lead others well, people look down on taking money for that?

CALLICLES: Yes, they do.

SOCRATES: Because real good makes people want to give something back. If there's no return, it's like no benefit happened at all. Right?

CALLICLES: Right.

SOCRATES: So, what kind of service do you want me to give the city? Do you want me to be the kind of leader who tries to make the citizens better? Or just someone who flatters them and gives them what they want? Tell me honestly, like you did before.

CALLICLES: I say you should serve the state.

SOCRATES: So, as a flatterer? That's quite the invitation.

CALLICLES: Call it what you want, Socrates. But if you don't, you know what will happen—

SOCRATES: Don't repeat the usual warning: "Someone will kill you and take your stuff." I'll just say again: if someone kills me, they're the bad one. They'll misuse what they take, and they'll be harmed by their own evil.

CALLICLES: You act like nothing bad can ever happen to you. Do you really think you'll never be taken to court, even by someone petty and cruel?

SOCRATES: Oh, I know it can happen, Callicles. In this city, anyone can suffer anything. If I'm brought to trial, I already know the kind of person who would do it—a truly wicked man. No good person would accuse someone innocent. And if I'm sentenced to death, I won't be surprised. Want to know why I expect it?

CALLICLES: Sure, tell me.

SOCRATES: I believe I'm the only one left in Athens who truly practices real politics. I'm the only one who tries to lead people toward what's actually good—not just what's popular. That's why, if I were taken to court, I'd have nothing fancy or flattering to say. You could compare me to a doctor being judged by a bunch of little kids, while the person accusing him is a candy maker. Imagine the candy maker saying, "Look, boys, this man hurts you! He cuts and burns and starves you, gives you bitter drinks, and never lets you eat treats like I do!" What could the doctor say in his defense? He'd have to admit it all and explain that it was for their health. But the kids wouldn't understand—they'd just shout at him.

CALLICLES: That sounds about right.

SOCRATES: He wouldn't stand a chance. And the same thing would happen to me if I ever had to defend myself in court. I haven't spent my time making people happy with pleasures, which they consider benefits. If someone accuses me of confusing young people or being rude to older people, even if I respond truthfully and say, "I only do this to serve justice and help you," no one will want to hear it. So who knows what could happen to me.

CALLICLES: Do you really think someone in your position is safe?

SOCRATES: Yes, Callicles—if he has the kind of safety we've already agreed is best: if he has done no wrong to anyone, not to people or to the gods. That's the best protection. And if I ever fail at that and someone proves I've been unjust, I'd be ashamed, whether it was in front of many people or just myself. Dying because I can't flatter or speak smoothly? That wouldn't upset me. The only thing to really fear is being a bad person. Dying with an unjust soul is the worst thing. And to prove it, I'd like to tell you a story, if you're okay with that.

CALLICLES: Go ahead, and then we'll be done.

SOCRATES: Alright, listen to this tale—it might sound like a myth, but I believe it's true. Long ago, the gods Zeus, Poseidon, and Pluto divided the world among themselves. Back in the days of their father Cronos, there was a law in heaven that said: if a person lived a just and holy life, after death they would go to the Islands of the Blessed and live in peace. But those who lived unjustly would be sent to Tartarus, a place of punishment.

At that time, judgments about people's lives happened while they were still alive. The judges and the people being judged both had their bodies, their clothes, and even their reputations—things that could hide who they really were. Some people looked good on the outside or had money and fame, so they got judged unfairly.

To fix this, Zeus made a new rule. First, people would no longer know in advance when they were going to die. Second, they would be judged after death, when their souls could be seen clearly. The judges would also be dead—just souls—so they could see the truth in others. He made three judges: Minos and Rhadamanthus for Asia, and Aeacus for Europe. Minos would make the final decisions when needed. That way, judgment would finally be fair.

From this story, I believe that death is simply when the soul separates from the body. The body stays as it was—tall or short, fat or thin, scarred or broken. And the same goes for the soul: its qualities—good or bad—stay with it. When a soul goes before the judge, the judge won't know who it belonged to in life—only whether it's good or bad.

Let's say Rhadamanthus sees the soul of a king, but it's covered in scars from lies and crimes, twisted by selfishness and arrogance. He'll send that soul to punishment, where it belongs. Because the point of punishment is either to help someone improve or to be an example to others. Those who can still change are corrected through pain. But those who can't be helped are punished forever so that others can see and learn.

Most of the worst offenders are powerful people—tyrants, rulers, and public leaders—because they have the most chances to do harm. That's why even Homer talks about people like Tantalus, Sisyphus, and Tityus—big, powerful names—suffering forever in the afterlife. You won't find stories of minor crooks or nobodies suffering like that, because they didn't have enough power to do much damage.

But even among the powerful, there are rare people who stay good. And they deserve great respect, because it's hard to be just when you have the power to be unjust. Athens has had a few, like Aristeides. Still, most powerful people end up doing wrong.

So when Rhadamanthus judges a soul, he doesn't care who the person was or where they came from. He just sees whether they were good or evil. If the soul is pure and just—often someone who focused on their own work and lived honestly, like a philosopher—he sends them to the Islands of the Blessed.

I believe all of this is true, Callicles. That's why I try to live in a way that keeps my soul clean and ready to face judgment. I don't care about winning awards or chasing power. I care about learning what's true and doing what's right. And I hope to die without regret.

That's what I encourage everyone to do—including you. I challenge you to join in the true battle of life—not for fame or fortune, but to become a truly good person. When your own day of judgment comes, I hope you're ready. Otherwise, just like I'd struggle in a court full of politicians, you'll struggle in the court of the afterlife, where no lies can hide you.

Maybe you'll say this is just a silly old tale. But unless someone can prove there's a better way to live, this is the path I choose. You, Polus, and Gorgias—smart as you are—haven't shown that any other way of life is better in both this world and the next.

So the truth stands: it's worse to do wrong than to suffer it. Real virtue is more important than just seeming good. If someone is unjust, it's best that they be punished and learn to be better. We should avoid flattery—of others and of ourselves. Everything we do, even public speaking, should serve justice.

So come with me, Callicles. Follow this way of life. It will make us happy in this world and in the next. If people mock you or hurt you, don't worry. If you live with true virtue, nothing can harm you. Once we've learned how to live well, then we can talk about politics or anything else. For now, let's not act like we know everything. We're still learning.

Let's follow the argument, which shows that the best life is one of justice and virtue. That's the path I'll take—and that's the path I urge you to take too. Because your way, Callicles, isn't worth following.

The End

Euthyphro

Plato

Foreword

A Divine Dilemma: Plato's Exploration of Piety, Morality, and Reason

Plato's Euthyphro stands as one of his most concise yet philosophically rich dialogues. Set just before Socrates' trial, the scene captures an unexpected encounter between Socrates and a self-proclaimed religious expert named Euthyphro. Their conversation begins with a seemingly simple topic: the nature of piety. But as is common in Plato's dialogues, this modest beginning soon opens up into deep metaphysical and ethical territory. By the end, the reader is left not with a definitive answer, but with a sharpened understanding of how difficult it is to define moral concepts clearly and consistently.

Despite its brevity, Euthyphro poses one of the most enduring questions in moral philosophy: Is something good because the gods love it, or do the gods love it because it is good? This question—now known as the Euthyphro Dilemma—has echoed through centuries of theological and ethical debate. At its core, the dilemma exposes a profound challenge to any theory of morality that bases right and wrong solely on divine authority.

Beyond this central dilemma, the dialogue is also a model of Socratic inquiry. Socrates does not lecture or declare truths; instead, he asks questions—often deceptively simple ones—that gradually reveal inconsistencies in his interlocutor's claims. Through this process, Plato demonstrates the value of dialectic: a philosophical method that seeks truth not by appealing to tradition or authority, but through reasoned debate.

At the same time, Euthyphro is not a dry exercise in logic. It is infused with irony, humor, and dramatic tension. The backdrop of Socrates' impending trial adds a layer of poignancy to the discussion. Euthyphro, confident in his divine knowledge, is prosecuting his own father for murder, believing it to be the pious thing to do. Socrates, meanwhile, stands accused of impiety—a charge that will ultimately lead to his death. This juxtaposition invites the reader to consider what true piety is, and who among the two men better embodies it.

In this introduction, we will explore Euthyphro through three lenses. First, we will examine the dramatic and historical context of the dialogue, situating it within the events surrounding Socrates' trial and death. Second, we will analyze the philosophical structure of the dialogue, focusing on the definitions of piety offered and Socrates' method of critique. Finally, we will reflect on the broader implications of the Euthyphro Dilemma for religious ethics, moral autonomy, and the role of reason in matters of conscience. By the end, readers will not only understand the key arguments of the dialogue, but also appreciate why this short text continues to shape the way we think about ethics, theology, and human responsibility.

Socrates and Euthyphro at the Porch of King Archon: Setting the Stage

The Euthyphro takes place outside the court of the King Archon in Athens, one of the magistrates responsible for religious and homicide cases. Socrates is there to respond to charges brought by Meletus, who accuses him of corrupting the youth and introducing new gods. Euthyphro is there for a very different reason: he is prosecuting his own father for the death of a laborer. This unusual act of familial accusation immediately sets the tone for the dialogue. Euthyphro's confidence in the righteousness of his actions contrasts sharply with Socrates' humble and inquisitive posture.

The dialogue's setting is more than mere background. It reinforces the themes of justice, piety, and moral responsibility. Both men are involved in legal proceedings with religious overtones. Yet their approaches to the divine are markedly different. Euthyphro claims to have precise knowledge of what pleases the gods and what constitutes piety. Socrates, in contrast, professes ignorance and seeks to learn. This difference frames the entire conversation.

From the outset, Socrates expresses amazement at Euthyphro's certainty. He gently mocks Euthyphro's confidence and positions himself as a student eager to learn the truth. This dynamic reveals a key aspect of Socratic irony: Socrates often claims ignorance to expose the ignorance of others. By asking questions and accepting answers at face value, he encourages his interlocutors to articulate their beliefs more clearly—often with unexpected and uncomfortable results.

As Euthyphro attempts to define piety, the dialogue proceeds through a series of proposed definitions. Each time Euthyphro offers an answer, Socrates exposes its shortcomings. The first definition—piety is doing what Euthyphro is doing, namely prosecuting wrongdoers regardless of their relation to us—is too narrow and offers only an example, not a general account. The second—piety is what is pleasing to the gods—is challenged by pointing out that the gods often disagree. If the gods are in conflict, then the same action could be both pious and impious depending on which god one consults.

Euthyphro then proposes a refined version: what all the gods love is pious, and what they all hate is impious. This leads directly to the famous dilemma: do the gods love piety because it is pious, or is it pious because the gods love it? Socrates' point is subtle but profound. If the gods love piety because it is pious, then piety must be defined independently of the gods' approval. If, on the other hand, piety is pious solely because the gods love it, then morality becomes arbitrary—it depends entirely on divine whim, and we lose the ability to judge right and wrong independently.

This challenge strikes at the heart of divine command ethics, both in ancient Greek religion and in modern theologies. Can morality be reduced to obedience to divine will? Or is there a higher standard—perhaps rational or objective—that even the gods must recognize?

Euthyphro is unable to answer the dilemma. He grows increasingly frustrated and eventually excuses himself, leaving the question unresolved. Socrates remains in his typical position—not triumphant, but still searching. The dialogue ends without a clear answer, but with the reader drawn deeper into the questions.

The Euthyphro Dilemma and the Foundations of Moral Thought

The central philosophical problem of Euthyphro—the relationship between the divine and the moral—has never lost its relevance. The so-called Euthyphro Dilemma poses a challenge to any ethical system based on religious authority. If morality depends entirely on divine will, then it becomes arbitrary: anything could be deemed good, including cruelty or injustice, if the gods happened to approve it. On the other hand, if the gods recognize something as good because it is already good, then morality must exist independently of divine command.

This dilemma has sparked countless responses in philosophy and theology. Some thinkers, particularly in the monotheistic traditions, have attempted to resolve the dilemma by redefining God's nature. For example, some argue that God is identical with the Good, so that whatever God wills is necessarily good—not because of arbitrary preference, but because God's will is the expression of perfect goodness. Others maintain that human beings, through reason or conscience, can discern moral truths independently of divine revelation, suggesting that ethics is autonomous rather than theonomous.

Plato himself does not offer a definitive answer to the dilemma. But his formulation of the problem challenges readers to think critically about the source and justification of their moral beliefs. It invites us to ask: Are we acting rightly because it is inherently good to do so, or merely because someone in authority told us to? And if the latter, how can we be sure that authority is just?

The dialogue also raises important questions about the nature of definitions and the limitations of language. Euthyphro repeatedly offers definitions that seem clear at first, only to collapse under Socratic scrutiny. This process reveals how difficult it is to define ethical concepts in a way that is both precise and universally applicable. It also shows how philosophical inquiry can uncover hidden assumptions and contradictions in our thinking.

Moreover, the Euthyphro serves as an early exploration of metaethics—the study of the nature and origin of moral values. It anticipates later debates about moral realism (the idea that moral truths exist independently of human beliefs) versus moral relativism or subjectivism. Socrates' questioning suggests a commitment to some kind of objective moral order—one that can be discovered through reason rather than dictated by tradition or authority.

In this way, Euthyphro is not just a religious or ethical text—it is a foundational work of philosophical method. It teaches readers how to ask the right questions, how to follow an argument wherever it leads, and how to live with uncertainty in the pursuit of truth. It models a kind of intellectual humility that is both rare and essential.

The Irony and Legacy of Euthyphro: Philosophy at the Crossroads

One of the most poignant aspects of Euthyphro is its dramatic irony. Socrates, the man on trial for impiety, is the one who approaches questions of piety with sincerity, rigor, and depth. Euthyphro, the supposed expert in religious matters, proves to be superficial and confused. This reversal invites the reader to reconsider what true piety entails. Is it blind adherence to custom and tradition? Or is it a thoughtful, rational commitment to justice and truth?

The contrast between Socrates and Euthyphro also highlights Plato's critique of Athenian society. The city that will soon execute Socrates for corrupting the youth is the same city that allows someone like Euthyphro to prosecute his father on religious grounds with no clear understanding of the principles involved. In this light, Euthyphro is not only a philosophical text, but also a political and cultural critique.

The dialogue's legacy is vast. Its questions have been taken up by Christian theologians like Augustine and Aquinas, by Enlightenment philosophers like Kant and Hume, and by contemporary thinkers in ethics and philosophy of religion. The Euthyphro Dilemma continues to be a staple of debates about divine command theory, secular morality, and the role of reason in ethics.

But beyond its intellectual legacy, Euthyphro offers something more intimate and enduring: a vision of philosophy as a way of life. Socrates does not claim to have all the answers, but he refuses to stop asking the questions. He is not interested in winning arguments, but in pursuing truth. He does not appeal to authority or tradition, but to reason and dialogue. In doing so, he embodies the philosophical spirit at its best.

For readers today, Euthyphro remains an invitation—to think more clearly, to question more deeply, and to live more honestly. It challenges us to examine our beliefs, to seek better reasons for our actions, and to approach the great questions of life with both rigor and humility. Whether one is religious or secular, traditional or progressive, the dialogue speaks to the universal human struggle to understand what is right, what is just, and what is worthy of our devotion.

In a world often dominated by noise, certainty, and dogma, Euthyphro reminds us of the quiet power of asking the right question. It shows us that philosophy begins not with answers, but with wonder—and that the search for truth, though often incomplete, is itself a sacred act.

Characters

Socrates and Euthyphro

Location: The porch of the King Archon

Euthyphro

Euthyphro: Socrates, why are you here instead of at the Lyceum? What are you doing at the court of the King Archon? You're not involved in a trial, are you?

Socrates: Not exactly a trial—it's called an impeachment. That's the word Athenians use.

Euthyphro: What? Someone is charging you with something? That's surprising. I'd never expect you to be the one pressing charges.

Socrates: No, I'm not the accuser.

Euthyphro: So someone else is accusing you?

Socrates: Yes.

Euthyphro: Who is it?

Socrates: It's a young man named Meletus. He's not very well known, and I barely know him myself. He's from the district of Pitthis. Maybe you've seen him—he's got a hooked nose, long straight hair, and a scruffy beard.

Euthyphro: Hmm, I don't think I know him. But what's he accusing you of?

Socrates: It's quite a serious charge. Honestly, I think it shows some boldness on his part. He claims to know how the youth are being corrupted and who's doing it. Since he thinks I'm not wise, he believes I'm the one harming young people. So, he's taking me to court to protect them. He must think of himself as a great public servant, starting with the youth, like a good gardener removing weeds. If he keeps going this way, maybe he'll try to "fix" the adults next. Who knows? He might end up thinking he's saving all of Athens.

Euthyphro: I hope he doesn't go that far. Honestly, Socrates, I think he's harming the city, not helping it. But what exactly does he say you're doing to corrupt the youth?

Socrates: He claims that I invent new gods and don't believe in the traditional ones. That's what he says I'm guilty of.

Euthyphro: Ah, I see. He's upset about the "divine sign" you've mentioned before—the one you say sometimes guides you. He's accusing you of having strange religious beliefs. And I bet he knows that's a popular way to get people against you. I've been through that myself. Whenever I speak in public about religious matters or predict the future, people laugh and say I'm crazy. But everything I say is true. They just get jealous of people like us. We just have to be brave and stand up to them.

Socrates: Their laughter doesn't bother me much, Euthyphro. What worries me is when people stop laughing and start getting serious. The Athenians don't care if someone is wise—until he tries to teach others. Then they get angry, maybe out of jealousy.

Euthyphro: Well, I won't be testing their patience. I keep my wisdom to myself.

Socrates: That makes sense. You're quiet and don't often share your knowledge. But I talk to everyone and would even pay someone just to listen to me. That's probably why the Athenians think I talk too much. If they only laughed at me, like they do at you, I'd be fine with it. But if they're serious, only the gods know how this will end.

Euthyphro: I think everything will work out fine, Socrates. I believe you'll win your case—and I'm sure I'll win mine too.

Socrates: What case are you involved in? Are you the one being charged or are you the one pressing charges?

Euthyphro: I'm the one bringing the charges.

Socrates: Against whom?

Euthyphro: You'll probably think I'm out of my mind when I tell you.

Socrates: What, is it someone hard to catch?

Euthyphro: No, he's too old to run anywhere.

Socrates: Then who is it?

Euthyphro: My own father.

Socrates: Your father?! Seriously?

Euthyphro: Yes.

Socrates: What are you accusing him of?

Euthyphro: Murder.

Socrates: Wow, Euthyphro. Most people wouldn't dream of doing that. You must be very certain you're doing the right thing.

Euthyphro: I believe I am.

Socrates: So, the person your father killed must've been a close relative, right? Otherwise, I doubt you'd bring such a charge.

Euthyphro: I find it funny you think it matters whether the victim was related or not. The point is this: if someone is guilty of murder and you continue living with them as if nothing happened, you become impure too. What matters is whether the killing was justified. If it was, then you let it go. But if it wasn't, even if it's your own father who did it, you must act. The man who died worked for us as a laborer on our farm in Naxos. One day, when he was drunk, he got into a fight with one of our servants and killed him. My father tied him up and threw him into a ditch. Then he sent someone to Athens to ask a religious expert what to do. But while they were waiting for an answer, my father didn't take care of the man at all. He figured the man was a killer and didn't deserve much concern. The poor guy died from cold and hunger before the messenger came back.

Socrates: And your family is upset with you for charging your father?

Euthyphro: Yes, they're angry. They say my father didn't actually kill him, or even if he did, the man was a murderer anyway. They say I'm being disrespectful to my father and acting in an unholy way. But this just shows how little they understand about what's truly right or wrong in the eyes of the gods.

Socrates: Euthyphro, you must be very sure of your knowledge about religion and morality to be so confident. Aren't you even a little worried that you might be doing something wrong by bringing your father to court?

EUTHYPHRO: The best thing about me, Socrates, and what makes me stand out from others, is how well I understand matters of religion. What use would I be without that knowledge?

SOCRATES: My dear friend, it sounds like I should become your student! Then, before my trial with Meletus, I'll tell him this: "You say I have strange beliefs about the gods. Well, I've now become a student of Euthyphro, who everyone agrees is an expert in religious matters. If you approve of him, then you should approve of me. But if you think I'm wrong, then you should go after my teacher instead. After all, he's the one teaching me and even correcting his own father. Surely that's more serious than influencing the young." And if Meletus won't listen, I'll repeat the same thing in court.

EUTHYPHRO: Absolutely, Socrates. And if he tries to charge me instead, I'll be ready to point out his mistakes. The court will end up focusing more on him than on me.

SOCRATES: That's why I'm eager to learn from you. It seems no one else notices your wisdom—not even Meletus. But he found me right away and charged me with being impious. So please, tell me what you know about piety, impiety, murder, and other sins against the gods. Isn't piety always the same, no matter the action? And isn't impiety its opposite, and just as constant?

EUTHYPHRO: Yes, that's true, Socrates.

SOCRATES: So what exactly is piety? And what is impiety?

EUTHYPHRO: Piety is doing what I'm doing—prosecuting anyone guilty of murder or other crimes against the gods. It doesn't matter if it's your father or mother or someone else. Not prosecuting them is impiety. I'll even give you a great example to prove I'm right: People say Zeus is the most just of all the gods. Yet they also admit that he punished his father, Cronos, because Cronos swallowed his children. Cronos had done the same to Uranus. But when I charge my father with wrongdoing, everyone gets upset with me. They clearly don't hold humans to the same standard they apply to the gods.

SOCRATES: Maybe that's why I'm being accused of impiety—because I question these kinds of stories about the gods. People think I'm wrong because I don't accept them. But since you believe in them and know so much, I'll trust your expertise. I admit I don't understand these things well. Just tell me, for the sake of Zeus, do you honestly believe these stories are true?

EUTHYPHRO: Yes, Socrates. And I know of even more amazing stories—most people don't know them.

SOCRATES: Do you really believe the gods fight, argue, and go to war, like the poets say? We see these scenes everywhere—in temples and on artworks, like the robe of Athena that's carried to the Acropolis during the big festival. Do you believe all that really happened?

EUTHYPHRO: Yes, Socrates. And as I said, I can tell you many other things about the gods that would amaze you.

SOCRATES: I'm sure you can—and maybe another time you can tell me more. But right now, I'd prefer a clear answer to my question. You said piety is doing what you're doing—charging your father with murder. But that's just one example. Isn't it true there are many different pious actions?

EUTHYPHRO: Yes, of course.

SOCRATES: So remember, I wasn't asking for just a few examples. I want to know what piety is in general—what makes all pious acts pious. Don't you agree there's one single idea that defines both piety and impiety?

EUTHYPHRO: Yes, I remember.

SOCRATES: Then please tell me what that idea is. That way, I can use it as a guide to figure out whether any action is pious or not, including your actions or anyone else's.

EUTHYPHRO: Okay, I'll tell you.

SOCRATES: Please do.

EUTHYPHRO: Piety is whatever is loved by the gods. Impiety is whatever the gods hate.

SOCRATES: That's a helpful answer, Euthyphro. Now let's see if it's really true. You say that what the gods love is pious, and what they hate is impious. These are complete opposites, right?

EUTHYPHRO: Right.

SOCRATES: And you also said earlier that the gods sometimes disagree and argue, correct?

EUTHYPHRO: Yes, that's true.

SOCRATES: And when people disagree, what do they usually argue about? Not things like numbers—we can solve those with math, right?

EUTHYPHRO: Yes, we just do the calculation.

SOCRATES: And if we argue about size or weight, we can measure or weigh and settle it.

EUTHYPHRO: Exactly.

SOCRATES: So what kind of disagreements can't be solved so easily? I'll help you here: we tend to argue about justice and injustice, good and bad, honorable and shameful things. And when we can't agree, that's when fights happen. Wouldn't you say that's true?

EUTHYPHRO: Yes, that makes sense.

SOCRATES: And you said the gods argue in the same way?

EUTHYPHRO: That's right.

SOCRATES: So they must disagree about justice, goodness, and what's honorable—just like humans do. If there were no disagreements about those things, they wouldn't be fighting, right?

EUTHYPHRO: Correct.

SOCRATES: And don't all people love what they believe is just and good, and hate what they think is the opposite?

EUTHYPHRO: Very true.

SOCRATES: But since people often see the same thing in different ways—some calling it just, others calling it unjust—that's why we argue.

EUTHYPHRO: Yes, that's exactly why.

SOCRATES: So if the same things are both loved and hated by the gods, then some things must be both pious and impious?

EUTHYPHRO: I suppose that's what it means.

SOCRATES: Then, my friend, I'm surprised. That's not what I was asking. I didn't want an example of something that's both pious and impious. But according to what you just said, it sounds like something could be loved by one god and hated by another. That would mean when you punish your father, it might please Zeus but upset Cronos, or be fine with Hephaestus but not with Hera. The gods could easily disagree with each other.

EUTHYPHRO: But I believe, Socrates, that all the gods would agree that someone who has committed murder should be punished. I don't think they would argue about that.

SOCRATES: Let's think about this from a human point of view, Euthyphro. Have you ever heard anyone claim that someone who did something bad shouldn't be punished?

EUTHYPHRO: That's exactly what people argue about all the time—especially in court! People do terrible things and then try to defend themselves.

SOCRATES: But do they admit that they're guilty and still argue they shouldn't be punished?

EUTHYPHRO: No, they deny being guilty in the first place.

SOCRATES: So they won't say, "Yes, I did wrong, but I shouldn't be punished." Instead, they argue that they didn't do anything wrong, right?

EUTHYPHRO: Exactly.

SOCRATES: So people don't argue about whether wrongdoers should be punished. They argue over whether someone really did wrong, and what exactly happened?

EUTHYPHRO: That's true.

SOCRATES: So if, like you say, the gods argue about what's just and unjust, then they must also disagree on whether some specific action is right or wrong. Because neither humans nor gods would ever say that someone who acted unjustly should go unpunished—right?

EUTHYPHRO: Yes, that makes sense.

SOCRATES: So it's not the idea of punishment that's debated, but the details—who did what, and whether it was right or wrong?

EUTHYPHRO: Exactly.

SOCRATES: So tell me then, Euthyphro—how can you be so sure that all the gods agree that your father did something wrong when he chained up the servant who later died? Are you sure they all think it was unjust? Are you confident they all approve of you pressing charges against your own father? If you can prove that every god agrees with you, I'll admire your wisdom forever.

EUTHYPHRO: It might be hard, but I could explain it clearly to you if you were willing to listen.

SOCRATES: I get it—you mean that I'm slower to understand than the judges, and that you'll have an easier time convincing them that your father's action was unjust and offensive to the gods.

EUTHYPHRO: Yes, as long as they actually listen to what I say.

SOCRATES: And they will—if you're a good speaker. But a thought just came to me: Let's say you do manage to show that all the gods hate what your father did. Would I actually understand piety any better? Even if everyone agrees your father's act was offensive to the gods, we've already seen that what the gods hate might still be loved by other gods. So I don't think your explanation helps much.

SOCRATES (continued): But let's try this: instead of saying piety is what all the gods love and impiety is what they all hate, maybe we should say that what all the gods agree to love is truly pious, and what all of them agree to hate is truly impious. If they disagree, then the action is neither fully pious nor impious. Would you be okay with that definition?

EUTHYPHRO: Sure, why not?

SOCRATES: I have no problem with it either. But does it really help you teach me what piety is, like you said you would?

EUTHYPHRO: I think it does. I say piety is what all the gods love, and impiety is what they all hate.

SOCRATES: Should we just accept this statement, or should we investigate whether it's really true?

EUTHYPHRO: We should definitely investigate. I believe it will stand up to the test.

SOCRATES: We'll find out soon. First, I want to understand something clearly: Do the gods love what is pious because it is pious? Or is it pious because the gods love it?

EUTHYPHRO: I'm not sure what you mean.

SOCRATES: Let me explain. Think of things like carrying or being carried, leading or being led, seeing or being seen. In each case, there's a difference between the one doing the action and the one receiving it. You understand that, right?

EUTHYPHRO: Yes, I think I do.

SOCRATES: Then isn't something that is loved different from the one who loves?

EUTHYPHRO: Yes, of course.

SOCRATES: Now tell me this—when something is being carried, is it in that state because someone is carrying it, or is there another reason?

EUTHYPHRO: It's in that state because it's being carried.

SOCRATES: And the same goes for things that are being led or being seen?

EUTHYPHRO: Yes, the same.

SOCRATES: So, a thing isn't seen because it's visible; it's visible because it's being seen. A thing isn't carried because it's in the state of being carried—it's in that state because someone is carrying it. I think now you can see what I mean. Any state like being carried or being changed comes from something happening to it first. Something isn't becoming because it's in the process—it's in the process because it's changing. The same goes for suffering—something suffers because it's actually being harmed, not just because it's in a state of suffering. Would you agree?

EUTHYPHRO: Yes, I agree.

SOCRATES: So wouldn't you say that something that is loved is in a state of being loved—like being affected by love?

EUTHYPHRO: Yes.

SOCRATES: And just like the other cases, it's loved because someone loves it—it's not that it's loved first and then someone loves it?

EUTHYPHRO: Right.

SOCRATES: So let's go back to piety. You said earlier that all the gods love what is pious, right?

EUTHYPHRO: Yes.

SOCRATES: And they love it because it's pious, not that it becomes pious because they love it?

EUTHYPHRO: Correct.

SOCRATES: Now let's talk about what's "dear to the gods." Isn't that something they love? Something is dear to them because they love it?

EUTHYPHRO: Yes, that's true.

SOCRATES: Then we've got a problem. The pious is something that the gods love because it's already pious. But what is dear to the gods is something that becomes dear only because they love it. So these are two different things.

EUTHYPHRO: I don't quite follow. Can you explain?

SOCRATES: Sure. You agreed that what's pious is loved by the gods because it's pious. But what's "dear to the gods" is dear only because the gods love it. So that means they're not the same thing. The pious is loved because it is what it is—it's worthy of love. But what's dear to the gods becomes dear only after the gods love it. Do you see now? You described piety by just saying that it's something the gods love, but that only tells us how they feel about it—not what it actually is. So, please, tell me again: what is piety itself? Don't worry about whether it's loved by the gods or not—just tell me what it really is. And also, what is impiety?

EUTHYPHRO: Honestly, Socrates, I don't know how to say what I mean anymore. Every time I try, our answers keep going in circles or running away from us.

SOCRATES: That sounds like something my ancestor Daedalus would do. He built statues that moved on their own. If I were the one giving these answers, you might say the arguments are moving because of my family background. But you're the one saying them, Euthyphro, so we'll need another reason for why your answers keep shifting.

EUTHYPHRO: No, Socrates, I still think it's you who's like Daedalus. You're the one who makes the arguments move. I wasn't moving them—they would've stayed right where they were if it weren't for you.

SOCRATES: Then I must be even better than Daedalus. He only made his own inventions move, but I somehow make other people's ideas move too. And honestly, I wish I didn't! I'd gladly give up all the wisdom of Daedalus and all the riches of Tantalus if I could make arguments stay still and not twist around. But let's drop that for now. Since I see you're getting tired of this, I'll try to help by showing you how you might teach me what piety really is. I just hope you won't mind making the effort. So tell me—would you say that everything that is pious is also just?

EUTHYPHRO: Yes, I would.

SOCRATES: Then is everything that is just also pious? Or is it that all pious things are just, but not all just things are pious?

EUTHYPHRO: I don't quite understand what you're getting at, Socrates.

SOCRATES: And yet, you're younger and wiser than I am! But maybe that's the problem—maybe your wisdom is making you lazy.

Try to focus, because this isn't really that hard. I'll explain using something I don't agree with. There's a line from a poet that says:

"Zeus is the cause of everything—

Where there's fear, there's also reverence."

Now, I don't think that's quite right. Do you want to know why?

EUTHYPHRO: Yes, please tell me.

SOCRATES: Well, I don't think that everywhere there is fear, there's also reverence. Lots of people are afraid of things like poverty, sickness, or death, but they don't show reverence for them.

EUTHYPHRO: That's very true.

SOCRATES: On the other hand, where there is reverence, there's always some fear—people who feel shame or respect are usually afraid of doing something dishonorable.

EUTHYPHRO: That makes sense.

SOCRATES: So we were wrong to say that fear always comes with reverence. Instead, we should say that reverence always involves fear, but fear doesn't always involve reverence. Fear is a bigger idea, and reverence is just one part of it—kind of like how "odd" numbers are just one type of number. Do you follow?

EUTHYPHRO: Yes, I get that now.

SOCRATES: That's exactly the kind of thinking I was using when I asked if piety is always part of justice or if all justice is pious. I was wondering if there are just actions that aren't necessarily pious. So maybe piety is just one part of justice. Do you disagree?

EUTHYPHRO: No, that sounds right to me.

SOCRATES: Then if piety is a part of justice, let's try to figure out which part it is. Just like if you asked me what "even" means in numbers, I could tell you it's the kind of number that can be split into two equal parts. Do you agree?

EUTHYPHRO: I do.

SOCRATES: So now I'd like you to explain which part of justice piety belongs to. That way, I'll be ready to tell Meletus that he's wrong to accuse me of being impious, because now I understand what piety is, thanks to you.

EUTHYPHRO: I'd say piety is the part of justice that deals with our responsibilities to the gods—just like the rest of justice deals with our duties to people.

SOCRATES: That's a good answer, Euthyphro. But I still need a little more detail. What do you mean by "dealing with the gods"? Because when we say someone takes care of horses, for example, we mean something specific—and only someone skilled in horses can do that properly, right?

EUTHYPHRO: Yes, exactly.

SOCRATES: So the skill of horsemanship is what lets someone care for horses?

EUTHYPHRO: That's right.

SOCRATES: And not just anyone can take care of dogs—it has to be a trained hunter, right?

EUTHYPHRO: Yes, that's true.

SOCRATES: So hunting is the skill needed to care for dogs?

EUTHYPHRO: Yes, that's correct.

SOCRATES: So, just like a cattleman knows how to take care of cows, you're saying that piety is how people take care of the gods?

EUTHYPHRO: Yes, that's what I mean.

SOCRATES: But doesn't taking care of something usually mean doing what helps it? Like horse trainers help horses get better, right?

EUTHYPHRO: That's true.

SOCRATES: And hunters help their dogs, and farmers help their cows. Everything we take care of, we try to make better, not worse?

EUTHYPHRO: Of course.

SOCRATES: Then does piety help or improve the gods? When we do something holy, do we somehow make the gods better?

EUTHYPHRO: No, definitely not. That's not what I meant.

SOCRATES: I didn't think so. That's why I asked, to be sure. So, what kind of care is piety then?

EUTHYPHRO: It's more like how a servant takes care of their master.

SOCRATES: Ah, so it's more like serving the gods?

EUTHYPHRO: Yes, that's exactly it.

SOCRATES: Like medicine serves health, and shipbuilding serves the making of ships?

EUTHYPHRO: Right.

SOCRATES: And building homes serves the goal of creating houses?

EUTHYPHRO: Yes.

SOCRATES: So what's the goal or result of serving the gods? If you really know about religion, you should know the answer.

EUTHYPHRO: I do, Socrates.

SOCRATES: Then please tell me—what important thing do the gods accomplish with our help?

EUTHYPHRO: The gods do many great and beautiful things, Socrates.

SOCRATES: Sure, but just like a general's greatest goal is winning battles, and a farmer's is growing food, what's the main thing the gods do?

EUTHYPHRO: To explain all that would take a long time. Let's just say that piety is knowing how to please the gods with our words and actions—through prayers and sacrifices. That's what keeps families and cities safe. And doing the opposite—what displeases the gods—brings destruction.

SOCRATES: You could have answered my earlier question more simply, Euthyphro. It seems like you don't really want to teach me. If you did, you wouldn't have gone off course just when we were getting close. If you'd just answered clearly, I would already understand what piety is. But I have no choice but to follow where you lead, since I'm the one asking. So I'll ask again: is piety a kind of knowledge about how to pray and sacrifice?

EUTHYPHRO: Yes, that's right.

SOCRATES: So, praying is asking the gods for something, and sacrificing is giving them something?

EUTHYPHRO: Yes.

SOCRATES: Then piety is about giving and receiving between gods and humans?

EUTHYPHRO: You understand me perfectly, Socrates.

SOCRATES: That's because I pay close attention to your teachings. But tell me—what exactly are we giving the gods? We know what they give us: everything good. But what can we possibly give them in return? If they give us everything and we give them nothing useful back, then we're getting a much better deal than they are.

EUTHYPHRO: You don't really think the gods benefit from our gifts, do you?

SOCRATES: Then what's the point of giving them anything?

EUTHYPHRO: We give to honor them. We offer what pleases them.

SOCRATES: So, piety is about pleasing the gods, not benefiting them?

EUTHYPHRO: I'd say it's the thing they love most.

SOCRATES: So we're back to saying that piety is what the gods love?

EUTHYPHRO: Yes, that's what I believe.

SOCRATES: And yet, you see how the argument keeps circling back to where it started? You can't really blame me for making it move—it's your own ideas that won't stay put. Earlier, we said what the gods love isn't necessarily the same as what's holy. Don't you remember?

EUTHYPHRO: Yes, I do.

SOCRATES: And now you're saying again that what the gods love is what's holy. But that's the same idea we already showed didn't work. So either we were wrong before, or we're wrong now.

EUTHYPHRO: One of those must be true.

SOCRATES: Then we'll have to start over and ask again: what really is piety? I'm never going to stop asking this, Euthyphro, so please don't get tired of me. You're the one person who truly knows what's holy and unholy—otherwise, you would never have dared to accuse your own father of murder. You wouldn't have risked making a huge mistake in the eyes of the gods, and you'd have cared more about what people think. So I trust that you must know what piety really is. Please, don't hold back—tell me everything.

EUTHYPHRO: Not now, Socrates. I'm in a hurry. I really must go.

SOCRATES: Oh no, my friend! Are you really going to leave me here, unsure and confused? I had hoped you would teach me what piety truly is. Then I could have defended myself against Meletus, and told him I've learned from you and stopped questioning the gods. I was ready to live a better life—but now you're leaving me in the dark.

The End

Thank You for Reading

Dear Reader,

We hope this timeless classic has sparked your imagination and enriched your literary journey. Now that you've turned the final page, we want to share a vision for the future of reading—one where every classic you've ever wanted to explore is at your fingertips, in a format that best suits your life.

We'd like to invite you to gain immediate, unlimited digital & audiobook access to hundreds of the most treasured literary classics ever written—along with the option to secure deluxe paperback, hardcover & box set editions at printing cost. Together, we can spark a new global literary renaissance alongside our small, independent publishing house called "The Library of Alexandria."

Thousands of years ago, the Library of Alexandria stood as a beacon of knowledge—until it was lost to history. We aim to reignite that spirit of preservation and discovery right now, in the modern age—only this time, it's accessible to all, in every language and every format.

Picture a world where every timeless classic, novel, poem, or philosophical treatise is not only available to read but also updated for today's readers—modernized, translated into any language or dialect, and ready to enjoy in any format you choose, whether that is in an eBook, audiobook, paperback, or deluxe hardcover & box set version a printing cost.

By joining our movement to rebuild the modern Library of Alexandria, you become part of an unprecedented mission to offer:

- **Unlimited Audiobook & eBook Access to the Greatest Classics of All Time**

  Instantly explore thousands of legendary works, from Plato and Shakespeare to Jane Austen and Leo Tolstoy. All are instantly ready to read or listen to, giving you a complete literary universe at your fingertips.

- **Paperback & Deluxe Editions at Printing Costs:**

  Purchase any title in a paperback, deluxe hardbound, or deluxe boxset edition at printing costs, shipped right to your doorstep. Curate your personal library of Alexandria with editions worthy of display—crafted to last, designed to captivate, and delivered straight to your door.

- **Modern translations for Contemporary Readers in all languages and dialects**

  Discover a vast selection of classics reimagined in clear, current language—no more struggling with outdated phrases or obscure references. Next to the original versions, we aim to offer translations in as many languages and dialects as possible.

  As we continue our translation efforts and add new languages, readers everywhere can connect with these works as if they were written today. By bridging linguistic divides, you're contributing to ensuring that these timeless stories become more meaningful, accessible, and inspiring for people across the globe.

- **Your Personal Library of Alexandria:**

  Over the months and years, you'll curate a unique physical archive of classics—each volume a testament to your taste, curiosity, and love of knowledge. It's not just about owning books—it's about curating a cultural legacy you'll cherish and pass down for generations to come.

- **Join a Global Literary Renaissance:**

  Your support fuels an ongoing mission: allowing us to reinvest in offering deluxe print editions (including special boxsets) at their true cost, broaden the range of available formats and translations, and extend the reach of these works to new audiences worldwide. By joining today, you're not just preserving a legacy of masterpieces; you set in motion a powerful wave of literary accessibility.

  We are more than a publisher—we're a movement, and we can't do it alone. Your support lets us scale our mission, preserving and reimagining history's greatest works for tomorrow's readers.

Become a Torchbearer of knowledge.

Thank you for picking up this book and allowing us into your literary journey. As you turn the pages, know that you're part of something larger: a global effort to keep these stories alive, share their wisdom across borders and generations, and spark a true cultural revival for the modern era.

If this resonates with you—please consider taking the next step by visiting:

www.libraryofalexandria.com

With gratitude and a shared love of knowledge,

The Modern Library of Alexandria Team

Visit:

www.libraryofalexandria.com

Or scan the code below:

www.ingramcontent.com/pod-product-compliance
Lightning Source LLC
Chambersburg PA
CBHW011652010726
47499CB00010B/3222